The chain around Josh Culhane's neck tightened

The two Amazon warriors pulled him into Princess Litra's chamber, and Culhane saw the huge bed dominating the center of the room. A large golden ring, like the kind that might be used to tether a prize bull, hung from the headboard.

Culhane felt the chain bite into his neck as the guards dragged him to the bed and pushed him down. He heard the clink of metal against metal, and he realized that the chain had been fastened to the ring.

He could feel his legs being spread wide, and he looked down the length of his body to see the Amazons snapping manacles around his ankles. He tried to pull his legs free, but they were bound fast to the bed.

Helpless, Culhane lifted his head and saw Litra standing beside him, a gleam of anticipation in her eyes. She was nude except for her bracelets and a finely-worked golden chain at her waist.

Culhane swallowed. He was about to be raped.

**By Jerry and S.A. Ahern
from Gold Eagle**

THE TAKERS RIVER OF GOLD

JERRY AND S.A. AHERN

A GOLD EAGLE BOOK FROM
WORLDWIDE

TORONTO • NEW YORK • LONDON • PARIS
AMSTERDAM • STOCKHOLM • HAMBURG
ATHENS • MILAN • TOKYO • SYDNEY

For all the Saturday heroes who made the frontier and the world of outer space safe for at least another week.

First edition May 1985

ISBN 0-373-62402-6

Printed in Canada

Acknowledgments

River of Gold is a book that involved considerable and sometimes bizarre research on topics as diverse as the Brazilian jungles, nuclear material and how much gold can be carried in a suitcase.

By far, the most important aspect of *River of Gold* was to get the feel of the Brazilian interior, especially the area bordering on the Amazon River. Without the help and patience of Martha Little, this would have been impossible. Martha Little spent more than twenty-five years in Brazil as a Christian missionary, and some of her adventures there make the exploits of our hero and heroine, Josh Culhane and Fanny Mulrooney, pale in comparison. Martha Little mastered Brazilian culture and language; she got the rhythm of the Brazilian pulse. She shared all of this with us.

Thanks also to Dacor and Tekna, whose involvement with diving is well-known. Their assistance in familiarizing ourselves with the techinques and hardware involved when going beneath the waves was invaluable. Special thanks to B&D Trading Company— "Executive Edge." The responsibility for any errors in factual data continues to reside with the authors.

A special thanks to Captain Jack, as well, and as before, without the help and patience of Jason and Samantha, the book might have been written faster but the process wouldn't have been as much fun.

Jerry and S.A. Ahern
Commerce, Georgia
March, 1985

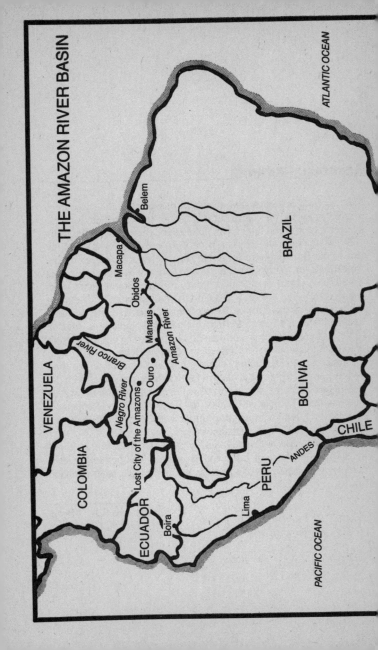

THE AMAZON RIVER BASIN

ATLANTIC OCEAN

Belem

Macapa

Obidos

BRAZIL

Branco River

Manaus

VENEZUELA

Negro River

Amazon River

Lost City of the Amazons

Ouro

COLOMBIA

BOLIVIA

CHILE

ANDES

ECUADOR

PERU

Boira

Lima

PACIFIC OCEAN

Prologue

Xanthos, like all scientists, was probably an alarmist.

The Ural truck began to lurch, Kruglovitch holding tight to the dashboard as the fat woman fought the wheel.

"Ice, Comrade Major," she explained.

The mountain road a few miles inside the Turkish border was barely the width of the truck. To the right was a high wall of jagged rock along which the truck traveled. To the left was a drop. Kruglovitch didn't know how many thousand feet, and he did not wish to learn firsthand.

The truck stopped swaying, lurched violently once more and ground ahead and upward.

"You drive this road frequently, comrade?"

"This time of year, Comrade Major, the ice is sometimes there and is sometimes not."

"Oh."

The truck rounded a bend in the road and started veering right. Kruglovitch was momentarily seized with the same feeling of mild panic as before, but he realized then that it was not another unexpected patch of ice but a branch road. It seemed impossible, he thought, but this road was worse than the other one, and even steeper.

Through the mud-spattered windshield he could see perhaps five hundred yards ahead. The road broadened into a plateau.

Kruglovitch forced himself to relax. The woman hadn't gotten him killed yet.

He could parachute from any number of aircraft at various altitudes. He could rappel from helicopters. He could swim underwater in climates as divergent as the subarctic and the tropics. But driving with this fat comrade made him uneasy.

They finally reached the plateau, and for a moment he was seized with what it must be that drove a man like Miklos Xanthos. Dominating the center of the plateau were broken columns. If they had stood erect, he imagined they would have towered some fifty feet. But they were scattered now; the broken columns surrounding what appeared to be massive flagstones. And at the center of these was what was unmistakably an ornately carved altar of vast proportions.

The truck moved across the plateau past dozens of men armed with shovels, tiny whisk brooms, and brushes. Kruglovitch could now see the columns in greater detail, and logic and appearance branded them as being several thousand years old. There were more men near the altar, and Kruglovitch recognized one of them. Tall, lean, steel-gray hair and matching beard, a heavy coat. Kruglovitch had seen the man's heroic visage in magazines and newspapers for decades.

The truck slowed, stopped, and Kruglovitch turned to the woman driver. "Thank you, comrade, and good day to you."

"And to you, Comrade Major."

Kruglovitch grabbed his hat and stepped down from the truck. The stones beneath his booted feet seemed to radiate cold upward through his body. He pulled his fur hat onto his head and searched the pockets of his coat for his gloves. But he left the right glove off. The gloves were too thick, so he couldn't satisfactorily handle a pistol while wearing them. Kruglovitch's orders had spoken of some unspecified danger, and he was an experienced man.

He stabbed his right hand into the slash pocket at the side of his leather coat as he marched toward Xanthos. Great white clouds formed as Kruglovitch breathed, and he could feel moisture condensing and freezing on the mustache that covered his upper lip.

Xanthos apparently saw him, Kruglovitch deduced. The bearded man gestured a dismissal to two others and came forward in long determined strides.

Kruglovitch stopped walking. He waited, staring at the toppled columns once more. He was no expert on ancient architecture, but to him they looked Greek. The altar looked very old.

Xanthos stopped. Kruglovitch bowed slightly, but did not render any sort of salute.

"You are Major Kruglovitch?"

"Major Engineer Fyodor Kruglovitch, Professor Xanthos. It is a great honor to meet you at long last. I have been an admirer of your work for many years. I have always harbored a secret interest in archeology. It is so beneficial to mankind—learning the mysteries of the past in order to better understand the present."

"You are an unconvincing liar. And you should have brought your troops."

Kruglovitch exhaled loudly, the white cloud enormous. "My troops are available to join us if necessary, Comrade Professor. In less than five minutes. We are a special airborne unit. I would know the nature of your discovery before provoking a diplomatic incident with Turkey. I have the appropriate clearances and have been given my orders by personal radio communication with Marshal Kamenov."

Beyond the columns were rows of dome-shaped khaki

tents, and Xanthos gestured with one long arm toward them.

Kruglovitch bowed slightly again. "Would you lead the way, Comrade Professor?"

Xanthos began his long-strided walk once more, Kruglovitch keeping abreast of him but with effort. "You are curious as to what this place is?"

" 'Was' might seem more accurate, Comrade Professor."

"A temple to the goddess Diana."

Kruglovitch laughed out loud.

"You do not find this important?"

"Hardly warranting the presence of my men or an incident with Turkey, Comrade Professor."

"Ah—so you know nothing at all then of what I have found?"

"Only that you deem it of paramount importance. Marshal Kamenov was no more specific."

"How old are you, Major?"

Kruglovitch stopped as Xanthos stopped. "Forty-three—soon, forty-four."

"I am sixty-one, though I am often told I look younger. That is merely because I was gray at thirty, and have always been tall and thin. I have looked the same more or less for thirty years and as the years have advanced against me, my chronological age has simply caught up with my appearance."

"I fail to see, Comrade Professor, what—"

"What great importance could be associated with this temple? Why I discuss your age and mine?"

"Yes."

Xanthos laughed, then walked on, continuing toward the row of tents. "It is the way of things that one generation grows old and is replaced by another, and this in turn by another and yet another, and for all death comes unavoidably, since the beginning of time."

"Yes, it is the way of things . . ."

"What if there were no means of regenerating conventionally through sexual reproduction, yet a specific race went on and on for ages, perhaps forever?"

"To survive without end?"

"I was never a Communist. Working with the Soviet Union has simply suited my purposes and continues to do so. I was raised a Christian. We called it eternal life. Do you get my meaning?"

"But that is impossible!"

Xanthos laughed again.

They reached the row of tents, and Xanthos turned left along the line of dome-shaped structures toward the largest of the tents. Kruglovitch noticed for the first time that the flag that drooped in the temporarily windless mountain air was not the red Russian flag but the Turkish star and crescent.

As if Xanthos read his mind he said, "We display the Turkish flag in case we are observed from the air. Come inside." Xanthos stopped before the flap of the large tent, wrenched it open and disappeared through the doorway. Kruglovitch followed him inside.

Diffused light from the gray sunlight made the tent's contents only dimly visible at first. Long shadows from the tent ropes and poles streaked across the urns, vases and pottery shards laid out across tarpaulins covering the entire floor surface.

One very large urn was at the far side of the tent. Xanthos picked his way with obvious care through what Kruglovitch considered centuries-old trash, then stopped and stood beside the urn. Kruglovitch followed, standing on the opposite side of the urn, and looked at Xanthos in the half light. The Greek scholar was smiling. "Eternal life—right in here."

Kruglovitch laughed. "In this pot?"

"It is actually a wine jar. Beneath the crust you see, which is caked mud and sediment, it is made of gold."

"A golden wine bottle that contains eternal life?" Kruglovitch laughed again.

"Come—you will see." Xanthos picked his way back across the rubble toward the tent flap. Kruglovitch followed. As they passed out of the tent Xanthos said, "You are an educated man, Major?"

"I consider myself so."

"Of the many disciplines you studied, was Greco-Roman mythology among them?"

"Children's stories only, to delude the peasant workers into believing in the false concept of gods and other divinities to better exploit their labor. The story is the same today as it was—"

"Yes—party line. Quite. But what do you know of these capitalist divinities?"

Kruglovitch shook his head. They were walking along the row of tents toward one near the far end where a man stood carelessly holding a rifle. Kruglovitch assumed it was Xanthos's own tent. "There were deities associated with the natural phenomena and with various human activities—a means of interpreting them before the dawn of science," he said finally.

"This is a temple to Diana. She was the goddess symbolizing what pursuit?"

Kruglovitch was surprised that he remembered. "The hunt, Comrade Professor?"

"Very good," Xanthos enthused. "You get high marks for that one, Major. But Diana is a borrowed name. Like most things Roman that involved culture, she too was borrowed from us Greeks."

The guard at the tent did not snap to attention, salute, or anything else. He merely stepped aside, his bolt-action rifle dragged by the butt across the stones and dirt. Xanthos went into the tent, opening the flap himself, Kruglovitch following.

This tent was small but still large enough to stand in comfortably, and Xanthos crossed the tent in the half-light, sitting down beside a card table in a folding canvas-backed chair. At the center of the table was a wooden box the size of a small child's coffin.

There was a second chair opposite Xanthos and Kruglovitch took it. Xanthos lit a propane lantern.

Yellow light bathed the walls and ceiling of the tent, making Xanthos's face somehow evil-looking, Kruglovitch thought.

"Her name was Artemis, at once the goddess of chastity and fertility, and the goddess of the hunt as well. She had a famous group of worshipers—"

"I did not come to discuss mythology, Comrade Professor."

"You are suggesting that I should get to the point of my discovery?"

"Yes, Comrade Professor. Only then can I determine what troops would be necessary to safely escort whatever it is you have found into Soviet territory."

"I should have been more specific when I called for military protection, Major. For this is perhaps the most important find in the history of archeology, in the history of mankind—"

There was a loud noise like an explosion outside the tent, and Kruglovitch was up and moving, biting off the glove from his left hand, his right hand reaching for the Czech semiautomatic under his jacket.

"They must not find this!" Xanthos shouted.

Kruglovitch, half out of the tent, turned back to Xanthos. The small coffin-shaped wooden box, which had been on the table between them, was now clutched against Xanthos's chest like a mother would protect a child.

"Who—"

"The bandits, Major!"

Kruglovitch said nothing and ran from the tent. Armed men ran from the far side of the excavation site, rifles and submachine guns in their hands. Some of the excavation workers Kruglovitch had seen before were fleeing, others were falling under the gunfire.

The guard with the bolt-action rifle was running away from Xanthos's tent.

There was another explosion, and the center of the temple floor heaved upward.

Kruglovitch worked off the safety of his pistol. "You! Halt!" Kruglovitch fired twice into the back of the fleeing guard, then shouted to Xanthos as he came from the tent, "Come with me! Hurry—pick up that rifle, Comrade Professor!"

Kruglovitch shifted the CZ-75 9mm to his left hand, firing toward the bandit invaders. In less than a minute they would reach the tent. Kruglovitch found his radio where it was clipped to his belt beneath his coat. He depressed the talk button. "Digger to Guardian—come in! Digger to Guardian—assault option now! All speed!"

A voice started coming back, then there was a burst of automatic-weapons fire and Kruglovitch felt something thudding heavily against him. Xanthos, blood streaming from his left hand, pawed at Kruglovitch as he fell.

Kruglovitch shoved the archeologist back and away from him and thrust his pistol forward, the radio falling from his right hand. Bandits. Six of them. Closing. Kruglovitch fired. One man down, a 2-round semiautomatic burst into the neck. Another down, the man clasping his chest with both hands. Another bandit, spinning away, blood spurting from the left side of the face.

A blur—a rifle butt.

Kruglovitch felt the explosion in his head and stumbled away from it, trying to fire his pistol again. Like a low roar came gunfire, very close to him suddenly, something burning inside him, but Kruglovitch couldn't tell where. He had been shot before and he knew the feeling. His head throbbed, and the stone floor of the temple was coming up to meet him as he closed his eyes against the pain consuming him.

"Lie still, Comrade Major!"

"Mikhail—the professor?"

"He has lost much blood, Comrade Major, but he lives and will recover," replied Senior Sergeant Mikhail Tibilovski.

"The casket?"

"What, Com—"

"A small box made of wood, Mikhail—the professor was carrying it."

"There is no box, Comrade Major. The bandits—the Comrade Professor spoke of them in his delirium—stole everything. Even your pistol and wristwatch, Comrade Major—even your boots. Most of the others...their throats were slit. The bandits must have thought that you and the Comrade Professor were dead..."

"Get us into Soviet territory, Mikhail. If I pass out, contact Marshal Kamenov. Have the Comrade Marshal alert the Committee for State Security. The wooden box must be recovered at all cost—at all cost! Do you hear me, Mikhail?"

"Yes, Comrade Major." Senior Sergeant Tibilovski had very large dark eyes that usually looked sad. Kruglovitch thought that now the eyes only looked confused.

Book One_____

The Pandora Ransom

Chapter One _____

As best as M. F. Mulrooney could figure it from her phrase book, the Turkish word for "okay" was pronounced like the baby word for "shit" in English, but she stared at the almost black, inquisitive eyes of the bellman and told him, "*Kaca*."

She smiled, then looked away quickly to her leather-trimmed blue canvas bag and started searching through it for her wallet. The bellman was waiting. His hand wasn't outstretched, but he withheld the key and she knew what he wanted. Finally she inverted the bag over the double bed. The bellman still stood expectantly beside her suitcase. She grinned at him. She'd had the wallet when she had used her American Express card at the front desk. She found a lipstick she'd lost more than a month ago. She set that aside to the right of the pile. The little wooden dowel piece—the martial-arts name for it escaped her, but Culhane had given it to her "Just in case, Fanny"—and her leatherbound notebook. "My wallet!"

She opened her wallet. She started to give the bellman a five-lira note, but she remembered that was worth about thirty cents. The taxi driver who had taken her from Yesillkoy Airport had sneered at the fifty-lira note she had offered as a tip. She shrugged, compromising on twenty lira.

The bellman took it, bowed icily and walked toward the door, setting her key on the table near the doorway.

She heard the door close and sagged back onto the bed, stretching across it. Her mother would have criticized her—"You don't stretch your legs out like that when you're wearing a dress. Do you want the whole world to see your panties?"—but M. F. Mulrooney was alone in the Istanbul hotel room, and she didn't care if the lecherous ghosts of any former occupants of the room were watching her. She sat up, the gray crocheted shawl remaining on the bed, her all-but-bare shoulders turning to gooseflesh in the air conditioning. She stood up, kicked off her heels and walked to the door, turning the dead-bolt lock and putting on the chain.

She picked up the key and stared at it for a moment. She would put the key in her purse after restoring some order to the contents. She dropped the key instead into the left-hand patch pocket of the navy-blue sundress and walked back to the bed.

Mulrooney picked up the telephone and an operator answered, "*Evet?*"

"*Merhaba,*" Mulrooney managed.

The operator said something besides "Yes" this time, and Mulrooney was out of her depth with Turkish.

"*Affedersiniz—anlamiyorum*...English? Do you speak English?" Mulrooney said at last.

"*Bir dakika, lutfen,*" the operator answered, and Mulrooney knew she was on hold.

"May I help you, madam?" The man had a sexy voice, she thought.

"Yes. I will need a taxi in an hour. I'm going to Kapalicarsi—is that close?"

"The covered bazaar—yes, it is not far. There are many shops there that a woman would very much enjoy and—"

"I'm here on business," she told him abruptly. The voice wasn't all that sexy.

"Kapalicarsi is five minutes from here except during the high-volume traffic times."

"An hour then—thank you. I'll be downstairs for it—no reason to call."

"Very good, madam." The line clicked off.

Mulrooney hung up the receiver. Where was Culhane when you really needed him, she thought. If he didn't speak Turkish already, give him ten minutes and he'd manage it.

She stood up. The purse could wait until a shower and a chance to wash her hair.

Mulrooney found her robe and toiletries in her suitcase, snatched her comb and brush from the bedspread and started into the bathroom. She slipped out of her dress. Wearing her bra, panties, panty hose and slip, she began combing out her hair.

Where was Josh Culhane when she really needed him?

But of course she really didn't need him now—except in the ways she'd always needed him since the first time she'd met him. And after seeing what Balthazar Muhammed was so excited about, she would fly to Brazil and wait for him to join her after his damned treasure-hunting expedition. She was mildly worried about him. Culhane was a good scuba diver, but from what little she had read of treasure diving—and of course she had always watched Lloyd Bridges in "Sea Hunt" when she was a little girl—it could be dangerous. Reefs. Sharks. Old ships with holes in their walls—bulkheads, she mentally corrected. She searched for the magic combination of hot and cold water that would neither scald nor freeze her as she stepped into the shower.

Something about a ship that was Libyan? No—Liberian, she thought. But it was really a Russian ship, and it had gone down in some storm off the coast of Brazil. Josh Culhane was diving on it with some man named Burroughs. She had met Burroughs in Miami with Culhane—and Burroughs's wife, Melissa. "Yecch," Mulrooney snarled, rinsing the shampoo from her hair and beginning to apply more shampoo for the second wash. Melissa Burroughs had tried covering Culhane like a tent. There was one language Mary Frances Mulrooney had picked up a bit of over the years—Spanish. And there was a good word for Melissa Burroughs in Spanish—*puta*. Slut.

She rinsed out the shampoo, then squeezed some conditioner into her hair.

"Sean Dodge," she groused. That was the name of Culhane's hero in his adventure series *The Takers*. She tried remembering which one Culhane was writing now—Number 18? She shook her head, massaging in the conditioner. He was always trying to live up to Sean Dodge—living up to someone who didn't exist, to a character of his own creation. Was it pathological? She thought not, it was just that Josh Culhane had never grown up. Mulrooney found herself smiling. She was a fine one to talk about never growing up. Mulrooney liked that about Culhane. And she appreciated the way that he had eased up on kidding her about her books on unexplained phenomena—but had not quite stopped.

She began thinking about her own latest book, *Warrior Women*. That was the whole purpose for going to Brazil after Istanbul, that and Culhane. In 1542 Francisco de Orellana had reportedly witnessed a battle between two warring Indian tribes. Fighting like demons, wielding massive war clubs against their enemies, were a group of women. They battled so bravely that they—the women warriors—seemed to be forcing the men with them to fight on.

And hence de Orellana had named the region he explored "Amazon" after the legendary warrior women of Greco-Roman mythology.

Mulrooney wondered what Balthazar Muhammed had. He had tried her at the apartment she still kept in Athens, Georgia, got the change of telephone number to Culhane's house on Lake Lanier near Gainesville, Georgia, and had called her there. "You work on a book called *The Warrior Women*, no?"

"Just *Warrior Women*—no 'the.' How'd you know, Balthazar?"

"Ah—a man in my business knows many things. I have something for you—something of very great value."

"What is it?"

"Miss Mulrooney, it is not something to be discussed by telephone—hmm?"

"And you're not planning a trip to Georgia, right?"

"Istanbul is always lovely—even the one week each year when there is snow along the Bosphorous—but there will not be snow for a great deal of time yet. You could visit my shop in the Kapalicarsi? You could bring a certified check in U.S. funds, hmm?"

"How big a certified check?"

"Ahh—I am too modest to mention the sum, but surely something in excess of five thousand of your dollars would be marginally adequate...."

"Where the hell am I supposed to get a loose five grand? It isn't even a royalty month!"

"But surely, Miss Mulrooney, your publisher would perhaps—"

"Him? Ha!"

"It is a find of inestimable value. The sum I reluctantly mentioned indeed only approaches covering the expenses entailed in its acquisition. But our long-standing friendship...."

She had told Balthazar Muhammed she'd come up with the money somehow. And she had. Her publisher had coughed up the money Muhammed had wanted. If it was worth what it was cracked up to be worth, the cost would be absorbed. If not, it would be advanced against royalties for *Warrior Women*. Mulrooney had agreed.

She shut off the water and snatched the towel from the rail on the outside of the glass door, a cloud of steam hanging in the bathroom. She stepped onto the mat, toweling her body dry, then wrapped the damp towel around her body, covering her torso from cleavage to crotch. She took a second towel, dried her hair with it, then wrapped that one over her hair turban fashion. Barefoot, she walked from the bathroom to the closet, unzipped her dress bag and wondered what to wear. This was a Muslim country, and women who showed too much skin didn't make points. She left the second sundress—pink—on its hanger in the closet and decided on the khaki dress with the straight skirt and all the buttons. She snatched it off the hanger and opened her suitcase to search for underwear. She took the towel from around her and tossed it into the bathroom through the open door, then started dressing.

Mulrooney thought about the time Balthazar Muhammed had produced the stainless-steel sphere found in the bottom of a well in North Africa. Dating it had been inconclusive. She wondered if the next book after *Warrior Women* should be called *Relics from the Future*?

"*Relics from the Future*...hmm." She liked the ring of it. The stainless-steel sphere made a great paperweight, and it weighed about as much as a bowling ball. She thought of that metal column that never rusted somewhere in South America; she couldn't remember the place. "Hmm...*Relics from the Future*..." Mulrooney made a mental note: talk to Balthazar Muhammed about *Relics from the Future*. But only if this thing for *Warrior Women* worked out all right.

Her hair was still damp, but she guessed she was running out of time. She checked that her earrings—tiny gold balls—hadn't worked loose, then she walked back into the bedroom and sprayed some Chanel No. 5 in her cleavage and some behind her left ear. She gave it a minute to dry while she searched the pockets of her blue dress, then she threw the key to the hotel room into the pile on the bed. She put two gold chains around her neck. She pulled the khaki dress over her head, buttoning it up the front but not quite all the way to her neck, buttoning the cuffs as she walked back into the bathroom to check her hair again. It was still wet, but better.

Mulrooney looked at the pile on the bed—she had a feeling she'd better hurry—and began indiscriminately tossing the items from the bedspread back into the blue shoulder bag. She opened the lipstick she had thought she'd lost a month earlier and, staring at herself in the mirror by the dresser, put it on. Tossing the lipstick into her purse, she slung the bag over her left shoulder and started to the doorway.

"Balthazar Muhammed—here I come," Mary Frances Mulrooney said out loud and laughed. For some reason she didn't—couldn't—verbalize to herself, she wished one other thing were in her purse: the removable center pouch with the built-in holster, and in the holster, her little snubby .38 Special.

IT WAS NOT A TAXI but a *dolmus* that awaited her—an automobile turned into a bus. A black stripe circumscribed the car; a black stripe or a yellow stripe, she had read in the guidebook, designated it a *dolmus* as opposed to a taxi. But she was its only passenger. She divided her attention between the guidebook and looking out the window. If she had the time, she wanted to visit the archeological museum where the supposed sarcophagus of Alexander the Great was kept. She smiled to herself, imagining herself for a moment as the woman of Alexander the Great. They made love and he whispered in her ear, "You were great."

"Here, lady."

She looked up from the guidebook. Garish signs and neon lights burning in the daylight. *Carsi* meant marketplace, she knew—and this was certainly a marketplace.

"Where you go, lady?"

"The shop of Balthazar Muhammed. Do you know it?"

"Yes."

"How do I find it?" She had read in the guidebook that there were hundreds of small streets and some five thousand shops inside Kapalicarsi.

"Walk down here—" the driver pointed into the main section of the bazaar "—and stop beyond the shop of Mehmet Bey, who is a leather merchant. Walk along the narrow street on the left, and you will see the sign of Balthazar Muhammed."

"Do you know him?"

The driver only grinned and shrugged his shoulders. She took out the fare and added a little over fifty lira as the tip. "Could you give me a receipt?"

"Ree-ceet? What is this?"

"A piece of paper with...."

"Ahh...wait." And he pulled a scrap of paper from the passenger-side sun visor and the pen from behind his right ear—there was a cigarette behind the left one—and leaned toward the dashboard, pushing away some of the litter of Styrofoam cups. She stared past him at the busy street as he wrote.

"Here, lady—you need taxi back to hotel?"

"Maybe."

"Phone number there. Have good time shopping." And he smiled.

She was tempted to ask for the tip back. If one other person insinuated she had traveled to Istanbul to shop... "Thank you," she said, and she climbed out, stuffing the guidebook into the center section of her bag, closing the Velcro tabs together and carrying the bag high, her left arm clutched against her.

She looked back once at the taxi, reminding herself she had stuffed the receipt inside the guidebook as a marker, then walked ahead.

Mulrooney stopped at the first stall. There was a really pretty green cardigan that was all wool, and she thought it would look nice on Josh Culhane.

Mental note: stop and buy sweater after seeing Balthazar Muhammed.

M. F. Mulrooney walked on and on and on, finally finding the sign for Mehmet Bey, Exotic Leather Goods. She looked at the shop window a moment—staring at a black leather bra and matching panties, holes where the nipples and the crotch would be, and what looked like rhinestones surrounding the holes. She could see why he used the word "exotic" in his advertising.

She found the street on the left. More like a narrow alley, she turned down it, looking for the sign of Balthazar Muhammed. She had visited him in Turkey once before, but at his second shop in Izmir on the Aegean, never here.

The alley was not straight, but twisted and snaked as she kept following it. A man stepped from a doorway, blocking her way as he stood between the doorway and a closed stall. "Hello, lady."

He was tall, dark and smelled of something slightly repellant.

"Hello, gentleman," Mulrooney said, grinning, trying to walk past him.

"You looking for something? Maybe I help find you?"

Mulrooney looked at him a moment. Guys like him were high on the list of the many advantages the world held for a woman who traveled alone a great deal.

She considered the list of responses she had built up over the years:

"You're annoying me. Please go away."

"I'm here on business for Interpol, so get the hell out of the way."

"I'm in a terrible hurry. My husband is waiting for me down the street."

"They taught me how to take care of creeps like you in the Marines."

But her musings ended as he reached out his hands to her shoulders and started to touch her hair. It was hard to do in a straight skirt, but she tugged it up as her right knee smashed upward into his crotch. Then she snapped her right leg down and spun ninety degrees to her right, her left elbow smashing into the side of his head.

Culhane had taught her that.

She let the guy fall, smiling as she stepped around him, saying under her breath, "Fuck off, buster—on somebody else."

She walked a little faster—just in case—but ahead she could see the sign, very plain, almost dignified looking: Balthazar Muhammed—Dealer in Rare Objects of Value. Beneath the sign hung three balls. It was also a pawnshop, she guessed, unless the three balls meant something else in Turkey, but that symbol was pretty universal, M. F. Mulrooney reflected as she stopped beneath the sign, put her hand to the tarnished brass door handle and pushed the door inward.

A bell tinkled and there was the hum of an electric fan somewhere.

A short man with a round sallow face peered up from behind a glass display case along the far wall that housed numerous pieces of jade and ivory. He was not Balthazar Muhammed. "Hello. I'm M. F. Mulrooney. Balthazar Muhammed is expecting me to call."

The round face smiled. "Indeed Dr. Muhammed does expect M. F. Mulrooney, madam—but he had not indicated that M. F. Mulrooney was a beautiful woman."

She felt herself smiling at the little man. "Thank you, you're sweet."

"I shall tell Dr. Muhammed that you have arrived. But first—might I offer a chair?"

Mulrooney smiled again, shaking her head. "I'll just browse around the shop if I may?"

"You honor these humble premises, madam." And the little man disappeared through the curtain behind the case displaying the jade and ivory. Something brushed past her right leg and she almost screamed, but it was a cat, the cat looking up at her.

She stooped beside the animal, stroking the back of its head cautiously at first. "You are a pretty one," Mulrooney cooed, and then she noticed the eyes. One was green as it should be, but the other was blue. Mulrooney stroked the cat for another moment or so, then stood and walked toward the counter with the ivory and jade. She had seen enough of both to know that this wasn't the really good stuff.

In the next case over were several daggers, their

sheaths, like the cigarette holders and the small mirrors sharing the case, done in silver filigree.

"Miss Mulrooney!"

It was the voice of Balthazar Muhammed. She turned on her left heel and looked toward it. "You grow lovelier each time that we meet, if you will forgive my boldness."

"You are very nice to say that," Mary Frances Mulrooney answered. "Your assistant—he referred to you as *Doctor* Muhammed?"

"It is an earned degree. I sometimes use the title when it suits me. I trust you had little difficulty locating my establishment?"

"Only a little difficulty," she smiled, thinking of the man she'd had trouble with. She felt the cat rub at her legs again, and she looked down at it. "This cat...he has one blue eye and one green eye."

"The cat is one of the cats of Ankara. One eye is always blue and one is always green—green like your eyes, if I may be so bold."

Mulrooney felt herself smile again. He was warming her up for the five thousand dollars he wanted, but flattery was nice however you got it, she reflected.

"Please," Muhammed effused, "I have the information you seek and have taken the liberty of having had prepared some refreshment. The food served on airplanes is sometimes so colorless, so tedious."

He parted the curtain, and Mulrooney walked between the two glass cases, past Balthazar Muhammed and through the curtained doorway into a small hallway. From behind her Muhammed said, "Along the hall and up the stairs and through the doorway. Or would you wish that I lead?"

"I can manage," Mulrooney told him, smiling at him over her left shoulder. Her bag swung on its strap at her left side now; there was no more danger. She followed the hallway to the stairs, then took these upward, crossing the small landing and following the stairs to the top.

There was a doorway on her left and she went through it, Balthazar Muhammed—she could hear his labored breathing—puffing behind her.

"Welcome to my real shop and to my apartment."

She stood in the doorway not moving, hearing Muhammed laugh. Sculpture, the interior kind only since Islam forbids the fall of the shadow of a manmade object. Tapestries. Sarcophagi. Paintings. Enamelware. Silver filigree far more delicate and much more beautiful than the humble items in the shop beneath. And jade. And ivory. The good pieces, exquisite in their detail, in their fineness. Mary Frances Mulrooney found herself at the far end of the room, almost unaware that she had traveled the length of it.

She could hear Balthazar Muhammed saying, "You appreciate art, then, Miss Mulrooney." And he laughed.

Mulrooney looked back at him, "I'm sorry, I, ah, you have some very beautiful things here. Treasures, genuine treasures."

"That iron miniature of the Great Sphinx is perhaps the rarest of my treasures. During the Ottoman Empire, as you would call it, in the period after the sixteenth century, metal objects regardless of artistic merit were melted down for use in the manufacture of arms. This Great Sphinx is fourteenth century, so it is rare indeed." He cleared his throat and continued. "You must see the handwritten copy of the Koran illuminated with gold. It, too, is quite old and very beautiful."

"Yes, I'd like that."

"You will take refreshment with me, then?" And he gestured toward a dais at the far side and beyond the room in which they currently stood, nearer still to what would be the street side.

"Yes, but only something little. My body is still on Daylight Savings Time or whatever it was," Mulrooney said.

He clapped his hands, and from the end of the room opposite the dais, a curtain parted and a young boy in baggy pants, a short blue vest, and a small blue skull cap appeared. Muhammed spoke to the boy in rapid Turkish, and the boy vanished through the curtains. "Come, then, Miss Mulrooney, we can take wine and taste of lamb's brain salad while we wait. And talk, too, of my find."

Lamb's brain salad, she thought. Yecch. "Yes, I would like that," she said, and he gestured toward the dais and she walked toward it, setting her purse on a third empty chair as he eased her chair into place, then seated himself opposite her.

"I drink raki, but you might not care for the taste of the aniseed. May I suggest a fine Kavaklidere from the oldest winery in Turkey, of course, and a very good vintage." He raised the bottle nearest her.

"Yes, please. May I smoke?"

"Of course. The lamb's brain salad will be but a moment."

"Wonderful," she said with a smile, opening her bag and searching for her cigarettes. She found the pack and was lighting one as Muhammed offered his own lighter. "No, thank you. I have it," she said, exhaling a long stream of smoke upward toward the slowly rotating ceiling fan overhead. "What is it that you have found that will be worth five thousand dollars to me, Balthazar?"

"Americans—Allah bless them—so direct. Well, yes, then I shall get right to the point, and perhaps, Miss Mulrooney, you will enjoy this humble repast all the better—the curiosity sated before the palate, eh?'' Then he raised his own glass and said, ''But first a toast—to pleasant business dealings, and to a most beautiful lady.''

She let him sip at his raki first, then she tasted her Kavaklidere. She liked the taste but found it slightly heavy.

''Your latest book—*Warrior Women*—''

''Right—no 'the'—you have a good memory.''

Muhammed smiled. ''The title would suggest that at least some small part of the work might at least allude to the legends that have persisted throughout the centuries regarding those archetypal women warriors, the Amazons. Is my assumption correct?''

''Yes, of course it's correct, Balthazar.''

''And of course you are aware that their origins are near the Black Sea. We sit between it and the Sea of Marmara even as we speak.''

He certainly did have a good memory, Mulrooney thought. When last they had met, her sense of geography hadn't been exactly perfect.

''You are also aware that the Russians view science in a broader spectrum as it were, than scientists of your own country.''

''I know they do a lot of things with mind control, remote viewing, telekinesis. And then there was a story years ago that they found a woolly mammoth embryo frozen and preserved somewhere in Siberia and placed it in the womb of an elephant. I never heard what became of it.''

''Perhaps I may be so fortunate as to locate it for you someday,'' Muhammed said with a small laugh. ''But my humble discovery touches upon still another scientific discipline the frontiers of which our Soviet friends seek to advance. Archeology.''

"This sounds like the beginning of Josh Culhane's favorite movie."

"I speak specifically—" he smiled "—of a recent archeological find just inside the Turkish border...in the mountains, where it is very cold and there are many dangers and much remains unexplored."

"Noah's Ark?"

"Alas, no, but perhaps even more interesting to you. And more profitable to me. Forgive me a moment." Muhammed pushed his chair back from the table and rose, walking a few steps to what in an American home she would have labeled a window seat, but it was built out from the wall beside the table and not from a windowsill. He stood there, looking down at the wooden box that rested upon it. It was of the size someone might expect for a small child's coffin and roughly the same shape.

"Inside this box is a find of rare magnitude. But for reasons of business and health, the original contents will be returned to their original owners—after a small service charge has been negotiated, of course. I have copies. You should know more than anyone how painstakingly difficult it can become to photocopy scrolls that have been rolled for centuries and which, if bent the slightest way wrong, will fragment into dust. Great effort was needed to secure accurate and legible copies. I have them here." And from behind the small wooden casket he picked up a large manila envelope. "And—you will forgive the attempt at humor—well aware of your natural gift for languages, I took the liberty of providing an interlinear translation of the documents."

He walked back to the table and sat down opposite her, handing across the manila envelope.

Mulrooney stubbed out her cigarette and lit another one with her lighter, leaving the cigarette in the ceramic ashtray and starting to open the envelope. In it were dozens of sheets of paper, stapled together at the top left corner, English scrawled between lines of some language she could not decipher. "It's Greek to me—what is it?"

"Greek—exactly. Classical Greek, but the differences between ancient Greek and the modern language are very subtle. Only a true scholar would be aware of them. As you will read the translation you will doubtless detect that it is a narrative. It is very complicated and would take considerable time to read. May I synopsize for you?"

Mulrooney looked over the papers at Balthazar Muhammed. She had already read a fragment of the interlinear translation from the first sheet, something about the ultimate fate of the most devout followers of Artemis. "What is this?"

"The story of the Amazon women—who they were and where they disappeared to thousands of years ago. And where they might still be. You will notice one of the sheets toward the very end is a map. When the map is considered—" she leafed through until she found it "—in conjunction with the textual material, the meaning of the map is clear. Did I not say a find of great importance?"

Mary Frances Mulrooney looked up at him, across the map. His eyes sparkled as he downed the raki, then he laughed.

Mulrooney laughed, too. "You cute Sidney Greenstreet look-alike, you. . ." She set down the papers and replaced them in the manila envelope as Balthazar Muhammed reached across the table and refilled her glass of Kavaklidere.

"What is contained in that envelope, Miss Mulrooney, is a link between past and present. Perhaps the

Russians have interest in it for some hope of eternal life, or of Amazon treasure. I do not know their desires, nor do I hold interest. But the story is magnificent. May I tell it to you?"

"Please do."

The boy came with the lamb's brain salad. Mulrooney was so excited it didn't even make her feel too nauseous to look at it—but nauseous enough that she wouldn't eat it.

The boy left. The way Muhammed smiled at the boy, she absently wondered if her host were homosexual, but she really didn't care.

"Very well, then. This was found inside an urn, an urn made of gold and sealed against the centuries beneath the altar in the recently uncovered ruins of a temple built to honor the goddess Artemis. In Rome she was called Diana, but in the Greek culture, especially in those early days, she was both the goddess of the hunt and, incongruously, goddess of fertility and chastity at once. The perfect description, one might say, for a race of female warriors who eschewed the companionship of men, yes?"

Mulrooney wondered if Muhammed had rehearsed his lines.

He continued. "The Amazons engaged in warfare with the legendary Thersus, Thersus triumphing over them and carrying off their Queen Antiope. After their subjugation, the Amazons saw their race doomed. But Phoenician sailors they had captured had told them stories of a land mass far to the west, where only primitive people dwelled, and where there was much gold, as well. And the Amazons felt that this land could be reached by sailing west from the coast of Africa.

"A fleet of thirty of their light, small, but very fast warships and three heavy treasure ships was assembled,

and some two thousand of the warrior race set out,''
Muhammed said, stopping for a moment to sip at his
raki. Mulrooney could feel her blood pressure rising.
She lit another cigarette and downed another half glass
of the Kavaklidere.

"The story goes on that the Amazon women located
the land mass after encountering many storms. And on
this land mass, they found a native population quite
easy to subjugate, racially different from them from the
descriptions of the features—"

"What did they look like?" Mulrooney interrupted.

"Like Red Indians, it would appear."

"Go on," said Mulrooney.

"They traveled inland along a great river. Where the
river parted into two great rivers—one of which ran
black—in a land of many smaller rivers and dense
forest, they found the place where the sun shone from
within—"

"'The sun shone from within'?"

"This is how it is spoken of, Miss Mulrooney—shall I
go on?"

"Yeah, yes, please, Balthazar. Continue."

"After all this had been accomplished, three hundred
warriors were sent back along the route over which
they had come, and six of their light ships were sent
out to carry them. But when the ships returned, perhaps
traveling along the Bosphorous, these warrior women
learned that their remaining numbers had been crushed
by their enemies, pursued, slaughtered and hunted to
the last. The three hundred warrior women were unable
to turn the tide against their enemies. They took to the
mountains, building with their last efforts one final
temple to their goddess whose protection they sought.
Finally—their ships burned, their cities destroyed, their
number reduced to dozens when once there were tens of

thousands—a last few took refuge at their temple, the male armies hunting them like beasts stalk their prey. One of these survivors, before her death, set down the record of which you, Miss Mulrooney, presently have a copy. The evident intention was that the record remain for future Amazon warriors who might return from the new land, that they might avenge the deaths of their sisters. The last lines of the record, from the deterioration, seem to have been written in something that might have been blood.''

Balthazar Muhammed leaned back from the table, folding his hands over his ample midsection, a pleased smile raising the corners of his mouth. "And there you have it, Miss Mulrooney—but there is one other thing."

"Wait—how did you—"

"Bandits, in truthfulness. They raided the camp of the Soviet archeological team working on the site, stole that wooden box, and once they learned the contents were old documents, eventually the papers came into my possession. I merely charge the Russians a fee for the trouble I incurred in securing them from the bandits. Scurrilous thugs, these mountain bandits."

"What is the other thing you began to mention?"

"An associate on occasion—a Brazilian of Italian extraction named Sergio Celini—lives on a small ranch but has a house near the town along the Amazon river, beyond Manaus. You are aware that the Amazon in Brazil, the river, the region itself were named because of one man's observation—Francisco de Orellana. He witnessed—"

"Warrior women. I know that story."

"Then perhaps you, Miss Mulrooney, will be less surprised than I was when Sergio Celini communicated his discovery to me."

Mulrooney smoked, very excited.

"My sometime associate found a woman in the jungle near his mine. She had been injured. He did not provide the details, but she lives even as we speak. Very tall, very strong, stronger than two normal men. She carried a bow and a quiver of arrows and a spear. She wore nearly nothing: a breechcloth of some type and a halter to restrain her breasts. The woman—she is white but deeply tanned—was delirious for a time, and she spoke to Sergio and his associates. She spoke to them in Greek."

Mulrooney dropped her cigarette and bent over quickly to pick it up before it burned a hole in the magnificent Oriental rug beneath her chair. Suddenly there was the sound of glass shattering and she looked up. Wine was dribbling over the edge of the table, and she slipped out of the chair onto her knees on the floor. Where her back had been against the chair there was now a hole. And it was from a bullet. There was a loud booming sound and her ears rang with it. Then Balthazar Muhammed cried, "Miss Mulrooney! We must get out of here!" She crawled on hands and knees under the table to beside the chair where her purse was. There was another of the booming sounds and she looked up. Balthazar Muhammed's white suit jacket was crimson along the length of the left sleeve. In his right hand was a revolver. His fez had fallen from his head to the table, lying amid the spilled wine and the broken bottle of Kavaklidere. Then the glass of raki shattered. Mulrooney reached onto the table for the manila envelope.

Suddenly there was a coughing sound and a hole almost magically appeared in the manila envelope's center.

Mulrooney looked toward the door. Two men stood there holding pistols in their hands with long things at the ends that a lot of movies and TV and the fact that she had heard no shots told her had to be silencers. Beside her there was another of the loud booms, and she glanced to her left. It was Balthazar Muhammed's gun, a flash of light from it as it boomed again. She looked to the door as she threw herself past the table and to the floor; her left hand clutching the strap of her bag and her right the top of the manila envelope with the bullet hole in it.

There was a scream from near the doorway, and as she rolled onto the floor and started to crawl toward the couch at the far end of the dais for protection, she could see the boy servant crumple to the floor, the center of his tanned forehead beneath his flowing black hair suddenly gush blood.

Another boom sounded, then another. One of the men in the doorway fell, and for the first time Mulrooney noticed that this was apparently the second man Balthazar Muhammed had claimed. The first man was draped across a half-shattered glass case containing small pieces of jade.

"Run—that way!"

She looked at Muhammed, then looked to where he pointed and saw a small doorway. She pushed herself to her feet and ran for it, a vase—it looked like pictures she had seen of Ming-dynasty pieces—shattering just in front of her.

She kept running, sagging against the door, twisting at the knob. It came off in her hands.

"Balthazar!" she screamed.

He was reloading his revolver. Two more men stood in the doorway. Both fired at him simultaneously, and his body rocked back and across the table, the table collapsing under his bulk.

Mulrooney threw her weight against the door, and for the only time in her life wished that she weren't one of those people who could eat everything, metabolize it and never gain a pound.

But the door rocked inward and she half fell through the doorway after it, down on her knees, a bullet dimpling the knobless lockplate.

"Shit," Mulrooney snapped, pushing herself to her feet and running. She was in a small corridor and at its end were stairs. A glass globe for a light fixture shattered beside her head. She didn't look back, but kept running, shifting her purse to her shoulder, clutching the manila envelope in her left hand, the stairwell near to her now.

She raced toward it, catching herself back at the railing just in time. The stairs were gone; only the skeleton of the framework remained.

Mulrooney looked back. There was one man at the doorway and a second man nearly halfway down the corridor, one of the automatic pistols with a silencer held in his right hand.

Mulrooney shrugged her shoulders and ran toward him, screaming at the top of her lungs.

She could see it in his eyes—hesitation. He stopped, turned on his heel and ran in the other direction.

Mulrooney spun around, ran back toward the stepless stairwell, and peered down. The runner had stopped at the doorway and was raising his gun to fire.

Mulrooney threw the manila envelope down the stairwell into the broken blocks of concrete at its base, then crawled under the railing and onto the skeleton of the missing stairs. A sharp end of the wooden corridor floor stabbed her left hand, and she lost her balance and fell away from the floor.

She caught herself with both hands and hung between the side ribs from the missing stairs.

"All right, M.F. Think of somethin'!"

She swung her legs out, cursing the tightness of the straight skirt of her dress, and entwined them around the framework of the stairs, finally finding footing with her left foot. High heels weren't made for this stuff, either, she thought. She was climbing down now, using the framework like a ladder.

Mulrooney looked up and saw the face of the man she'd unnerved in the corridor. His gun was pointing down at her, and he shouted something she didn't understand. It wasn't Turkish, she'd bet anything it was Russian.

Mulrooney let go of the framework where she held it and dropped, landing on her knees in the pile of broken concrete blocks, trying to roll with it, sucking in her breath, screaming with the pain in her knees and her hands as she landed, tumbling downward.

She shook her head, looking up again. Her left hand snaked out for the manila envelope as chunks of the concrete blocks powdered and sprayed toward her.

She hadn't broken an ankle, she figured; she was running too fast.

She heard something behind her that was unmistakably a curse and looked back. One of the gunmen had jumped to the bottom of the stairwell.

Mulrooney realized she was outside, in an alley of some kind. Behind her, toward Balthazar Muhammed's shop, the alley was blocked. She ran toward the opposite end, the alley narrowing like a funnel's mouth.

She shrieked involuntarily. A figure stepped out of the doorway near her. It was the man who had tried grabbing at her, the one she had kneed in the crotch and elbowed in the head.

"Lady, I no like—" There was a knife in his right hand as she dodged past him, his left hand reaching out for her. Mulrooney felt the right sleeve of her dress rip as she tried to break away from him.

She wheeled toward him then, ready to hammer her left fist into his face if it would do any good, but his eyes were suddenly wide and blood poured from his mouth as she stumbled back and he fell toward her. She tripped, falling to her knees. Both kneecaps were already scraped raw, and blood streaked her legs beneath her stockings as she tried to stand.

"Hold it!"

She looked up. It was the gunman from the corridor, the one who had jumped after her. His pistol was aimed at her head.

"What do you want?" she said.

"May I have the envelope—please?" He didn't smile.

The envelope was under her right hand, and as she started to pick it up, she noticed that under the envelope was the knife her now-dead assailant had wielded toward her. It looked like a long, thin pocketknife, the handle black plastic, the blade shiny.

The gunman crouched in front of her. "The envelope—okey-dokey?"

"Sure," Mulrooney said, smiling, raising the envelope with her left hand. The knife in her right hand, she threw her weight forward against the gunman, burying the blade into his neck as the pistol discharged beside her.

The man's eyes were fixed. He fell back, and she let go of the knife.

Mulrooney held the envelope in her left hand. In her right hand she picked up the fallen pistol.

She read what it said on the side of the pistol: Carl Walther Waffenfabrik. It looked, she thought, kind of like the gun James Bond always used in the movies.

Another man was running down the alley toward her,

a gun in his hand, and she stabbed the automatic pistol with its silencer out toward him, pulling the trigger. She pulled the trigger again and again and again, and then nothing happened.

The other gunman wasn't moving anymore.

Mulrooney looked at the gun in her hands, wanting to throw it down because it was empty. Still on her knees, she wiped off the butt of the gun with her skirt to get rid of her fingerprints.

Her prints would be all over Muhammed's place, but she could explain that away all right. Like Culhane always said, you weren't a writer for nothing.

The knife was deep in the dead Russian's neck—at least she assumed he was Russian.

She got up, her knees smarting. She lifted the wide part of the man's necktie from his bloodstained chest and wiped the handle of the knife with it.

The envelope—she had that.

She looked down the alley from where she had come. No one was coming after her . . . yet.

Mary Frances Mulrooney started running toward the opening in the alley. It was stupid to go back to her hotel, she knew, but that pink sundress was new. And she wasn't going to fly all the way to Brazil with her legs all full of blood and her dress ripped half off.

It was stupid, she told herself again. She had her passport, her money, her credit cards, and her airline tickets in her purse. She'd traveled light, packing only the bare necessities for a few days in Istanbul. The rest of the things she would need she had had shipped to Brazil.

A taxi stood at the end of the alley. She passed it up— just in case. She'd seen movies where the bad guys would disguise themselves as taxi drivers. Culhane used stuff like that in his books all the time.

She kept running.

Mulrooney turned right out of the alley and saw stalls and shops. She was back in the Kapalicarsi.

She slowed her pace. People were looking at her already.

A sign almost just above her read Dafik's Discount Dresses.

She turned into the store. If he had running water so she could clean off her legs, she was in business.

"Hello, lady!" a smiling fat man with a heavy mustache greeted her.

Mulrooney looked down at her bloody knees. "Show me something with a midcalf-length skirt."

"Betcha, lady—right away!"

Somehow she knew that Dafik's Discount Dresses was her kind of store.

Chapter Two _____

Melissa Burroughs was sitting in the booth in the galley, and the way she stuck her bare right leg across the companionway, Josh Culhane had three choices: step over it, crawl under it or ask her to move it. He decided to step over it, and as he did she raised her leg and her toes were rubbing against his crotch through his tennis shorts.

"Hey, Melissa. What are you doing?"

"Is that what Sean Dodge would say, Josh?"

"Probably," he told her, nodding his head and trying to smile at her. "Yeah, that's probably what he would say."

"And what would Sean Dodge do if the lady just kept rubbing his crotch with her big toe?"

"He'd whip out his Bali-Song knife, cut off her toe, then glance at the luminous black face of his Rolex Oyster Perpetual Sea Dweller and tell her he was supposed to be on deck two minutes ago."

Melissa Burroughs didn't remove her foot. "But I don't see your knife, Josh—"

"See? Right here..." Culhane tried reaching down to his pocket with his right hand, but her other foot was resting against his hip.

"Go ahead—move my foot. You can move my foot."

"I don't want to move your foot, Melissa. I want *you* to move your foot. *Both* of them, okay?"

"And what if I won't and you can't get to your knife—what would Sean Dodge do then, huh?" And she laughed, sipping at the beer from beside her on the galley table.

"Are you auditioning for the nymphomaniac character in the next *Takers*? C'mon—I gotta get topside."

"I'd love to try out for the nympho. Jake's doing a test dive later this morning. How about your cabin?"

"You're a married woman, Melissa."

"I'm left-handed, too—no big deal."

"Look, you met Fanny Mulrooney in Miami. Fanny and I, well—"

"Sean Dodge wouldn't care."

Culhane grinned at her. "Sean Dodge doesn't know Fanny."

"'Know'—I like that word in the Biblical sense—why don't you get to know me, Josh?"

There was a shout from topside. It was Jake Burroughs. "Hey, Culhane! Give us a hand!"

Culhane reached down to her left foot and ran his fingers fast along the sole. She started to giggle and her foot drew back reflexively. He pushed the other foot away and got past her, but he could hear her behind him, calling in a loud stage whisper, "This is a small boat, honey."

Culhane took the companionway steps two at a time, coming out into the sunlight past the aft bulkhead into the cockpit, then he flipped up onto the coach roof where some of the diving gear was laid out.

"Any problems below?" Burroughs asked, looking up from adjusting an air-tank cylinder band. Burroughs's gray eyes squinted hard. Culhane doubted it was the sun.

"Nothing I couldn't handle," Culhane told him, not smiling.

Burroughs had to know about his wife, Culhane had reasoned after the first night aboard *Seacutter*. Culhane had also guessed that Melissa Burroughs had accompanied them on *Seacutter* if for no other reason than Jake couldn't trust her alone on shore. "What can I help with?" Culhane asked, breaking the long silence. "Melissa was telling me down there you're planning a test dive. I thought we did that already yesterday."

"Yeah—but I did another test dive again this morning before you were up. Before Melissa was up. No, I got no more test dives planned. I need all the tanks double-checked for pressure. That wreck's about a hundred feet down, so we should have only a quarter of actual tank capacity considering the pressure. I want each tank to maximum and all things that can go wrong checked before they do go wrong. Not too deep a dive, but that wreck ain't in the best shape, neither."

Culhane thought for a moment, running the "no decompression" table in his head. "So we're talking about twenty-five minutes unless we want to do a timed ascent."

"Yeah—and at this stage there's no sense wasting time for that. I wanna go down, scout her out and then plan out tomorrow's dives. We'll pick up plenty of timed-ascent time once we start cleaning her out—unless we wanna hang around here for the next six weeks."

The black man squatting on the coach roof laughed. "That's if this here Liberian freighter really got all these fucking computer chips and shit."

Burroughs looked at him. "Look, Blackie—when Colby couldn't make it, he told me you were a terrific diver. All I seen you do is drink. All I heard you do is complain. Hell, if we were goin' much deeper than a hundred I wouldn't let you suit up. You'd have so much booze in your system you'd be dancin' upside down with the raptures, so shut the fuck up."

Blackie only laughed again. Culhane felt uncomfortable with the man—and with the name that sounded more like a racial slur than a nickname.

Lundy, crouched beside Burroughs, looked at Blackie and rasped, "Man—you're the kinda guy what gives us all a bad rep—go below and get sober, huh?"

Lundy scratched his chocolate-brown chin and the gray stubble there and looked away.

Culhane watched as Blackie got unsteadily to his feet and walked aft.

Burroughs began to talk again. "I found some blood in the head last night. I think Blackie's snortin' coke—"

"Aww, shit, man," Lundy groused.

"Hey, if he's got the membranes in his nose irritated, hell, he'll have a mask full of blood."

Culhane cleared his throat, saying, "How many do we need down there, d'you figure?"

"I can dive on this, man," Lundy volunteered.

"Who's gonna mind the store up here? Anyway, your heart. . ."

Lundy looked at Burroughs. "We been all through that, Jake—why'd you take me along then?"

"'Cause you're the best dive master goin' and if we do get in trouble, then fine, go risk your heart and come and bail out our asses. Otherwise, stay topside."

"Hell."

"Look," Culhane interrupted.

"What?"

Culhane looked at Burroughs. "Does Melissa dive?"

"Yeah—Melissa dives. Not too good, but she dives. Whaddaya got in mind?"

"Fine. You want two of us on the wreck and a third diver outside, right?"

"So?" Burroughs snapped.

"So, the deal with me coming along was I got to explore the wreck with you. You and I go in. Melissa stays outside in case there's any trouble. Blackie stays topside with Lundy to give Lundy a hand."

Burroughs let out a long, loud sigh. Then he turned to Lundy. "Get Melissa's beer away from her, put a lock on the icebox and pour some coffee into Melissa—and Blackie, too."

Then Burroughs turned to Culhane. "You got a deal, Josh." And Burroughs lit a cigarette. . . .

BURROUGHS USED ONLY DACOR EQUIPMENT and so did Culhane, but Culhane's budget was bigger, and he had the new aluminum tank that held eighty cubic feet of air rather than the older-style chrome-molybdenum steel tanks that Burroughs and his wife still used and which were customarily filled only to a hair over sixty-four and a half cubic feet.

He was descending slowly now, the sound of his air bubbles comforting to him as he exhaled a little into his mask to equalize pressure. As he looked up, he spotted the Portuguese man-of-war again, reminding himself to watch for it on his ascent. Its sting was in some ways similar to the effects of nerve gas on the respiratory system. Occasionally fatal. He had no desire to become a statistic.

Culhane was moving his jaw and swallowing against ear squeeze, but he was not experiencing pain. For a diver he smoked too much. But he was only an occasional diver. And for a writer, compared to some at least, he smoked too little.

Below seventy-five feet and slowly descending still, all that was around him—the ocean floor beneath him, the dim outline of what was the wrecked Liberian freighter—all was a deep blue, all other color diffused away. He checked his Rolex Sea Dweller against the Tekna dive timer; they were on the money with each other, he decided. He exhaled more air into his mask against face pinch, seeing Jake Burroughs to his right and Melissa Burroughs to his left evidently doing the same.

He heard a sound. Culhane glanced toward Jake Burroughs. Burroughs's diving knife, one of the big Wenokas that with the size distortion of the water looked the size of a Bowie knife, was tapping against his tank. Culhane watched him a moment, Burroughs using hand signals to gesture toward the hulking shape of the wreck perhaps a hundred yards to Culhane's left. Culhane nodded broadly, twisting the head of his Tekna Lite 8 into the "on" position. The blue seemed only brighter, but he could see the bottom better now. He leveled off his descent and swam a few feet over the wormlike tendriled plants that waved up at him. In the light of the flashlight the tendrils came alive in yellows and oranges and reds. He worked his flippers harder, resting his arms. They had used the DV-3X shuttle the previous day and would have used the shuttle today, but Blackie had been assigned to supervise and had neglected it, and there had not even been time for the three-hour fast charge.

So they swam unaided.

Culhane swung the light beam ahead of him again. There was more definition now to the wreck, and he could see more clearly than the day before, when there had been silt in the water, the gaping, jagged hole in the hull from the boiler explosion Burroughs had talked about.

Culhane had decided Burroughs was a contract man for the CIA. He had to be. He spoke so confidently of the position of the wreck, something a satellite could have confirmed. He spoke so confidently of the boiler exploding. How Burroughs had known that, Culhane had consciously avoided trying to guess.

The contents of the wrecked freighter—this, too, would have been hard to know, but Burroughs claimed he knew and had not been wrong yet. On the world market, ten million dollars' worth of computer chips and the same amount in missile electronics. All for Cuba.

Burroughs claimed he was not only seeking to enhance his wealth with the operation, but he was a patriot as well. ''Keep the Commies from getting their things back, keep that bastard Castro from getting his hands on them,'' he'd told Culhane.

What Castro needed with computer chips and missile electronics was another story. Culhane had already decided to send Sean Dodge into Cuba, perhaps in *Takers* Number 19. But he wasn't certain. It would be useful to the story to actually get into Cuba himself. The State Department wouldn't be fond of the idea, but if he could somehow get Canadian ID manufactured for himself...

Culhane lost his train of thought. Burroughs was rapping his knife against his tank again.

Burroughs was carrying on a frantic hand-and-arm-signal conversation with Melissa. Finally he put his mask against the side of her pink hood—it was the only hot-pink wet suit Culhane had ever seen—and was apparently shouting to her.

Culhane looked away, flashing his light through the hole in the hull.

Burroughs had elected to do something any experienced diver would consider unsafe: abandon going through the conventional means of entrance and enter the ship through the hole in the starboard side amidships.

Culhane shook his head at that. Daring was fine; stupidity something else.

They had agreed that since Culhane's air tank was larger and his air supply could better take the exertion of a long swim, Culhane would circumnavigate the wreck before entering and scouting it.

Culhane tapped on his own air tank with his light and Burroughs looked toward him. Culhane gestured toward the wreck, then made a circular motion. Burroughs nodded broadly. Culhane would let Burroughs fight with his wife in private. He started swimming toward the freighter's stern.

He shifted the position of his Bali-Song knife taped under his wet suit. He was getting a pressure pinch and would most likely have a nasty welt there. But he had decided to bring it. Maybe it was Blackie's attitude; maybe it was the way Burroughs eyed him after coming up on deck fresh from another encounter with Melissa Burroughs.

Culhane kept moving, shining his light along the hull, then he started to swim the length of the ship from above before continuing to circumnavigate the hull. The part about the freighter going down in a storm seemed true enough, although the damage evident could have resulted from something else. He stopped over the main hatch, shining his light downward off the port side. Nothingness. A void. That was another part of the dive that less than enthused him.

The freighter rested on the lip of a precipice and what seemed to be a bottomless trench beyond it. If the sandy bottom beneath the freighter were to shift with a sudden powerful current, the freighter would roll over into the abyss. And whoever was inside would be crushed by the pressure before having the chance to die from impact.

A sobering thought, Culhane reflected.

For some reason he thought about Fanny Mulrooney.

She should still be in Istanbul with that pirate Balthazar Muhammed filling her head full of crap about secret archeological finds and similar drivel, he thought. She was a good writer. He'd tried getting her to do a novel, even to start one. But she insisted on writing about monsters and legends and devils and flying saucers.

After completing the dives with Burroughs, Burroughs would drop him on the coast and he would fly inland to meet Fanny in Belém. Then they would go up the Amazon, Fanny searching for fragments of information and mysterious bones and relics for her book *Warrior Women* and Culhane searching for... He didn't know quite what. Material for another of Sean Dodge's adventures. At least that was what he told himself.

Culhane doubled back from the forecastle, traveling up along the full-dress ship line, then down again toward the stern, swinging out to cover the portside hull along the waterline, avoiding looking down. Into the abyss. He had no fear of heights, but he had no desire to become disoriented, either. There was a strong downward current here, and Culhane found himself getting caught up in it. "Shit," he snarled into his mouthpiece, letting the current carry him for an instant. Suddenly it twisted him and he lost his orientation. Groping out with his light, he could see the shape of the forwardmost end of the propeller shaft. He let the light fall from his hand on its lanyard around his wrist and reached for the shaft.

He had it, dragging himself in toward the shaft, holding on with both hands now.

His body swung with the current, sucked at by it. Culhane popped the seal on his mask, letting water in to make an impromptu level.

He closed his eyes then opened them, working his way along the underside of the hull now and forward.

It was dangerous what he did, he knew. Even the slightest shift of the hull and he would be crushed beneath it. But the current leading down into the abyss was sudden death.

He wondered if that was why he had been sent to scout the far side of the hull rather than merely because of the increased capacity of his tanks.

But Culhane dismissed the idea. Burroughs wouldn't kill because of his wife's desire to get someone besides her husband into her pants. If Burroughs did, he would be a mass murderer.

Culhane kept going, continuing his reasoning to avoid thinking about the tons of wrecked freighter that at any second could crush him downward into a smear of flesh and wet suit and mangled steel. He kept moving, kept thinking. He was letting his imagination get away with him; it was a writer's occupational hazard. If you wrote espionage, you saw intrigue in everything. If you wrote mysteries, everyone was a potential cold-blooded murderer.

He shook his head and glanced at his pressure gauge. He was fine. He shook his head again—

"Nitrogen narcosis," he murmured into his mouthpiece. But at only one hundred feet, there had to be a reason for it. He laughed a little but still worked his way ahead. Fear. Perhaps the fear of the abyss when he had been sucked in by the current.

He stopped. He held on to the underside of the hull and to the rocks against which the hull was wedged. There was one sure remedy for it. He tried remembering what it was. He laughed at himself.

There were ladder rungs ahead and Culhane started for them, finally remembering. Ascend.

He started up the ladder rungs, the current tugging at his back. He thought about the current and laughed, saying into his mouthpiece, "Not gonna get me!"

He kept moving. To ascend would reduce the level of nitrogen in his blood and sober him up.

Culhane made a mental note to quit smoking for a week before his next major dive. Maybe that would help.

He could see the outline of the ship's rail above him now. He grabbed at it, half climbing, half swimming over it, then he pushed himself off, swimming upward. For some reason he checked his time. He still had ten minutes to go before he had to start up for real.

He kept ascending and could faintly see the shapes of Jake Burroughs and Melissa Burroughs beside the hole in the hull.

Culhane studied his watch face as he ascended, forcing his brain to work.

$E = MC^2$—but what does it really mean, he wondered. Energy expressed in units called ergs is equal to the sum of the mass of an object multiplied by the speed of light squared. Aw, boy.

He stopped his ascent at seventy-five feet or so and realized he'd been breathing rapidly.

Culhane forced himself to be calm.

"Calm," he said into his mouthpiece. He found his light on his lanyard and turned it on, aiming it into the distance. There was something moving. Maybe a shark. He hoped it wasn't a shark. He'd done a stint in a shark cage once, and it had been an unnerving experience, especially after the shark had nearly eaten half the cage and him with it.

Killer whales, he thought, because whatever it was it was a school of them, and killer whales traveled in packs when they hunted. They rarely—if ever—attacked man.

He told himself to relax, the effects of the excess nitrogen clearing now. He ran the eights through his head. "Eight times nine is seventy-two. Eight times seven is fifty-six. Eight times—"

Men.

They were men moving through the water, and what had not happened when the current had sucked at him happened now. He could almost physically feel it. Adrenaline.

It was flowing now, his head clearing almost instantly.

Men—maybe a dozen of them. Black wet suits. Spear guns. Some type of underwater shuttle—but really large.

Culhane shook his head one more time.

He started down, slamming his flashlight against his air tank to try and attract Burroughs's attention.

Melissa Burroughs in her hot-pink wet suit was turning around. Culhane whipped his light to his left toward the divers, toward the shuttle. She waved back at him. Culhane tapped at the tank again with his light.

He looked left. The divers were angling down toward the wreck of the freighter, the diffused light from their shuttle casting a gray wash on the water ahead.

Culhane exhaled into his mask, evacuating more of the water he had let it partially fill with earlier. He swam toward Jake and Melissa Burroughs at full speed.

Russian freighter. Russian divers. "Shit," he snarled into his mouthpiece.

Burroughs was turning around now from the hole in the freighter's hull. He'd seen the Russian divers, too. Burroughs treaded water as he snatched his massive diving knife from the sheath on his right leg.

Culhane decided that was a good idea. It wasn't really a *good* idea, but it was better than nothing.

Culhane shifted the flashlight's lanyard to his left wrist, snatching his Tekna knife, the sheath that was integral with his compass, depth gauge, pressure gauge and digital dive timer.

It was a small knife, about the size of a good boot knife. But it felt right through the reef glove that covered his right hand.

One of the spear guns fired, just missing Melissa Burroughs. Jake Burroughs picked up the spear that had bounced off the hull, holding it in his left hand and the knife in his right as the divers approached.

Culhane closed with the lead divers at the same time, grabbing at the nearest Russian's air hose and hacking it with one of the serrated upper edges of the knife. In a flurry of air bubbles, Culhane's right foot pushed the diver away, and he slashed his knife across the man's chest, his left hand ripping away the face mask. Blood filled the water.

A cloud of darker water.

Culhane twisted left, one of the Russian divers coming for him, a spear gun firing with a whoosh and a trail of bubbles, the spear passing inches from his head. Culhane threw himself forward against the man, the diving knife in Culhane's right fist pumping into the diver's abdomen, then back out, then in again. Culhane pushed the body clear.

Melissa Burroughs's body contorted and slammed against the hull of the freighter. A spear was protruding from her abdomen now, dark reddish-black streaks washing across the hot-pink wet suit, the cloud all but obscuring her as it grew and grew.

Jake Burroughs was using his knife well, one diver then another floating away from him as he fought his way toward his wife.

Culhane felt something slam against him, and he was pitched forward. His right shoulder hit the sand at the base of the hull, a cloud of sediment rising around him.

He looked up. There was a flash of bright light and Culhane's ears suddenly ached with the sound waves. Something huge and dark was drifting downward.

A shape shot past his face: a shark. Its length was about eight feet, and suddenly it and Melissa Burroughs seemed one, and then as quickly they were separated and the bottom half of her body was gone, one leg floating upward, a cloud of blackness enveloping Culhane and he wanted to retch.

Another of the Russian divers swam toward him, and Culhane stabbed the man in the left side of the neck, using the diving knife like a rapier. There was another cloud of blood and Culhane pulled back. The dark shape drifting down from above was uncomfortably close—and he knew what it was.

Seacutter and she was down.

Burroughs was beside him treading water, his face turned toward his dead and mutilated wife.

Culhane grabbed at him and shook him. He stared into Burroughs's face mask; the eyes were fixed and glassy, as though he was already dead.

Culhane held on to him, prying the knife from Burroughs's right fist lest Burroughs suddenly snap out of it and use the knife against him. He locked his left fist around Burroughs's right wrist and dragged him from his dead wife. His small Tekna knife was back in its sheath; the massive Bowie-like diving knife he had taken from Jake Burroughs was clenched in his right fist.

He glanced back at the bottom as he began his ascent. Some of the Russian divers were setting charges against the hull of the sunken freighter.

Culhane looked up. There were more Soviet divers descending.

There was only one place to go now, Culhane thought as he wrenched Burroughs along with him. He headed toward the still settling hull of *Seacutter*, her main mast overturned, a hole in the port bow large enough to drive a small truck through.

Culhane aimed toward her stern.

The nitrogen narcosis was gone now; adrenaline had replaced it, a high that could save the body.

Dragging Burroughs was slowing him, but he would not leave the man.

A Soviet diver, his diving knife large, was fast approaching.

The knife hacked toward Culhane, and he loosed Burroughs's wrist for a moment, shoving Burroughs away as the Soviet diver's blade cut within inches of Culhane's throat.

Culhane twisted his body to the right. Another lunge was coming, and Culhane reached for the arm, his action slowed by the natural drag of the water. But his attacker's movement was slowed, as well.

Culhane's borrowed blade cleaved downward across the inside of the man's right elbow, ripping back. Blood spurted outward, the diving knife falling from the Russian's right hand, the fingers limp, blood pouring across them from the wound at the elbow.

Culhane was ready for a final thrust, a kill. But he was knocked aside by a shark. If anything, this one was larger than the one before. The Soviet diver's mouthpiece fell from his lips and for an instant Culhane could see the look of horror and then the right arm was ripped away and the shark twisted violently, the Soviet diver's body lurching, the shark ripping at him.

Culhane looked behind him for Burroughs.

Burroughs was swimming back into the knot of Soviet divers beside the hull of the freighter.

Culhane snarled curses into his mouthpiece. He couldn't leave Burroughs; it wasn't right. Practical had never been a meaningful word for him, Culhane knew. Practical was a cop-out.

He started down after Burroughs, two of the Soviet divers already falling on him. Burroughs straight-armed one man in the face and ripped the mask from another.

Culhane swam against a third man, ramming Burroughs's knife into the man's right kidney, shoving the body off the knife.

He grabbed at Burroughs, and Burroughs instinctively swung at him, but the water slowed him down enough for Culhane to duck the blow.

He shoved the knife toward Burroughs, and Burroughs took it.

Culhane grabbed his own knife.

They were back to back, the sound of their air tanks

clanging ominously in the blue blackness of the deep beside the hull of the sunken freighter.

Russian divers closed in from both sides, Culhane fending off one man with his knife, then another.

A spear gun was raised, Culhane ready to dive for the man.

But suddenly the spear gunner was pushed against the hull of the freighter by a shark, and seconds later his body was locked in deadly combat, the spear firing uselessly upward.

Culhane turned to grab at Burroughs, to signal for them to ascend, but Burroughs's body was sinking forward. As Culhane twisted him around, he could see the shaft of a spear protruding from Burroughs's chest, a cloud of blood surrounding him.

And through the face mask Culhane saw the look of death in Burroughs's eyes—and this time the look of death was real.

Culhane swam away, a shark punching at him and knocking the wind from him for an instant, but the shark ignored him, going for Burroughs's blood.

Culhane looked up. Still more Soviet divers were coming to help their comrades, and Culhane swam for the portside hull of *Seacutter*.

He glanced at the dive timer near his chest; nearly the full twenty-five minutes was gone. There was a margin for safety, but it would be slight.

He swam faster, ignoring his own accumulated wisdom from personal experience and the experience of other divers. He swam for the hole in the hull.

Jake Burroughs had shown him the new stainless-steel .45 he had. Once he got to the surface—he refused to think the word "if"—Culhane could expect only one thing. Careful of his gear, he swam through.

He was inside where the portside V-shaped berth had

been and opposite a hanging locker. He started aft, toward the stateroom he had shared with Lundy.

The Tekna knife ahead of him like a wand, he stopped suddenly. Jammed into the doorway of the owner's head he saw Blackie. Blackie's eyes were staring, his arms floating, the door into the head binding his legs there. Protruding from his right arm was a needle.

Culhane swam past, wrenching open the door to his cabin, swimming up and coming into an air pocket. Culhane left his regulator in place. He rifled through his black nylon flight bag. His passport. His wallet. His money, which he counted daily, considering Blackie's habits. His keys. From a pouch at his weight belt, Culhane tugged free a Ziploc plastic bag, inserted the things between the sealing lips and ran his gloved fingers along the edge, locking the bag, making it watertight.

The rest of it there was no time for, no need for.

Culhane swam down from the upper bunk, across the flooded companionway to the stateroom.

The desk in the far corner by the bulkhead was thrown over like the rest of the furnishings of the ship's largest stateroom. Culhane tore open the middle drawer. Burroughs thankfully had not kept it locked.

The stainless Randall LeMay model. A spare magazine. From the weight of the gun, it was as Burroughs had last left it: loaded except for the chamber. The spare magazine was loaded, as well.

Culhane started ripping through the drawers, searching for a box of spare ammunition.

Prolonged exposure to saltwater could render it useless, but the time hadn't been that long.

Books and papers floated everywhere around him, but there was no sign of the log book. He would have taken that.

No sign of more ammunition.

And then Culhane heard it. He had heard the sound in movies, read accounts of others hearing it in real life.

It was the sound of a mine being placed on the hull.

The starboard hull. He forced himself to think. The mines on the freighter—they were going to blow both ships over into the abyss.

Culhane's palms sweated inside his reef gloves.

He jammed the Randall under his wet suit top, the spare magazine wedged beside it.

Through the stateroom door, forward now, past the dead body of Blackie with his needle still stuck in his arm. Past the dinette table, a beer can floating up from the garbage can.

Culhane came to the hole in the portside hull. He swam through it, and out.

Around him there was carnage. The Soviet divers battled a group of blood-crazed sharks.

Culhane started his ascent, then thought for a second. He swam for the deck of *Seacutter*. If Lundy had gotten into a tank setup before the ship had gotten too far down, he might be alive, trapped.

Culhane swam over the coach roof, looking from right to left—and then he saw him.

The only other gun aboard the ship was still in his hands, locked there in death. Lundy clenched a stainless Ruger Mini-14 in his dead hands, his eyes staring, the top of his skull split wide.

Culhane swam to him. As yet no sharks had found the body.

Culhane reached out to him. He tore the reef glove from his right hand and let it sink away, his thumb working down first one, then the second eyelid. Into his mouthpiece, Culhane murmured, "Rest in peace, Lundy."

Another of the thudding sounds. Culhane swam for

it, ditching his weight belt, controlling his breathing. He didn't want to look at the dive timer. Going up.

Up. Below him the Soviet divers were moving off.

Up. He could feel the pressure changes.

Up. His head broke the surface and he spat the mouthpiece away, gulping the cool fresh air. Far to his right, perhaps a half mile distant, was a freighter. It would be the base of the Soviet divers.

And it was his only prayer.

Culhane found his mouthpiece and tucked down under the surface, swimming for it now.

His limbs stiff, aching, his mind telling his body to keep moving, his body telling his mind where to go. He kept swimming.

And suddenly the sea around him ripped upward, Culhane's body buffeted with it, twisting, wrenching, punched at by pressure waves as he fought his way to the surface, a rain of spray pouring down on him.

He knew what had happened. The Soviet wreck and the wreck of *Seacutter* were both down in the abyss now.

There was no time to think. If the Soviet freighter toward which he swam was to get underway before he reached it, he was a dead man.

Chapter Three

It was interesting to watch the rich, for he had never been one of them but had often been near them. In one way, they lived like the people in Saigon had lived. As if each day were perhaps the last. But they were unlike the people in Saigon, for they did not want.

Damascus Santini lit a Camel, flipping the lighter in his hand. It was the same lighter he had carried throughout the war, and it carried the Special Forces insignia.

All the men on the team of which he had been a part had been given one of the lighters by the team leader, each man's name engraved on the opposite side from the crest.

He studied the lighter, reading his name.

He pulled up the hem of his alb and found the slit in the right side of his cassock that allowed access to his pants pocket, and stashed the cigarettes and the lighter there.

"Should be nearly there, Father Santini. Once we're within the limit, I'll be told."

He nodded. "Hope it's not too quick, Captain Porter. I just lit up here."

"I don't mean any disrespect, Father," Porter began, his florid face lighting with a grin that could only be Irish, "but you're an odd sort for a priest. The wisecracks...I can't put it into words, but, well, more like a normal..."

"A normal man?" Santini smiled. "Yeah, well—if you don't let the word get around, I am. No lie." Porter started to laugh and Santini let himself laugh a little, exhaling a cloud of cigarette smoke.

"So you and Scott Palmer, Jr., were in Vietnam together. You been a chaplain long?"

"I was never a chaplain."

"Medic, then?"

"I was part of a Special Operations team—all Special Forces except every once in a while we'd get a couple of Navy SEALS or some CIA guy. Used to be Sergeant

First Class Damascus Santini. Now it's Father Santini—same man regardless of the uniform. In most ways, anyway."

"So you and Mr. Palmer. . ." Porter didn't finish his question, just let it hang.

"He was the youngest guy in Captain Culhane's outfit, but he was a good trooper if that's what you were asking."

"This Captain Culhane—I didn't see him on the guest list—didn't make it back?"

Santini laughed at that. "No. They've never made the bullet that'll get old Jeff Culhane."

"That name rings a bell. Is he a writer or something?"

"You're thinking of Josh Culhane, the guy who writes adventure novels."

"*The Takers*, right? Get 'em in the ship's bookstore."

"Josh is Jeff's twin brother. Never met him, but Jeff used to talk about him a lot. I don't know what Jeff does these days. I think he moved over into less vigorous government work. I haven't talked to him in about two or three years, and he didn't talk about his business then. No—Scott's the only one of us that made it into the big time, inheriting all that money and everything."

Porter exhaled long and loud. "Mr. Palmer is a very rich young man, Father—I'll say that."

"That didn't sound like a compliment," Santini remarked, flicking ashes from his cigarette.

He didn't expect a reply and he didn't get one.

The buzzer rang and Captain Porter snatched up the telephone receiver. "Porter here."

Under his breath Santini rasped, "Saved by the bell, Captain."

"Very good, Mr. Snow—give us a smooth ride."

Porter hung up the phone, turned away from the wind-screen and looked at Santini. "My chief officer has just informed me that we have passed into Brazilian coastal waters as per the request of Mr. Palmer's fiancée, so the wedding can begin." And then Porter laughed. "Funny for me to watch a shipboard wedding. I've married a lot of people myself."

Santini grinned. "As a Catholic priest, I should re-mind you that unless they were married by a priest they were not married in the sight of God. Civil ceremonies don't count, even at sea." Santini slapped Porter on the shoulder. "But that'd be a pretty hard-nosed attitude, wouldn't it?"

The captain laughed, shaking his head as he walked away, Santini straightening out his chasuble.

He could hear the captain spreading the word that the ceremony was about to begin, and Santini looked along the cruise ship's sun deck forward and toward the stack. Standing like the two figures atop a wedding cake but one to port and one to starboard, surrounded by their attendants, were the bride and groom. Santini started walking toward them, holding his book from which he would recite the marriage vows to them.

Palmer wore a white three-piece suit, his blond hair blowing slightly in the breeze.

Palmer's fiancée was the epitome of what the beauti-ful bride should be: dark hair flowing past her shoulders all but masked by the longer flowing veil; the white dress an artful combination of yards of lace and yards of silk; the bridesmaids ooing and aahing around her, looking like the varied petals of some multicolored flower—one blue, one pink, one yellow, one green.

Santini ascended the small platform erected for the ceremony. Palmer owned the cruise-ship line, one of the many elements of Palmer Industries, Inc. He had personally chartered the ship for his wedding party to the beautiful and very European-looking girl named Amelina. The captain of the flagship of Palmer's line was giving away the bride in lieu of her father. Each guest, aside from receiving a free cruise and all the food and champagne he or she could consume, was given a specially struck gold coin commemorating the wedding that bore the likenesses of Scott Palmer, Jr. and Amelina. The gold was from Palmer Industries mines in Brazil.

As Scott Palmer waited now beside the newly fabricated altar rail, Amelina was brought forward by the captain, who raised her veil. Amelina kissed the captain on the cheek, and Santini winked at his old friend Scott.

Santini began, "Dearly beloved..."

And at least one of them was to him, as beloved as any man's comrade-in-arms could be.

SANTINI FELT CONSPICUOUS; he was the only man in a black suit. In the old days in Chicago a guy had felt well dressed with a clean T-shirt and a pack of cigarettes that was still at least half full rolled into the sleeve. He shrugged his shoulders, stabbed his hands into his trouser pockets and mingled.

He had walked over much of the ship, watching the revelry. It was tough being a priest at a party. There wasn't anything wrong with dancing, but people always looked at you strangely if you did—"Look at that priest with his hands on that woman!"—and if you drank too much, that got them started on all the old sacramental wine jokes.

He stood by the bar now, overlooking the upper-level pool. "Can I get ya somethin', Father?"

Santini turned around. The bartender was addressing

him. "Well, I suppose I might try something," Santini said, smiling.

"Maybe a glass of white wine?"

"How about a shot of Jim Beam and a Michelob?" Santini answered, letting the smile turn into a grin.

"Sure thing, Father—back in a second."

While the bartender poured the shot and opened the beer, Santini lit a cigarette. Scott Palmer, Jr., married, he thought.

"Here ya go, Father. If ya need somethin' else, just check with me."

"Gotcha," Santini nodded, slugging down the shot of bourbon and setting the empty on the bar. He left the glass for the beer and took the bottle, sipping a pull of it and giving the bartender a wave.

Orchestras played all over the ship, and if you listened hard, Santini reflected, when the wind was just right you could hear two songs at once. He kept walking, finding an ashtray for his cigarette and stubbing it out after a last drag, then continuing on. He could see Scott Palmer and the new Mrs. Scott Palmer just ahead beyond a small forest of white dinner jackets and pastel garden-party dresses. He skirted the forest and walked straight for his ex-Army buddy. Scott had been a second lieutenant, but that was because Scott had been rich enough to go to college before the Army.

"Hey—Lieutenant!"

Scott Palmer turned around so fast he almost spilled his champagne, and Damascus Santini laughed.

"Damascus—come on over here."

Santini shouldered past a few white dinner jackets and stood flanking Amelina with Palmer. "I didn't get to kiss the bride," Santini said, and she leaned up toward him and he buzzed her lightly on the lips.

"Sometimes you civilians have all the luck," Santini joked.

"You're right there—I do have all the luck. Ever since I met Amelina."

Amelina was either very quiet by nature or had little to say. Santini was not sure. Her English was excellent although she was Brazilian by birth and education. "You two need to have a reunion for all of your Army friends. I can tell that by just listening."

"You know, she's got a point there," Palmer agreed, running his left hand through his thick blond hair.

"Yeah, well, there'll be no reunion without me, and I'm gonna be outta circulation for a while up the old Amazon," said Santini, taking another pull of his beer.

"I still can't figure a guy like you being sent way back in the jungle to mind a Catholic mission for two years."

"Look, missions in a Brazilian jungle can't be too much different from missions on the South Side of Chicago, only here they're supposed to be a little more backward. Just switchblades—they haven't gotten into guns yet."

Palmer leaned across his wife and slapped Santini on the shoulder. "In two years, then, we'll have a reunion—but it won't be the same."

Santini just looked at him. "Do you know something I don't know?"

"I mean with Jeff gone and all—"

"Jeff?"

"Yeah, why the hell do you think—excuse me—why do you think he wasn't here, Damascus?"

"Jeff Culhane dead? Shit." Santini reminded himself to do a penance for that one. "What happened?"

"God, Damascus, I missed the funeral, but I heard about it a couple of days later. I tried contacting his

brother Josh, but he was away on business or something. But it was in all the papers.''

"Not the Chicago papers. What happened?''

"They put him down as working for some computer
software outfit in Virginia, but I checked. Jeff was CIA,
you know.''

Santini nodded. He knew. "Business?''

"Nobody'd ever give me the truth, but I put two and
two together. It looked like some people assassinated
him. I thought you knew. Gee, man—I'm sorry,
Damascus.''

Amelina interrupted. "Look, both of you, this is a
wedding. I'm sorry, Father, about the death of your
friend. But this is a happy time. Please?'' And she
smiled up at him.

Santini took her hand and nodded. "Yeah, look, ah,
I'm gonna go for a walk—catch some sea breezes and
stuff. See you guys later, okay?'' Santini didn't wait for
an answer; he just walked away.

He didn't know where he was going, and he didn't
know enough about the layouts of ships to get there if
he had. A rubber raft? He knew them inside and out.
And the rowboats in the lagoon in Lincoln Park—he
was pretty good with those.

This thing was too big, an ocean-going hotel. The
captain had told him it normally carried almost seven
hundred fifty people plus over three hundred staff.

But today the ship was running with a full crew and
only three hundred intimate friends of Palmer and his
bride. The odds between the rich and the poor were
pretty even for once.

Santini kept walking. He was going forward along the
right-hand side of the ship. He remembered the term
was starboard. They weren't too big on nautical ter-
minology in the seminary.

He kept walking, thinking about Jeff Culhane. It was the first time he used a word like—like that out loud in maybe four or five years. But Jeff dead. He told himself he'd write a letter to Josh Culhane when he hit the beach and give Josh the address for the mission. He had to tell Jeff's brother how sorry he was and find out more about how it happened. But he could never tell Jeff's brother just how sorry he was.

"Hey, Father, I could use your help!" said a familiar voice.

Santini stopped and turned around. "What's up, Captain?"

"We're trying to keep it down—"

"What?" Santini asked, cutting the distance between himself and Captain Porter to just a few yards. He stopped, leaning against a lifeboat and glancing overboard. "The boat spring a leak?"

"Don't even say that in jest, Father. No, look up ahead."

Porter pointed forward, and Santini leaned over the rail ahead of the lifeboat and peered out to sea. He saw what looked like a small powerboat. "Dead ahead in the water out there. It looks like a couple of bodies aboard her. Once we see what's up I'm having a radio message sent to the Brazilian authorities. I've got the chief engineer slowin' her down enough so we can get near enough to get a line on it and haul it alongside."

"If they're Brazilians, odds are they're Catholic. I'll get my gear for the last rites just in case and meet you— where do I meet you?"

"Back along the fantail, Father. These babies don't stop on a dime, you know. It's lucky we were just meandering along or we would have been on them before we could have stopped."

"Okay. Where's the fantail?"

"Back end of the boat," Porter said, and grinned.

"Gotcha," Santini nodded, and took off at a run in the direction of his stateroom....

SANTINI WAS STARTING TO FEEL BETTER about things—at least a little. Some of Scott and Amelina Palmer's guests had stopped their drinking and partying long enough to do more than just gawk over the rail into the small boat and had offered to help. Captain Porter tactfully ordered them to stand by in case they were needed, and proceeded to conduct the rescue effort with his crew. There were only two bodies: a man in swimming trunks and a woman in a bikini. The man was collapsed beside the controls of the small cabin cruiser, and the woman was lying in the back of the boat. Santini supposed there could be more people below.

"What do you think happened?" Santini asked the ship's doctor beside him.

"Hard to say, Father," the man answered with a deep Southern drawl. "Could have been a freak storm. From this distance the bodies don't look badly sunburned, so they can't have been out here like this for long. Maybe food poisoning. That happens a lot with small boats that don't have adequate refrigeration. And in these waters the temperatures get awfully high awfully quick. Have to wait and see, I suspect."

Santini only nodded but then added, "I hope it's a job for you and not for me—if you know what I mean."

"Yeah, I know what you mean, Father." The doctor went on puffing his cigar.

Santini riveted his eyes back to the small boat. The motion of the cruise ship was making him a little seasick now, the engines at dead stop. He decided that the bigger the ship, the more you felt her rock in the water.

"Got her!" a seaman called. He was hanging off a

small scaffolding immediately below them, a boat hook at the end of his outstretched right arm.

"Bring her alongside, Peterson."

"Aye, Captain."

A second scaffolding appeared, and a second boat hook was whipped out from it by another crewman. The small boat was being pulled forward and closer to the cruise ship's hull. "The woman's breathin', Captain! She's alive!"

Santini really felt better now, and from the passengers and crew lining the rail there was a spontaneous cheer.

A third crewman hanging from a third scaffolding jumped and made it onto the craft, landing less than gracefully. He caught up a line and tossed it upward toward one of the men on the scaffolding. "Securing, Captain—she's secure!"

"Get another line on her," Porter called down.

As the sailor started to turn to reach down for another coil of rope, the body of the woman suddenly animated, rolling off the seat in a flash, and Santini recognized what was in her hands. It was a MAC-11 submachine gun. "Nobody does a damned thing or a lot of people get really dead real quick!"

Her male companion was throttling the seaman to the deck now, a pistol jammed against the sailor's head. "And he dies."

Two more people, both clad in black clothes with ski masks, came from the cabin of the cruiser, MAC-10s firing short bursts into the air. Then they pointed them along the rail, causing screams from some of the female passengers around Santini.

And then he heard the gunfire and the screams from behind him. Santini grabbed as many people to him as he could and threw himself and them back from the rail as the submachine guns opened up from below.

And there was gunfire everywhere now. The ship's doctor had a gaping hole at the center of his forehead, the cigar still clamped between his teeth.

Santini heard Captain Porter shouting, "My God—what's happening?"

Santini got up and ran. Palmer was a good man in a fight. Maybe between the two of them they could do something. He skirted the lower-level pool, taking the stairs up three at a time. Palmer and Amelina had stayed near the upper-level pool with the rest of their guests after the captain had advised everyone that watching at the rail represented more of a hindrance than a help.

He saw Scott Palmer. And he saw armed men everywhere in orange wet suits, their faces covered with black ski masks and diving masks with snorkel tubes attached to them hanging from around their necks, MAC-10s and MAC-11s in their hands, firing.

Palmer reached for one of the men, and a submachine gun slammed across his face and put him down. Amelina screamed. Santini reached out, collaring one of the armed invaders, dropping him to the deck with a double tae kwon-do kick to the back of the knees. Santini's hands acted automatically, catching up the MAC-10 and ripping the sling from the body, bracing the weapon against the invader's larynx. His right knee hammered into the man's backbone between the shoulder blades. Santini realized he was killing the man and he stepped back, the submachine gun falling from his fingers and his shaking hands.

He looked at the thing that was called a squirt gun years ago. He could take one apart and put it back together blindfolded. He'd used one of these more than an M-16. How many men he had killed with one of these he didn't remember, but he had counted their faces lots of times, lots of nights....

THEY WERE SO FAR THE HELL NORTH of the DMZ that sometimes he thought they were going to China. He looked at Jeff Culhane. "Hey, Captain—where the hell are you and the lieutenant takin' us, anyways?"

"To a ball game, Damascus. You like baseball, right?"

"Shit, Captain, best damned hitter you'll ever see."

"Yeah, my ass. Remember the time—"

"I'm hit—Jesus—but I'm all right—" Palmer shouted.

Santini wheeled toward the gunfire and started shooting, the MAC-10 in his right fist, the .45 automatic in his left, ripped out of the leather tanker rig across his chest.

They were coming with bayonets and he kept shooting and the bodies kept piling up and up and Palmer cried out, "I'm bleedin' over here, guys!" But the bodies wouldn't stop piling up and Santini opened his eyes and there were dead eyes staring into his and he felt blood on his face and he knew he was alive and there was a dead woman on top of his own body.

He pushed her off. The front of her frilly pink dress was covered with splotches of red.

He sat up. His head throbbed with pain. This wasn't Vietnam. There weren't women in pink party dresses in Vietnam....

He heard the scream again. It was Palmer. "Leave her alone, you motherfuckers!"

Then came a woman's scream and a loud thudding sound.

Santini freed his legs of another corpse, this one a man.

He tried to stand up but pitched forward, his face inches from the pool. There were three bodies floating in it.

The shouting was coming from the little deck below the sun deck where the wedding ceremony had taken place.

Santini rolled back from the edge of the pool so if he fell he wouldn't fall in.

His head was exploding, and he knew that the blood he felt on his face was his own.

To his knees. A priest was good at that, he thought.

To his feet.

There were only dead men and dead women around him near the pool. He looked toward the fantail. He didn't try to count the bodies.

He shook his head to clear it and staggered back, dropping to one knee. The pain.

Gotta get up there, Santini thought. He started for the stairway, but then he dropped into a crouch beside the steps and slid under them. A man with a ski mask and a submachine gun was at the top of the steps. God didn't want him to kill, he figured. But knocking a guy around a little with some karate or some street fighting or some boxing in a good cause . . . ? He peered out from beneath the steps. He could get up behind the guy if he turned around, then toss the gun to Palmer.

He waited, listening.

"I was going to tell this to Palmer, so I'll tell it to you—"

"My passengers! My crew!" It was Porter.

There was a sound of knuckles contacting bone. "Shut up about your goddamned ship!" The voice had a French accent.

Santini didn't bother to listen to the rest. There was another way up by going along behind the lifeboats and climbing up. He slipped under the steps, stuffing his shoes in his pockets as he ran.

A man stood about six feet from the lifeboat. Santini

watched him. If he jumped the man, chances were good that the submachine gun would start spraying. That wouldn't be so good.

But God was on his side, he reasoned.

The French voice called out, "Phillipe! Get over here!"

The man with the submachine gun trotted off, and Santini flipped from the rack that supported the lifeboat and jumped to the deck. He ran forward in stocking feet, flattening himself against the interior wall just behind the sun deck.

He could now see and hear.

Scott Palmer was sprawled on the deck, blood dripping from his nose and mouth, and a dark bruise on the left side of his head. Amelina was handcuffed and being held by the woman in the bikini from the boat that had been "in trouble." The MAC-11 was pointed at Amelina's head.

Captain Porter was on his knees, a pistol muzzle against his head. The man from the small boat held it.

"You just give this message to Palmer when he wakes up," the Frenchman said through his ski mask. "You can lose anything, anyone, but do not lose this message. If you do, his new wife dies. Do you understand?" He slapped Captain Porter's face. Porter looked up from his knees, his hat gone, his bald head oozing a line of blood. He nodded.

Santini assessed his chances. He could not jump one of the terrorists—or whatever they were—without another of them killing a hostage.

"Your radio has been smashed. I could smash your lifeboats, too—"

"Why—"

"Silence!" Again the Frenchman cuffed Captain Porter across his face. And then Santini heard it, something he'd been half expecting: the sound of heli-copter rotor blades. He could see the faint shape on the horizon as he peered around the corner. The noise of the machine grew in intensity, and Santini heard the sound of objects splashing into the water on both sides of the ship. He stole away from the corner and back toward the lifeboat, peering down over the rail. Their ski masks gone, diving masks in place, snorkels set, flip-pers in position, their weapons in clear plastic bags, in pairs the terrorists were jumping ship and swimming off.

Santini could no longer hear the splashing sounds. From the horizon line shoreward, power launches began to appear. He didn't delude himself that it was help. Merely transportation for the terrorists. Some of them were already clambering aboard the small boat still moored aft, the small boat the cruise ship had stopped to help. Santini fought at the hatred building in him, filling him.

But the sound of the powerboats was gone now, and the roaring sound of chopper blades very close.

Santini ran from the lifeboat, toward the corner from where he had first observed. The helicopter hovered low over the sun deck. Amelina was wrestled down to her knees, her handcuffed wrists drawn up high, her head pushed down. A bag was thrown over her head, like a flour sack, then tied around her neck.

The Frenchman was shaking Porter, shouting some-thing to him that Santini could not hear. Two guns were trained on Amelina as she was dragged along the deck on her knees, the once-beautiful wedding dress ripped and bloodstained. Amelina was pushed to her feet and half thrown into the waiting helicopter, the woman and the man from the small boat beside her, their guns still trained on her.

Porter held a plastic-bagged envelope in his hands, the Frenchman slapping him back and forth across the face. And then the Frenchman and the last guard ran toward the helicopter, their submachine guns aimed at Porter. The guard clung to the float beneath the chopper's fuselage, the chopper climbing now, a burst of gunfire lacing across the deck, but Porter sat unmoving, staring up at it.

Santini ran from hiding, dropping and skidding on his knees to be beside Porter. "What did he say, Captain?"

"Explosive devices are planted all over the ship!" Porter shouted, weeping. "The radio's destroyed! All communications cut! The charges should start going off any minute. God help us!"

"The Lord helps those who help themselves, remember? Let's get everyone that's still alive into the lifeboats. Do you have radios—emergency radios?"

"Yes—yes—"

"What about Amelina?"

"This—" Porter brandished the envelope "—for Mr. Palmer."

And Santini turned to Palmer, cradling Palmer's head in his lap for a moment. He breathed evenly enough, but he was unconscious. He had been pistol-whipped. Santini rose to his feet. "I'm getting Scott into the nearest lifeboat, then I'll help you. Start organizing to abandon the ship."

Porter stumbled to his feet. Soon his voice came over the intercom: "Now hear this! Now hear this! This is Captain Porter speaking. All officers and crew members, report to your lifeboat stations and prepare to abandon ship. This is not a drill. Cruise and culinary staff—each of you make yourself responsible for one of the wounded. This is not a drill. I repeat: This is not a drill. Move with order to your lifeboat stations immediately and assist any and all wounded persons or injured. This is not a drill.''

As Santini shouldered Palmer down into the lifeboat, he began murmuring, ''Hail Mary full of grace, the Lord is with thee, Blessed art thou amongst women and blessed is the fruit of thy womb, Jesus. Holy Mary, mother of God, pray for us sinners now and—''

And he said the words out loud: ''—now and in the hour of our death.'' Klaxons sounded around the ship, the noise deafening as he ran to help Porter with the evacuation. The lifeboats would not be crowded; so many were already dead....

THERE WAS A STORM MOVING their way, the clouds dark and ominous and huge and fast. Santini aided the still-bleeding woman into the lifeboat, careful of her poorly bandaged left arm. He looked to his right. The captain, his head and face a mass of cuts and bruises, and the chief purser, his left arm hauling on the winch for a lifeboat, his right arm covered with blood, were lowering away another of the lifeboats.

Santini turned to the boat nearest him and shouted to two of the men aboard; one of them had a bleeding head injury. ''Get this thing winched into the water and do it in time with each another. Otherwise, you'll pitch into the sea.''

''But what about you, Father?'' the injured man called back.

''There might be more survivors, but you get outta here—and God bless you all.'' He did a quick sign of the cross over them and ran.

''That's everybody that's still alive,'' Porter said to him.

''We didn't check the chapel,'' said the purser.

"I'll do it. Where is it?" Santini called.

"Come on!" Porter started to run, the chief purser loping beside him, Santini falling in with them, Porter shouting again, "Father—down those steps and to your right, then down one more deck and on your left."

Santini shot past the purser and the captain, and reached the steps. He ran halfway down, then jumped down the remaining steps, coming to his feet in a crouch, pushing himself up, swinging around the next landing and taking the steps three at a time, running, jumping the last six. He found the double wooden doors to his left and wrenched at them. A woman, very young, very pretty, her clothes drenched with blood, turned from the small altar rail where she knelt.

"Get out of here!"

"My husband, Father—he's dead."

"Get out of here!"

"No, Father."

Santini raced up the chapel aisle and grabbed the woman at her shoulders, wrenching her to her feet. And then he noticed her hands and knew why she was covered with blood as she sagged forward against him.

She had been holding in her intestines. She was dead.

Santini lowered the woman to the chapel floor. He prayed for her, and he prayed for them all—and he prayed for himself. . . .

THE FIRST OF THE EXPLOSIONS HAD BEGUN, the ship listing at the bow, waves rolling across it as Santini, Porter and the chief purser ran. It was running uphill, the deck partially awash beneath their feet now, the lifeboats already away and safe, Santini prayed.

The last lifeboat was ahead of them, Porter slipping, Santini catching him, the purser, younger than either of them, sprinting past, toward the lifeboat winch. "You get in, Father—Captain!"

Santini looked back. A wall of water was rolling toward them, and beneath his feet he could feel the deck tremble. He grabbed Porter and threw himself and the captain against the interior wall. Another explosion.

Santini looked behind. The wave was crashing down. "No time! Run for it! We're gonna swim for it!"

It was the purser shouting as they ran, Santini pushing Porter ahead of him. "I don't know how to swim, Father—leave me!"

Santini laughed, shouting at him, "Relax. I used to teach swimming at the YMCA to get some pocket money in the summers when I was studying for the priesthood—"

Santini looked back once more. The water was closing now, but the rail was closer still.

He shoved Porter toward it. "Jump, Captain!"

Porter started climbing over the rail, then was gone. Santini was at the rail, the chief purser beside him. "I wasn't kidding, Father—I can't even tread water or float."

Santini wrenched the chief purser up by his uniform jacket and hurled him over the rail. "Right behind you, my son," shouted Santini, and he flipped the rail one-handed and closed his eyes for a second, hitting the water feetfirst and going under, then bobbing to the surface. The waves were building as the winds increased, rain falling now from the storm clouds overhead. He could see Porter, swimming away from the ship. He couldn't see the chief purser.

Santini tucked down under the water. He saw a shape and swam toward it, bobbing up again, reaching into the water and grabbing. He had a handful of hair and he yanked it up. The chief purser's head was beneath it; he was coughing, choking on water. Santini threw his left arm across the chief purser's left shoulder and under his injured right arm.

"Just relax. See? Isn't swimming terrific?" He didn't wait for an answer. Another explosion ripped out a section of the hull, the big ship uncomfortably close. Santini dragged the purser beneath the waves with him for an instant, then up, the purser choking again. "When we go under, shut your mouth and hold your breath." Again Santini hauled the purser beside him, swimming with his right arm and his legs only, dragging the floundering man with him. Chunks of burning wreckage and debris filled the ocean surface around them, the waves still building with the storm.

He looked back. The bow of the cruise ship was completely awash now, the ship almost vertical in the water. He knew that once it went down, it might flip—and they would be killed. He kept swimming, not seeing Porter anymore. He closed his eyes for an instant, praying that the captain would survive. As he opened his eyes he saw one of the lifeboats rowing toward them.

"Come on, Father, just a little more!" It was Porter.

Santini coughed up water and kept going. "Not much farther now, son!"

Santini dragged himself through the whitecaps, the lifeboat there one instant, gone the next. He asked himself if he were imagining it.

His right arm burned with the exertion, but he kept going. He was glad he'd kept himself in shape, working out daily, religiously. He laughed at the thought. A priest did almost everything religiously.

"Not much farther now, son," he shouted to the purser whose body he still clutched against him. "Hang in there! God's on our side—we're the good guys!"

Santini kept going.

There was a roar behind him, then a mighty metallic-sounding groan. He didn't look back. If the ship were coming to crush him to death, it would do no good. He started the Lord's Prayer in his head, swimming, holding the terrified chief purser.

And he bumped his head.

Santini looked up and saw the injured man with the bandage around his head. Hands grabbed for him over the edge of the lifeboat, and Santini reached up with his right hand. A hand locked around his wrist and he was being pulled inside.

He rolled down into the lifeboat. "Watch out—watch—"

"He's all right, Father."

Santini closed his eyes. He felt something in the pocket of his suit jacket he didn't remember being there. It was the plastic-bagged envelope for Palmer—the ransom demands.

He tried remembering when Porter had given it to him.

He could not. The chief purser was beside him, coughing and sputtering. "Your second lesson'll be even more fun," Santini cracked. Catching his breath, he looked at the people who had saved him. Captain Porter wasn't there. "Where's Porter? His boat was real close to me. I saw him and it kinda kept me going. He was reaching out for us. What boat's he in?"

One of the women in the lifeboat began to cry.

"I thought—thought you—" the chief purser was coughing, spitting up seawater into the bottom of the boat, and Santini folded his arm around the man. "Father, I saw him when I hit the water. He split his head open against the hull when he dived in. Captain Porter's dead—he never surfaced."

Santini realized he was sitting. He dropped to his

knees and crossed himself. He didn't want to consider now how the envelope in its plastic bag had gotten into his pocket—or what he had seen in the lifeboat that had urged him on. He prayed instead as the cruise ship disappeared beneath the waves.

Chapter Four _____

Culhane squinted his eyes tight shut a moment to read his watch's luminous dial in the total blackness, trying to synchronize his head with the movement of his wrist, the deck of the Soviet freighter rolling beneath him. He had been asleep for something over six hours, he judged. The light that had bled through between the gunwales of the inverted lifeboat and the deck was gone completely, and Culhane realized suddenly that what had awakened him was not the violent motion of the ship but the clattering of the rope in the bow eye. Something was moving it in more rapid time than the shifting of the deck, and the low whistling sound that came through the crack that had admitted light earlier was high wind. He could smell rain, feel it. He shivered slightly, his hair wet under the hood of his black wet suit, wet with sweat.

Before allowing himself to assess his chances, Culhane assessed his weapons. The Tekna knife was all that remained of his lost diving gear. He still had his Bali-Song, the Filipino Butterfly knife taped inside his wet suit near his abdomen.

But he had no gun of his own. The revolvers that he had brought to Brazil to carry when going upriver with

Fanny Mulrooney were stowed with the rest of his gear at the hotel in Belém. Burroughs had originally offered Culhane a ride on *Seacutter* on the long run down from Miami, but Culhane had not been able to go. Time and deadlines were always his enemies: *Takers* Number 18 was going to be late.

He started to laugh under his breath. If he couldn't find a way to somehow get safely away from the Russian freighter and then safely to shore, *Takers* Number 18 would be forever late.

The gun stuffed into the front of his wet suit was Jake Burroughs's. Culhane wished Burroughs had purchased more than one spare magazine to go with the little Randall .45. But there were only two, each holding six rounds, one up the butt of the pistol, the other stuffed beside it under his wet suit.

He figured that the freighter's crew plus the survivors of the underwater battle would number about a hundred. Math was never his strongpoint, so he settled on the arbitrary figure of one hundred eight; it divided nicely. With each 185-grain bullet he would somehow have to kill or disable nine Russians in order to shoot his way off the freighter.

There would have to be a better approach.

What would Sean Dodge do?

Josh Culhane thought about that for a moment. The logical thing—that was what Sean Dodge would do: leave the safety of the inverted lifeboat and cautiously move along the forecastle aft toward the bridge. Culhane stripped away the reef glove from his left hand— the right was already gone—and stuffed it inside the top of his wet suit. His right hand closed on the butt of the Randall, and his left hand closed over the slide, very slowly, very cautiously drawing it back over the loaded magazine. There was no need to first check the chamber; Burroughs had said he never left it loaded. Slowly, to avoid some betraying sound, he edged the slide forward, chambering the top round from the magazine. His right thumb upped the safety. Nearly prone beneath the lifeboat, he edged all the way over from his right side to peer beneath the lifeboat's gunwale, raising the edge slightly with both hands.

His smelling of the rain was confirmed. It now lashed the deck in torrents, windblown sheets driving aft.

No one was visible in the forecastle. Culhane regrasped the .45 and pushed up on the lifeboat enough to slide between the gunwales and the deck. He crouched there for an instant, surveying the ship in the wind-driven rain. The salt spray in the air bathed his face, and his eyes squinted tight shut against it. A wave split in two around the jackstaff in the bow, the forward anchor light obscured completely for a moment, the impact of the tons of water crashing him down flat against the deck plates.

Culhane shook his head to clear it. He had been in storms on land and at sea, once weathering the butt end of a hurricane on the coast in the Carolinas, but the wind and the height of these waves seemed more intense.

He pushed himself up, the Tekna knife in his teeth pirate fashion, the .45 clenched in his right fist, his right thumb poised over the safety, ready.

Halfway along the forecastle was a large, indeterminate object covered with a lashed tarpaulin, and Culhane threw himself behind this as the bow of the Soviet freighter stabbed downward and into the swell. He half choked as his mouth filled with seawater, suddenly icy cold in the high winds that whirled around him.

Prone beside the tarp-covered object dominating the

deck, Culhane spat the water from his mouth, then peered beneath the tarpaulin. Only blackness, but with his left hand he felt upward: two handles on either side. It was a deck gun. "Damn," Culhane rasped, pulling out from beneath the tarp with his head and left hand as another wave crashed down over him. Culhane squinted his eyes against it, but it was too late, the water swamping him. When his eyes cleared he scanned aft again. Towering over the superstructure was the bridge, the wheelhouse light visible well below and forward of the yardarm and the meager light of the signal blinker. Culhane pushed himself to his feet, running for it, the deck too slippery to continue to hold the Tekna knife in his teeth, the knife now clenched in his left fist, the pistol cocked and locked still in his right.

He ran toward what he recognized as a fire-control station.

Another wave crashed over the bow, spilling along the forecastle with the force of a fast-running mountain stream as he plastered himself against the gray metal plates of the fire-control station, the water tearing at him.

He started moving again, planning to work his way still further aft, but he froze for an instant as he rounded the edge of the bridge superstructure. He threw himself down in at least two inches of standing water. Off the starboard side from the main deck below he could see a whaleboat being lowered into the swells, a half-dozen men working the winches and guiding the craft downward from the superstructure.

Aft of the whaleboat another was starting down, and behind that one there were more men on his deck level negotiating them downward.

There was no way to go but up, and to get there he needed to move aft and nearer the yardarm and the signal blinker he had seen earlier. He got to his feet and, his body flat against the bulkhead, inched along, watching the crewmen as they maneuvered the whaleboats into the water, praying no one would see him and sound an alarm.

Culhane kept moving, the ladder nearer now. He glanced at his right hand. His fist was so tightly clenched on the butt of the pistol that his knuckles were white. Culhane shifted the Tekna knife back to his teeth, taking the ladder two rungs at a time, his left foot slipping once in the wet suit's boot, but he regained his footing and continued upward. Taking no time to look along the superstructure, Culhane swung through between the vertical stanchions for the rail and dropped into a crouch, the knife still in his teeth, rain streaming down his face from the wet suit cowl that covered his head, the pistol stabbing the darkness ahead of him like a wand.

He ran forward, taking the companionway steps up to get to the level of the wheelhouse. He had seen lights there, and if he could somehow determine why the whaleboats were being lowered, there might be some way to smuggle himself aboard and escape. He stopped just below deck level, the yellow light from the wheelhouse casting faint streaked shadows against the bridge wing.

Saltwater dribbled from his face into his mouth, and he brushed the water from his lips with the back of his right hand still holding the pistol.

In a low crouch, Culhane moved ahead, grateful for the black of the wet suit that would help the darkness beyond the shafts of yellow light to conceal him. Culhane edged close to the wheelhouse windows, the noise around him deafening now as the howl of the wind seemed somehow—impossibly—to have increased.

Beside the water-streaked windows now, Culhane edged slightly closer and peered inside.

Two men stood at the wheel, but standing hardly described it; they fought the wheel and it fought them. A third man's hands moved with frenetic agility over a control panel of some sort. But the fourth and fifth men fascinated him. The fourth man was almost a stereotype of a sea captain—burly, seeming to exude strength through his lined face, a battered cap cocked back over a shock of wet curls, a yellow slicker on the chair back beside him. The chair was on casters and rolled back and forth to slam against the bulkhead nearest him and then his thigh, but it evidently didn't bother him.

The fifth man most fascinated Culhane. Looking like a villain from a 1930s movie in a broad-brimmed, high-crowned fedora and belted, nearly ankle-length, rain-splotched gray trench coat, the man's face was thin to the point of being gaunt, the cheekbones high and prominent. Beneath the hat was a fringe of ragged blond hair that looked poorly cut. He was taller than Culhane by several inches, the shoulders very broad, the set of the neck pointing to body building or some other strenuous form of exercise. And his hands—both clasped over a leather briefcase—were massive, the fingers long and wide, pressing the plastic-wrapped briefcase to his chest and abdomen. It was obvious that whatever the briefcase contained was more than important.

Trench Coat—Culhane dubbed him that—turned suddenly toward the windows, and Culhane ducked back. Culhane barely heard what perhaps Trench Coat had only sensed, and the sound was hardly audible outside the wheelhouse. Men—six of them—shouted as they walked, shouted to one another to be heard over the roaring sea and the keening of the wind.

Culhane hid in shadow, the blackness of his wet suit his only protection against their seeing him. Six men in yellow slickers and sou'westers walked together in twos, all six in almost perfect step, AKS-74 assault rifles slung beneath their right arms, muzzles down against the rain. The AKS-74s—Culhane had never seen one in the flesh before—were the newest type made for Soviet military use. And according to the data he had researched for one of Sean Dodge's adventures, only Special Forces and crack Airborne elements were issued them.

The rain continued to drip down from the hood of his wet suit and across his face and into his mouth and eyes. He rubbed the back of his right hand across his eyes again, still clutching the .45.

A man who looked KGB—Trench Coat. Six men— perhaps more—who looked Special Forces or Airborne. The diving team that had cost the lives of the crew of *Seacutter* and forced Culhane to seek refuge here aboard the Russian freighter. The lowering of the whaleboats into such unremitting seas.

These men were going ashore.

Josh Culhane realized that his one chance to stay alive was to somehow go with them. The six men disappeared inside the wheelhouse, and Culhane pushed himself away from the bulkhead and ran aft, toward the companionway steps, down one level, then started for the safety rail. Beside him, at the base of the steps, one of the gray watertight doors opened. Culhane threw himself around the corner, flattening himself against the bulkhead beneath the now-silent fog whistle.

Two men, clad like the other six in yellow slickers and hats, AKS-74s carried beneath their right arms, walked past him. Rain lacerating his face, Culhane held his pistol leveled toward their backs as the two men fell into single file to move up the companionway steps, their bodies swaying from side to side as they fought for balance against the rolling of the freighter.

For a moment, when the first man attained the upper level, Culhane thought he would have to shoot. But the man never turned completely. Culhane gambled he had not been seen.

Culhane started past the now-closed gray door as the two men disappeared from view. But there was more shouting—the sound of someone coming up the ladder Culhane himself had used after observing the departing whaleboats.

There was nowhere to turn except the gray watertight door. Culhane wrenched at the lock and shoved the door inward, slamming it behind him. The bare bulb overhead was so bright after the darkness outside that Culhane squinted against it.

There was no one in sight, but he heard voices from the bend the companionway took some ten yards distant. The man or men would be up the ladder outside; going into the storm would get him nothing.

A cabin door was on the right. The knife in his teeth, Culhane's left fist wrenched at the knob. It turned under his hand and he went through, closing the door instantly behind him.

A man stood at the far side of the cabin. He was half into or half out of his pants; one leg was bare. His mouth opened to shout as his left hand reached toward an AKS-74 leaning against the lower bunk, but the sling was twisted over a metal brace of the bunk to keep the rifle from being tossed about the cabin.

Culhane crossed the cabin in two steps, his right fist hammering upward and out, the butt of the pistol like a massive roll of quarters. His fist made contact with the base of the jaw as the first note of the cry for help issued from the man's lips. The man's head snapped back and the body fell, the head slamming hard against the bulkhead, the body sagging, the eyes closed.

Culhane dropped beside him, his pistol to the Russian's head. He felt the neck for a pulse. The man was alive.

Culhane took the knife from his teeth, ready to slash the throat—but he didn't. Sean Dodge killed more indiscriminately. Culhane did not. Real life was not fiction.

He crossed the cabin and secured the lock on the door. Beside the man again, he reached over to the bunk and set down the pistol and the knife. Culhane reached inside the front of his wet suit and stuffed the reef glove into the unconscious man's mouth to gag him.

He scanned the room. A small locker. Culhane moved to it swiftly, opening it.

Nothing hung there, but there was a duffel bag. Culhane opened it. Soviet jungle fatigues, but there was no insignia on the fatigues, not even rank. Stuffed into the top of the duffel bag as they were, they might have been just removed. They felt slightly warm.

Culhane glanced around the cabin and saw a cotton sweat shirt and gray tennis shoes. The pants the man had been getting into or out of were work pants. "Changed from fatigues into civies—hmm," Culhane murmured under his breath.

He took the fatigue pants and blouse from the top of the duffel bag and walked back to the unconscious man, methodically tying the man's hands and arms with the fatigue pants, thinking as he did, Russian commandos—what are they doing invading Brazil? The freighter couldn't have made much progress in the storm, enough progress to get up or down the coast to invade still another nation. There were not enough of them for a full-scale invasion, and coming ashore in a howling storm made little sense. None of them seemed Cuban—and if it was an invasion, there would likely have been Cubans with them. After all, Latin America was Castro's stomping ground.

Culhane finished with the hands and arms, and began tugging the trousers off the man's right leg. He threw these onto the bunk, using the fatigue blouse to bind the man's ankles tight.

Finished, he started to reach for the pillow on the bunk to cushion the man's head. But if the unconscious man rolled over, he could smother. Fatal kindness.

Culhane left the Russian's head lying as it was.

He reached inside the top of his wet suit, ripped away the waterproof black tape and freed the Bali-Song. He tossed the spare magazine for the Randall .45 and the Bali-Song on the bunk beside the automatic and the other knife, then tore away the toquelike hood of his wet suit. As he stripped, he was suddenly cold. Sweat drying on his body was all it was, Josh Culhane told himself. . . .

THE ROPE LADDER LEADING DOWN to the aftmost of the whaleboats swung nauseatingly. Culhane stared down a moment, his duffel bag—borrowed—slung over his yellow slicker, the raincoat borrowed as well.

The man in the rowing thwart amidships of the whaleboat was looking up at him—quizzically, Culhane thought. This one would have to be killed.

The man said something in Russian.

Culhane spoke Russian well, and he answered the man in Russian, trying to avoid the man seeing his face. This was not one of the commandos, he reasoned, but a seaman instead. No rifle.

Culhane dropped into the tossing whaleboat, setting down his duffel bag as the sailor spoke again.

Culhane raised up from his bag and smiled, saying, "Josh Culhane." Culhane's right fist hammered up, tipping the base of the sailor's jaw, then his left hand snapped forward, the Bali-Song already opened, the blade gouging through the seaman's raincoat and biting into flesh up to the hilt, blood spurting from the Russian's chest. Culhane wrenched the knife clear and the body slumped forward. Culhane's right knee smashed upward into the head, launching the body out over the transom to starboard of the motor, the sailor lost instantly in the waves that washed over the gunwales and thudded heavily against the freighter itself. The whaleboat banged against the hull as well, and Culhane nearly lost his footing.

He looked forward to the other two whaleboats. No one had apparently seen what had happened, the two other boatmen huddled on their rowing thwarts like wet lumps of yellow rubber.

Culhane slipped the duffel bag overboard, then unslung the AKS-74 and tossed it into the swells as well. He was supposed to be a seaman—not one of the commandos—and the rifle and duffel bag didn't fit the part.

He sat on the rowing thwart, huddling in the slicker, pulling the yellow hat lower over his face, the drenching rain having already washed the blood from the blade of the Bali-Song. He one-handed it closed, securing it in the pocket of his borrowed trousers through the slash pocket of the slicker.

He waited. It was all he could do.

He did not know how long he sat there; his Rolex was in the other side pocket of his pants. Soviet merchant seamen didn't wear thousand-dollar watches.

He waited, the storm seeming to grow in intensity around him rather than abating. What if the shore party were scrubbed? He already knew the answer. He would start the whaleboat toward shore if he could make the direction; he had no compass, and there was no way to tell with the thunderous low black clouds obscuring the sky, the rain nearly obscuring the clouds.

He waited..

"Ah-llo!"

Culhane looked up. Glaring down at him from above was Trench Coat, the coat no longer gray but black with wetness, the hat crushed down low on his head, the plastic-bagged briefcase clutched against his chest in the massive left hand. The man was gesturing to him. He wanted Culhane to hold the rope ladder steady.

Culhane watched his balance as he stepped toward the bow of the whaler, throwing his weight down on the ladder as Trench Coat started down.

In seconds, the man was beside him, smiling. "Thanks!"

"Don't mention it," Culhane said in Russian, nodding good-naturedly, looking up along the rope ladder again.

On deck was a huge man, older than the captain Culhane had seen earlier but at least the captain's size, perhaps bigger. A chief, Culhane guessed, to take charge of the shore party. Culhane started to take hold of the ladder again, but the chief shouted down, "Don't bother!"

Culhane nodded and let go of the ladder, stepping over the sailing thwart and going aft to the transom where logic dictated he was supposed to be. The whaleboat tossed and pitched, and Culhane again nearly lost his balance, a wave swamping over him and the boat as he sat. He looked forward along the freighter's hull. The other two whaleboats were filling as well, these with the men he had pegged as the commandos.

Culhane looked back to the rope ladder. Following

the chief down the ladder were six of the commandos, their AKS-74s suspended on their slings across their backs as they descended, the chief catching and stowing their duffel bags on both sides of the rowing thwart to balance the boat.

Eight people to kill—in order to stay alive, Culhane thought.

The chief nodded and shouted something Culhane could barely hear over the wind as the huge man undid the heavy rope from its mooring. It meant "hurry up," but Culhane didn't know to where. Without thinking, he did what he would normally do before starting an outboard, he checked the transom clamp screw. Automatically he set the clutch lever. The power on, he held the throttle arm and pulled the starter rope, but the engine didn't catch. He let it snake back on rewind, then tore at it, and this time the engine caught. Culhane steered the whaleboat away from the hull of the freighter, eyeing the other two boats, seeing aft now three more identical boats. The farthest forward of the whaleboats was starting off at close to a right angle off the starboard hull and Culhane—shooting in the dark— followed suit, fighting the waves as he tried to steer away from the focus of their impact. The wind if anything seemed worse, and waves crashed over the whaleboat, swamping passengers and gear.

The chief sat on the forward of the three seats beside Trench Coat, gesturing ahead into the raging darkness. Culhane steered as best he could. The whaleboat rolled up over a wave to be caught in the curl of another, the passengers including Trench Coat and the chief bailing with their hands and caps and anything that would hold water. Culhane was ankle-deep in seawater. Far to starboard were faintly detectable lights. Perhaps a city? Culhane started aiming the prow toward them.

The chief turned back suddenly, shouting, *"Nyet, Ivan!"*

Culhane bore to port again, at least two of the other five whaleboats still in sight. The wind-driven spray chilled every exposed centimeter of his flesh. More gradually now, he aimed the prow toward the lights. Holding a straight course was impossible in any event.

It was not a lighthouse, but the lights of a town.

The chief shouted in Russian again.

Culhane started to answer, but then he saw it: a wall of water higher than anything he had ever seen on the sea. He shouted, pointing toward it, but the chief had turned away.

One of the Russian soldiers shouted something that Culhane mentally translated as "My God!"

Culhane cut the steering-throttle arm toward him, giving the engine all it had, angling the craft harder to starboard now. He saw the lights of the city in the distance and the wall of water crashing toward them. Suddenly looming ahead was a field of jagged rocks jutting high into the darkness, the rocks black and shining with spray and rain, the wind suddenly calm.

Culhane looked up. The gaunt-faced man in the trench coat was standing by the sailing thwart, his body shifting back and forth, balancing against the motion of the boat. In his right hand was a Walther P-38. "You take us to the city lights!" He screamed the words in the comparative stillness since the wind had died. He screamed the words in English.

Culhane did the only thing he could. Years ago, he had spent two weeks with a circus performer, learning the man's art. Now he used it, the Tekna diving knife sliding from his sleeve into his right palm, his right arm snaking forward, the knife underhanding from the hollow in the palm of his right hand, his thumb releasing it as his hand reached the level of the man's chest.

The knife plunged, but not into Trench Coat; instead it stabbed one of the six soldiers as the man stood up from the rowing thwart and swung his AKS-74. There was an almost inaudible shot as the body of the impaled soldier sagged against the muzzle of Trench Coat's P-38.

Culhane shot a glance to port. There was no escaping the wall of water. He loosed the throttle and hurled himself overboard into the water, gulping air as he dived, the surface of the water erupting over his head as he looked up, darkness surrounding him now, inky blackness as he swam downward, fighting the eddies and flows of the water, the water tearing at him as he wrenched his arms free of the slicker, swimming out of it, ripping the hat from his head.

There was a roar—like a thousand thunderclaps, he thought—mentally logging away the simile to use in his next book. If he ever wrote another book. It was the wall of water, the ocean above him suddenly bright and almost white, the underside of the whaleboat's hull visible in stark relief, then the whaleboat upending, vanishing, Culhane's body rocking, as if invisible walls slammed against him, thrashing him, the breath being driven from his lungs.

He started upward, swimming toward where he thought the rocks were. His lungs burned, his head was beginning to ache and his limbs were heavy, stiff and unresponsive. Culhane's head broke the surface, and as he gulped for air, he started to choke, a breaker crashing over him, driving him down. But he fought against its force, raising his head above the water again. He was vomiting into the water, vomiting the seawater that had inundated him. He gulped air, choking, coughing. The rocks were ahead. He looked around him;

there was no sign of the whaleboat. He started swimming, the wind heightening again, the waves around him hammering at him.

Culhane looked to his right. Another wall of water was rolling inexorably toward him. He could not dive below the surface to escape it. The rocks were too close, and the water would hurtle him against the rocks, killing him. He quickened his pace. His only chance was to reach the rocks and take shelter among them.

The water was coming. He squinted his eyes—the rain and the salt spray and the smaller waves almost blinding him—but ahead now, he could see the glistening blackness of the rocks. He swam harder.

The wall of water was almost upon him. His right knee slammed into something hard. The rocks. Culhane reached out, his hands finding the roughness of them, his feet scrabbling against them for a hold, then he was up, running and slipping, trying to stay ahead of the wall of water.

Culhane threw himself forward, his right shoulder hitting the highest of the rocks near him, his body rolling. At a hollow in the rock his hands reached out. Culhane splayed his legs to stop his roll and crawled forward. He burrowed his head beneath his hands, sucking in breath as the wall of water crashed over him, hammering the breath from him, tearing at his sweat shirt and his pants. He felt one of the borrowed shoes torn from his right foot.

The hammering stopped. Culhane gasped for air and looked up.

His left arm at a bizarre angle, the chief from the whaleboat stood beside him. The man in the trench coat stood less than ten feet away, leaning heavily against one of the taller black rocks.

The slouch fedora was gone, but the pistol wasn't.

Trench Coat raised his right arm and extended it. Culhane pushed himself up on his hands and rolled right, grasping for the butt of the Randall .45 that he hoped the waves hadn't torn from the waistband of his trousers.

Grabbing it, wiping down the safety, twisting his body at an awkward angle to get the pistol on line, firing a single shot, then another and another. The man in the trench coat fell, his pistol discharging as his back slammed against the jagged black rock. Culhane twisted right to find the chief with the muzzle of the .45, but suddenly pain was radiating upward from his right wrist, the .45 flying from his grip.

Culhane rolled back as a second kick came hammering toward him, missing his head by inches. He drew back to his knees now, the chief throwing himself toward Culhane, hands open wide, fingers splayed, rage etched across the coarse Slavic features.

Culhane's body reacted before the giantlike chief contacted him. He threw himself prone along the rocks, a scissors kick for the chief's leading leg, then he rolled away, the chief toppling sideways and away.

Culhane was up and he started to reach for the Bali-Song, but the chief was up too, lunging for him. Culhane started to sidestep, then saw the look of terror in the chief's eyes. Culhane glanced behind him. A third wall of water, at least as high as the first two, was seconds away from the rocks.

Culhane threw himself to his left, toward the higher rocks, the wall of water catching him too soon, his body ripped from its angle of flight, thrashed downward, hammered against the rocks, his hands reaching out, grabbing, his nails trying to dig into the rock surface, the water tearing him from the rocks, the sound of his heart hammering louder than the crashing of the waves in his ears.

And then the wave was gone. Culhane raised his head and saw the chief beside him. Culhane rolled from the kick, but the foot caught his left shoulder. Involuntarily Culhane screamed with pain. The right foot came again, but Culhane's head dodged it as he rocked up and back to his haunches. The right foot launched for his face again, but Culhane's hand reached out, grabbing the foot at the instep, twisting as Culhane wrenched his own body left, dragging the man down against the rocks. Culhane felt unbelievably powerful hands gripping his shoulders and his neck.

His arms were becoming numb. Culhane snapped his right arm back, the elbow making contact with something hard. There was a scream of pain, and the grip on his neck and shoulders loosened. Culhane snapped the elbow back again, causing another scream of pain. Culhane rolled left and away, getting up to his knees, then to his feet. Waves were lashing across the rocks, tearing at his legs and feet.

The chief was up, throwing himself forward, Culhane twisting half right, his still shod left foot snapping outward, hitting the massive midsection, the chief's body rocking back but not falling.

The immense Russian shook his head, growling, *"Nyet—nyet!"* He charged, Culhane feigning a quarter twist right and another roundhouse kick with his left foot, but pulling out, sidestepping across the Russian's path. Culhane's right fist rammed against the Russian's left temple, sending him down.

Culhane started for him—but stopped. The Russian's broad face was seamed with laughter, and in his right hand was the gleaming Randall .45. Culhane reached for the Bali-Song, starting a one-hand opening, knowing he'd be too late. The Russian waved and said, *"Dasveedanyeh—"*

The pistol discharged as Culhane threw himself to his right, the Bali-Song open in his hand now, the pistol on line with his head. The gaping muzzle was blacker than the night. Culhane felt the impact throwing him forward, his right hand still gripping the Bali-Song. There was a shriek of terror from the Russian's lips, the sound of the .45 discharging again, and then all sound vanished in the roar of the wave that flooded over Culhane. He braced himself against the rock, the other shoe ripped from his left foot now, the water surrounding him. Culhane struggled up to his knees to breathe as the water fell away.

The dead man who wore the trench coat, his body was gone, washed away.

And the chief—Culhane thought that somewhere in the darkness he heard a scream for help, and he waited in the rocks, peering into the darkness, waiting for a sign of the Russian who had tried to kill him. But there was no sign, no more sound, and he was alone on the rocks as the storm lashed around him.

Chapter Five

Santini had left his shoes behind on the cruise ship, and with a blanket wrapped over his wet clothes, he walked the decks of the freighter, the storm lashing at him as he dodged from one impromptu lean-to to the next, offering a word of comfort, encouragement or consolation. He was drenched, and he finally aimed himself for the wheelhouse to see if he could get a cup of coffee. All of the survivors rescued by the small Brazilian freighter had been seen to. Of the lifeboats, only nine had managed to stay together. The fate of the others he did not know, but with the howling winds and the waves that ripped upward from the seas to crush down anything in their path, he doubted any more lived.

The door to the wheelhouse nearly ripped from its hinges as Santini opened it, then pressed it with his full body weight to close it.

"Damascus—where's Amelina?"

Santini let the wet blanket fall from his shoulders. He crossed the wheelhouse, grabbing the offered cup of coffee from the crewman's hands and nodding a thanks, then dropped to his knees on the floor beside Scott Palmer. Only the unconscious had been brought into the wheelhouse or any of the other confines—the unconscious and the obviously dying.

Santini studied the look on Palmer's ashen face for a moment. "She's safer than we were. The terrorists—or whoever they were—took her in their helicopter. They gave the captain this, and Porter gave it to me somehow—I, ah—can't explain it."

Palmer took the plastic-bagged envelope from Santini's right hand and ripped open the bag, then tore the envelope inside it. Santini watched his eyes as he read it.

"What does it say you're supposed to do?" Santini asked him.

Palmer didn't answer.

"What does it say, Scott?"

No answer.

Palmer was reading it again; Santini watched Palmer's eyes drifting across the page.

"What does it say, Scott?"

Palmer looked up from the note. "I'm not supposed to tell anybody—even you."

"Can I help you?"

Santini watched Palmer's eyes in the yellow light of the wildly swaying overhead lamp.

"You can take this note, but promise me you won't read it, swear to God you won't—like it's the confessional—that you won't read it. And then ball it up and throw it overboard for me and never mention it."

"But you're going to have to have the note to follow their instructions, or to give to the cops, Scott—"

"No, I memorized it. No police." And Palmer forced a hollow-sounding laugh. "You know me—always a quick study. Got all the details in my head. All of it."

"What do they want?"

"I can come up with it."

"You won't tell me."

"Jesus, Damascus, I can't tell you—or anybody."

"You'll need a delivery boy. At least you can trust me not to snatch it. I don't like playing games with scumbags like that, but I'll do it."

"I couldn't ask you to, to have it on your conscience when you . . ."

"When I what, Scott?"

"Just throw the note away, and swear to God you won't read it, or ask me any more questions. Swear it, Damascus—on Jeff Culhane's grave, okay?"

Santini looked at him, studying Palmer's eyes.

"Swear it, Damascus, or so help me God, I'll get out to that rail myself and throw it overboard! On Jeff Culhane's grave—swear it to God!"

Santini took the note and crumpled it in his left fist. "I swear it to God. On Jeff's grave, man. But this isn't the priest talking now—just a friend. You're a fool, Scott. And if you do something that you know is wrong, you'll be a fool that's damned for it."

Santini squeezed his fist tighter over the note, then

got up and downed half his coffee as he started for the door, handing the half-filled cup to the seaman who had given it to him.

He wrenched open the wheelhouse door, the rain driving at him as he slammed it behind him, the wind tearing at him as he walked to the rail. Leaning heavily on it, water filling his mouth, salty spray soaking him as the waves crashed over the bow, he threw the note into the sea.

Chapter Six

"Bom dia, menina!"

She guessed he was saying, Hi, how are you. Mary Frances Mulrooney gave him her best smile and asked, *"Fala inglês, senhor?"* She had her fingers crossed that he did.

"Of course, miss. How may I assist you?"

"My name is M. F. Mulrooney—"

"Ah—Miss Mulrooney. *Muito prazer em conhecê-lo.* Oh, I am sorry, miss—you do not speak any Portuguese?"

"No—no, I'm, ah, no. . . ."

"But of course we have your reservation, Miss Mulrooney," the desk clerk said with a smile. "If you would care to sign this card for me. . . ."

"My things, and Mr. Culhane's things, they have arrived?"

"Ah, yes, I remember that indeed they did, miss. The customs broker transferred them to our care upon the letter of authorization."

"I lost most of my luggage," Mulrooney said, raising the purple carryall in her right hand, then gesturing to her purse. "Mr. Culhane isn't here yet, is he?"

"No, miss, sad to say he is not. Last night there was a terrible storm along the coast—"

"Nothing happened, did it...?"

"There has been no report to that effect that I have heard. Were you expecting him?"

"No. Is my room ready?"

"Yes, miss. The room for you and Senhor Culhane has been ready since your overseas call alerted us. Can I have a bellman assist you with your things?"

"No," Mulrooney told him, "I only have these." She looked down at the purple wool bag and gestured again to her purse.

She began filling out the registration card, handing the clerk her passport but telling him she wanted it back.

MARY FRANCES MULROONEY SAT at the dressing table. It was a typical Josh Culhane rented "room"—the most expensive room in the hotel, a suite. He'd told her more than once that when all the pluses were added up, staying in the best hotel you could find and renting its best room was always the best bargain. Somehow, her natural feminine thrift denied this reasoning. But if he was paying for it...

As she brushed her hair, wearing only panties and a strapless bra, she thought about Culhane some more. She wished his damned treasure-diving expedition were over. After coming up to the room, she had called the American consulate and inquired after the fate of *Seacutter*. It had taken several attempts to get through, but eventually the man she'd spoken with told her that there was no word of *Seacutter* having encountered difficulties in last night's storm. There had been a disaster, although the details were unclear. The *Duchess of the Caribbean* had gone down with hundreds of lives lost. The storm had been terrible, but in the area where Mulrooney had told him *Seacutter* was supposed to be, there were numerous spots where a seaworthy craft could ride out the storm in relative safety. And in any event, the storm had been at its worst along the coastline, little better than a squall farther out to sea.

This eased her mind—but not a great deal. She considered trying to place a call via radio to *Seacutter*. But it wouldn't look good for Culhane to have her checking up on him, especially with Melissa Burroughs aboard.

She had showered and washed her hair instead.

Mulrooney had bought two dresses at the shop in Istanbul. She had hated them both, but both had been long enough to cover her skinned and bloodied knees.

Her knees hadn't healed overnight, but among the things she had shipped down for the anticipated lengthy stay in Brazil were several dresses that were long enough to cover the scabs. A call from the airport to the hotel before she had left Istanbul had elicited a pledge that her things would be packaged and sent to her post-office box in Athens, but the clerk had insisted that Athens was in Greece, not Georgia. If the package ever made it to her, she would be surprised.

The telephone rang and she got up to answer it, sitting on the edge of the bed.

"Yes?"

"Menina Mulrooney?"

The caller started speaking in Portuguese, and Mulrooney interrupted, "I don't speak Portuguese, *senhor.*"

"*Desculpe, menina.* Forgive me, Menina Mulrooney. I am Sebastiao Oliveira, the friend of Senhor Josh Culhane—"

"Sebastiao—yes..."

"The assistant manager of the hotel—he call me and say you want to see me."

"Yes. Can you meet me in the lobby in ten or fifteen minutes?"

"Is there something wrong?"

"No, nothing's wrong. I just need to see you right away."

"Yes, Menina Mulrooney, in the lobby, then—in ten or fifteen minutes."

The phone clicked and Mulrooney hung up. Josh Culhane would be angry, but she couldn't wait for him if the Russians had the original of the map, which she assumed they did.

Mulrooney sat on the bed, thinking. A real Amazon. She had picked up a Greek phrase book at the airport. If the woman really did speak Greek...Mulrooney shivered a little. It would be meeting history, talking with someone from the past.

She stood up, walked across the room to the closet and rifled through it, but her mind was elsewhere. Another place and maybe another time....

THE ELEVATOR DOORS OPENED and she stabbed her hands into the pockets of the midcalf-length white skirt, her eyes scanning the lobby for someone who looked like he should be a backcountry guide. She'd met quite a few of the type, but unfortunately they rarely looked alike in any aspect except the way their eyes lit up when she would tell them she was traveling alone. But this man she should trust; he was someone Josh Culhane knew. She caught a glimpse of herself in the mirror on the far wall of the lobby opposite the registration desk. The full skirt looked as though it had enough material in it to make six tablecloths, but the pink short-sleeved knit shirt clung a little too much. She fiddled with the bottom of the shirt to blouse it out a little more as she stopped in the center of the lounge area that dominated the high-ceilinged lobby.

No guide type was in evidence, but she heard a voice from behind her. "Menina Mulrooney?"

She turned around to see a very skinny man with a very bony face and a white straw cowboy hat in his hands.

"Yes?"

"I am Sebastiao."

She walked toward him as he walked toward her, her hands thrust back into her pockets. She was wearing flat sandals, but she was still an inch or so taller than he was.

She took her right hand from her pocket and offered it. "Hi—nice to meet you."

He took her hand. The grip was all right, not a crusher or a fondler, she thought. And the palm was dry.

"It is my honor, *menina*. Please to sit down?"

He gestured toward the couch near him, and Mulrooney sank into it, arranging her voluminous skirt. Sebastiao perched on the edge of the couch beside her. "Senhor Culhane is not with you, then?"

"No. He's treasure diving off the coast—research for one of his books. We were going to go upriver together, but I can't wait for him now."

"It can be very dangeorus, *menina*—"

"I've been in jungles before."

"*Sim, menina*. Yes, but the Uruentes. . .they are. . ."

"Who are the Uruentes?"

"It is said, Menina Mulrooney, that the Uruentes still hunt for the heads of men."

"Yeah, well, I read the tabloids, too."

"What is that, Menina Mulrooney?"

"The newspapers that talk up all that garbage. Anyway, I'm not interested in Indians. There's something more important than that. Natives usually leave you alone if you leave them alone, right?"

"Yes, this is correct, but—"

"I need you to take me upriver to Ouro. There's a man there that I must see."

Sebastiao took a half-crumpled package of cigarettes from his shirt pocket and a box of matches. "It is permitted?"

"Only if you light one for me." She grinned. Mulrooney fished her cigarettes from her left pocket. She shook a Salem loose from the package and held it while Sebastiao struck a match. Sebastiao lit his own cigarette, and through a mouthful of smoke he told her, "You want to go to Ouro? But you do not need a guide to take you there. Any pilot can fly you. It is a short ride."

"But he has a ranch," she told him. "Away from the town. And after that there is another place I must go— between the Negro river and the Solímões. Deep back into the jungle."

"How far back?"

"How far can we travel through the jungle in a day?"

"It depends on the terrain, *menina*. On foot, very little. If a car can be used, or if we can travel by boat—it is hard to say."

"Plan to be out for several weeks. Can you take me?"

"But Senhor Culhane, he will be very infurious—"

"Infuriated," Mulrooney corrected him. "But he'll understand. I'm leaving a message for him so he'll know where to meet us. Will you do it? Take me upriver?"

"And if I say that I cannot—you would still go?"

"Josh must talk about me a lot," Mary Frances Mulrooney said, and laughed.

And for the first time, Sebastiao laughed as well. She watched as he flicked ashes into his cupped left hand. Mulrooney inhaled again as she watched him.

"*Sim, menina*. I will take you."

"Do you carry a gun? Upriver, I mean."

"It is necessary. I know some North Americans think that revolvers are—"

"Not me," she cut in. "Josh's guns are here in the hotel. But my gun is too small to get back into the country if I took it out. He said you could find me a gun."

He looked over his shoulder nervously. "It is legal, but much work of papers—"

"No. You buy yourself an extra gun and just lend it to me. I don't have time for paperwork. Josh said maybe you could do that. He said—wait a minute—" Mulrooney fished in her right pocket. She had written it down on an empty matchbook when they had talked about it, and she had kept the matchbook just in case she reached Brazil considerably earlier than he. "A Rossi Model 68/2 .38 Special—in stainless steel. He said that was like my Smith & Wesson."

"*Sim, menina*. I will get this, and you can borrow it."

"And he told me the ammunition. Federal Nyclad," she read.

"I cannot buy this. I do not know the name. But I get you some other."

"All right. When can we leave?"

"A few days...to prepare?"

"Tomorrow morning?"

He leaned back. His eyes seemed to register genuine shock. "But—"

"All right, at noon or so, okay?"

"It must be morning. The plane leaves then."

"Can you get the tickets?" she asked him.

"Sim."

"You'll need money, for that and—"

"I can make the arrangements, *menina*, and give to you the bill—"

"All right," she interrupted. Mulrooney stood, Sebastiao standing, as well, his hat dropping to the floor. She reached for it for him and he reached for it and she bumped her head against his forehead and she started to laugh. "What a great beginning, huh?"

"Sim," Sebastiao said, smiling. "Great, yes, *menina*."

She could live with being called *mademoiselle*; in fact it sounded rather nice. *Señorita* was okay. *Fräulein* she didn't like. But *menina* definitely had to go. "First step toward greatness: it's Mary Frances—that or M.F.— whichever feels better."

She watched Sebastiao's eyes as he thought for a moment. "M. F.—Menina M. F.!"

Mulrooney shook her head, inhaling on her cigarette again. "Just M. F., Sebastiao—just M. F."

"Sim—okay."

She sure hoped it would be.

Chapter Seven

Josh Culhane opened his eyes and squinted against the glare of the sun reflected off the sand beneath his head.

His head had been resting beside his left arm, and automatically he looked at his wrist. But the Rolex wasn't there.

He remembered now—all of it.

He touched his left front pocket, pushing himself up a little, and felt the familiar shape of the watch. He half expected it to have smashed against the rocks, but the watch seemed to be in one piece and was ticking as he held it up to his left ear. The time read almost noon and the date had changed, so he assumed everything was still working.

Culhane sat up and looked around him as he secured the watch to his wrist. In the sand near him was his Bali-Song knife. He picked it up, wiping the sand from it against his trouser leg. The pants were torn at the knees, and the left leg was ripped at the seam from cuff to crotch along the inside.

He closed the Bali-Song and flipped closed the lock, tossing the knife in his right hand for a moment.

"Watch Sean Dodge top this one," he said out loud, and laughed.

And then he heard the voice behind him. *"Mãos ao alto!"*

Another voice, the Portuguese laced with authority, *"Deita as armas!"*

Culhane turned his head slowly and saw two men in dark suits and sunglasses, each man holding an Uzi submachine gun. One man was less than ten yards from him on the sand, the second in the rocks above. The muzzles of the Uzis were angled for his gut.

Culhane spoke Spanish well and could get by in French, but he didn't speak much Portuguese. He did, however, understand the men's commands. He dropped the Bali-Song to the sand. He raised his hands.

"Há aqui alguém que fale inglês?" He gave the men a big smile.

"We each speak English together," the man shouted down from the rocks.

Culhane nodded. He decided to try Portuguese again. *"O meu nome é Josh Culhane—"* And then Culhane collapsed into English. "Ever read any of my books—*The Takers*? You know—Sean Dodge?"

Neither of them answered. "Aw, shit," Culhane murmured under his breath.

It was the one from the rocks who spoke first: "See-ann Dod-gee?"

It took Culhane a second. "Yeah—See-ann Dod-gee—I write See-ann Dod-gee—I'm Josh Culhane—*The Takers*, huh?"

The man standing ten feet away from him dropped the Uzi on its sling and ran forward, laughing. "See-ann Dod-gee—ha!"

Culhane looked skyward and murmured, "Thank you, Sir."

Chapter Eight _____

Scott Palmer stared out the window. He watched Damascus Santini getting into the taxicab. He had offered Damascus a boatload of supplies for his jungle mission. Damascus had labeled it a bribe for Palmer's conscience. But Damascus had taken it anyway.

His people needed the supplies.

As the taxi pulled away, the telephone rang. Palmer's body became rigid. He turned, looked at the telephone and walked toward it, stopping in the middle of the suite's living room, staring at the telephone for a moment. Then he sat down on the couch and picked up the receiver.

"Hello?"

"Scott Palmer, Jr.?"

He didn't answer for a moment.

"Senhor Palmer?"

"Yes. Who is—"

"I am Gunther Hoevermann, chief inspector with the Brazilian State Counterterrorist Department. I'd like to come up and chat for a few moments. I'm only five minutes away by automobile from you."

The voice was slightly German accented, the English perfect.

"Look, Inspector, I told everything I know to the São Luis police, to a representative of your unit."

"Ah, yes, but since I am in charge of the investigation, I beg a bit of your time merely to sort out a few details that will aid my grasp of the situation. It is to the best interests of you and your kidnapped wife that we meet, *senhor*."

Palmer didn't know what to say.

"I have a gentleman with me who is the brother of a dear friend of yours, I understand," Hoevermann said. "I'll bring him along. A friend at this particular time might be most welcome."

"Yes, yes—come on up," Palmer said, and hung up the telephone without waiting for a reply.

SCOTT PALMER SMOKED A CIGARETTE. He had given up smoking after getting out of Vietnam alive, but he had started again after getting a cigarette from one of the crewmen in the wheelhouse.

When the door vibrated with a knock he called out, "Just a minute," and he got up, walking quickly across the living room to the small hallway and putting his right hand on the knob. He took a deep breath. "Shit..."

The brown hair, a little reddish in the sunlight from the window in the hallway. The lean face. The brown eyes. Everything about the clean-shaven face. Palmer took a step back from the door, still holding the knob to steady himself. A ghost. The height, over six feet. The build, lean and muscular.

It was Jeff Culhane. But Jeff Culhane was dead.

"I'm Josh—Jeff's brother. I heard about your troubles." And the man who looked like a Xerox copy of Palmer's dead friend extended his right hand.

"Josh Culhane—I—"

"And I am Inspector Hoevermann. I regret meeting you under such unpleasant circumstances, but it is a pleasure nonetheless."

Palmer released Josh Culhane's hand and took Hoevermann's. "A pleasure to meet you, Inspector. Come in—both of you." Palmer found himself still staring at Culhane. Damascus wasn't the only one who prayed. And his—Palmer's—prayer was answered.

"God—you look just like your brother," Palmer said, walking behind them into the living room. "Sit down. I'll pour you both a drink."

He watched as Josh Culhane dropped easily into a corner of the couch. Culhane was wearing blue jeans that were too big for him in the waist and too short for him in the legs, and the shirt was a faded blue workshirt. No socks, just a pair of running shoes. Hoevermann took the opposite side of the couch, and the couch visibly sagged. Palmer rubbed his hands together once and walked toward the small bar opposite the couch. "Bet you'd like a salty dog minus the salt just like Sean Dodge in the *Takers* books, right?" he said, forcing a laugh and looking back at Culhane.

"Most people don't keep grapefruit juice at their bar. Anything'll do."

"How about Myers's rum—dark?"

"Fine, but not too much, please. It's kind of early," Culhane said.

"Inspector, how about you?" Palmer asked.

"In novels and movies the detective always says, 'Nothing for me, thanks—I'm on duty.' But that rarely bothers me. However, it is too early. Nothing for me, thank you."

Palmer consciously willed his right hand to stop shaking as he poured the rum and another CC for himself.

He turned around, a glass in each hand, and walked back toward the couch. He set Culhane's glass on the coffee table, then settled back into the overstuffed chair opposite Culhane's side of the couch and sipped at his drink.

"I won't bother you, Senhor Palmer, with reviewing the details of the attack on the flagship of your cruise line, or the kidnapping itself. I'll come straight to the point. The terrorists must have made some demands, either there aboard the boat or since. For the safe return of your bride, ah, Amelina, is it?"

"Yes," Palmer replied. "Amelina. And, yeah, they made a demand. I'm taking care of it."

Culhane spoke. "The dive party I was with—we were attacked by Russian UDT people or whatever. I barely got out alive. Maybe these were the same—"

"No—they aren't Russian."

"I understand the one man had a French accent. Is that true?" Hoevermann asked.

"Yes. But who told you . . ."

"Father Santini, I believe. But he said he had no knowledge of the demands other than the fact that he assumed there had been demands. And that you were aware of them—perhaps. Are you aware of the demands, Senhor Palmer?"

"Yes, I said I am, and I'll take care..."

"It is only natural, *senhor*, that you wish your wife returned unharmed—as we do, in the Brazilian police. And I'm sure Senhor Culhane does, as well." Hoevermann nodded toward Culhane. "But you should be aware of two factors. Terrorists—and we are quite experienced with them—rarely keep their part of any bargain. And if whatever they demanded of you should in any way aid their activities, you would be in violation of Brazilian law by cooperating."

"I'm a rich man, Inspector. I can handle it."

"Back up," Culhane interrupted. "Damascus Santini was here? My brother told me about him—best damned sergeant there ever was, my brother said."

"He was, but not any more. He's a priest now—a Catholic priest. Heck of a good guy. You know I was your brother's second lieutenant—"

"And you saved his life that time. It always sounded like you and Jeff and Santini and the other guys—like you were brothers. It seemed that close when Jeff would talk about it."

"One more question, please," Hoevermann interjected. "I'm sure you have a great deal to discuss between you. But what is the demand of the terrorists? I assume, of course, that they threaten the death of your wife if you do not comply."

"First a question," Palmer asked, feeling his hands sweat. "How many people died?"

"If no more of the lifeboats are spotted, three hundred fifty-eight. The purser counted how many persons he and the late Captain Porter and Father Santini placed aboard lifeboats."

"I'm not telling you a damned thing, Inspector—and you can't make me. You can arrest me, your guys can

beat the crap out of me—but I'm paying the ransom.
I'm getting my wife back."

Hoevermann stood up. "We are a civilized country,
Senhor Palmer. Only rarely do we beat the 'crap' out of
people. I shall confer with you later when you are
perhaps a little more settled." Hoevermann turned to
Josh Culhane. "If I should fail to contact you before
you leave our city, please contact me. Good day." He
turned back to Palmer. "I'll find my own way out. And
my best wishes for the return of your wife—safely."
Hoevermann walked past Palmer's chair, and Palmer
held his breath until he heard the door open and shut.
He finished the rest of his CC in one swallow.

"What do you want to ask me?"

He looked at Josh Culhane. "Was it that obvious?"

"Yes."

"I'll lend you some of my clothes. If you need any
money or anything..."

"No, I'm fine. But I could use a set of clothes. I'll
return them to you after I get some things of my own."

Palmer started to get up.

"Wait a minute."

Palmer stood, staring down at the couch at Josh Culhane. "I want you to take the ransom upriver."

"Why didn't you ask Damascus Santini?"

"He's a priest. It would be against his scruples to
deliver a ransom. Will you do it? I have to send somebody alone. But I'm cheating on that a little. I'm sending a woman along—Helene Chavez. She's a doctor.
Just in case Amelina, ah, in case she was—"

"You don't have to say it."

"You leave from Belém. I can give you the details
when I give you the ransom."

"What is it?"

"I don't have it yet. It's on the way."

"What is it?" Culhane asked again.

Palmer took a deep breath. "You said it yourself—I saved your brother's life." He got sick inside asking like that. "Will you just hang in—and take the ransom? I'll tell you in Belém. Tomorrow, okay? For Jeff?"

"I'll have to keep Fanny out of it—"

"Fanny?"

"M. F. Mulrooney. She writes books about the supernatural, the occult, UFOs—things like that. Anyway, Fanny's kind of my, ah . . ."

"And she's with you?"

"I'm supposed to meet her sometime this week in Belém and go upriver with her. I'll have to keep her out of this."

"I'll help. If there's anything . . ." Palmer cleared his throat. "Please, Josh?"

Culhane nodded. "You got any cigarettes?"

Chapter Nine

Culhane and the other guy—he couldn't get a clear look at the man's face—were in the cockpit of the fighter. It looked like a curious hybrid of Korean War-vintage aircraft and the F-18. Gray slushy snow was everywhere as the warehouse doors opened and the fighter plane, the cockpit canopy cover still up, began taxiing up the ramp from the warm darkness of the warehouse and into the dirty snow of the streets, the grayness of the snow and the gray blueness of the sky and the steel gray of the towering office buildings lining both sides of the street. And Culhane was very cold.

They were being pursued, and dark cars were starting to fill the streets ahead of them to cut them off—

The telephone. Josh Culhane rolled over and caught it on the first ring. "Right—I'm up, operator—"

"Senhor Culhane. This is not the operator, I'm afraid. Did you ask for a wake-up call?"

Culhane unwound himself partially from the sheet and leaned up on his elbow. "Hoevermann?"

"You have a good memory for voices. Would you meet me downstairs for a drink and some dinner? Unless you have plans, of course."

Culhane looked at his watch. "Are you downstairs now?"

"Yes. I'm sorry to wake you, but it's sort of important that I talk with you."

Culhane realized he was still staring at his watch. He shook his head. "Give me twenty minutes. In the lobby, okay?"

"You're sure you're awake?"

"Hmm—yeah, I think so."

"Twenty minutes, then." And the line clicked dead.

Culhane leaned back. The air conditioning was up all the way, and he was cold now from sweating under the sheet and the blanket. He lay there a moment, staring up at the ceiling.

He was holding his eyelids up by force of willpower. He sat up lest he fall asleep again. "Ohh—boy," he groaned, kicking the sheet and the blanket down and throwing his feet over the side of the bed. He had sealed the window drapes shut, and it was dark in the blue-walled room. He walked barefoot and naked to the windows, and opened the dark heavy drapes and the sheers between them. He peered out, squinting against the late-afternoon sunlight. "Baah," he snorted.

Culhane walked back across the room, toward the bathroom.

HOEVERMANN'S APPEARANCE WAS UNMISTAKABLE. Culhane stuffed his hands in the pockets of the borrowed white slacks and walked across the bar toward the bulky figure. As if Culhane had called out, Hoevermann turned around. "You look better than you sounded. You must have gotten some sleep after all."

"Not enough," Culhane sighed, finding his cigarettes in the breast pocket of the light blue sport shirt. He'd rolled up the sleeves; Palmer had shorter arms. "When do you sleep?"

Hoevermann laughed, clearing his throat as he lit another cigarette from the one he'd just taken from the left corner of his mouth. "I don't sleep." Hoevermann grinned and winked. "I leave the sleeping for the young fellows like you."

Culhane sat on the barstool beside Hoevermann, the bartender coming up. "On my bill, please," Hoevermann said. It was an order, not a question.

"Fine," Culhane said, nodding. "Can you make a salty dog minus the salt?" he asked the barman.

"Sim, senhor," said the barman and walked away.

"I've got a table for us. When you get your drink let's go over to it, all right?"

"Are you the Brazilian welcome wagon, or is this police business?"

Hoevermann laughed again. "Friendly police business—let's put it that way, okay?" The cigarette left Hoevermann's mouth long enough for a swallow of what looked like something with gin or vodka to enter. Then the cigarette returned. "Not often do I meet a famous personage in my line of work—at least one who isn't in need of VIP protection."

"Goes to show I'm not *that* famous, I guess." Culhane let himself smile.

The salty dog came, and Culhane tasted it and nodded to the barman, and the barman left.

"What do you say we eat something?" Hoevermann was up and moving, Culhane grabbing up his cigarettes and following him. The white shoes Palmer had lent him were the right size, but Palmer had a narrower foot and Culhane's feet hurt slightly as he walked.

Hoevermann crossed the bar and nodded to the maître d', who picked up two large menus and started down the three steps into the dining room. Hoevermann glanced back once. "Right behind you," Culhane said. The big inspector stopped at a table overlooking a lush hanging garden, and the maître d' pulled out his chair, Hoevermann sagging down into it.

Culhane caught his own chair and sat down opposite him, taking a sip of his drink as he stubbed out his Pall Mall in the ashtray. Immediately a busboy came and the dirtied ashtrays were replaced by a clean one that Hoevermann promptly dirtied.

Culhane glanced across his menu at Hoevermann. "What would the chief inspector of the counterterrorist division want with me?"

The waiter arrived, but Hoevermann waved him away, reaching inside his left breast pocket and handing a folded piece of paper across to Culhane.

Culhane took it and opened it. The words were Portuguese. "Not one of my languages, I'm afraid."

"I had my secretary type it up. I should have thought of the language thing. *Saúde.*" He raised his glass, and Culhane raised his. "Those are the most important Brazilian laws concerning smuggling. Thought you might appreciate them."

Culhane flashed him a grin.

"I shall have it translated for you, Senhor Culhane."

"You don't have to bother."

"Really, Senhor Culhane, it wouldn't be any trouble at all."

Culhane gestured toward the massive, open menu. "What would you recommend?"

"Any of the seafood—the catch is always fresh." Hoevermann read the menu silently for a few moments. "You can get yourself into a great deal of trouble helping Scott Palmer, Senhor Culhane."

"Smuggling? I wouldn't get involved with smuggling. And I had seafood yesterday, so I'll try something else."

"You're going to help Palmer, aren't you? He asked you to, didn't he?"

Culhane said nothing.

"I can have you deported very easily."

"Why? Because maybe I'm going to help him get his wife back? Maybe?"

"Maybe is a rather awkward word. Whatever those terrorists want, it can't be to the best interests of my country. Senhor Culhane, paying the ransom is helping the terrorists, and that is a crime. I have every available man and woman in my section working to find some lead as to the actual identity of the terrorists and where the woman might be being held...and we are very good at this. In North America you read about terrorism in the newspapers—or in adventure novels. Here it is not the same, I'm afraid. Terrorism has pervaded South American life for many years, and we know how to deal with it."

"You seem like a nice guy," Culhane began. "Let me ask you a question. Do you have a brother?"

"Two sisters—what does that have to do with it?"

"I had a twin brother. His name was Jeff. He worked

for—well, some people—their initials get attention any time you mention them.''

"I understand.''

"I don't know if you do. Jeff died. Scott Palmer was the youngest guy in my brother's outfit in Vietnam. Despite the fact that Palmer was loaded—hell, he had a Mercedes that he kept garaged in Saigon—my brother always talked about him as a decent guy. One time my brother got wounded, Palmer fragged the VC that did it and hauled Jeff three miles through the jungle until he could get help. He saved my brother's life. Now some assholes kidnap Palmer's wife on their wedding day and he asks me to deliver the ransom. I don't even know how much. The only way I can get near enough to her to get her out and maybe croak some of these terrorists is to take the ransom upriver. And I'm the only one who can do it. If he sends you guys, he'll lose his wife for sure. If he hires some guy off the street, chances are he'll hand over the money or the diamonds or whatever, and that's the last he'll see of him. Kiss off Palmer's wife. Sure you can deport me. But that doesn't get Amelina back, and it doesn't get you any dope on the terrorists.''

"I have read one of your books. It was very exciting reading. An excellent adventure story.''

"Thanks.''

"The point I'm trying to make, Senhor Culhane, is that what your character Sean Dodge is able to do isn't necessarily what you can do. This is more a job for a highly trained secret agent rather than for someone who only writes about one.''

Culhane suddenly felt on the defensive. Hoevermann was very good, he reflected. He was probably a superb interrogator.

"I can take care of myself,'' Culhane said, realizing after he said it how juvenile that sounded.

"Can you take care of Uruente tribesmen? The last of the headhunters some say. Over the last dozen years or so, no government workers sent out to find the Uruentes have come back. How are you with poisonous snakes? Piranha? Have you fought many bandits lately?"

"What's next? Gonna try scare tactics?"

Hoevermann began to laugh, then snapped his fingers for the waiter. "If you don't want fish, I'd recommend the chicken cordon bleu with wild rice. You'll have enough of our more ethnic entrees as you travel up-river."

Chapter Ten _____

Mary Frances Mulrooney felt slightly ridiculous—like an extra for "Ramar of the Jungle"—in the broad-brimmed fedora-style hat that was the same khaki color as her shirt, her bush shorts and her knee-high socks. But when she had been a Brownie and later a Girl Scout, it had been drummed into her head that you wore a hat in the woods to keep out ticks and other unpleasant little critters. So she wore the hat.

Mulrooney stood on the dock, her backpack and maroon stuff sack beside her feet, her blue canvas bag over her shoulder, a cigarette going.

She not only felt ridiculous, but conspicuous.

Sebastiao had contacted the hotel that she should meet him by the dock, that the floatplane would have the words "Spirit of East St. Louis" written in script along the right side of the fuselage.

But there was no pilot and no Sebastiao.

And M. F. Mulrooney felt dumb.

There were several planes moored along the Belém docks, and several medium-size powerboats. If Josh Culhane had been with her, she thought, he could have told her the exact sizes of the boats and the types of engines they had. He could have told her why the pontoons under some of the airplanes were different and that when the water was just right you could see wheels beneath them.

But he wasn't there. She had resisted the impulse to contact him again. If she had reached him, she would have been reluctant to speak over a telephone about anything having to do with the map to the lost Amazon city. "Lost Amazon city" sounded like something from pulp magazines, and she made a mental note not to use the phrase in talking about the place.

She'd left a note for him at the hotel. It explained everything. He'd be angry when he read it, but by the time he caught up with her he would have cooled down and they wouldn't fight.

That was very important to her. She loved him—and she felt almost silly realizing it was the most important thing to her.

Loving him.

"Menina Mulrooney!"

She turned, and coming along the dock under what looked like an impossible array of burdens was Sebastiao. Beside him, carrying a battered briefcase and an even more battered suitcase, the suitcase plastered all over with peeling travel stickers, was the man she assumed was the pilot.

He was an American, that was obvious. Tall, curly brown hair, a Tom Selleck mustache and pilot's sunglasses. Mulrooney stubbed out her cigarette on the dock planking and ran toward Sebastiao to help him. He looked as though he were about to collapse.

Sebastiao and the pilot stopped, Sebastiao resting his burdens on and around his feet. Mulrooney slowed her run, trying to look less flustered than she felt. The pilot was really good-looking.

She walked now, calling to Sebastiao, "I was beginning to worry about you."

"Jes' walks slow's all," the pilot drawled. His Deep South accent was heavier than anything she'd ever heard in Georgia.

"Hi—I'm Mary Frances Mulrooney." She stuck out her right hand. The pilot shrugged his shoulders, dropping his briefcase and shook her hand. The grip was kind of weak. Mulrooney remembered her mother talking about beauty being only skin deep. "You're..."

"Cal Cummings. And I ain't got all day. Get y'all crap over into the airplane and we'll fly on outta heah." Never a smile, not even an offer to help Sebastiao with his burdens. He picked up his briefcase and walked on.

She stuck her tongue out at him as he walked past her, then she looked at Sebastiao. "Where the hell did you dig him up?"

"It was not easy to find a pilot, Menina Mulrooney."

"You said you were going to call me M.F., remember?"

"Yes—Menina—M.F.—"

"Where the hell does that creep get off carrying his damned briefcase and his suitcase and leaving you stuck with all of this?" She promptly started picking up Sebastiao's backpack. It was heavier than she'd thought, but she took it anyway. It was then that she noticed the rifle slung from his right shoulder. "What kind of rifle is that?" She wasn't really interested, but it was the sort of question men liked answering and Sebastiao looked as though his ego needed reinforcing.

She took up a small canvas sack—it was heavy, too—
and walked beside him along the dock toward the airplane.

"A Steyr-Mannlicher Model M, M.F. It was a present
from Senhor Culhane many years ago after I lost my old
rifle when we were pursued by bandits. It is a .30-06."

Mulrooney made herself smile. "It's a very nice-
looking gun, Sebastiao. Did you get my gun?"

"Of course, M.F. It is in my pack, which you carry in
your hand."

She nodded, setting the backpack and the canvas sack
on the dock beside her own backpack and stuff bag.

Sebastiao clambered up to the fuselage door and
called back to her. "If you could hand me the things,
M.F.?"

"You bet," she answered confidently, then she tried
lifting the large canvas laundry bag Sebastiao had been
carrying. "Got your bowling-ball collection along, have
you?"

"It is food for our journey and some medical supplies. There is a car waiting for us in Manaus."

"Right." She managed to use all her body weight to
propel the bag into a pendulum motion far enough
across the gap between the dock and the fuselage that
Sebastiao could reach out for it. He snatched the bag
with one hand and swung it out of sight into the aircraft. She repeated the procedure with another equally
heavy laundry bag and with his backpack, the smaller
canvas bag, her backpack and the stuff bag.

He extended his left hand to her and she screwed her
hat down tighter on her head and jumped, her right
hand in Sebastiao's left, her left hand grasping what
looked like a ladder rung. She stepped inside and down,
bumping her head as she tried to stand to her full height.

"Get strapped in so we can get the hell airborne,

lady," the good-looking, foul-mannered pilot shouted back.

"Hold your goddamned horses, flyboy," she snapped, waiting beside the fuselage door as Sebastiao handed her his rifle and then swung himself in and down. He pulled at the door and it closed.

She found a seat—there were only three—and sat down, finding the seat belt ends and mating them. Sebastiao sat himself across from her after giving a last bit of attention to the gear. His rifle was between his legs, the barrel pointing upward toward the roof of the fuselage.

His pack was on the seat beside him and he was digging inside it. "For you, M. F. It is a present from me." He handed her a box with Amadeo Rossi written all over it and she opened it. In it was a little stainless-steel revolver that looked almost identical to her own Smith & Wesson that was locked in Josh Culhane's safe at his house on Lake Lanier. The grips were the normal size for a small revolver, she decided. She liked the fatter grips Culhane had put on her own gun better. "And this."

A box of ammunition. She read the end flap. Remington .38 Special—158-grain Round Nose Lead. She took out the gun and looked it over. It smelled as though it had been fired.

"I fired the revolver to make certain that it was as it should be," Sebastiao said, and smiled.

She noticed him unbuckling his gun belt as she began loading the gun. Five rounds, just like her gun back home. She closed the cylinder and set her purse across her lap, opening the center compartment with the special insert. A friend of Culhane's had made the purse for her, and she placed the Rossi revolver into the little built-in holster. The fit was fine.

The props started turning, and reflexively she gave her seat belt a good-luck tug. "I hope this guy's flying is better than his mouth," she muttered.

Chapter Eleven

"Nicolai must never have had a chance, I think. The radio message from the freighter—that he was found tied up..." He was searching for a cigarette.

"But Nicolai lives. The man who fought him must have been a demon, I think."

"The others..." Corporal Agronski found his cigarettes and lit one. "The storm—it was very bad."

Corporal Illyevitch began to answer, but Mikhail Tibilovski cut him off. "If we spend all our moments talking about the dead, we shall soon be among them."

"But Sergeant—"

"But nothing, Illyevitch. Whoever this demon was he was not on the freighter and is not among us now. He is dead. The proper place for demons, I think."

The voice he heard made him stop and turn. He always listened to it. Major Kruglovitch. "Twenty-four of us remain. That Nicolai cannot be here is indeed unfortunate. That the man the Committee for State Security had us bring in for their own project has died is unfortunate for the sake of their project, whatever it may have been. But it affects not at all our primary mission."

Tibilovski turned his attention to the strangely accented voice. "We must locate the archeological site according to the map. We must ascertain if the area still possesses any inhabitants. If such inhabitants exist, they must be captured, interrogated and returned with us to the Soviet Union. That is our mission.''

Major Kruglovitch laughed out loud. ''You make it all sound so terribly simple, Comrade Professor Xanthos. I have briefed the men. There is no need to speak obliquely of the focal point of the mission. That lives have been lost tracing after Amazon warriors is something I personally consider a waste, a horrible waste. And I shall make my sentiments known to my superiors in the Special Forces command upon our safe return.''

Xanthos smiled, plucking at his beard with both hands as though combing it with his fingers. ''Have you told your men we may return with the secret of eternal life?''

Major Kruglovitch stopped closing the front of his fatigue blouse. None of his men made even the slightest sound now as they stripped away their civilian clothes and donned their unmarked jungle fatigues.

Tibilovski could hear the jungle birds, hear the buzz of insects. A warm breeze blew, but despite its warmth, despite the heat of the jungle that surrounded them now, he was cold. It was not good for men to speak of living forever, as though they were gods.

The major sat down on a fallen tree trunk and began adjusting his boots, his fatigue blouse still half open, sweat pouring from his forehead. ''Stories,'' the major began. ''You have found what you have found, Comrade Professor. And perhaps indeed the Amazon women warriors once existed as you claim. And perhaps, too, they traveled great distances by sea from Africa and discovered this continent could be their home. But if they ever did exist, they do not now. They were mortal, as are we—as were the men who died in the storm to bring you here, Comrade Professor. If any of their numbers exist today, they are only the mongrelized descendants of those women. If a city existed once, it is buried under thousands of years of jungle. But I, like my men, am a soldier. And I was ordered to bring you here, to protect you, to help in your search for this city however I can. And like any soldier who is worthy of the name, I follow my orders. But do not ask me to believe in fairy stories of eternal life, Comrade Professor. Nor should you ask my men.''

Kruglovitch stood, Tibilovski watching as his superior officer, his friend, strapped on his pistol belt, mechanically checking the CZ-75 9mm automatic as he continued to speak, "And so, we shall take you on your tour of the Amazon jungles, Comrade Professor. And perhaps some of us will succumb to the dangers ahead. Perhaps not. We will follow your map. And perhaps, too, we shall successfully intercept the American woman journalist. And silence her. But when it is all through, the world will not have changed.''

Senior Sergeant Mikhail Tibilovski was shocked— and a little frightened. But Comrade Professor Miklos Xanthos merely threw back his gray-maned head and howled with laughter.

Chapter Twelve _____

Josh Culhane closed his eyes, feeling his hands shaking as he held the note. He looked at it again.

Hi, Josh:
Balthazar Muhammed came up with the greatest thing! A map leading to an old Amazon city in the

jungle—real Greek Amazons. He stole it from—
well, some people. And they killed him in Istanbul,
and I got away and came here. Couldn't wait. But I
took Sebastiao with me, so don't worry. If you can,
follow us. Manaus is the first stop and a little town
called Ouro between the two rivers and some guy
named Sergio Celini. He has a ranch outside of
Ouro and a house there in the city. And at his ranch
he's got this Greek girl—a real Greek. That's all she
speaks, I guess. And she was dressed like an
Amazon and living in the jungle. This could be real
big, darling!

Whenever she called him darling, she was aware of
the fact he was most probably furious.

The only problem in all this is the people who
killed Balthazar. Now sit down and don't get
upset. You know what that does to your stomach
and then you smoke too much. Balthazar stole
the map from the Russians and they stole it back,
so I guess they have a copy of the map, too. But
I don't think they know about the Amazon on
the ranch and how she only speaks Greek and
everything, so there is absolutely nothing to
worry about. Sebastiao got me a gun, and he
seems like such a nice little man. I can see why you
like him.

I love you—bye,
M.F.

"Shit," Culhane snarled, looking at the puzzled
desk clerk. "Why the hell did you let her go?"
"But, *senhor*—I, ah..."
Culhane looked back at the bottom of the note.

P.S. Hope you had a great time on the boat going after the sunken treasure and didn't get yourself an ear infection with all that diving. Love ya.

Culhane camly folded the note and put it in the pocket of the bush jacket he'd bought in São Luis. "When did she leave?"

"The airboat this morning, *senhor*."

"Is there another floatplane I can get to go after her?"

"They would all be gone, *senhor*—until tomorrow morning. And they will not go beyond Manaus where the young lady said she was going. But only because there is no gasoline."

"So she hired some guy—"

"It was the guide called Sebastiao, *senhor*."

Culhane lit a cigarette. "Fuckin' wonderful. Excuse me."

"I have another note, *senhor*."

Culhane took the envelope. It was from Scott Palmer. An invitation to an early dinner. He pocketed the note and checked his watch. It was almost time to meet him. "Can you have my stuff taken out of storage and sent up to the room I reserved for Miss Mulrooney and myself?"

"Of course, *senhor*, and is there. . ."

"Yeah—check around the docks and find out the name of that pilot."

Culhane returned the registration card and the pen and took his room key. He imagined it was still warm from being lost in the depths of Mulrooney's purse.

He wanted to strangle Sebastiao.

THE WOMAN SITTING ACROSS FROM SCOTT PALMER was stunning, Culhane thought.

He waved away the maître d' and walked out onto the

veranda, crossed the flagstone patio floor and made his way toward the table.

Palmer stood when Culhane reached the table. "Helene, this is my old friend's brother, Josh Culhane. I was telling you about him. He's a writer. And, Josh, this is Dr. Helene Chavez."

Culhane took her proffered hand. She had a solid grip for a woman.

"I've read your books, Mr. Culhane. Quite exciting," she said.

"Drop a note to my editor. He loves to hear that kind of stuff," Culhane said, and smiled. He sat down next to Palmer, and Helene Chavez began speaking.

"Perhaps I should explain a little bit about myself since we'll be traveling together. I'm employed by Palmer Industries as one of their medical officers. My father was Argentinian and my mother Brazilian. They were divorced. Quite scandalous at the time. So I grew up in both cultures, speaking both Spanish and Portuguese. And I went to college and medical school in America, which accounts for my English." And she smiled.

"You're very direct," Culhane told her.

"I've found that it's a wonderful time-saver. You're very handsome."

"I've found that to be a wonderful time-saver, too," Culhane told her.

"You are also very direct."

Culhane turned to Palmer. "So—give me the information. I've got problems, too, now. Fanny Mulrooney went upriver on her own, and she's got some guys chasing her, and I'm going to have to catch her on the way upriver with the ransom."

"Josh—this is a complication. The kidnappers said—"

"I don't think that an extra woman along will bother the kidnappers," Helene Chavez interjected. Culhane turned to face her. Her blue eyes were piercing. Her almost black hair cascaded in waves to her bare shoulders and beyond, the white dress she wore accentuating the deepness of her tan. "Call it intuition. The important thing is that the ransom gets upriver just as they directed, and that there be no police. We can always leave Mr. Culhane's friend at one of the river stations if we have to."

"Gee, Fanny would love that," Culhane muttered. "You bet." And he turned to Palmer. "What's this about getting upriver 'as they directed'?"

"That's part of it, Josh. You take a plane up to Manaus. There's a river station just beyond there, and you transfer to a boat. They even said which one."

"I have to go beyond Manaus—to Ouro."

Helene Chavez spoke. "The riverboat stops near there, but that is well past Manaus."

"I have to get Fanny!"

"She'll be all right—you can probably catch her at Manaus. If you don't, then get this boat to let you off near Ouro and rent a car or buy one—whatever you need. Whatever kind of person she is, she can't get in that much danger in just an extra day or two."

Culhane looked at Palmer. "You don't..."

"I think it's wonderful that you're so devoted to your friend," Helene Chavez said. "But your brother was Scott's best friend, his commanding officer, I understand. And Scott's wife, Amelina...we know she's in danger. And if we don't keep to their schedule, the terrorists will kill her."

Culhane looked directly at Palmer. "What is it I'm taking upriver? Money? Diamonds? What is it?"

"Gold," Palmer answered after a moment. "A

million dollars' worth, more or less. One hundred forty-six pounds of it. It'll be carried in two suitcases. Each ingot is the size of a house brick. The terrorists were very specific.''

"Do you have any idea what group this is? What their track record is?''

"No—and they told me not to try to find out.''

Culhane nodded, stubbing out his cigarette, sipping at the glass of ice water in front of him. A cool breeze blew, but the sun on the veranda was hot.

"The man in charge of the riverboat is not involved, but he'll have a note for you," Palmer continued. "Read it, and follow the directions in the note to the letter. Please, Josh.''

"Scott told me that the directions should tell us how far to go up the Negro.''

Culhane looked hard at Helene Chavez. "Dr. Chavez, have you ever done anything like this before?''

"No, I haven't. I was upriver once a few years ago. But no, not really.''

"I've never delivered a ransom, but I've been into a few things. This could get very dangerous. I don't know how much Scott mentioned about that.''

"I'm prepared for whatever risks I must take. Scott's father was a fine man. My father worked for him, as I work for Scott now. I'm doing this because I want to— not because Scott threatened to fire me or something if I didn't.''

Culhane signaled to the waiter. He wasn't hungry, but he figured he should be.

Chapter Thirteen _____

"Hell," Culhane snarled, slamming the hotel-room door behind him. He was sorry he had agreed to help. He found himself staring at the bed. Mulrooney had slept there. Where she slept tonight he didn't know. He felt like wringing her neck, except wringing her neck would hurt her and he wanted to do just the opposite—to protect her from harm. He would wring Sebastiao's neck. Sebastiao should have known better. He would take the rifle he had given Sebastiao and break it over his...

"Shit," he snarled again, walking to the center of the room and taking out his Bali-Song to cut the rope around the packages that contained his guns. He cut the cord, then used the knife to cut through the heavy wrapping tape. He dropped into a squat on the floor beside the partially opened packages, ripping away the wrappings, pretending he was ripping away someone's face instead.

The shoe box with the taped lid. He reached back to the bed for his knife, using it to cut through the tape. He ripped off the lid. Packed in newspaper was his Metalife Custom six-inch-barreled Smith & Wesson Model 629 .44 Magnum. A piece of newspaper was stuck in one of the trapezoidal Mag-na-port slots flanking the front sight. He plucked the newspaper free, then opened the cylinder, checking its empty condition. He closed the cylinder, his right fist closing over the Pachmayr gripped butt.

"All right, Sebastiao—you take a defenseless woman—never mind she's crazy—but take her into the jungle, huh?'' He double-actioned the empty revolver toward the blue sky beyond the drawn-back drapes covering the balcony doors. Finally he set the revolver down. Packed in the box with it was its custom-made full-flap holster, the wide, double-billeted Safariland gun belt and the three now-empty hinged dump boxes that would soon hold six rounds each. In the box, too, was the black-handled Gerber MkII fighting knife, with its black sheath that also nested the sharpening steel for it. The sheath, the holster and the belt were all the color of his mood. Black. He set these aside and emptied the box. The Break Free CLP to clean and lubricate his weapons. The Cattle Baron Leather Cattlehide Cream, to preserve his holster and belt, even his boots. The jungle's oppressive humidity made the cream and lubricant a necessity. The two-foot-long Collins machete and the Cattle Baron back sheath to house it.

He pried open the other box. He had sent the rifle to his friend Ron Mahovsky to be Metalifed before taking it into the jungle. But when he opened the box—there had been no time to open it before shipping it—he didn't recognize the gun. It had been a very ordinary, very nicely blued Browning B-92 lever-action .44 Magnum. He had always liked the idea of a handgun and a rifle using the same cartridge. He was a Western buff right down to his cowboy boots, he realized.

There was a note inside the box and he opened it.

Dear Josh,
You may feel kind of upset. Your girl friend Fanny asked me to do this. If you don't like it, I'll trade it back from you for a standard B-92. But I tried it, and the gun works great with the trick lever and the

set screw. And the laser engraving Laser Creations did on the stock is real pretty.

It was signed by his friend Mahovsky.

Culhane lifted the rifle out of the box to examine it. The lever had been replaced by an oversize bow-shaped lever, the kind John Wayne had used on his rifle. In the trigger-guard position of the lever was a set screw. Culhane turned it by hand. When turned in, it would contact the trigger when the lever was closed. When turned out, it would not. When turned in, each time the lever was worked, the gun would automatically fire. The Metalifing had made all the metal surfaces a dull-silver color, and small silver eagles were just forward of the barrel band inset on each side of the front stock. The underside of the front stock was deeply laser engraved: JOSH CULHANE. The right side of the butt stock was engraved with a large eagle with wings outspread, a banner in its talons reading The Taker.

He shook his head. The rifle was almost too pretty to use. But he'd take it upriver after he cleaned it and saw to his other gear. And after a good night's sleep—

He laughed at that. He was very worried about Fanny. After he thanked her for the beautiful rifle, he'd punch her in the mouth. But the trouble was, Culhane sighed, that he knew he wouldn't, no matter how much she deserved it.

Chapter Fourteen _____

It was hot inside the floatplane. Mulrooney stood up, remembering just in time that fuselages taper as they go from front to back and ducking her head before hitting it. She grabbed the ridiculous hat and started forward, catching up her purse over her shoulder and stopping at the hatch. She stuck out her head. It was nearly dark, the sun setting upriver. She shouted to the pilot, "How's it going?"

But he didn't answer her.

Sebastiao, standing on the wing stem behind Cal Cummings, explained, "It is a fuel line, M.F. He is fixing it."

"Wonderful." Mulrooney shrugged. "This may seem like an insignificant problem, but I have to go to the bathroom."

Sebastiao looked at her.

The pilot turned his handsome face up from the engine cowling and looked at her. "I got a Porta-Boat—not a porta-potty. Y'all wanna take a leak, lady, get Sebastiao to break out the dinghy and row ya ashore."

"You're a prince, you know that, Cummings?"

He didn't answer her, turning back to the engine cowling and taking the flashlight from Sebastiao.

THE GREEN FOLDING BOAT WAS SECURED along one internal portion of the fuselage, and Mulrooney had helped Sebastiao get it by the hatch and into the water, folding it open and placing the two seats inside it. It had suddenly gone from something the size of a large surfboard to a three-man boat that could be used with a motor or oars. All they had were oars, and though Mulrooney had offered, Sebastiao had rowed her ashore. He had offered to accompany her and stand nearby, but she had told him she'd been going to the bathroom by herself for a long time.

She had a flashlight that Sebastiao provided, but it wasn't so dark that she really needed it yet, and she walked away from the shore, carefully picking her footing.

There were strange noises—but they really weren't strange noises, Mulrooney told herself. They were just strange to her. Jungle noises. Her footsteps were really the alien sounds. She held that thought as she found a sufficiently secluded-looking spot.

One of the strange noises was really starting to sound strange—and close.

She finished, but she left her purse open while she adjusted her clothes and straightened her knee-high stockings. Mary Frances Mulrooney refused to be intimidated by the moaning noise she heard from the jungle.

As she tugged at the brim of her hat, something half the size of a B-52 and twice as loud buzzed past her ear. "Hang tight, M.F.," Mulrooney told herself. Calmly she started walking back toward Sebastiao.

The moaning sounds were louder. The light around her was purple now, the shadows long.

Something swatted at her face and she jumped. It was only a broad leaf, half in shadow, half in light.

She tried whistling. Something touched her right arm beneath the short sleeve of her shirt. Another leaf, she told herself and looked down.

It was a hand—hairy and huge—and it started to

close around her forearm. She looked into the darkness past the hand, along the massive furry arm and into eyes that seemed almost to emit light. They were staring at her.

"An overactive imagination," Mary Frances Mulrooney told herself.

But the eyes still stared at her out of the darkness, and she could feel the hand on her arm. She pulled her arm away from the hairy hand and screamed, "Sebastiao!" Then she started to run.

"Sebastiao!" She could hear noises behind her, something huge crashing through the jungle after her, almost feel breath on the back of her neck, her hair stuffed up under her hat.

"Sebastiao! Sebastiao!" The moaning noises were louder, closer. "Sebastiao—ow!" And she fell against Sebastiao's chest.

"*Menina*—what is it?"

"Some big hairy monkey tried grabbing me! He's—"

Mulrooney edged behind Sebastiao, and he raised his rifle to his shoulder. She stared into the jungle.

But nothing was there and the moaning noise was gone.

Sebastiao made the sign of the cross.

"What is it?"

"The mapinguari."

"The maping-what?"

"The mapinguari." And he crossed himself again. "*Menina*, the legends are told of the monkeys. No one has seen them but women, and these women have never been seen again to tell of them. They kidnap women in the night and drag them off into the jungle—perhaps for. . ."

"You're pulling my leg."

"The stories of the mapinguari—they have been told for generations, M.F."

"I just decided I want to see how Mr. Congeniality is doing—let's get outta here." And despite the heat of the jungle, as she held Sebastiao's arm all the way back to the dinghy, she couldn't help shivering.

Chapter Fifteen _____

He checked the face of his gold Rolex President. Josh Culhane was running late. The bellman had brought Culhane's luggage down ten minutes before. Most of it was packed in Palmer's customized Mercedes convertible—he kept company cars everywhere—along with Helene Chavez's luggage, and Helene Chavez. Two suitcases were flanking his chair. Every bandit on the river, every hoodlum in every city would have heard of the kidnapping of his wife and know that a ransom would be paid. It was why Palmer needed a man like Culhane to get the ransom upriver in the first place.

The elevator doors opened and Palmer stood up, seeing Culhane as he stepped out and into the lobby. Culhane noticed him, grinned and waved, then started across the lobby.

Absently, Palmer thought Culhane looked like Sean Dodge from *The Takers* books. Tall, lean, a full-flap military-style holster at his right hip, partially covered by his khaki bush jacket, the jacket open, the belt stuffed into the side pockets. Faded Levi's were bloused over black Vietnam-era G.I. combat boots. What looked like some kind of musette bag hung at Culhane's left side, partially concealed beneath the bush jacket, and below the bush jacket Palmer could see the bottom portion of a long black knife sheath. In his left hand, Culhane carried a broad-brimmed, low-crowned Confederate-gray Stetson. At least it would be a Stetson if Culhane were true to Sean Dodge in the books. The gun in the holster would be a customized 629 .44 Magnum. The knife would be a Gerber MkII. And somewhere on his person would be Dodge's Bali-Song. The musette bag—he remembered from the books it was really a Norwegian army engineer's bag—would hold the top-of-the-line Victorinox Swiss army knife, a G.I. lensatic compass, an extra package of Pall Malls, a small leather notebook, a pen, a Cutter snake-bite kit, and a red-and-white box of Federal .44 Magnums for the revolver.

Culhane shifted the Stetson into his right hand and ran the fingers of his left through his brown hair, then pulled the cowboy hat on low over his eyes as he stopped in front of Palmer.

"Sorry I'm a few minutes late. I tried calling the Manaus hotel Fanny and I were going to use. They haven't seen her. Checked with the police up there, too. She hasn't gotten into any trouble they know of."

"You'll find her—and you'll get Amelina back for me. I have confidence in you," Palmer told Culhane, letting himself smile.

Culhane only nodded. Then he glanced down at the cases. "That it?"

"That's it. Your pack, your other gear and your rifle are already in the car. Helene's waiting for us. Figured I'd drive you down to the docks and see you safely aboard the plane."

Culhane nodded again, picking up one of the suitcases. "Seventy-three pounds plus the weight of the suitcase, right?"

"Right."

"I can feel every ounce of it," Culhane said, grinning, then started across the lobby and toward the revolving doors.

Palmer noticed a few of the guests staring at Culhane's gun as he left the hotel. But Culhane would be like Sean Dodge; all of the paperwork would be in order for the gun.

Palmer hefted the second suitcase and started after Culhane, following him out into the street. Culhane stood at the curb. "I'm going to put these on the back seat and on the floor. Otherwise your trunk'll get weighed down."

"Good idea," Palmer said, nodding. Culhane set one of the cases on the seat between where he would sit and Helene Chavez already sat. Palmer watched her eyes as she looked at the suitcase. Palmer leaned in, putting the second suitcase on the floor beside Helene Chavez.

He climbed into the car behind the wheel, finding his driving cap on the seat and pulling it on. "All right, buckle up. I'm a reckless driver." He forced a laugh, fired the engine and glanced behind him, waiting for a break in traffic.

He could hear Culhane talking to Helene Chavez. "I'll assume you're armed, Dr. Chavez."

"Please, as I told you last night, it's Helene."

"Helene."

"And yes, but I'm afraid nothing as big as what you seem to have there. Just a little .25 automatic I always carry for protection—here in my purse."

"Don't shoot anything that can shoot back with one of those."

Palmer saw his break and took it, peeling away from

the curb, calling over his shoulder, "We talked about it last night some, Josh, but every crook in Brazil should be after this ransom."

"And they'll know I've got it, with you driving us to the docks."

"I shoulda thought—I'm sorry..."

"They'd probably know anyway. Good thing I work out with weights, or otherwise I wouldn't be able to carry it," Culhane said, laughing. "And you relax—I'll find Amelina."

"I know you will, Josh. I'm really counting on you—more than you realize."

Palmer took the left and turned off toward the docks.

Culhane found the ashtray and lit a cigarette, his hands cupped around the lighter's flame. Helene Chavez was talking. She seemed to do that a lot, he reflected. "This should be quite an adventure—up the Amazon, wild animals, river pirates, terrorists. I bet this will be in one of your books someday."

"Probably," Culhane agreed.

"Maybe I can be the heroine."

Culhane looked at her and smiled. "Would you like that?"

She actually giggled. "It would be kind of fun."

"Tell you what I'll do," Culhane began. "If I write it that way, I'll—" But he stopped, losing the thought. A hearse was coming up fast behind them, a black Cadillac of early 1970s vintage. Culhane asked Palmer, "Scott, are there any cemeteries out this way—or any funeral homes?"

"Neither one, at least I don't think—"

Culhane turned to Helene Chavez. "You're a doctor—how do they usually pick up a corpse? Ambulance or hearse?"

"An ambulance usually, but—"

Culhane reached to his right hip, popping the snap on the flap holster, drawing the 629, his fist closing over the Pachmayr gripper stocks. "Get down between the seats! Hurry!" he told Helene Chavez. "Scott—get us outta here!"

"Right!"

Culhane pulled the Stetson from his head, tossing it into the front seat beside Palmer, the revolver across his lap now as he eyed the hearse.

Culhane could hear the whine of the Mercedes's engine. The scenery on both sides of them—rundown houses, yards—was all a blur as he kept his eyes focused tightly on the Cadillac hearse. It was speeding up.

From the corner of his eye he saw them coming. First one, then a second and then a third. Motorcycles, big powerful-looking machines.

"Got a gun, Scott?"

"Yeah, a little thirty-eight snubby. Holy Jes—"

"Hand it back here to Helene!"

Helene Chavez's head popped up, her right hand reaching over Palmer's right shoulder.

She took the gun. "What do you want me to do with it?"

"If I need a second gun fast, give it to me. Otherwise, stay down and keep it beside you," said Culhane, shoving her down between the seats.

The big motorcycles were closing in, the roar of the Cadillac hearse's engine loud now.

What looked like a moon roof opened over the driver's seat of the hearse and a body popped up. Culhane recognized the shape in the hands. "Scott, swerve her right and left—fast!" Culhane threw himself across the seat, submachine-gun fire opening up from the moon roof of the hearse. Culhane peered up, snapping his big gun over the seat back and across the folded-back top of the Mercedes and firing, the .44 Magnum rocking in his hands. He ducked, hearing the sound of submachine-gun bullets hitting the Mercedes's body. "Keep down as low as you can, Scott!" Culhane shouted. He assumed Palmer was still alive since the car wasn't out of control; there was no time to look. Culhane shoved the revolver up again and fired, the subgun still firing from the hearse.

Lighter, higher-pitched cracks—it sounded to Culhane like a 5.56mm—were coming from the nearest of the motorcycles. Culhane peered up. It was an assault rifle. "He's a good biker," he mumbled under his breath. Culhane pushed up, snapping the .44 Magnum out to full extension and double-actioning the trigger. The shot tore the biker from his machine, the assault rifle firing skyward. "Was, anyway," Culhane remarked, ducking, more submachine gun fire exploding from the hearse. Culhane edged over farther from Palmer's side to draw fire away from Palmer. He looked up. The downed bike had skidded along the street and into the front porch of a small house. The porch and the bike were on fire.

Culhane ducked. Another gun was opening up from one of the two remaining motorcycles—a pistol by the sound of it.

Culhane pegged the shots as coming from the one on the left of the Mercedes. He pushed up, firing the .44 Magnum, missing, pulling the gun out of recoil and, on target again, double-actioning a second shot. The biker's body snapped from the saddle and was impaled on a chain link fence running alongside the curb. The bike spun out across the middle of the street, and the third biker tried to jump it, the bike in midair as Culhane fired his sixth shot. The bike exploded, the gas tank hit.

Submachine-gun fire from the hearse shredded the convertible top and its cover, thudding into the front seat back behind Culhane. "You still with us, Scott?"

"Still with ya!"

Culhane snatched one of the Safariland Speedloaders from the bag at his left side, dumping the empty brass from the Magnum onto the seat, ramming the loader against the ejector star, charging all six chambers. The Speedloader shoved into his bush-jacket pocket, Culhane slammed closed the cylinder and fired toward the windshield of the hearse—one shot, then another and then a third, his wrist taking it, his hand hurting. The Cadillac hearse swerved but kept coming. Before he ducked under a hail of gunfire, Culhane noticed that a chunk of glass the size of a grapefruit was out of the hearse's windshield on the right-hand side.

He could hear the roar of the Cadillac's engine now— louder.

"They're speeding up. I can just see 'em in the rear-view mirror," Palmer shouted over the slipstream and the gunfire.

"Helene—gimme the second gun—quick!" His left hand found the butt of the revolver. "Scott, when I shout—no gas for a count of ten, then give her everything she's got. Okay?"

Culhane rose to his full height, standing now between the front and the back seats, the little snubby revolver in his waistband. The Magnum was in both fists. Culhane fired once, then again, then again. Another chunk of the Cadillac's windshield was blown out. A headlight was gone.

Culhane very deliberately took aim on the Cadillac a fourth time, but he knew there wasn't another shot left.

"Now, Scott—no gas!"

The Mercedes started to slow, Culhane balancing

himself, the Cadillac shooting forward. The subgunner's face was visible now, a leering grin, exposing yellowed teeth and black eyes.

Culhane threw the Magnum to the seat, raising his hands into the air. The Cadillac was beside them. Culhane kept counting. "Ten!" The Mercedes slammed forward, Culhane throwing himself down across the shredded convertible top, the little Colt .38 Special in both fists, his finger pumping the trigger again and again and again until there was nothing but a click. The subgunner's body had crumpled back across the moon roof opening, swaying from side to side, the subgun clattering to the street, the Cadillac skidding, jumping the curb, crashing through a wooden fence, and coming to a stop.

Culhane dropped into the seat. "Drive like hell, Scott!" He remembered to breathe....

Chapter Sixteen _____

Manaus had seemed like a good-size town. Mulrooney made a mental note that after she found the Amazon girl and located the lost Amazon city, she should stop there on the way back to do some shopping.

But they were out of the city now, the obnoxious pilot just a memory, faithful Sebastiao at the wheel of the Ford Bronco, and high, grassy savannah on both sides of the well-paved road.

Sebastiao had slept aboard the aircraft, as had Mulrooney, and they had been driving since before dawn. Mulrooney had noticed that the speedometer was printed in both miles and kilometers, and the miles-per-hour figure was high. She saw another reason why Sebastiao got along well with Culhane; he was also a crazy driver. The needle hadn't dipped below eighty for the past two hours.

"Would you, ah, like me to drive? I've got an international driver's license. Got a Brazilian license, too—you must be tired."

"I know the roads, *menina*—it is better for me to drive. Soon we will leave the good road and be on one that is dirt and sometimes washes out. It is better that I drive, *menina*."

"Remember—no more of this *menina* stuff, okay?"

"Yes, M. F.—I remember."

She looked away from his little face and back at the Greek phrase book in her hands. "Hero polly," she said out loud, reading the phonetic pronunciation.

"M. F.?"

"Hero polly—it means 'Delighted to meet you' in Greek. How about that?"

Sebastiao didn't answer.

IT WAS NEARLY DUSK when she opened her eyes and stared around her for a moment, trying to wake up. Sebastiao still sat at the wheel of the Bronco, and the dashboard lights were on now. She could feel the roughness of the road. The speedometer hovered at seventy. "What time is it, Sebastiao?"

"Nearly seven, *menina*."

"We've been on the road for...what...fourteen hours?" She remembered their last stop at around three o'clock, Sebastiao on one side of the road beside a bush and herself off in the brush. "How much farther?" she finally asked, yawning, stretching her arms up to where her hands touched the roof of the

Bronco, her feet pressed out against the floorboards.

"Ouro is maybe another ten miles, M.F.—and the place of the man Sergio is twenty miles beyond the town, I think."

She laughed, glancing at the speedometer. "Another five minutes or so then, huh?"

"There are no traffic police like you have," he told her, smiling. She could barely see his face in the reflected lights of the dashboard.

"You know, I have to say this, Sebastiao—you're okay."

"Thank you very much, *menina*—you are okey-dokey, too."

Mulrooney laughed, feeling around in her purse for her cigarettes and lighter. She wondered if Culhane had gotten to Belém yet and read her note. She almost hoped he hadn't, but in a way she hoped he had and that he was in hot pursuit. He would be angry. That was putting it mildly, she thought as she lit her cigarette. But it would be nice to see him. She smiled.

"You hungry, Sebastiao?"

"*Sim, menina.* A little."

"Hang loose, pal." She twisted around in the seat onto her bruised knees, the filter tip of the cigarette clamped in her teeth as she started fishing in the big orange container in the back of the vehicle.

Maybe Sebastiao was only a little hungry, she thought, but she was starving.

THE TOWN OF OURO was like some of the smaller towns in Georgia; it could be driven through without really noticing it, especially with darkness full and complete suddenly upon them. They had driven on, resuming Sebastiao's breakneck pace for a time, and then, after turning on to what she would have labeled a ranch or farm road, he had slowed to fifty. Mulrooney could feel the vehicle slipping and skidding along the road's surface, but she said nothing.

Looming ahead of them just inside the boundary of their headlights was a house. It was tall, and grayish looking in the shadowy light, and ornately Victorian, bedecked with intricately patterned woodwork. Beneath the Bronco's tires she could now hear the crunch of gravel.

Sebastiao was slowing the Bronco. Mulrooney thought she could just barely detect a light in one of the first-floor windows.

The Bronco slowed still more, skidding a little, Mulrooney hearing gravel flying and pelting at the undercarriage of the Bronco, the vehicle finally stopping.

"I think this is the place, *menina*. I do not like it."

Mulrooney opened the Velcro tabs holding together the center compartment of her bag. Her right hand touched lightly at the grips of the Rossi revolver. "It'll be all right, Sebastiao—don't worry," she told him.

He had already gotten out of the car, his door open and the dome light on. He'd rebuckled the gun belt at his waist, then walked around the front of the vehicle and to her side, opening the door.

"Thank you," she told him. She had worn a sweater across her shoulders since a few minutes after awakening and had left it there, the night air chill. Her purse hung from her shoulder beneath the sweater. She left her hat on the seat.

Sebastiao walked beside her as Mulrooney pushed her shoulder-length hair back from her face. Another light came on in the house, and then another in what was apparently a hallway.

Mulrooney and Sebastiao stopped at the foot of three concrete steps that led to the wide, long front porch. The door opened.

A man was framed in the doorway, backlit so Mulrooney could not see his face or features. He said something in Portuguese, and she looked at Sebastiao as he answered.

And then the voice from the doorway—she noticed the hand that belonged to it held some kind of big gun, maybe a shotgun—said in English, "So you are the one Balthazar knows."

"Knew," Mulrooney corrected Sergio Celini. "He was killed a few days ago."

"I should ask you why, no?" His English had an Italian accent.

"It had something to do with an ancient artifact he had acquired. There wasn't time to ask any questions. I just ran for my life."

"And so," Celini said after a long pause, "you come to see the girl? No?"

"Yes. I'm M. F. Mulrooney—well, I guess you know that."

"You write about this girl?"

"Yes—maybe. If she's genuine. I've got to see her to know. Talk with her."

"You speak Greek?"

"I have a phrase book. I'll get by."

"I speak Greek. I will help you. We go in my car. If we drive through the night we will be there shortly after dawn. She is on my ranch."

"Maybe I'm confused," Mulrooney began, looking up at him across the porch. "But I thought this was your ranch."

"No—it is many miles. We will go then quickly."

"Sebastiao, just get what we'll need." She turned to

Sergio Celini. "Unless you want us to all go in Sebastiao's car."

"He does not go. I told Balthazar Muhammed I would take only you—nobody else, *signorina*."

"M. F.—just call me M. F., Mr. Celini."

"Sergio, then."

"Thank you." Mulrooney turned to Sebastiao. "Why don't you wait for me in Ouro—"

"No, *menina*—Senhor Culhane—he will . . ."

"I'll be all right."

"He can wait for us at the river station above the fork where the one-legged man Raphael runs the bar."

"I know the place," Sebastiao volunteered. "But I do not like this."

Mulrooney reached out in the darkness, found Sebastiao's left arm and held it tight. "I'll be all right. Don't you worry a bit. And have a drink for me at the one-legged man's bar."

Sebastiao turned his face toward her. Celini must have moved, shifted his position in the doorway, because she could see Sebastiao's face clearly in the yellow light. "It is not a good thing, M. F."

She still held Sebastiao's arm. "I'll be all right." She turned and looked at Celini. "Got a bathroom I could use—to freshen up?"

He stepped out onto the porch. "Yes."

Sebastiao stepped onto the porch before she could say anything. "After the *menina*—me, too."

"All right."

Mulrooney started up onto the porch. She paused at the doorway, in the light there still not seeing Celini's face but seeing his gun—a short double-barreled shotgun. "That looks like something out of a Western movie."

"Rossi makes it," Sebastiao said absently.

Mulrooney stepped inside. She regretted opening her mouth about the bathroom, but it was too late to back out.

Copies of all the American tabloid newspapers she could think of were stacked against both walls of the hallway, index cards sticking out periodically from each stack. She imagined it was some sort of reference system.

"The bathroom is through the room on your right, Signorina Mulrooney."

She turned around and finally saw Sergio Celini's face. His face was dirty looking, as if perspiration had turned to grease. And his black beard—there was some gray in it—was unkempt. The khaki shirt he wore had large sweat stains under the armpits, but they were not as large as the salt stains where sweat had dried. She estimated the shirt got washed as often as he shaved.

Turning to her right, she entered what was probably the house's dining room but which now served the function of a library. Paperback romance novels littered the tables and chairs, some of them decades old from the clothes of the women on the covers. She walked past, and through a small doorway.

It was the bathroom.

"I'll be right out," she said, closing the door behind her, not touching the doorknob any more than she had to.

"Ugh," Mulrooney murmured, and shivered involuntarily. She stood in the middle of the floor, mentally going through the motions of doing what she had to do. She wanted to be there a reasonable time, and had no desire to offend Celini. But she wondered if he were capable of being offended. The toilet tank was covered with tabloid newspapers. She saw no toilet paper.

There was no soap on the sink, and she wondered if the sink had been turned on at all recently.

She decided she had been in the bathroom long enough. She tried looking in the mirror, but it was too dirty to return a clear image.

She balanced on one booted foot and worked the handle on the toilet with her other foot.

At least it flushed.

Carefully, touching it as little as possible, she turned the doorknob and let herself out.

Mulrooney put on a big smile. "I feel better now—"

Sebastiao walked past her and closed the bathroom door behind him. There were times, she reflected, when being a man was a decided advantage.

Alone with Celini, she tried making conversation. "Balthazar was never too specific. How did you find the girl?"

"In the jungle."

"But—"

"She had fought with some wild animal, I think. She was—how do you say the word—unconscious, no?"

"Yes—I mean, that's how you say the word."

"*Si*—unconscious. We took charge of her, cleaned her up. She waits for you there. You think she is a real Amazon?"

"I don't know. It would be nice if she were."

"*Si*. How much you pay for story in papers?"

"If she's the genuine article, you'll be well paid. But I have to see her, to talk with her. Did she recover from her wounds?"

"Yes, very quickly. She healed."

"How does she feel about..."

"About what?" Celini asked. Mulrooney eyed the shotgun he held casually in the crook of his right arm. Josh Culhane wasn't much of a shotgunner, but she had always thought that to be safe the gun was always broken open. This one wasn't.

"Well—I mean—how did you get her to stay?"

"We have locked her in a cage—a wild animal cage. She is a wild animal. You will see."

Mulrooney heard the toilet flush through the bathroom door and heard the door opening.

She looked over her shoulder at Sebastiao. "I think I will come along, Senhor Celini," Sebastiao began.

"Then nobody goes."

Mulrooney stepped between them. "Sebastiao will wait for me at that bar you talked about." And she looked at Sebastiao, into his eyes. "If we get to Mr. Celini's ranch by early morning, I can meet the girl and—" Mulrooney looked into Celini's black eyes. They were watching her. "How long a drive is it from your ranch to the place on the river where Sebastiao will meet us?"

"Six hours, maybe seven."

"Can you take me there by nightfall tomorrow?"

"*Si*—yes. I can do this thing."

Mulrooney looked back to Sebastiao. "Then I'll see you tomorrow night. Wait up for me."

Sebastiao nodded and she saw the look in his eyes. He understood. She knew he did.

"We go then," Celini said. He turned on his heel and walked past the litter of romance novels and into the hallway.

Sebastiao took her arm, "*Menina*—do not do this."

"If I'm not there tomorrow night, bring in the Marines, okay?" And she leaned up and kissed Sebastiao on the cheek.

Then she walked after Sergio Celini.

Chapter Seventeen _____

Culhane had showered and changed and slept a long but uneasy night. A million dollars in gold in two suitcases beside his bed hadn't made for untroubled rest. And he was beginning to think he was as attractive to women as he made Sean Dodge to be in *The Takers*. First it had been the ill-fated Melissa Burroughs. And now Helene Chavez. She had invited him into her room and he had declined.

He was a victim of the modern age, Culhane thought, walking back and forth on the veranda in front of his room, waiting for someone from the boat crew to come and help with his luggage. No matter how hard he tried—and he didn't try that hard—he could not convince himself that it was acceptable for a man to cheat on a woman and unacceptable for a woman to cheat on a man.

Fanny Mulrooney was faithful to him. He lit a cigarette. And he was faithful to her. Goddammit.

Culhane heard footsteps along the veranda and he turned, expecting to see one of the boat crew. It was impossible for him alone to carry his pack, his stuff sack, his rifle and the two suitcases.

But it was a priest—black shirt with dog collar, wrinkled black suit, a full head of dark hair, and a face that looked very Mediterranean. The priest looked ridiculously physically fit.

And the priest looked up from apparently studying his shoes. He stopped. "Jeff—they said—"

Culhane swallowed hard. "Sergeant Santini?"

"You're—"

"Josh—Josh Culhane. Damascus Santini?"

The priest jogged toward him, and in the next instant Culhane found the man pumping his hand. "My God, and I really mean it when I say it, you look, well, just..."

"Just like him."

"You're the kid brother—"

"By a few seconds—twins."

"Jeff always said you were the last one to get up. God. I can't believe it. Your brother. I'm sorry, man— he and I—we were, well, like this." And he brought the first and second fingers of his right hand together. "You know?"

Culhane laughed. "Yeah—I know." He realized he was smiling. "I talked with Scott Palmer. He told me you'd become a priest. I had no idea you were coming upriver."

"Mission work." Santini kept shaking his head. Then he clapped his hands and threw his arms around Culhane. "God, I miss your brother."

Santini stepped away.

Culhane looked at him, into the deep-set eyes. "I miss him, too."

"How the hell did it happen?"

"Oh—he, ah—he burned to death. He'd been shot. Some—some assholes—I'm sorry, Father—"

"It's Damascus. Your brother was my best friend. Like my brother, only I never had one. But when I met him I did. And I'm your friend if you want me."

Culhane extended his hand to the man, and this time it wasn't like being on the receiving end of a pump handle. It was a hard, firm, dry grip that somehow exuded something Culhane had found too rarely in the world— trust, honor, even strength. His throat was tight. "Do you drink?"

"Yeah—maybe too much."

"Have a few drinks with me before we get upriver. Then I'll tell you all of it."

Santini nodded. "You got a deal, my friend."

Culhane was unable to talk for a moment. He lit a Pall Mall, offering one to Santini. Santini took it and lit it with his own lighter. Culhane recognized the lighter. He had buried his brother with one just like it.

"You met Scott. I was on that boat. Those terrorists—it was a massacre."

Culhane looked into Santini's eyes again. He needed an ally—or he would. Fanny liked to talk about sixth senses and things like that. But maybe she was right and there was one. "Guess what I got in that—and in that." Culhane gestured to the two suitcases.

"Aw, man—he got you?"

Culhane nodded. "He saved Jeff's life. What could I say? Anyway, I don't like terrorists."

"Sounds like something Sean Dodge would say."

"You read my books?"

"God help me, yeah."

Culhane laughed. Then he got serious. "I got it—in there."

"What? Diamonds?"

"One hundred forty-six pounds of gold in ingots the size of house bricks."

"That must be—"

"A million bucks, Father."

"I told you—Damascus. A million dollars...!"

Culhane looked at Santini. "You're supposed to be a shepherd to your flock, right?"

"Yeah—"

"Help me shepherd this. Give me a chance to close my eyes once in a while. Keep an eye on my back."

Santini's eyes flickered downward. Culhane could

hear a parrot call from off in the rain forest beyond the river-front hotel above Manaus.

"I, ah, I don't have one of these anymore," said Santini, tapping Culhane's full-flap holster.

"I've got a spare in my pack."

"Yeah, but see—I can't, ah—'cause I might use it, you know, and—"

"Using your eyes is okay, isn't it?"

"My eyes," Santini said, squinting through a cloud of exhaled cigarette smoke. "My eyes—they're your eyes, man."

Culhane just looked at him. His brother's friend. Now his friend.

Chapter Eighteen

He had called from the lobby after tracking Scott Palmer to Belém. Palmer had said he was tired. Palmer had said many things, but Gunther Hoevermann had been insistent and Palmer had relented. Hoevermann knocked again on the door to the hotel suite, and it opened under his hand.

It was impossible, perhaps, but Scott Palmer, Jr., seemed to have visibly aged since their first meeting in São Luis along the docks when Hoevermann and his people had boarded the ship to interrogate the crew of the freighter and the passengers who were fit to talk. It had been a brief meeting. Hoevermann had not identified himself beyond offering condolences. Palmer did not even remember it—that had been evident when Hoevermann had brought Culhane to

Palmer's hotel room—and Hoevermann had not mentioned it.

"Good morning, Senhor Palmer."

"Good morning, Inspector. What can I do for you? I'm trying to run a business and make the telephone company rich at the same time here," Palmer said, smiling.

"You own enterprises all over the world?"

"Yes—more or less. Please come in." Palmer stepped back from the door. Hoevermann passed him, smelling the cigarette smoke and looking to Palmer's right hand where an unfiltered cigarette had burned almost to Palmer's flesh.

Hoevermann lit a cigarette of his own, sitting unbidden on one of the cushioned white wicker chairs by the balcony windows. The sunlight felt pleasantly warm in contrast to the air conditioning of the room.

"What did you come to see me for, Inspector?"

Hoevermann looked up from his hat, flicking ashes from his cigarette into the ashtray on the glass table between the two chairs. "I understand from the police reports that you, a woman whose last name is Chavez and the American writer Josh Culhane were set upon by robbers yesterday."

"You've read the reports with the local police. I can't tell you anything more. You want more, talk to Mr. Culhane when he gets back from upriver."

"Yes," Hoevermann said, "but by then it would be too late. Culhane carries your wife's ransom. That is clear. And everyone along the river knows it. That is obvious."

"He wanted to help."

"I'm sure. What did you smuggle in?"

"You may as well know. A large sum of money. They promised to return my wife."

"Even if it were a million of your dollars," Hoevermann said, "it would not guarantee her safety." Hoevermann noticed Palmer's cigarette. It was dead in Palmer's fingers. "All any money paid these terrorists will do is guarantee more misery for the people of Brazil, more misery for people all over the world. I wish to know their instructions to you."

"I won't tell you."

"I can have you arrested."

"Go ahead. I can close down every plant I own in Brazil. Every shipment of components I sell into Brazil can be canceled."

"You threaten to damage my nation's economy on one hand and to cause many innocent deaths on the other. As a policeman and not an economist, the deaths concern me more," Hoevermann declared. "If I lock you up, if I confound your lawyers, at this stage it will yield nothing. If you will not talk to me here, I doubt you will talk to me from behind bars." Hoevermann exhaled a loud sigh and stood up, stubbing out his cigarette as he did.

He settled his hat on his head. "But I will discover the exact nature of the ransom and where its point of entry was if it did not originate in Brazil— and I think it did not. And I will return and you will tell me what I need to know. For I have never doubted that you are an honest man. Under the circumstances, I would most likely do what you are doing were my wife—we've been married thirty-eight years—or one of our children in jeopardy. Or one of my grandchildren. I would most likely do what you are doing. Good day, *senhor*." He walked past Palmer and left the room, going back toward the elevator.

He would probably do exactly what Palmer was doing. But somehow he felt that what Palmer did was unspeakable.

Chapter Nineteen

Culhane sat in the darkness beside Damascus Santini, the sounds of the river current lapping against the boat the only distinct ones, but thousands of other sounds from the shore on both sides made a background to the night.

Santini smoked a cigarette, molding a tip from the ashes, the tip glowing against the plastic ashtray between his legs.

Culhane leaned his head back against the gunwales.

Part of the quiet resulted from their relative aloneness. Helene Chavez was forward, talking with the captain of the boat crew. He could hear her husky alto now and then. Aside from Santini, Helene Chavez and himself, only the captain and his crew had remained aboard, the other six passengers going ashore to the river-station inn.

Culhane had chosen sleeping on the hard deck to a soft bed perhaps filled with lice inside a room possibly filled with roaches and flying insects. Not many people traveled the Negro tributary of the Amazon much above Manaus. Those who could pay for plush accommodations were farther downriver where ocean-going vessels could still travel.

"So, you and this Fanny Mulrooney sound pretty tight," Damascus Santini said finally.

"I checked with everyone I could. She never stayed in

Manaus. And the pilot returned to Belém. I couldn't get hold of him. I have to figure she went out after this Greek girl she was so hot about.''

"Fanny sounds like quite a woman."

"She is," Culhane said, laughing. "Good journalist. Good writer, you know—but, God—she's always after this cockamamie weird stuff. Amazons—boy, I tell you..." Culhane shook his head, lighting a cigarette.

"What are you going to do?"

"At the next river station the boat captain says there's a guy who runs the bar there—a fella with one leg. The captain says the barman knows someone in the interior who's probably the man Fanny was alluding to. Celini—Sergio Celini."

"You want me to watch the gold while you go into the interior after Fanny Mulrooney?"

"Yeah. The captain said he can stall things for a few days. It'll get the rest of the passengers pretty ticked off, but he can stall things long enough. Scott gave him a bundle to take me upriver, so the captain's eager to please."

"All right. I'll watch the suitcases. But like I told you—if push comes to shove, I don't know."

Culhane laughed. "You're the best shot I have. And if Fanny's got Russians on her trail, I can't let her be out there all alone."

He looked at Santini, and Santini nodded. "I'm going for a walk. Want to join me?"

"Naw," Culhane said, laughing. "Already saw the front of the boat—go ahead."

Culhane looked up as Santini got to his feet. Helene Chavez was coming aft, down the ladder from the cabin roof. She had changed from the bush shorts she had worn throughout the day into a short-sleeved blouse and loose-fitting midcalf-length skirt. She smiled at Santini and sat down in the spot on the port side of the riverboat that Santini had vacated.

Culhane thought he caught Santini grin as the priest walked forward.

"You and Father Santini—how lucky for you to find a friend way out here."

"Damascus Santini and my brother, Jeff, were in Special Forces together in Vietnam."

"What does your brother—oh, Scott mentioned it. He's dead, isn't he?"

"Yes."

He felt her hands on his left forearm as he stubbed out his cigarette. "Sometimes, well, things are easier if you share them," she whispered, and he felt her hands leave his arm, felt her hands on his cheeks. He turned to look at her, and in the darkness he could barely see her face. But he could feel her mouth press hard against his. His left arm closed around her waist. Her mouth left his and he could feel her hot breath on his face. "I share the cabin with the other woman. But she is ashore tonight. Come share my bed with me so I am not alone."

Culhane could see little of her face in the shadow. "I'm not going to. And don't tell me I'm stupid—I know I am."

She pulled away from him. "You speak Spanish—no?"

"Yes."

"*Hijo de puta.*" She was up, running across the deck, then she disappeared in the shadows heading aft.

He guessed she had a right to call him what she called him. He knew what Sean Dodge would have done. And maybe that was who Helene Chavez really wanted....

"JOSH—WAKE UP."

Culhane opened his eyes. He'd been dreaming. He shook his head. The face above him was Damascus Santini's. Culhane looked at his wrist. It was almost four in the morning.

"Something on shore—I heard something. Men moving in the jungle. That's what it sounded like."

With almost anyone else, Culhane would have asked if he were sure it wasn't just an animal or something. The standard jungle adventure-movie question. But his brother had survived in North Vietnam, fought in the jungles, been hunted—and made it home. And Santini had been with his brother. So he didn't ask. "Any idea how many?"

"Can't tell. The sound of the water around us gets in the way."

Culhane sat up, sweating from being under the lightweight sleeping bag. Not having any mosquito netting to cover him, he had slept under the bag despite the discomfort. He pulled the zipper down and slid his legs up and out. "All right. You keep an eye on the suitcases and Helene Chavez. I'll get the captain up and some of his men. We can strike out toward the riverbank. We'll have to use those aluminum rowboats we've been towing; there are too many gators, crocs and piranha to swim it." Culhane buckled his gun belt around his waist, falling back onto his butt as he shook his combat boots and socks, and started putting them on.

"Bandits after the you-know-what?" Santini said.

"Maybe," Culhane rasped. "Maybe the terrorists and they really don't want me getting it upriver. This route crap they gave to Palmer—I don't like it. Never did."

One boot was tied. Culhane began working on the other one. "Get the gold down below with Helene," Culhane went on. "Then if the boat gets scuttled, it'll make it just that much harder to fish up the gold." He was tying the second boot now. "And just in case things *really* get bad and you need it to save somebody's life—not the suitcases—there's another Smith 629 in my backpack.'' And he looked at Santini as he started forward, Santini heading for the portside rail, Culhane for the starboard. "Hey, aren't you supposed to say something religious and inspirational?"

"Consider it said, okay?"

"You bet." And Culhane half tripped over the first of the boat crew, but it was a good way to start waking the guy up.

THEY HELD THE OARS near the blade portion of the shaft, using them like paddles. This increased the risk of something sticking its mouth out of the water and grabbing for a hand, but it also reduced the noise. Culhane had set a book in Brazil once, and he remembered some of the Portuguese phrases he'd had Sean Dodge use on a commando raid. Under his breath he started reciting them to be ready when they beached the two rowboats and headed inland to the river station, which was about an eighth of a mile back from the riverbank.

He had heard no noises in the jungle, but Santini had stopped hearing them as well.

When Culhane had awakened the captain, the captain had said that perhaps if there were men in the jungle, they were the river pirates of José Maria de Jesus, a murderous butcher.

The irony of the name was not lost on Culhane. Joseph. Mary. Jesus.

Culhane's rowboat beached, and he jumped from the rowing thwart and waded through the water and up onto the mud, the others with him, tugging the boat onto the land.

The second boat beached, and Culhane signaled "*Silêncio!*" in a low whisper.

There was no noise now from the jungle. He could see the captain's eyes a little in the intermittent light. High clouds were scudding overhead. A pale hint of dawn glowed downriver.

What had Sean Dodge told the Brazilian commandos when they had prepared to penetrate the secret Nazi chemical-warfare plant? He remembered, and hoped he pronounced it right. He must have, because to a man, each of the six crew members and the captain drew their blades: cane knives, machetes, flashy-looking Bowies, and Arkansas Toothpicks. Culhane unsheathed the Gerber from his belt, ready. He whispered for the men to follow, and he started ahead toward the river station, the men close behind.

MARY FRANCES MULROONEY, despite her ready-to-burst bladder and her gut-level fear of Sergio Celini, realized she had been asleep. Celini was talking to her.

She shook her head. "I'm sorry. I must have dozed off."

"It is nearly dawn, *signorina*—that is all I said. Soon we will leave the Land Rover."

"I thought we were driving to your ranch."

"We have been on my ranch for the last two hours, *signorina*, but she is not at the ranch itself, but at a mine at the north corner. That is where we keep this wild girl. Friends protect her there."

"What kind of a mine?" Mulrooney asked him.

"The mine is none of your concern, *signorina*. You want to see the Greek girl and you will see her, and then if you want story you will pay very much money to me before it goes in your paper."

"I write books."

"A woman who writes books? You write romance novels, then. So why do you want to see the Greek girl?"

"Didn't Balthazar tell you? And besides—a lot of women write other things besides romance novels." This guy was a pig in more ways than one, Mulrooney thought. She took a deep breath. "Why do we have to leave the Land Rover?"

"There is a small mountain, *signorina*. If we drive around it, it takes three hours. If we walk over it, it takes one hour. If you must be at the river by nightfall, then we must walk over it. We will be there before full light."

"What about animals? I thought animals were on the prowl at night in the jungle."

The Land Rover lurched to a halt, and Celini bounded from behind the wheel. He caught up a bolt-action rifle and slung it on his shoulder. There was a telescopic sight on the rifle. "We walk now."

Mulrooney climbed from the Land Rover. "I'll be right back." She took her purse and started away from the Land Rover. The night was clear enough to see well, except when some of the high clouds blew past and darkened the sky. It felt good to get away from Celini for a few minutes. He made her skin crawl.

THEY HAD WORKED THEIR WAY along the riverbank, Culhane in the lead, the captain beside him and slightly behind.

Culhane raised his left hand to signal a halt, the crunching of branches and the sloshing of the sticky riverbank mud stopping as Culhane held his breath to listen. He could hear movement in the jungle ahead: careless woodsmen, like the men he traveled with. Perhaps more careless. If they had heard him and the boat crew, they would have stopped.

Culhane checked the luminous black face of his watch

against the widening line of pink and gray downriver. It was nearly dawn.

He edged forward, signaling the others with his left hand to stay back, the knife in his right fist held like a rapier.

Insects buzzed around his head, and there were little noises of the jungle night that still clung to the land. The water of the Negro River was shimmering in the pale light.

Culhane stopped at the edge of the heaviest vegetation. He looked inland along the runwaylike clearing cut in the jungle that led from the riverbank to the single-story, peaked-roof river station: a hotel, restaurant and bar—all of it under one partially sagging roof.

Six passengers from the riverboat were inside: a Brazilian girl named Magdelena, and five men, two of them engineers heading to the recently discovered mountain chain deep in the jungle, well beyond even Culhane's destination. There was gold there.

His attention wandered from the night and whatever moved about in the jungle. In a country full of gold, why was he carrying two suitcases filled with it? Palmer Industries owned mining facilities elsewhere. Did they own any in Brazil? Was there something Palmer wasn't—

The roof of the restaurant and half of the river station blew away in huge chunks, fire belching through the picture window that opened off the restaurant and bar onto the river. Culhane shouted over the roar of the explosion for the boat crew to follow him, and he started to run. If bandits—this José Maria de Jesus and his men—were attacking the river station, it was for one reason only: the gold. And it was Culhane they were after.

Gunfire from the jungle erupted from both sides of the clearing.

Culhane saw a man rushing out of the undergrowth and racing toward the steps of the hotel porch. In the man's hands was an assault rifle, long tongues of flame spitting from it into the night. Culhane stopped, bringing his revolver up in both hands and settling the muzzle against the silhouette of the man. He double-actioned the .44 Magnum once, and the body fell through the flames that poured from the blown-out picture window and was gone from sight.

Culhane started running again, smaller explosions deafening now as either grenades or sticks of dynamite exploded on both sides of him. He kept running for the river station. There was nowhere else to take cover, nowhere to hide and return fire.

As he ran, he kept glancing behind him. The boat crew, rifles and pistols and shotguns firing, were storming along the clearing behind him.

A figure darted from the hotel. It was a woman, her clothes on fire. Another figure jumped from the steps, tackling her and bringing her down. The second figure rolled the burning woman across the ground, then tore away her clothing as Culhane got closer. The man had a knife in his teeth. Culhane snapped the muzzle of the 629 on line and fired, the body of the man blowing back.

Culhane ran the few more yards and fell to the ground on his knees beside the woman.

She was dead, burned, blood dripping from a gunshot wound in the chest across her scorched blouse.

Culhane was up, jumping to the level of the porch, flipping the railing on his left hand.

A figure stepped from one of the doorways, an assault rifle opening up as Culhane dropped to both knees and fired the .44 Magnum, gut-shooting the man.

Culhane stabbed the revolver into the holster and

grabbed the dead man's assault rifle. It was an AK-47. Russian. There was an interesting story in that, he thought, running the length of the porch, his footfalls loud like hammer strikes, the crackle of flames from the building itself louder still. He heard a scream from one of the rooms. Culhane stopped, wheeled toward it, took a half step back and, with a double tae kwon-do kick to the lock, sent the door smashing inward. A woman—the riverboat passenger Magdelena— was on her knees at the feet of one of the river bandits, the man's right hand locked in her dark hair, his left hand ripping her nightgown from her as she screamed and stabbed his left thigh with something that looked like a boot knife.

Culhane didn't know the Portuguese for it, but he yelled, "Hey—asshole!"

The man wheeled, letting go of Magdelena's hair. The girl fell back, clasping the shredded nightgown over her breasts. As the bandit went for the revolver in his belt, Culhane pumped the trigger of the AK-47, a 3-round burst, cutting into the chest and abdomen and the body of the bandit, and slamming him against the burning wall.

Culhane was across the room in three strides. He hadn't spoken to Magdelena at all during the trip. "Speak English?"

"Yes. Do you speak Portuguese?"

He looked at her and smiled, then set down the AK-47 and unbuttoned his shirt, pulling it from his shoulders and placing it across hers. "Get into that and stay with me."

"Yes."

The AK-47 in his hands again, Culhane was up and moving to the door. The bandit's pistol had been on him when the body had fallen into the flames.

Culhane looked at the Brazilian girl. He couldn't give her his .44. "Use a rifle much?"

"Yes. A little. Is it like a shotgun?"

"More or less," he said, and handed her the AK-47. "When you pull the trigger, let go immediately or you'll blow the whole magazine away. Understand?"

"Yes."

"Ever say much of anything besides yes?"

"Yes."

"Stick with me. When I tell you to run for it, do it. Let's go!" Culhane was through the door and onto the porch, the smoke thick now. The 629 in his right fist, he edged along the porch.

The door to his right smashed open. Culhane slammed the girl against the wall and stabbed the .44 Magnum into the doorway, double-actioning the trigger, a bandit falling through, a .45 automatic clattering to the porch surface. Culhane picked it up. He pointed the .45 toward the bandit and pulled the trigger. It was loaded all right. A pistol in each hand, he kept going.

Assault-rifle fire came from inside the hotel. "They are killing everyone!" the girl cried, her English good but heavily accented.

"They'll kill us, too, if we don't get outta here. Come on!" Culhane vaulted the railing, followed by the girl. "Stay with me!" Culhane shouted. The fire was crackling loudly; the roof would collapse any second.

On the ground a few yards ahead, he recognized the body of one of the boat crew.

Culhane kept going. From the jungle shadows, the sky a pinkish-gray now, a figure jumped for him. Culhane fired both pistols simultaneously. The slide of the .45 was locked back, empty, and Culhane threw it down; he had no spare ammo for it.

He saw the captain of the riverboat and shouted, "Captain—take the girl!"

The captain turned, running toward him, a single-action Army Colt in his right hand, a machete in his left. "Two of my men dead here."

"Take her and get your remaining men back to the riverboat! I'm going back inside!" Culhane rasped, reloading the 629. "Did you see any of the other passengers?"

"I think behind the station, Senhor Culhane. The bandits have some they make to talk."

"Did you see this de Jesus guy?"

"In the fighting—but not now. He is tall—he has—how you say it—" He tugged at his chin as though stroking a beard.

"Gotcha! Run for it!" Culhane turned to run back, but felt Magdelena tug at his left arm. He looked down at her, and both her arms circled his neck and she kissed him hard on the mouth. Then she ran after the captain.

Culhane smiled as he started to run. Fanny Mulrooney would understand, he told himself.

The roof of the hotel portion of the river station fell in as he reached the porch. Smoke was billowing around him now, the heat of the fire intense against his bare chest and back. At least the smoke would keep the bugs away, he told himself.

He edged ahead, the 629 up and ready.

Culhane threw himself across the corner of the porch in a roll, gunfire ripping into the already smoldering timbers of the porch, Culhane's 629 firing once, then again, the body of the gunman thudding hard against a corner of the building, then sprawling back.

Culhane was standing, snatching up the AK-47 from the dead man, moving ahead, taking no time to search the body for spare magazines. Culhane looked skyward.

The sky was more pink than gray now, with broad streaks of blue in it.

He kept moving.

He reached the far edge of the porch.

He edged off from the corner, toward the rail, stepping ahead, the AK-47 ready to fire—but there was no guard. At the edge of the jungle, perhaps twenty-five yards behind the river station, he could see them.

He saw a tall man with a beard. As Culhane watched, the man wielded a machete downward, his face and the blade of the machete washed the color of blood by the flames of the burning river station. Culhane saw the head of one of the riverboat passengers roll away into the jungle, a fountain of blood spraying from the severed neck.

Culhane raised the AK-47 to his shoulder, the 629 holstered now. He sighted on the bearded man, whose name was a mockery, and screamed, "Son of a bitch!" He pulled the trigger, but the bearded man had thrown himself down, Culhane's bullets thudding into the headless corpse.

Culhane vaulted the back porch railing now, the rifle at his right side in an assault position. A bandit with a rifle fired into the group of hostages and missed. Culhane fired, the bandit going down. The Russian-made rifle was empty and Culhane threw it down, drawing his revolver. He ran toward the hostages, firing at a third bandit with his revolver. The hostages' hands were bound behind them, their eyes blindfolded.

Culhane ripped away the blindfold of the nearest man—one of the engineers—and spun him around. His hands were wired together, his wrists bleeding. "They killed Murphy," the man said.

"Was that the other engineer?"

"Yes. All of us were pulled out into the bar. They

killed Murphy when he went for his gun. The three of us are the only ones left.''

"You take one and I'll take the other. Hurry it up," Culhane snapped.

One of the blindfolded men—a Japanese—was shouting in good English, "What is happening?"

"Relax, you're okay." Culhane took the Japanese and pulled away the blindfold, then started to work on the wrists. He glanced at the engineer; the third hostage, the British chemist, was nearly free. "Find yourselves weapons! We have to get to the riverbank. Is there anybody alive left inside—does anybody know?"

"There is no one," the Japanese grunted, ripping his hands clear of the wire.

Culhane began reloading the 629 to have a full cylinder. "Who are these killers?" asked the Japanese.

"River bandits—at least that's what they tell me."

"There was a Brazilian girl with us," the Englishman said suddenly.

"Magdelena something," the American engineer added.

"She's with the captain," Culhane said quickly. "We lost two of the boat crew, so once we make it we've got some work ahead of us. Let's move it!"

If it had been one of the Sean Dodge books, even now the bandit leader would be rallying his men to pursue them to the river.

Culhane hoped life didn't imitate art.

He ran the width of the river station on the ground beside the porch, glancing behind him. The Japanese was coming, a knife in each hand, the American engineer had an AK-47, and the Englishman held a revolver of some kind. Culhane waved them past as he slowed, looking back. There was no gunfire now, only the crackle of the flames. But the bandits would come—he felt it.

He threw himself into a dead run for the riverbank, the Englishman outdistancing the Japanese and the American. Culhane caught up to the Japanese. "When we hit the riverbank, there should be one boat left. You're gonna be last into it, so once you're half aboard, start shoving off—but don't leave without me!"

"All right!"

Culhane slowed his run, looking back. From the sides of the river station two men were coming, and at their head in the dawn light Culhane could see the tall bearded leader.

Culhane stood his ground, raising the 629 in both hands. The distance was one hundred yards and dropping fast. He aimed and fired, but the bearded man dodged. One of the river bandits behind him stopped in midstride, his hands flying out from his sides, his arms spread wide, the body snapping back.

Culhane looked over his shoulder. The bandits were coming up fast, rifles blazing, a whine of bullets around Culhane's head now, plowing the ground on either side of him and behind him as he looked back.

He threw his body into the run, his hands at his sides, his head thrown back as he gulped for air.

Culhane looked back. The Japanese had turned off by the riverbank. The bandits were coming from the jungle on both sides now, closing in. He fired the 629 behind him, throwing himself forward.

At the riverbank he skidded on his heels, hurling himself toward the aluminum rowboat that was already shoving off. "Wait for me, guys!"

The boat was getting into the current now, Culhane running from the bank into the water. He threw himself over the gunwale, rolling onto his back, shouting, "Row like your lives depended on it!" Then he was up on his knees, three shots remaining in the 629.

The first of the bandits to break from the clearing and run along the riverbank—Culhane shot him dead.

Three more appeared, their assault rifles blazing, causing the water on both sides of the boat to churn furiously. "Down!"

Culhane ducked for an instant. There was a loud ping and he looked to his left. There was a hole in the gunwale and in the boat's bottom, the gunwale-side hole jagged, the one in the bottom neatly rounded.

Culhane snapped his revolver up and fired, then fired again. Another of the bandits fell, this time into the water. The water suddenly seemed alive. The snout of a crocodile grinning hideously, and the body, was dragged under.

Culhane looked into the river. The riverboat had started up, the captain and one of his crew on the port side now, rifles blazing shoreward.

"Row for it!" Culhane ordered, using his last loaded Speedloader to replenish the 629. When he'd reloaded, he fired toward the riverbank. More of the bandits, some of them running out into the shallows, were firing their assault rifles. "My God—my chest—" shouted the Englishman, and his body snapped back and into the water. Culhane reached for him, but the eyes were wide open and staring upward as the face sank beneath the water.

Culhane returned their fire, killing another of the bandits, the 629 coming up empty now.

He had more loose ammo but no time. The rowboat was close now to the riverboat, and Culhane reached out as a boat hook was extended. He caught the boat hook and pulled, the rowboat almost slipping from beneath him, the water ankle-deep now as he stood.

At the riverboat's starboard rail was Damascus Santini. Culhane reached out, Santini's hand locking on his right wrist. Culhane's right foot hit the deck planking and he was up and over the rail, Santini reaching for the others. "Your rifle—it's by the bench there!"

Culhane saw the gun Fanny Mulrooney had had made so fancy for him.

Culhane hurried across the deck into the stern, facing the riverbank, the rifle at his hip, locked there. His right hand held the lever, his left was firmly over the front stock. "Eat lead! Eat it!" Culhane started snapping the lever—down and back, down and back, down and back—the .44 Magnum lever action bouncing in his hands, the first two shots walking the water onto the targets firing from the shore. And then men started to fall as he emptied the rifle.

He stood there, the riverboat making good time now, the engine loud and protesting, but the riverbank and the river pirates were vanishing behind them.

Culhane took his rifle and sat down on the bench under the canopy and stared at the receding riverbank.

"You left your cigarettes and your lighter in the shirt, *senhor*," said a soft voice at his side.

He turned and smiled his thanks as he took the offered cigarette. But his hands were shaking, and Magdelena lit it for him.

Chapter Twenty

Mary Frances Mulrooney didn't know the legal status of submachine guns in Brazil. Culhane had explained the difference between submachine guns and regular machine guns to her once, but somehow she didn't think these men had them legally.

"It must be some mine," she said, walking beside Sergio Celini.

"It is a good mine, *signorina*. It is worth protecting."

"Right," Mulrooney said, smiling.

There was a low house that looked as though it could have been a ranch house in a very loose sense, but the windows were boarded up. And well beyond this—and beyond still another man with a submachine gun who saw them and waved to Celini who waved back—was a dark hole leading into a hill.

"That's the mine, right?"

"That is the mine, *si*."

He kept walking. She wasn't going to tell him her feet hurt. Not yet.

It had been less an hour's walk than an hour's climb, the jungle lingering up the mountainside, some of the trees thick-trunked enough that she had used them to help her navigate the rocky trail they had followed. Sergio Celini was always ahead of her, his rifle bouncing up and down off his shoulder as he walked.

She took off her hat. It was stained with sweat around the band and she put it back on. She guessed her hair looked just marvelous.

"How old is the girl?" Mulrooney asked, keeping up with him, trying to make conversation.

"About twenty-five perhaps, perhaps younger or a little older. She is very tall and very strong. She almost killed two of my men when they were trying to help her."

"After the encounter with the animal?"

"No, ah, later. It was after that, *signorina*."

"Right. Well, I hope she's up this early." It was just after dawn, the sky very pretty overhead, Mulrooney thought.

"I think this girl never sleeps," he said as though speaking some ultimate truth to her.

Mulrooney's eyes were glued to the mine entrance. She didn't like holes in the ground, especially when she was supposed to go inside them.

The man at the entrance to the mine—blond and wearing a white shirt—stiffened slightly as they approached, but it was nothing like a soldier coming to attention—just, she guessed, to show he was alert.

Celini called to the man and he answered, shouting back something that, to Mulrooney, didn't sound good even though she couldn't understand the words.

"We had better hurry," Celini said to her, and he broke into a jog, holding his rifle at the butt against his side, Mulrooney shaking her head, trotting after him.

"Hey—what's the big rush about?"

"The Uruentes," Celini called back.

"Uruentes . . . Uruentes—what are—" Then she remembered. The headhunters.

She ran faster.

At the entrance to the mine, the white-shirted guard was talking animatedly to Celini, slinging his submachine gun under his right arm so he could use both hands to gesture. Celini began what Mulrooney guessed passed for a running translation. "Two Uruente warriors were killed. Apparently they let us pass inside here. The mine and the house are surrounded. He says that the Uruentes are in the trees out there." Celini gestured beyond the mine and then back the way he and Mulrooney had come.

"Oh, wonderful—they do this all the time or is this something special?"

"One of my men—the idiot!—saw some of the Uruentes in the jungle beyond the mine and shot at them with his submachine gun. He killed two of them."

"Oh, great," Mulrooney said, closing her eyes, shaking her head. "Do these Uruente guys have guns?"

"What—I am sorry?"

"I said," Mulrooney repeated, "do these guys have guns—the Uruentes?"

"No, no—only spears, and bows and arrows, and poisoned darts from their very accurate blowguns."

Mulrooney leaned against the timber that supported the right-hand side of the mine opening. Celini was still talking with his guard. She finally pushed herself away from the timber and interrupted him. "Look, I gather we're going to have a real problem getting out of here alive, right?"

"That is correct, *signorina*. There is no radio, and the telephone line has never come this far."

"Great. At least let me die happy. I want to see the girl. That's what I came for. Right now."

Celini looked at her, scratching his beard and then looking off into the jungle. "*Si*—as you would say, why not?"

He said something else to the guard, but the guard only nodded. Celini picked up a lantern from just inside the mine entrance and raised the mantle. He struck a match on the butt of his rifle, put it under the mantle, and lit the wick. "Walk this way," he told her.

Mulrooney followed him into the mine, and the guard followed them, carrying a second lantern.

Reflexively, Mulrooney ducked her head. "You keep her down here all the time?"

"It is the only safe place, *signorina*," Celini's voice echoed back to her.

"The poor girl."

"Ha."

They walked on in silence. Mulrooney pulled the long-sleeved khaki bush jacket closer around her. It was damp and chill in the mine. Or perhaps it was nerves, she thought, as they made their way along the shaft, which angled steeply downward.

Celini still made her skin crawl.

"We will turn off from the main shaft now. It is like a room," Celini said, taking a right. It was the first turn-off she had seen, Mulrooney decided. She was memorizing the route, just in case.

All was in darkness as they stopped for a moment, black except for the cones of yellow light from the lantern in front of her that Celini held and the lantern behind her held by the mine-entrance guard. But coming from the darkness was a hissing sound—not like a gas leak, but like a cat, a big cat.

The cone of light behind Mulrooney moved and she sucked in her breath, but the guard was lighting other lanterns hung about the walls of the room. Gradually the cavern took shape out of the shadow, and Mulrooney could see something at the farthest end that reminded her of the picture of tiger cages she had seen in Vietnam War footage.

Vastly longer than it was wide, constructed of something like bamboo, the cage extended from the cinder blocks that supported it eighteen inches above the floor to perhaps six feet in height.

The last lantern came on, the one nearest the cage. At the farthest end of the cage, cramped back into the corner, legs set like coiled springs, arms at right angles, palms up, claws bared, hissing through brilliantly white, clenched teeth was a naked girl. In the light of the lanterns, Mulrooney flipped through the Berlitz phrase book she had taken from her purse. She had touched the butt of her gun before removing the book, just for reassurance.

"*Kahleemerah*," Mulrooney said, reading carefully.

The girl was very pretty. She had a tangle of waist-length black curls, the hair partially covering her breasts. She was tall, her body beautifully tanned. Mulrooney decided to try something besides "Good morning."

"*Poseestheeh?*"

"How are you?" was pretty dumb, too, she reflected. Mulrooney flipped pages as Celini started closer to the cage, unslinging his rifle. Mulrooney tried something else. No response. She flipped pages again. "*Eestheh endahksee?*"

The girl still said nothing, then Celini rammed the barrel of his rifle through the cage and into her abdomen. The girl screamed, but more like a wounded animal than a woman, clawing at him as he withdrew his rifle. The girl clawed at the air with both hand, sounds coming from her that somehow sounded the same in any language, almost like a stream of curses. But Mulrooney recognized some of the sounds from studying her little book. Celini laughed. "You see, I told you she spoke Greek!"

"Holy shit. A real Amazon..." Mulrooney whispered under her breath.

Mulrooney stuffed the Berlitz phrase book back into her purse and unslung the bag from her shoulder. "Let her out of the cage, Celini."

"I cannot. She would attempt to kill us all. I told you how she injured my men."

Mulrooney glared at him, stripping off her bush jacket. She reslung her purse and approached the cage, slowly, taking off her hat, shaking her hair loose. Mulrooney felt that the more feminine she looked, the less of a threat she would pose to this girl.

The girl edged back. She seemed more afraid of a woman than of the men. Mulrooney couldn't understand it.

Mulrooney took the bush jacket and stuffed it between the bars, using gestures to show the coat being put on. The girl did not touch it.

Mulrooney noticed the smell in the cage—and saw the reason why beneath it. She turned to Celini. "You let her out of here. You can't keep a human being like this!"

And then she noticed that the man with the submachine gun had left the room. "Where's your friend?"

"He has resumed his post—to guard for the Uruentes."

"Guard against," she corrected.

"*Si*," he murmured, his voice very low, as if he was trying to sound sexy. "We are alone."

"No, we're not—we've got the woman here. Now let her out."

"Maybe I will let her out. Later, eh?" And he leveled the rifle toward Mulrooney's abdomen. "Put down your purse, *signorina*. I think maybe you have a gun in there."

"You mess with me and you don't get paid a goddamned dime, Celini!"

"Some things, *signorina*, are more important than money. You have a good strong body—I can tell. You have long legs. The auburn color of your hair...the green eyes...you are very beautiful. Now set down the purse." He gestured with the rifle and she set down her purse.

"Look, Celini, you're a great-lookin' guy, but you're not my type." A flash of inspiration. "I've got herpes!"

"So do I, *signorina*."

"Aw, shit," Mulrooney moaned. "Would you believe there are six divisions of Israeli commandos who have this mine surrounded?"

"No."

"How about six Green Berets and a pack of attack dogs?"

"No."

"Ah—three Green Berets and a particularly vicious French poodle?"

He started walking toward her. "I like it when you remove your jacket. Now take off your blouse, *signorina*."

"It's cold down here."

"Take it off—or I shoot the woman in the cage."

Mulrooney looked at his black eyes. They looked dirty like the rest of him. She looked at the Greek girl, then back at Celini. He was working the bolt handle of the rifle. Culhane had a rifle that worked like that, and she knew what Celini was doing. He was getting ready to fire.

"All right," Mulrooney said nodding, stepping between Celini and the girl in the cage. Slowly, as slowly as humanly possible, Mary Frances Mulrooney started to undress. She wished the shirt had more buttons. "I'm terrible with buttons. My mother—"

Celini cut her off. "Perhaps we die—the Uruentes. But we will have these beautiful moments together, *signorina*."

"If you're going to rape me, we may as well be on a first-name basis, Sergio," she told him. All the buttons were open now, but mercifully the shirt stayed closed together in the front. "My name is Mary Frances."

"*Si*, Mary Frances," he repeated.

Where was Culhane when she really needed him? Another flash of inspiration. Celini was very close now, holding the rifle almost carelessly in his right hand at his side, his left hand reaching out to her. He touched the front of her shirt. "Culhane! Thank God you got here!" she screamed.

Celini's eyes flickered, and he turned his head toward the entrance to the subterranean room. Mulrooney's right knee smashed up hard, and she hooked her left fist across his jaw. But Celini, the rifle dropping from his right hand, grabbed at her, and she felt his hands at her waist and throat.

Celini dragged her to the floor, his eyes bright with lust and anger, and rolled on top of her. Mulrooney reached up with her free right hand; the left was pinned between their bodies.

Shots exploded from outside the subterranean room. Many shots. Bursts of submachine-gun fire.

Celini looked up. Mulrooney picked up a rock from the floor of the cave and slammed it against Celini's right temple. Celini's body fell to the left, and Mulrooney rolled over onto her stomach, then got to her feet, her shirt wide open. She reached for her purse, falling as Celini swept his left leg out.

But she had the purse. She reached inside, thanking God, Milt Sparks and Josh Culhane in that order as she grabbed the Rossi revolver free of the holster in the special center compartment. God for letting her reach her purse. Josh's pal Milt Sparks for creating the purse. Josh Culhane for giving it to her.

Celini was on his hands and knees, blood dripping from his left temple, his body lunging toward her. Mulrooney pulled the trigger.

A splotch of red appeared on his left shoulder and Celini fell back.

More gunfire from outside the subterranean room.

"It is—" he was panting, breathing hard "—the Uruentes. I go—to fight them." He reached out slowly for his rifle, Mulrooney holding the little Rossi revolver in both hands, aimed at his head, the muzzle following his head as he slowly picked up his gun.

He got to his knees, then to his feet, holding the rifle away from him. He backed toward the entrance to the subterranean room—and then he was gone.

Mulrooney remembered to breathe.

She looked at the girl in the cage.

Holding the revolver in her right hand, she found her phrase book with her left. She flipped to the dictionary in the back. The word for friend. She pointed to herself and then to the girl. "*Feeloss—feeloss.*"

And then Mulrooney pointed to the padlock on the cage. She read off another word: "*Elefthereeah.*" According to the book, it meant freedom.

She saw something in the girl's eyes—or thought she did.

She had the purse over her left shoulder and dropped the book inside. Mulrooney raised the revolver in both hands and aimed at the padlock, just like in the movies.

She fired.

There was a loud ringing sound and she remembered to open her eyes.

The lock was hanging loose, shattered.

"Way to go, M. F.," Mulrooney congratulated herself.

She went to the lock and tapped it free of the hasp with the butt of her revolver. It would be hot, she guessed.

The lock fell, and Mulrooney almost fell, stumbling back as the Greek-speaking girl jumped from the cage, their faces inches apart.

Mulrooney still held her gun by the barrel.

She tried remembering the Greek word, but she couldn't, so she said it in English. "Friend—friend." She gestured to herself, then to the girl.

"Fred—fred," the girl said.

Mulrooney figured that was good enough. She

reached past the girl and into the cage, picking up the bush jacket. She tossed it to the girl. "Fred."

"Fred." The girl nodded and took it. It looked for a second as though she didn't know how to put it on, but then she had it, pulling her hair free of it, tying the belt at the waist as one would a trench coat. The girl's waist was incredibly slender.

Mulrooney opened her purse and found the loose cartridges she had poured into it from the box Sebastiao had given her. She found two, opened the Rossi's cylinder, plucked the empties out with her fingernails and replaced them with loaded rounds.

She looked at the Greek girl and grinned. "Let's see Sean Dodge top this," she said, and grabbed one of the lanterns and started for the door leading from the chamber into the main shaft of the mine.

The Greek girl was running easily beside her.

Mulrooney slowed and stopped, reaching out to the Greek girl, the girl stopping. "What is your name?" Mulrooney hissed.

The girl's face looked puzzled. "Name." Mulrooney said it slowly, gesturing to herself. "M.F.—me, M.F."

The girl nodded, the light of comprehension in her eyes as she gestured broadly toward her magnificent chest. "Fred."

"Fred. Okay, you wanna be called Fred." And she looked into the girl's eyes, pointing to her. "Fred."

The girl smiled, nodding, saying, "Me-em-ef."

"Shit," Mulrooney snarled. She started ahead, the gunfire louder, but whooshing sounds audible now, too. Suddenly Mulrooney felt the girl grab at her arm.

"What?"

"Uruente."

"Right—Uruente."

"Fred." She pushed Mulrooney back and, crouched,

moving like the cat whose sounds she had imitated, went ahead, Mulrooney behind her now.

"Me-em-ef—" And Fred turned around and touched Mulrooney's chest. Mulrooney stopped again. "Uru-ente."

"Uruente."

"Fred—Me-em-ef—" Then the girl said something Mulrooney didn't understand.

Mulrooney tried to show puzzlement in her face.

The girl nodded, smiling. With her fingers, she made a walking motion—but very fast. Mulrooney did the same. "Run?"

"Fred—Me-em-ef—run!"

Mulrooney nodded. Culhane had taught her not to cock a revolver, just use it. She held it tight, her right first finger hard against the trigger guard.

"Run!" Mulrooney said.

Fred started bounding forward. Mulrooney set down the lantern and ran after her, daylight visible in a growing hole as they dashed along in the darkness of the main shaft, the gunfire louder, the whooshing sounds louder, too.

At the mine entrance, the air around Sergio Celini and the guard who had accompanied Mulrooney into the mine shaft was thick with flying arrows and spears.

Celini wheeled, screaming as he fired his rifle, the rock and dirt near Fred powdering. And then he was up and running, an arrow embedded in the stock of his rifle as he cut laterally from the mine entrance and toward the jungle.

The guard with the submachine gun was up, running after him.

Fred reached to the ground now, picking up a spear that was taller than she was.

"Run?" Mulrooney asked hopefully.

"Fred—Me-em-ef—run!" The Greek girl started after Celini and the guard, Mulrooney right behind her, running, clutching the pistol in her right hand, holding on to her purse with her left.

She heard sounds—inhuman sounds—and she looked toward the house. It was in flames, and running from the jungle were men, nearly naked, red bands around their heads, white necklaces that looked like they were made of teeth around their necks, muscles rippling under cocoa-colored skin glistening with sweat. The fronts of their bodies were painted with red designs. Spears were held high in their hands. Arrows filled the air.

As she looked back, perhaps a half dozen of them stopped and raised long skinny poles at least twice the length of the men holding them to their mouths. Blowguns, Mulrooney realized.

"Hey—Fred!"

Mulrooney threw herself into a run, wishing she were wearing track shoes rather than the heavy boots Culhane had insisted she have. Suddenly Fred turned, her right arm hauling back, the spear sailing from her hand. Mulrooney's eyes felt as if they were popping from their sockets. The spear passed over Mulrooney's head and Mulrooney followed its path. One of the Uruente warriors had been less than a dozen yards behind her and the spear was in his chest now.

"Hey, Fred, way to go!"

And Mulrooney ran for her life, Fred waiting for her, wresting a spear from the ground that had been hurled at her, then running. To Mulrooney, she didn't even look as though she were breathing hard.

Chapter Twenty-One _____

The bandits had taken pot shots at them from the river-bank until the boat had gotten out of range. Culhane, Santini, the American engineer and the Japanese had helped the captain of the boat and three of his crew members, and Helene Chavez and Magdelena had cared for a crewman with a bleeding shoulder wound.

Magdelena de Cunha sat with Culhane for a time while Culhane manned the tiller, the putting of the engine so incessant it was almost hypnotizing. She thanked him again for saving her life, and apologized for kissing him. He told her he had been happy to save her life—and that it was a good kiss and no apology was needed. He thanked *her*.

Since reuniting with Fanny Mulrooney, Culhane had discovered something else that was almost equally disturbing as the truism that if women were expected to be faithful, men were, too. It was that a man and a woman could actually speak as friends—and *be* friends.

And Culhane and Magdelena spoke as friends. She told him—apologetically—that she read very little in English and had never read his books, or even heard of them. And then she had told him about herself. She was a lawyer who worked for the Brazilian government. She had been assigned to travel upriver and go out to the new mining sites where the American engineer and the Japanese were bound for, to determine if fair labor practices were being adhered to concerning the employment of Indians.

Culhane stood now in the prow of the riverboat, the boat really a huge rowboat in terms of design, with a cabin built over the center section, and small living quarters for the captain and storage for goods being shipped upriver beneath the deck planks. But this trip there was much cargo and the boat traveled low in the water, the captain had explained—supplies for the mission of Father Santini donated by Senhor Scott Palmer. Some of the larger items were lashed down and stored on deck.

He watched across the bow as the riverboat glided noisily, sluggishly toward the bank.

Unlike the previous river station where rowboats had been necessary to get back and forth to shore, a well-built floating dock was available, and the riverboat aimed toward it.

Santini stood beside Culhane, the suitcases between them. Culhane held his rifle over his shoulder, the chamber empty, the screw set to fire when the lever was worked.

Santini held the forward mooring line, the Japanese held the aft line, and the captain was at the tiller and the controls for the engine. On the dock Culhane saw a familiar face. For a moment it brought a smile to his lips. But the face was alone. It was Sebastiao, but Fanny Mulrooney was not with him.

"WHY DID YOU LET HER GO, Sebastiao?"

"She told me that she would be safe, Josh Culhane."

"I don't give a shit what she told you," Culhane snarled, walking away along the dock. He turned around, glaring at Sebastiao. "Where is she?"

"There is a problem, *senhor*..."

"What! You don't know where she is?"

"The one-legged man in the bar, *senhor*, he knows where she is. He knows this man Sergio Celini." Sebastiao spat into the water.

"Let's go talk to him." Culhane picked up his rifle and thumbed his hat back up from his forehead. He started past Sebastiao, but Sebastiao wasn't coming. Culhane stopped. "There's something else you haven't told me," Culhane murmured without looking at Sebastiao.

"The Uruentes. When I arrived here last night there was much talk of them. They kill—they fight now."

"The headhunters?"

"*Sim, senhor*. They are killers—they fight like demons!"

"Fanny—M. F., I mean—she's in Uruente country?"

"*Sim*. I found two dead men—without heads—on my way between the house of Celini and the river station here."

"The Bronco gassed up and ready?" Culhane looked at it parked on the far side of the dirt street that ran parallel to the floating dock.

"*Sim*."

"Supplies?"

"*Sim*."

"Come on—we're going to go see this one-legged man." Culhane pulled his Stetson low over his eyes and shifted the rifle back into his right hand as he walked.

He crossed the dirt street. There was only one building large enough to be a bar, and he aimed himself toward it, backing off the set screw on the rifle as he walked. He might need the dramatic effect of working the lever but might not need to fire. He wanted information, not a fight, but life was rarely that easy, Culhane thought, mounting the single low wooden step, then the plank sidewalk. He glanced back once. Sebastiao was behind him, the flap of his holster open, his face grim.

Culhane pushed through the bat-wing doors and stepped inside. It was indeed the bar. He squinted his eyes, adjusting to the vastly lower light. The street was bright, the bar in semidarkness.

The doors opened and closed behind him. Sebastiao. "I am here, *senhor*."

Culhane nodded. "You know this one-legged guy?"

"*Não*."

"Know what he looks like except for the leg?"

"*Não*."

Culhane nodded again. Perhaps twenty men and two women patronized the bar, some leaning along the rail, others sitting at the small dingy tables. "I'm looking for the one-legged man," he announced in a loud voice.

No one turned around. "Sebastiao—tell them in Portuguese."

Sebastiao said that the American was looking for the one-legged man to ask him an important question.

No one turned around or looked up. "Must cater to deaf people here," Culhane muttered. He'd seen John Wayne do it a hundred times. Culhane flicked the rifle out of his right hand and roll-cocked it under his arm. It was dangerous and you could shoot yourself in the armpit or worse, he knew, but it had the desired effect. Faces turned, staring at him.

"Tell them what I want again—nice and loud, Sebastiao," Culhane whispered.

Sebastiao repeated the request in Portuguese.

A voice—in English but heavily accented—came from behind the bar. Culhane looked to the source. "I have one leg, *senhor*." The frame was immense; the shoulders hunched over the bar at least a yard from tip to tip. Culhane lowered the hammer on the Browning lever action and started across the room toward the bar itself. "I want to know how to find the ranch of Sergio Celini. I have a friend out there. My friend might be in trouble. The Uruentes are on the warpath."

Culhane stopped at the bar, resting the rifle across it, his right hand on the small of the stock, his right thumb near the hammer, his right first finger against the trigger guard.

"He is a private man, *senhor*. Celini is a very private man."

"I don't care. Where's his place?"

"I cannot tell you. He is my friend, and he would be very angry if I told anyone how to find his ranch."

"There is a mine there, no?" It was Sebastiao.

The big one-legged man said nothing.

Culhane thumbed back the hammer on the rifle. "I want to know. My woman—she's out there. I want to get her back before some Indian warrior chops her head off."

The big man laughed. "They rape women first, I think."

Culhane moved the muzzle of the rifle—fast. He touched it against the big man's throat, the Adam's apple bobbing up and down crazily. Culhane's finger touched the trigger. "All I have to do is twitch my finger, pal—where is Celini's ranch?"

"You will never reach it. The Uruentes are everywhere."

"Your concern touches me deeply. Tell me, and tell me the truth, or you'd better hope I don't make it back." Culhane stabbed the muzzle of the rifle harder against the one-legged man's throat.

The man swallowed hard, the Adam's apple moving very slowly and then very fast.

Culhane decided the one-legged man could be an eloquent speaker if given the opportunity and the right amount of persuasion.

Culhane moved the rifle. "Sebastiao, get to the door and cover my back."

"*Sim, senhor*." Culhane could hear Sebastiao's feet on the board floor, and then Culhane started backing away. . . .

CULHANE HAD LET SEBASTIAO DRIVE. He remembered the man's driving from his other time in Brazil, and Sebastiao if anything drove even more recklessly, the needle never dipping below eighty.

The needle on the speedometer finally dropped, and Sebastiao turned off and went up into the mountains. Santini had agreed to baby-sit the two suitcases, and the riverboat captain had pledged to pull out upstream to a point along the river roughly parallel to Celini's mine in the event he and Sebastiao were pursued by the Uruentes.

"How much is this car worth in American dollars in its present condition, Sebastiao?"

"Perhaps four thousand dollars, *senhor*."

"If anything happens, I'll give you four grand toward a new one. Deal?"

"You are not angry anymore?"

"Angry at myself. I should have gotten on to her more quickly, then none of this would have happened."

"If you do not mind me to say it, Josh Culhane, M. F. is a fine woman, I think."

"Are you saying she can take care of herself?"

"Yes—I think."

"She probably can. But where's she going to go? You said yourself this Celini guy seemed pretty rough. And the Uruentes. I can't see this guy laying down his life to save Fanny. Her only chance is the river. And we're her only chance of getting there."

Culhane snapped his head right, toward the jungle growth beyond the even narrower roadway climbing into the mountains. "Stop the car. Cut the engine! Listen!"

The brakes screeched, dirt and rocks flying from beneath the tires, then the engine stopped. Culhane jumped from the Bronco, the rifle in both hands, listening.

It had sounded like a child, but the voice was too deep.

"Bang—bang—bang-bang! Bang!"

Culhane turned and looked into the dense rain forest. Sebastiao was beside him.

Culhane, using the rifle to bat away the broad leaves of a vine, started in. "Keep an eye out behind us," Culhane whispered hoarsely. The voice was getting louder, Culhane homing in on it. "Bang—bang-bang! Bang-bang-bang-bang-bang!" Culhane stepped over a termite-infested deadfall log. The voice was so loud now he realized whoever belonged to it was close. He heard the familiar sound of a submachine gun bolt being drawn back and he froze, the rifle down to his hip.

But there was a click. "Bang! Bang-bang-bang-bang-bang!"

Culhane pushed aside a hanging plant with yellow petals forming the shapes of stars, then stepped into a small clearing.

A man—a grown man, his white shirt drenched with blood and sweat, his blond hair matted across his forehead with perspiration—held a submachine gun in his hands. Culhane saw the look in the man's eyes as he "fired," but the man wasn't seeing them. "Bang! Bang-bang-bang!"

"Do you speak English?" Culhane called softly.

The man did not answer. He did not seem to notice them. Culhane walked across the small clearing and stood beside the man who knelt there. "Sebastiao—ask him if he knows Sergio Celini."

But the face turned up toward Culhand, the eyes

flickering. "Sergio—him run away—far away—hah-ha!"

Culhane dropped into a crouch beside the man. "We'll help you."

"Uruentes help Sergio and the Amazon and the American girl—ha!"

"What American girl?"

The man only laughed again. Culhane grabbed the man's shoulders and shook him. "What American girl? A journalist—a writer? Mary Frances Mulrooney?"

"Mulrooney—ha!"

The man fell back onto the matted leaves that covered the ground. He aimed the submachine gun skyward. "Bang—bang—bang-bang-bang!"

"This is bad, Josh Culhane."

The man started shouting, this time in Portuguese. Culhane couldn't follow and looked at Sebastiao. "What's he saying?"

"He says they are coming—the Uruentes. They will never get—Culhane!"

Sebastiao lunged toward the ground, Culhane wheeling around, but the neck of the blond-haired man pumped blood and the eyes stared up at the sun.

Sebastiao fell back to his knees and crossed himself.

The blond man who had lost his mind had taken his own life.

If Sergio Celini had made it clear of the Uruentes, if Mulrooney and the Greek-speaking girl had made it, they would head for the river.

Culhane, his voice low, his left hand resting on Sebastiao's shoulder, told him, "Cut off toward the river as fast as you can. We're going to try and head 'em off. If it's just this Sergio Celini character, Fanny and her Amazon, Celini at least should know his only chance is to try for the river."

Sebastiao nodded. "Yes, the only chance, Josh Culhane." He got to his feet and walked to the edge of the clearing, then turned and looked at the corpse. He climbed a rubber tree, and began hacking down some of the large leaves. Culhane reached to his right shoulder, drawing the machete from its sheath, and began doing the same. They would cover the dead man. And Culhane, as he cut at the stalks, found himself praying that Fanny lived. Or if they caught her, that she died very quickly....

MARY FRANCES MULROONEY WAS HOT, tired and out of breath.

Two Uruente tribesmen had cut them off shortly after the women had entered the jungle, and Mulrooney had shot and killed one of them. The girl who spoke Greek killed the other with a spear. Fred picked up the bows and arrows of the two dead Uruente warriors, took their knives—Mulrooney was surprised that the knives seemed perfectly modern albeit sort of flashy—then slit their throats.

They had run on. And run and run and run.

From the sun being directly overhead, Mulrooney assumed it was about noon, but as they were so close to the Equator, she wasn't sure.

She had not seen Sergio Celini, but once she had heard a rifle shot. He was somewhere ahead. She had no words to ask the tall, muscular and very beautiful girl where they were going—or if they were just running. Logic dictated that they head for the river. Were they doing that? Or were they doing that only if Celini headed for the river? Was the Amazon girl on a blood hunt for Celini?

Mulrooney shook her head, her hat down low over her eyes to absorb the sweat and shield her eyes from the blazing sun. Her khaki shorts were grass stained, leaf stained and sweat stained, and the Uruente she had killed had been so close that her shorts were blood-stained, too.

"Me-em-ef!"

Mulrooney looked up. Fred had stripped away the khaki bush jacket and had somehow cut and tied it into a breechcloth, her breasts bare. Somehow it looked perfectly natural.

"Yeah?"

"Uruente!"

Mulrooney jumped to her feet, her revolver in her right fist. She gestured into the jungle. "Fred and Me-em-ef—where do we run?" She had given up on straightening out the girl regarding names.

"Fred—Me-em-ef—*run*." And the girl pointed in the direction they had been going before Mulrooney had forced them to stop.

Fred started into her long-strided trot, Mulrooney running beside her, knowing Fred was intentionally slowing the pace to avoid outdistancing her.

And now Mulrooney heard what Fred had heard moments before.

The Uruentes.

There was a blood-chilling scream, and arrows filled the air around them as Fred wheeled, the bow in her hands, and shot an arrow into the sky.

Then Fred shoved her ahead and loosed another arrow. Mulrooney aimed her little revolver into the jungle and fired at one of the cocoa-colored, red-painted bodies, a blowgun at his lips. The body fell across the path.

Mulrooney ran for her life, Fred right behind her.

Chapter Twenty-Two _____

The Ford Bronco skidded in the mud a little, Culhane jumping out before it stopped, nearly slipping but stepping clear. He tossed the rifle across the hood of the mud-spattered Bronco to Sebastiao, Sebastiao neatly catching it. From the Norwegian army engineer's bag at his left side he took the compass, opened it and let the dial settle to level. "Check your map."

"This is where the boat should meet us, *senhor*."

Culhane closed the compass. They were at roughly the same coordinates but parallel to Celini's mine.

"Let's go." He secured the compass in the bag. Sebastiao handed back the rifle, and Culhane shouldered into his pack. He had picked a distant peak barely visible across the jungle canopy to shoot his azimuth on. He drew his machete from across his back and pointed it out to Sebastiao. "We're about parallel to the Uruente village if the captain knows his stuff. If we don't intercept Fanny, we go there. If they capture her, they'd take her there if they're like most other headhunters—for the ritual murder."

"*Sim, senhor*."

Culhane looked into Sebastiao's eyes. He deeply respected the little man. There was terror written there, and yet Sebastiao had not wanted to stay behind.

Culhane started to run.

THERE WERE DRUMS IN THE JUNGLE. Mulrooney tried pretending that she was starring in an old Hollywood B-movie: headhunting natives pursuing her through the jungle, an Amazon warrior by her side, the jungle drums signaling death—or worse. Only this was no fantasy.

She kept running, not deluding herself that the Uruentes had been lost.

There was no choice but to follow Fred.

And then Fred stopped. She dropped to one bare knee and was examining a leaf. Mulrooney saw red spots on it, the spots bright and wet looking. "Blood," she whispered, and tapped the girl's shoulder. "Fred—" She pointed to the blood on the leaf. "Celini?"

"Celini!" And Fred was running, Mulrooney shouting after her, "No—we can use his help! Fred!"

The drums seemed louder now. Mulrooney told herself it was her heart pounding in her chest.

Mulrooney kept running, leaves and branches slapping at her, tearing at her shirt, at her flesh.

Fred was just visible turning a bend in the trail they had followed through the jungle.

And then Mulrooney saw him as she herself rounded the bend. Celini was on his knees, trying to raise his rifle to his hip from the ground beside him. His left thigh was bleeding where the shaft of an arrow protruded, his left shoulder soaked where Mulrooney had shot him in the cave.

Fred stood towering over him, her bow up, the arrow ready to fly.

"Fred!" Mulrooney screamed.

Fred remained motionless, then twisted left, firing into the jungle. There was a cry of pain, and a body tumbled from one of the higher branches: one of the Uruente warriors.

Mulrooney swung her revolver on line into the trees to fire, but there was no target.

Sergio Celini screamed and Mulrooney wheeled toward him.

His body looked like a pincushion. Tiny darts protruded from his chest and his cheeks and his left eye, more thudding into him.

Blowguns.

And then she saw them. Uruente warriors stepped from the trees into the small clearing, surrounding them.

Fred had another arrow ready. Mulrooney, her gun leveled at the Uruente, moved slowly toward Fred.

"Fred?"

"Me-em-ef."

"Run?"

Fred shook her head.

Mulrooney closed her eyes for an instant and licked her dry lips. She needed water. She needed rest.

Fred lowered her bow for an instant, drew one of the two knives she had taken from the dead Uruente warriors, then aimed the bow again. The knife was in her left hand beneath the tip of the arrow.

Mulrooney understood what Fred wanted her to do. She took the knife.

The knife in her balled left fist, the gun in her right, she placed herself against Fred's back. The other woman towered over her.

"You're a good woman, Fred. You don't understand me, but you're a good woman."

"Fred—Me—em-ef."

Mulrooney understood that Fred understood.

No blowguns were raised. No bows were drawn.

The Uruentes began to close the circle, spears held like quarterstaves out of a Robin Hood movie.

There was the twang of a bow. Mulrooney didn't

look. At that range, Fred could not miss. Another twang. Another and another.

There was a shout from one of the Uruente warriors. And Mulrooney noticed that the drums had stopped.

A scream. A war cry. The Uruentes rushed forward.

Mulrooney's little revolver bucked in her hand—once, then again and again and again and again, and then it was clicking empty. The Uruente warriors were clambering over the bodies of the men she had shot, and Mulrooney clubbed the revolver into the face of one of them. He fell back. The gun was lost. She rammed the knife forward blindly. There was a shriek of pain and the body fell and then another hurtled at her.

Mulrooney turned. She was shoulder to shoulder with Fred now, who held her bow in one hand like a club and was hammering at skulls and necks, her knife slashing from the other hand. Mulrooney caught at a spear as one of her attackers fell to her knife, and she tried hammering at one of them with it.

Fred was on her knees, a spear crashing down across her shoulders, then she fell facedown to the ground. Mulrooney stepped over her, fighting them away from the girl.

A spear....

Mulrooney couldn't close her eyes in time, but there was darkness anyway and her stomach churned and she closed her eyes.

Chapter Twenty-Three _____

Culhane slowed his run. The drums he and Sebastiao had heard had stopped ten minutes ago.

He had run toward the sound, shooting an azimuth on the origin of the drums.

Culhane handed his rifle to Sebastiao and checked the compass again. He was going in the right direction. He closed the compass, took his rifle, picked up his machete and they continued ahead. Few twentieth-century men had fought Indians. But in movies and books when the drums stopped... He sucked in his breath, forcing the thoughts from his mind.

The jungle undergrowth thinned, and he sheathed the machete, holding the rifle in both hands now.

There was a clearing and Culhane aimed toward it.

Sebastiao murmured, ''Be careful, *senhor*!''

Culhane nodded, his eyes flickering left to right, then he looked straight ahead.

There was something in the clearing, and Culhane started toward it as he broke from the foliage, looking up into the trees, the rifle's muzzle held out like a wand. Magic against death?

He saw the headless body.

''Sergio Celini,'' Sebastiao whispered hoarsely. ''Uruente—they are here.''

Culhane saw something flash in the sunlight, and he dropped to one knee beside it. Bloody fingerprints covered most of a two-inch-barreled stainless-steel Rossi .38 Special. He picked it up.

''Jesus...'' Culhane looked up into Sebastiao's face.

The man was crossing himself. "That is the gun of M. F., *senhor.*"

But there was no telling whose blood it was.

He forced himself to think clearly. If they had killed her, he would have found her decapitated body. And he would follow the Uruentes to the ends of the earth until he'd killed every one of them.

But there was no body.

They had taken her alive.

Culhane closed his eyes, still holding her blood-smeared revolver: *I'll find you—so help me. I'll find you. Believe in that sixth sense you talk about—hear me. I'll find you, Fanny.*

Chapter Twenty-Four _____

Hoevermann lit another cigarette with the burned-down butt of his last one. "And so, *senhor*, how much money did they give you?"

"It . . . my family . . . we are . . ."

"Then don't tell *me* how much, tell your superiors in the customs office. But money was exchanged. That is known."

"He said it was something very innocent . . . to help a young girl . . ."

"You are most noble," Hoevermann remarked, inhaling the cigarette smoke deep into his lungs. "Did you ascertain how much they helped this young girl?"

"Bricks of gold—ingots."

"How many?"

"I did not count them, Senhor Inspector. I . . ."

"How much do you think they are worth? In U.S. dollars."

Sweat dripped from the customs inspector's face, and his hands shook and his right eye twitched. Hoevermann imagined it was not the first time the man had taken a bribe, just the first time he'd been caught.

"How much gold did the agent of Senhor Palmer smuggle into this country?"

"I think—a million dollars, I think."

"*Only* a million dollars? That is odd. Perhaps, my friend, you can act as a sounding board for my suspicions—if you do not mind?" Hoevermann stood up and began to pace the white-walled, soundproof interrogation room, staring at his own reflection in the two-way mirror dominating the far wall. "Senhor Palmer is very rich. To him, a million dollars is very little. I think I read somewhere that ransom payments are deductible on U.S. income-tax forms. Why did they not ask him for more? A million dollars in gold must be very heavy. Those two suitcases Senhor Culhane seems wedded to, hmm? But why not fill those suitcases with diamonds? And if smuggling is to be done, why not smuggle in cash? There is gold aplenty in our nation, no? It is estimated that we have almost seven and a half billion U.S. dollars' worth of metallic gold scattered about Brazil." Hoevermann didn't wait for an answer. "Why smuggle it in?" He thought of the English colloquialism, carrying coals to Newcastle. "Why gold? If you were me, would you ask Senhor Palmer about this, my friend?"

The customs inspector said nothing.

Hoevermann shrugged. He was glad he had the man flown to Belém for questioning. Somehow he felt that he was running out of time. . . .

PALMER HAD NOT WANTED TO SPEAK with him, but Hoevermann had suggested that if Palmer did not agree to an interview in his hotel suite, suitable accommodations could be arranged at the municipal jail of Belém.

So Hoevermann sat in the same cushioned white wicker chair, beside the same glass table, filling the same glass ashtray with the remains of his cigarettes. "You are fortunate they asked for something that you have in such abundance—gold."

"Ah," Palmer said, smiling, lighting a cigarette. Hoevermann noticed that his hands trembled slightly. "You know, then."

"Yes, but I can't understand something. It is for this reason I came. A triviality perhaps. But why, when you own some of the most prosperous gold interests in Brazil, did you smuggle gold illegally into our country?"

Hoevermann made a smile appear on his face.

"Ah—I—I didn't want, well, I suppose I can trust you."

"Yes—oh, yes, indeed."

"I was trying to keep the ransom payment secret so there would be a better chance of getting it upriver. And then, too, I didn't want you to try and stop me. I'll gladly pay whatever fines I've incurred. I can have my lawyers—"

"How about the customs inspector who was only ten years from his pension?"

"I'll provide for his welfare."

"Will you pay for added police and military forces to counteract the help your ransom payment will give these terrorists?"

"If there is anything I can do—"

"You are so public-spirited, *senhor*."

He watched Palmer's eyes narrow, the handsome brow knit as Palmer bent forward, stubbing out his cigarette. Palmer rose from the chair opposite Hoevermann at the glass table. "I am a very rich man—as you seem so obsessed with reminding me. And terribly rich men have terribly influential friends."

"My job?"

"I didn't say that."

Hoevermann laughed. "I have been exceedingly fortunate throughout my career, *senhor*. Integrity is something I have never disavowed. I shall not disavow it now. You can have my job—I shouldn't think you would like it at all. The hours are bad; the pay is worse. It is fortunate for me that a small inheritance has helped sustain me all these years. I have lived frugally but well. Were I to lose my position tomorrow, neither my family nor I would want. And I would not give up. I would remind you of a basic fact relevant to those relatively few career police officers who specialize in counterterrorism. One usually does not take such a job because it is the safe route."

Hoevermann stood, stubbing out his own cigarette. "I shall pursue the reason why, *senhor*, you smuggled gold needlessly into this country. And when I find out the reason, rather than you harming me, there may be precious little I can do to avoid harm coming to you."

Hoevermann settled his hat on his head.

He didn't bother to say good-day. It wasn't one.

Chapter Twenty-Five _____

Damascus Santini peered over the gunwale. Bandits, but this time by boat. To attempt to flee would only yield a running gun battle, and staying at this point on the river was imperative if Culhane, his guide, Fanny Mulrooney, and any other survivors of the Uruente attacks Culhane might bring with him were to be saved.

He thought of Vietnam.

"Captain, we have company. Get your men ready."

"Yes, Father!"

He closed his eyes. There should be a prayer for people who were about to sin.

He would not surrender the gold. Evil could not win simply because it was unafraid of violence.

"Hurry!"

A salvo of automatic weapons' fire came from a riverboat almost identical to theirs except for the camouflage paint job. Santini estimated it was about 150 yards away. A voice floated over the water, launched from a bullhorn: "Give to us the ransom—and the two women. And you will live."

Santini, low behind the gunwales, had counted perhaps twenty guns. He looked beside him. The captain had dropped to his knees behind the gunwales, his deeply tanned stubbled jaw set, his eyes pinpoints of fear. Santini knew the look well. He had worn it on his own face many times.

"What's it to be?" Santini asked him.

"The ransom. I would give that to save the lives of my passengers. But he would kill them anyway. And he does not get the women."

"Good man. At this range, all they can lay over us is harassing fire. But harassing fire can kill just as easily as aimed fire. Keep everybody down. Use the packing crates and keep everyone behind them."

"If they shoot into the hull and the boat should sink—there are piranha in these waters."

"When they get in range, open fire on my signal." Santini's mouth was very dry and his hands perspired.

"You cannot—"

"It's my conscience. Let me wrestle with it. And they won't go for putting holes in the hull. As long as this boat's afloat, they've got a chance of getting their money."

"The things Senhor Culhane carries—what is in the cases? Diamonds?"

"I promised him I wouldn't tell anybody, but they'll sink if we go down."

The boat captain laughed. "We fight them!"

The voice of the bandit leader came over the water again, echoing from the jungle on both riverbanks. "You will die—all of you! I promise this!"

Santini thought back to the halcyon days when he could have visibly shown his answer with an upraised middle finger. . . .

THEY WERE USING A SMALL BOAT NOW, a long tiller off the outboard, the boat low in the water as it raced toward them.

Santini shouted, "Look out—firebombs!"

Gunfire came a fusillade from the pirate riverboat. Santini's force—the boat crew, the two male passengers and Helene Chavez and Magdelena—were too pinned down to fire.

Santini watched through a crack between two packing crates of supplies for the mission's kitchen. The small boat was heading right for them, the man at the tiller on his knees to keep his head low. A second man was in the prow, an AK-47 assault rifle firing, and a third man was standing, a wine or whiskey bottle in his right hand, a burning wick at its mouth.

Beside Santini, the Japanese shouted, "No, Mr. Archer!"

Santini wheeled on his knees. The American engineer was on his feet, the captain's bolt-action rifle in his hands. Santini started to reach for it, but the rifle discharged, and Archer collapsed into the cabin bulkhead, bullets from enemy fire slamming into his chest and neck, his wide-open eyes staring in death.

Santini looked to the river. The man with the Molotov cocktail was falling over the side of the little boat—and suddenly the water's surface was alive.

All gunfire stopped, and a scream more hideous than any Santini had ever heard pierced the air.

The water seemed to boil and then it stopped.

A skeleton of human bones floated to the surface for a moment and then was gone.

Santini stared.

"Piranha," the Japanese beside him whispered.

Santini turned to the dead American and began the last rites. And the gunfire began again, too.

THE RIFLE CLUTCHED IN BOTH HANDS—the rifle Fanny Mulrooney had had altered for him—Culhane ran. Chanting was audible in the distance, and smoke rose out of the jungle. And a scream—a woman's scream.

"*Senhor*—there are many of them! If you run into the village all will be lost!"

He kept running. Were they killing her? Was it the other girl—Mulrooney's Amazon—who had screamed?

His heart beat so loudly, the noise of it filled his ears and drowned out the chanting that he knew was still there.

He stopped running, gasping for breath. "Sebastiao...we get up there...we have to create...a diversion. Get the layout of the village real quick. I'll create the diversion—whatever it takes. You go for Fanny and the other girl."

"If they are dead, Josh Culhane?"

"Then—" Culhane stared at his hands. They trembled. It was not fear. It was rage. "Then you run like hell for the river and tell them all to get out of here. Ask Father Santini to take care of the suitcases for me—"

"Suitcases?"

"He'll explain. You help him."

"And you, *senhor*?"

"I won't be coming."

Culhane turned the set screw back in, ready with the rifle. And he started running again, taking an indirect route to the village.

There was another scream. He prayed—for Fanny and for himself.

MASSIVE CAULDRONS OF BLACKENED CAST IRON boiled, the smell sickening, sweet, nauseating. The cauldrons were mounted over flaming logs, and above each cauldron was an inverted V of wooden poles, the apex of the V fitted with a heavy rope. She had seen things like this before in artists' conceptions. Read of them. The dance, the ceremony, the chanting, the stares in the eyes of the Uruentes—it was all preparatory to boiling them, Mulrooney realized. And she couldn't help it. She screamed again.

Suspended from woven sashes at the waists of the Uruente warriors were shrunken human heads—*tsantsas*. The *tsantsa* was no mere trophy, Mulrooney knew. Shrinking the head of a foe is thought to prevent the *muisak*, the avenging soul of the victim, from killing the slayer.

The work is begun on the trail, starting with a cut up the back of the neck, and the scalp is carefully peeled off the skull. Then the skin is carefully stitched up and soaked in hot water. When dried, it shrinks to the size of a man's fist and is then blackened over a smoky fire, preserving it.

Mary Frances Mulrooney just couldn't stand to think of those toucan feathers decorating her hair for the rest of eternity.

But first the body would be killed.

Her body.

They would behead her, but only just prior to the moment of death. The water could not be hot enough to kill her instantly. She knew that her suffering would last an eternity in her mind. Tears streamed down her face and she fought them back, trying to hide her weakness from the Uruente tribesmen who danced around her, prodding at her with their spears, her hands bound behind her around a stake the thickness of a telephone pole, her ankles bound as well, her body weight sagging down, her knees too weak to support her.

She thought of Josh Culhane. She wanted to be in his arms, to have him awaken her from this bad dream, to have him kiss her, to feel his lips at her lips, at the tip of her nose as he liked to do, to feel his hands on her body.

She stared past the Uruente warriors. Ten or twelve feet from her was Fred. She was tied as Mulrooney was tied, and one of the Uruentes—a shaman, perhaps, judging from his dress—was coming up to her. She bit at him, snarled at him. Her head was tied back to the post, a cord bound around her forehead.

The shaman worked on Fred's face. Painting it. Red. Black. Stripes. Symbols. A small star.

And then the shaman was finished.

He started toward her, and Mulrooney screamed at him, ''No! No!''

The shaman dipped his fingers into a small wooden jar, the fingers emerging smeared with red. Mulrooney told herself it wasn't blood. It wasn't blood. It wasn't blood. He smeared it across her face and she remained motionless. It *was* blood. She could feel it and she screamed, ''Josh!'' But no one could save her. M. F. Mulrooney knew that. No one.

Chapter Twenty-Six _____

He had found her purse in the jungle along the trail, found the lipsticks and the comb and the brush and the pens and the other things he had always gently ridiculed her for lugging around everywhere. He had picked them up and put the purse into his backpack.

He had found spare ammo for her gun littered along the trail, as well. He had loaded the revolver, and now he gave the revolver and the few remaining loose rounds to Sebastiao. "If you get her out—give her her gun. It won't do a hell of a lot of good considering the way she shoots, but it'll be all right at close range. And if you get cornered, and if she won't use it on herself... Please?" Culhane looked into Sebastiao's eyes.

"Yes, Josh Culhane. This I promise my friend."

Culhane nodded.

He edged forward now, Sebastiao beside him. He could hear screaming.

He parted the feathery leaves of a fern and looked into the village, along the single semicircular street to the center of the village. He saw two cauldrons. And flames leaped up beneath them.

There was a half-naked woman tied to a stake.

The Greek girl?

And Fanny Mulrooney was being dragged toward the side of one of the cauldrons. She was kicking and screaming, and swearing like a foul-mouthed sailor. Her hands were raised over her head, and a rope swung beneath two poles tied to her wrists.

They were going to lower her into the boiling cauldron.

"Good luck, my friend," Culhane said to Sebastiao.

"And to you, my friend." Then Sebastiao was gone, running soundlessly along the village perimeter, his bolt-action rifle ready in both hands.

Culhane stood up to his full height and stepped from the foliage. He started walking down the street toward Fanny Mulrooney....

MARY FRANCES MULROONEY BUTTED HER HEAD toward the face of one of the Uruentes, but his head dodged back and she thought she heard him laugh. "You son of a bitch—gotta tie up a woman just to kill her? Bite it—all of you! Take your goddamned ceremony and shove it up your—"

And she sucked in her breath a moment as the rope that bound her wrists was drawn up and suddenly her feet were off the ground and she was swinging over the cauldron of the foul-smelling boiling water.

"Culhane!" She screamed for him.

And she looked to her left—at the end of the village street. She told herself she was dreaming. *"Culhane!"*

She wasn't dreaming.

He held the rifle skyward—the rifle she'd had fixed just for him—and fired more shots than she could count.

"If any one of you understands English," she heard him shouting, "all I want are the two women!"

There was a cry. She had heard it before: the Uruente war cry. Suddenly all the dancers were running, their spears held high in the air, blowguns being fetched up from the ground around her, bows, arrows—they were all running toward Culhane. "Get out of here! I love you!" she screamed, but she knew he could not hear her.

And she looked down to her feet. The shaman held a

knife in his upraised hands, a knife not like the ones the warriors carried, but carved, very old-looking, the blade long and curved, and he was driving the knife toward her abdomen.

Mulrooney tried swinging her feet against the knife to block the thrust, but it was too late. *"No-o-o-o!"*

Suddenly the shaman's body froze like a child in a schoolyard playing statues. And his knees buckled and the knife fell to the dirt from limp fingers.

She knew it couldn't be Culhane: the natives were charging down the street toward him. Mulrooney looked to her right. "Sebastiao—I could kiss you, Sebastiao!" she cried.

His face lit with a smile for an instant as he stepped from between two huts, slinging his rifle, his knife going into his teeth as he grabbed at her ankles, dragging her back from where she was suspended partially over the boiling cauldron. He hugged her legs to his chest and hacked at the rope that was hung over the poles shaped like the inverted V. She felt the line snap and she sagged forward, across his shoulder. Sebastiao lowered her to the ground. *"Menina*—it is good you are alive. We must go quickly now." He settled her over onto her back and cut the ropes binding her wrists. She wondered if she'd ever have the feeling back in her hands. He cut her ankles free.

Mulrooney looked at him. "Gimme that knife, Sebastiao!" She took the blade and used it to cut away one of her shirttails. She rubbed the fabric over her face to wipe off the awful colors. Then she threw it to the ground and put her arms around Sebastiao's neck and gave him the biggest first kiss she'd ever given any man.

"You're a good kisser, you know that?" She didn't wait for an answer. She was up on her feet, almost losing her balance, half running, half lurching toward the stake where Fred was tied still.

She cut the ropes binding Fred's wrists.

She dropped to her knees and cut the ropes binding Fred's ankles.

She stood up and hacked away the other front shirttail. "Fix your face," she said and handed it to Fred.

She turned to Sebastiao. "What's his plan? He's always got a plan. Sean Dodge always has a plan."

Sebastiao gave her the Rossi .38 Special.

Automatically she checked the cylinder. He handed her five more loose cartridges. "We will meet him at the river—hurry!"

"Fred—run!"

Mulrooney started into the jungle, looking back once to check that Fred was behind her. In Fred's hands were a bow and arrow. Mulrooney ran; Culhane would be in trouble. She could sense it. . . .

CULHANE WAS IN TROUBLE. He stopped his headlong lunge from the village street and wheeled, pumping the lever of the Browning, machine-gunning it, his left hand burning from the heat of the barrel where his palm grasped the rifle to steady it.

Four Uruente were down; dozens more were coming. Culhane turned and ran, a hail of arrows and darts filling the air around him. The shaft of a spear brushed at his left shoulder.

Behind him, at the far end of the village, he could see the cauldrons and the ceremonial square, but Fanny Mulrooney was nowhere in sight. He kept running.

Out of the village now, into the jungle, Culhane jumped a deadfall tree. His rifle empty, Culhane switched it into his left hand and snatched the four-inch

629 from its holster. He looked behind him, then fired once into the center of the path. An Uruente grasped his chest with both hands, the body collapsing. The spear he held clattered to the ground.

Culhane kept running.

The sun was beginning to set. The river was to the southwest, and he adjusted his direction accordingly. War cries filled the air around him. Culhane snapped off another shot from the .44 Magnum. He didn't look to see if he'd hit anyone. He just kept running.

His hat was low over his forehead. Sweat poured down his face from beneath the hatband, dripping into his eyes.

He kept running, the war cries getting closer.

Culhane snapped off a third shot. Something was nagging at him, telling him he wasn't going to make it this time....

"HURRY, M. F.!"

"We have to head him off," Mulrooney announced, hands on her hips, Fred standing beside her.

Sebastiao turned to look at her. She realized he was pleading with her. "But Senhor Culhane...he tells me that we must meet him at the river. These are his orders."

"You follow his orders, Sebastiao. I just know he's in big trouble and if we don't help him, he'll never make it! I *know* it. I *feel* it."

Sebastiao muttered something in Portuguese.

They heard a shot. It had to be Culhane.

"Let's go! This way, Sebastiao!" And over her shoulder M. F. Mulrooney yelled to the bare-breasted girl, "Fred—run!"

CULHANE FIRED TWO MORE SHOTS from behind the trunk
of a rubber tree. The revolver was empty. He swung
open the cylinder, punched out the empties, and reloaded. The Uruentes would be fanning out, and they
would encircle him if he waited much longer. His rifle
reloaded, the set screw still turned in, Culhane rammed
the revolver back into its holster and took up his rifle
from beside the tree trunk.

He fired two shots along the route he'd come and
started to run again. He tugged his Stetson over his
forehead with his left hand, dodging a lightning-struck
stump, running, tripping. He spotted a clearing ahead
and ran for it, jumping a tangle of vines. Once in the
clearing, he picked up his pace.

Culhane jumped over a huge deadfall, half eaten
away, landing on the mossy carpet of rotting leaves
behind it, stabbing the rifle over the top of the log, his
fingers automatically backing off the set screw. He
waited.

He worked the lever.

Uruente warriors streamed into the clearing, and he
let them come. Closer. Closer.

Sweat glistened off their dark bodies. The red ceremonial paint gleamed in the sun.

Culhane squeezed off his first shot.

One of the Uruentes dropped. Culhane worked the
lever again and fired, another Uruente going down.

He was going for wounding shots, the old combat
principle his brother had told him: wound the enemy
and it takes two of them to cart him away. Culhane
fired again and again and again, the Uruente warriors
falling back.

Culhane rolled onto his back and reloaded the rifle,
then set it down against the log.

His right hand found the flap of the holster, and he drew the six-inch-barreled .44 Smith. More waiting.

The Uruentes were coming again, their war cries like the cries of fierce birds. Culhane ducked down as the air was suddenly filled with darts and arrows and spears.

He stabbed the revolver up, firing once, then again and again. He sighted on one of the Uruentes, the man's bow poised to fire. Culhane fired first, the man dropping.

Culhane double-actioned the revolver, the gun bucking in his hands with recoil, and another Uruente went down, chunks of the rotted log exploding upward as a spear struck within six inches of his head. He fired the last round from the revolver at a Uruente who was grasping for his left arm. The warrior spun away like an out-of-control dancer.

And Culhane was up, the revolver rammed back into the holster, the rifle in his hands.

He nudged the lever closed, and the rifle fired, his right hand working the lever down and up, down and up, each time the lever closed, the set screw contacting the trigger, the rifle discharging.

He swung the muzzle left, then right, Uruente warriors falling with each shot—and then the rifle was empty.

Culhane turned and ran for the jungle again, a hail of arrows around him as he threw himself into the underbrush. He had to try to make the river. He reloaded the rifle as he ran. It was tougher than it looked in the movies, he thought.

"How far to the river, Sebastiao?" Mulrooney could hardly breathe any more let alone talk.

Sebastiao's voice panted from beside her. "Two kilometers, perhaps less—about a mile, *menina*."

Culhane would be behind them. She could hear his shots; she had heard them as they ran. The new rifle apparently worked. It sounded like a machine gun going off across the jungle.

Mulrooney stopped. A clearing opened before them, a few trees were scattered in the center around a long deadfall log.

"We'll make our stand here," she declared firmly. "Is that all right?" She looked at Sebastiao.

"It is as good as any place, *menina*."

Mulrooney nodded, then looked at Fred. "Me-em-ef—do you understand?"

Fred smiled. She had gorgeous teeth. "Uruente!" And Fred raised the bow over her head, twanging it into the jungle without firing an arrow.

Mulrooney nodded. "Uruente." And she ran her right index finger left to right, ear to ear across her throat in what she hoped was a universal gesture.

Fred was running into the clearing now, to one tree, then to the other. And then Fred was climbing, the bow clenched in her teeth, the arrow quiver across her back.

"I fight from behind the other tree," Sebastiao told Mulrooney.

Mulrooney nodded. "I'll fight from the ground behind the log. When Culhane jumps it I'll get him to drop."

"What if he does not reach this clearing?"

"It's big enough, and the shots keep getting closer." She heard another volley. "He'll come. I know it." She hoped. Mulrooney and Sebastiao ran into the clearing, Sebastiao positioning himself behind one of the trees, his rifle coming up, the flap on his holster open.

M. F. Mulrooney threw herself down behind the deadfall tree. "Yecch!" Bugs crawled all over it, and she picked up a clump of leaves and brushed them away, a worm falling from the leaves. Then she braced the pistol on the log. She looked up. Barely visible in the lush foliage, Fred stood ready in a large notch, her bow ready.

Mulrooney turned her attention back toward the far end of the clearing. She heard more shots. He was coming. She knew it would be Culhane.

"Don't shoot until Culhane jumps the log," she whispered loudly so that Sebastiao and Fred could hear her. "Then let 'em have it. Fred—Me-em-ef—" Mulrooney gestured with her revolver and held up one finger.

"Fred—Me-em-ef," the girl rasped back.

Mulrooney waited. . . .

CULHANE HAD FIRED OUT THE RIFLE, and there was no time to reload it now. The ground dropped suddenly, steeply, Culhane's momentum carrying him forward and down more quickly than he wanted.

Uruente war cries were behind him, arrows and spears flying everywhere.

The ground broke a hundred yards ahead. Heavy undergrowth rose from the depression; perhaps it was a stream course when the rains were very heavy. High trees rose, the trees intertwined with vines.

He could see the higher ground beyond the deep cut. If he went down into the cut, shooting at him would be piteously easy. He considered running to the right or left, but if the cut broadened or steepened he would be stranded. And if he ran parallel to the cut, his pursuers would close on him, cutting the distance to where their spears and arrows would not miss.

Culhane took the rifle into his left hand and wrenched his machete clear of the case across his back. He hurled the machete behind him as he ran, hoping it would hit somebody. He stabbed the rifle muzzle-first into the machete sheath, leaving both hands free as he reached the lip of the divide. Vines were everywhere. It was grabbing the right one that was the trick.

Culhane looked behind him as he stopped. The Uruente warriors were less than a hundred yards back.

Culhane grabbed a vine. "Edgar Rice Burroughs—I hope you knew what you were talking about!" On the last word Culhane jumped, hurtling himself out over the cut, swinging from the vine.

He couldn't resist it. He did his best Johnny Weissmuller Tarzan yell. The ground on the far side of the cut was coming up fast, and it was lower than the height of the opposite side from which he had come. Culhane let go as he swung over it, falling to his knees, rolling facedown.

His motion stopped. He looked up and smiled. "Hot damn—I did it!" Culhane pushed himself to his feet and started running, Uruente darts peppering the ground near him, arrows springing into tree trunks as he ran past. He turned once. The Uruentes were storming up the near side of the cut.

The river couldn't be too far, he told himself, and the chase he had led the Uruentes on would have given Fanny Mulrooney, Sebastiao and the girl a chance to get to the river ahead of him.

Culhane kept running, spotting a large clearing up ahead. The Uruente warriors—bowmen, spearmen, blowgunners—were almost at his heels, and he knew he'd be an easy target there. As he drew closer, he could see a massive deadfall log, the tree trunk enormous.

He propelled himself toward it. If he could jump the log, then hide behind it and fire at his pursuers, it would give him a chance to catch his breath for the final run to the riverbank.

If the boat were not there and close to the bank, he was a dead man.

He kept running, seeing something for an instant behind a tree to his left.

But there was no time to worry about it. If it were some new danger, he'd meet it when it met him.

Culhane looked back, the leading wedge of the Uruentes into the clearing now.

The log was coming fast, Culhane pouring on his last speed, using his last strength, jumping up and over the log, rolling onto the ground.

He looked up. "Hi, Josh. What's happening?"

Stunned, he looked into Fanny Mulrooney's face, but then she turned away.

Her revolver discharged, and from Culhane's right he heard the sound of a rifle. He looked to his right, behind that tree. Sebastiao.

A bow twanged, and he rolled onto his back, stabbing the 629 Smith skyward, but it was no Uruente. It was an impossibly beautiful, impossibly tall girl, naked except for a breechcloth. She was firing an Uruente bow as rapidly as most experienced shooters could handle a turnbolt rifle.

He shook his head. Bellying closer to the log, Culhane shifted the four-inch revolver to his left hand and snatched the six-inch from the holster at his hip.

"Hold your ears!" he shouted to Fanny Mulrooney as he opened fire.

The Uruentes were charging, their spears filling the air, the air already thick with arrows and poisoned darts from their blowguns.

But Uruente warriors were falling now, the hail of lead from the .44 Magnum revolvers in each of Culhane's hands hammering at them. He kept shooting, Mulrooney beside him reloading her revolver. Both 629s empty, Culhane set them onto the log and hauled the rifle from the machete sheath. His left hand already had what remained of the box of Federal .44s, and he started loading the rifle, rasping to Fanny Mulrooney, "Take some of this ammo and load up my revolvers—fast, kid!"

The Uruente charge was close now, very close. Culhane rammed the last round into the tubular magazine, and he stood up, working the lever of the B-92 down and up, down and up, swinging the muzzle from left to right, firing at the leading edge of the Uruente charge.

Sebastiao's rifle boomed again and again.

Arrows felled Uruente warriors from the girl up in the tree.

And then Mulrooney was kneeling beside Culhane, her revolver firing again and again.

Culhane's rifle was empty.

He put it down and snatched a revolver with each hand, emptying the gleaming stainless .44 Magnums into the Uruente charge.

Most of those who were still standing turned back, but a few kept coming. Culhane's revolvers were empty now, and he put them down, drawing the Gerber fighting knife with his left hand, flicking open the Bali-Song with his right. The Uruentes closed in. Culhane blocked a spear thrust with his left forearm, knifing the Bali-Song forward into his attacker's abdomen. He hacked with the Gerber, practically gutting him.

Mulrooney had his empty rifle and was swinging it like a baseball bat. She'd seen too many John Wayne films, he thought, but so had he.

There was a blur of motion to Culhane's left as two Uruente warriors closed in on him, then one of the Uruentes ripped away. It was the nearly naked girl, the spear in her hands used more like a rifle with a fixed bayonet, her glistening body moving like a dancer's, the point of the spear hacking at her opponents, the base of the shaft pounding at their bodies and heads.

Another shot exploded from Sebastiao's rifle, and then Sebastiao was beside him, his knife in one hand, his revolver firing from the other.

Mulrooney was holding Culhane's six-inch .44 Magnum and suddenly Culhane's ears rang and Mulrooney screamed and the Uruente nearest Culhane was done.

Culhane hacked at another. The boom of the .44 Magnum sounded again, and another Uruente went down.

And suddenly there was no one left.

Culhane looked at Fanny Mulrooney. They would have to run for the river. The Uruente warriors would return—and soon.

Mulrooney held the 629 in both hands. She smiled. "You always said the recoil with this thing was such a big deal. Ha!" And the revolver almost fell from her hands as she sagged to her knees beside the body of one of the defeated Uruente warriors. "It's a good thing I don't have any loose fillings, though."

Culhane pulled her to her feet, using his Speedloaders to recharge both revolvers. Mulrooney had only gotten two rounds into the 629.

He could no longer reload the rifle. There was no more ammunition.

Sebastiao reloaded his rifle. The nearly naked girl was gathering up arrows and spears, and she had two knives compressed between the breechcloth's waist and her abdomen.

"We should run, *senhor*!"

Culhane nodded to Sebastiao. Then he looked at

Mulrooney. Still holding his revolvers, he drew her into his arms and kissed her harder than he had ever kissed her.

As the kiss broke, he looked into her face—dirt-stained, dripping sweat, streaks of what looked like black and red paint. She looked all set for a Georgia Bulldogs game, he thought absently, or at least the colors were right.

"Did I ever tell you that you're beautiful?"

She laughed. "You're pretty beautiful, too." And she punched his chest lightly.

Culhane just shook his head. But Mulrooney was calling to the stunning girl, and Culhane couldn't really understand her. "Fred—Fred, Me-em-ef—run!"

"Fred—Me-em-ef—run!"

The girl—festooned with bows and quivers taken from the dead, spears in each hand—started to run, Sebastiao beside her, the girl outdistancing him almost instantly.

Mulrooney looked at Culhane. "Josh—Me-em-ef—run!"

Side by side, Culhane's empty rifle in the machete sheath across his back, a revolver in each hand, they ran. And behind them, Culhane could already hear Uruente war cries. They were coming....

THE DENSITY of the rain-forest canopy was increasing now, the light dimming. Culhane and Mulrooney were barely able to keep the fleet-footed girl in sight. Sebastiao would drop back from time to time to check that the Uruentes were not too close.

They had run for some ten minutes, Culhane figured. He imagined he could smell the water, but it was only his own sweat, he knew.

And suddenly the girl ahead of them disappeared. It

was as if she had dropped into a hole. Despite the darkness of the rain-forest floor, Culhane increased his pace, the revolvers clutched tightly in each fist.

And then he saw the river.

But no boat.

"Christ—where are they?" he panted.

Sebastiao came up behind them. "*Senhor*, we are perhaps two kilometers—maybe a mile below the position where the riverboat was to meet us."

Culhane nodded, trying to get his breathing closer to normal.

He heard the voice of the girl Mulrooney called Fred. "Me-em-ef—"

"Why the hell does she call you that?"

"It's a long story. Don't worry about it now."

"Me-em-ef!"

Mulrooney started in the direction of the girls' voice, Culhane and Sebastiao following. A tiny spit of land jutted into the river. Culhane watched for crocodiles or gators as Mulrooney jumped onto it, Culhane right behind her, Sebastiao staying on the higher ground as Culhane looked back.

And then Culhane saw the girl. And he blinked. She was standing beside six dugout canoes.

"Me-em-ef!" The girl was smiling.

"Fred!" Mulrooney clambered over to stand beside her.

Culhane just shook his head.

"Josh Culhane—they come! The Uruente warriors!"

Culhane snapped his head around. Sebastiao had jumped onto the spit and was running toward them. And Culhane heard it, too, now, the war cries—and very softly in the distance, the drums. He started shoving one of the dugouts into the water. "Sebastiao—get in!" There were carved paddles in the bottom of each canoe. "Take the girl with you!" Culhane turned to the powerful-looking girl, trying to keep his eyes off her magnificent chest. "Get in with him!"

Fred looked at him, puzzled. He shrugged, then repeated the command in Greek.

The girl's face lit up. She nodded her head and bounded into the canoe. Culhane thought for a moment she would upend it. Once in, she shouted something to Sebastiao.

Sebastiao turned and looked at Culhane. "What did she say, *senhor*?"

"She told you to hurry up—in Greek." And Culhane turned and looked at Mulrooney. "In Greek!"

And Mulrooney doubled over with laughter. "Eureka—an Amazon—ha!"

"*Modern* Greek," Culhane told her. Her face fell. "Some of the letters are pronounced differently from ancient Greek, and some of the grammar's different, too. Fred knows modern Greek. She's just a Greek-speaking, giant-sized girl who runs around more than half naked and lives in the Brazilian jungle. She's no Amazon, sweetheart."

"Shit," Mulrooney hissed, looking like a disappointed little girl.

"Get in the other canoe. Hurry it up, kid!" Then Culhane shouted across the water to the Greek girl and Sebastiao, not knowing the Greek word for spear. He swung his arm as if he held one.

One of the spears the girl had placed into the bottom of the canoe sailed back toward him, Culhane catching it in his right hand. His left hand held the four-inch .44; the six-inch was holstered.

"What the hell are you doing?"

"Letting the air out of their tires. Get the canoe ready to move!" Culhane rammed the second revolver into his belt. Hearing the war cries even louder now, he plunged the spear into the floor of one dugout after another, puncturing each several times so the boats could not be used.

Two more to go—and the war cries were louder. Culhane wheeled toward the water, shoving Mulrooney's dugout out toward the current. "I'll catch up to you—go on!"

"No!"

"Start paddling!" Culhane shouted, turning to the next dugout and attacking it with a vengeance.

The war cries were louder.

Three down, one to go, then the shaft of the spear broke. "Damn!" Culhane drew his revolver and fired into the bottom of the canoe twice, then kicked at the side, gouging a third hole.

He looked toward the river. Mulrooney's canoe was caught in the current now, and Sebastiao sat in the other canoe, the Greek girl standing, a bow in her hands, an arrow ready to fly. Culhane wheeled toward the jungle. The Uruentes were coming at him.

Sebastiao's rifle cracked.

Culhane emptied the four-inch revolver into four bodies, then ran downriver, paralleling the canoes. The crack of Sebastiao's rifle echoed again.

Ahead he could see rapids along the river. "Wonderful," he snarled to himself. The reason there was no riverboat was because they were on a fork of the river and not on the Negro at all. He knew there were no rapids along the Negro here. "Rapids ahead—watch out—turn back!" Culhane shouted as he ran along the riverbank.

Mulrooney nodded and began paddling fiercely, Sebastiao paddling, too, now, alternately firing his pistol shoreward.

Culhane kept running, trying to parallel Mulrooney's canoe. She was still headed into the rapids. "Lousy canoe paddler!" He kept running, drawing his six-inch .44 and snapping off a shot behind him, downing one of the Uruentes.

Mulrooney finally had the canoe holding its own. Culhane looked up. On the higher ground above the riverbank was a tree, the main trunk and a thick branch extending out over the water forming a Y-shape.

Culhane ran toward the tree, the six-inch back in the leather. He jumped, his fingers grabbing the low-hanging, long-reaching branch. He swung his legs up and rolled up onto the branch. There was no time now to crawl along its length. He was over the water and the slick rocks that fed out into the rapids from the riverbank, Uruente spears and arrows and darts zinging through the leaves around his body and head. Culhane fired the big .44 Magnum, then again and again and again. He had one bullet left, but four more Uruentes were dead.

He took advantage of the lull in the Uruente charge and crawled along the branch. He was nearly to the end of the thickest portion, perhaps thirty feet out over the river, Mulrooney at least another twenty feet away.

The canoe was holding back from the rapids, but Mulrooney seemed powerless to get it from the white water. Suddenly an alligator came toward the canoe, and Mulrooney raised the canoe paddle to beat it off.

She wasn't going to make it, he realized.

Culhane stabbed the revolver toward the alligator and fired—his last shot. The gator's body wrenched and twisted, coming half out of the water, then vanishing beneath the surface.

Culhane crawled another two yards, then jumped, a hail of Uruente arrows filling the air around him. Culhane's feet touched down onto the slick rocks, his hands going out, almost losing the revolver as he splayed out his arms and legs, slowing himself, stopping. He looked back to the riverbank. Uruente warriors fired arrows and hurled spears.

The rocks were as slick as ice. Culhane half ran, half skidded over their surface, stuffing the revolver into the leather, jumping the last three feet for Mulrooney's canoe. He realized now why it was not moving: it was wedged against the rocks. The upper half of his body inside the canoe, he dragged his legs after him. Something moved in the water around him as he pulled his body the rest of the way up and into the canoe.

He was soaked from midthigh down—and he was out of ammunition.

Uruente spears plunged into the water.

Some of the Uruente warriors were moving cautiously out onto the rocks.

Culhane grabbed Mulrooney's other paddle. "Do what I do but from your side of the canoe—and pray a lot!"

Culhane started shoving the butt of the paddle shaft against the rocks, trying to free the boat. One of the Uruentes had made it out along the rocks.

Culhane drew his empty gun and stabbed it toward the Indian. "Bang-bang, you bastard!" The Indian leaped into the water. Culhane guessed the Uruente preferred gators and piranha to a bullet. But the trick wouldn't work again.

The canoe lurched, and Culhane nearly lost his balance. "Paddle—fast—this way!"

He didn't look at Mulrooney, only heard her grunted agreement.

Gunfire blasted from Sebastiao's canoe, and more arrows sang from the nearly naked girl with him. Sebastiao and the girl had crossed to the far side of the river, and they were beginning now to pole their canoe along the opposite riverbank with their paddles to escape the power of the downstream current.

Culhane was hoping to do the same. "Paddle faster, Fanny!"

"I'm paddling as fast as I can!"

And then they were out of the strongest part of it, Culhane feeling the resistance change against his paddle, against the dugout itself, the water quieter. They were nearing the opposite bank. And they were out of range of the Uruentes.

Sebastiao and the Greek girl were moving out from the riverbank now, paddling upstream.

Culhane reached the far bank and dug his paddle into the mud, the dugout holding.

"You all right?"

"I think so. You're gonna get yourself killed someday and make me a widow before I'm a bride."

"Yeah, well. . ."

"Yeah, I know, Sean Dodge does this stuff before breakfast."

Culhane laughed, and grabbed her face with his right hand. He kissed her hard on the mouth, and then she buried her head against his chest. "I thought those Uruente guys had me—had us."

Culhane only nodded, still a little out of breath. "Let's go and catch up with Sebastiao and Fred." He shrugged out of his backpack and started to rifle through it, finally finding Mulrooney's blue canvas purse. "Thought you might like this back."

"They pulled all the stuff out."

"I found some of it. Hairbrush, lipstick—"

"Lipstick! Let me at it!" She started rifling through the bag. "Ha!" She opened it and pursed her lips.

"You realize how ridiculous this looks—you're a strange broad." But meanwhile he had found the spare box of ammo that was in the bottom of the pack.

Closing the pack, he started poling them upriver against the current, telling Mulrooney, "When you get through getting gorgeous, load my revolver and my Speedloaders, okay?"

"I can load the rifle, too. Is this water safe to wash my face with?"

"Watch out that nothing nips off the ends of your fingers. Better still, take the canteen off my pack and use some of that."

"Gotcha."

"And pass over the canteen when you're through. There's plenty of fresh water on the boat."

But he heard something as he poled them away from the bank and back into the deeper water. He heard gunfire, and as the roar of the rapids decreased, the sound of the gunfire became even louder.

The gunfire was ahead, beyond the bend in the river perhaps a mile away.

He closed his eyes for a moment, telling Mulrooney, "You might try and hurry up on those guns. And thanks for the rifle. So far, the field testing's going just great." And the gunfire ahead grew louder. It sounded like automatic weapons. The river bandits?

As they drew closer to the bend, Culhane could see the color of the water. It was the Negro, the river's color darker than the water in which they now traveled. He kept paddling. Sebastiao and the Greek girl's canoe slowed, and Culhane was nearly beside it now.

"The pirates, *senhor*?"

"Yes—I think so," Culhane called back.

"What do we do?"

"*Tin aftoh*?" asked the Greek girl.

Culhane looked at her. He couldn't think of the word for bandits. Then he looked at Mulrooney. She was doing some sign language, something like a gun being shot. A frown on her face. Her hands to her neck as though she were being strangled. Snatching her purse as though it were stolen.

The Greek girl smiled. *"Kleftiss!"*

"Charades," Culhane muttered.

Culhane looked downstream. The Uruentes had lit fires near the riverbank opposite them.

"What are they doing?" Mulrooney asked him.

Culhane took a pull from the canteen, then answered her. "Burning down trees. They can use vines to lash the trees together. The trees are small enough to burn quickly. Five or six together make a decent raft. They'll be following us as soon as they can."

"How long, *senhor*?"

"I don't know. I've never built a raft that way." But as if punctuating his words, there was a sudden snapping sound that could be heard above the gunfire. A tree was falling. "This is what they call the horns of a dilemma." The Greek girl looked worried. He told her not to be. And Culhane smiled. He was worrying enough for everybody.

They began to paddle, this time to make headway rather than merely to counter the current.

The bend in the river was growing in the distance, the gunfire more sporadic now. Culhane looked to the other canoe. Sebastiao was checking his rifle. He and Mulrooney paddled hard in silence.

They were nearly at the bend now, the darker waters of the Negro forming a downstream current. He was still trying to figure how they had gotten so far off position. He remembered fording a stream with the Bronco. Was that it . . . ?

Culhane stopped his musing. He saw ahead of them a camouflage-painted riverboat about the size of their own riverboat, gunmen hanging over the gunwales, firing, then diving down to cover. Parallel with them, off the nearer bank, was their own riverboat, guns popping up and firing, the white Ford Bronco parked by the bank.

It was no longer necessary to paddle except to steer as they turned into the bend, the current snatching the canoes like the claws of a ravenous animal.

Culhane drew the six-inch, ready.

Behind him, he heard Mulrooney working the lever of the Browning rifle.

Almost beside them and a little behind, he heard the bolt of Sebastiao's rifle being worked.

He glanced toward the second canoe. Sebastiao's face was set, grim. Behind him, poised on her knees with one of the Uruente spears in an upraised arm, was the Greek girl, the modern-day Amazon.

There was a novel in her, Culhane thought. Maybe he could get Fanny away from her crazy occult books to do some serious fiction. He thought about his own books: he was a fine one to lecture somebody about doing some serious writing.

"All right, Sean Dodge, let's see you top this!" Culhane rasped under his breath.

Behind him he heard Mulrooney's voice. "Hey—if we die or something, I love you."

"I love you, too, but we won't die. We're too tough."

"Sure we are." He heard her force a laugh.

The bandits' boat was anchored slightly upstream of the second riverboat. It meant that until Culhane and the others were very close, their canoes would not be seen. He judged the speed of the current. They would be sitting ducks for approximately three minutes—maybe four.

The current pulled them along. Two small motorized skiffs pulled away from the camouflaged riverboat, armed men firing from them as they made wide arcs, coming up on Santini and Helene Chavez and the others from both sides. Someone from Santini's boat fired, and one of the river bandits went down into the water, the water foaming with piranha. The second boat came alongside, the three men with guns jumping from it to the gunwales of the riverboat, one of them shoved into the water. Again there was the flash of white foam, then a scream.

But there was fighting aboard Santini's boat now. The second skiff came alongside and two men jumped to the riverboat, both skiffs then pulling back to their own boat. Culhane was tempted to snatch the rifle from Mulrooney's hands and fire at one of the skiff pilots, but it would have been a hard shot and given away their presence. He kept guiding the canoe instead.

The skiffs set out again from the bandits' boat as soon as they touched her port and starboard sides. More men were aboard. They were taking the fight to the deck of the riverboat.

Culhane steered the canoe and waited.

Their distance from the pirate vessel was perhaps fifty yards. At any moment they would be spotted by one of the bandits.

"Get ready, Fanny!"

"Be reckless!"

"Right—"

Culhane shot a glance toward the second canoe. Sebastiao still looked grim. The Greek girl's face seemed oddly at peace. He wished his Greek was better, so he could talk with her more. Culhane waited.

He saw a face by the portside gunwale of the bandits' boat, and saw an assault rifle leveled. Culhane stabbed the six-inch .44 Mag Smith outward and double-actioned the trigger. The bandit's body jackknifed, then snapped back and disappeared beneath the gunwale.

Culhane shoved his revolver back into the holster and shouted to Mulrooney: "Use the rifle. And keep down!" He started paddling, alternating his strokes from port to starboard to port again, Sebastiao's rifle cracking, another of the bandits down, the body toppling into the water. The Greek girl worked the paddle of the dugout. She could have rowed in the Olympics, Culhane thought.

Port. Starboard. Cut the paddle in. Knife it through the water. Port. Starboard.

Gunfire sprinkled the water around them, a hole now in the prow of the dugout. Culhane kept paddling, hearing the crack of the .44 Magnum rifle in Mulrooney's hands, earsplitting so close to him. The riverboat deck was a battleground. And he could see Santini, the priest who had been a Green Beret, taking on two of the bandits in unarmed combat on the roof of the cabin. Sean Dodge was supposed to be good at tae kwon-do. Santini, as Culhane watched, was better. He had the grace of a ballet dancer, the speed...Culhane was awestruck.

He dug in his paddle, the distance to the riverboat narrowing to twenty-five yards.

Mulrooney fired the rifle again from behind him, then again and again. One of the bandits splashed down into the river as Culhane looked back.

Less than twenty yards now. He dug in his paddle. Port. Starboard. He kept going.

The crack of Sebastiao's rifle again, then again and again.

Culhane looked to the stern of the riverboat. One of

the bandits was raising an assault rifle to fire at them. Culhane pulled in the paddle, drew the six-inch from its holster, double-actioned it once, then twice more, the bandit's body rocking with the last two rounds, falling.

Culhane holstered the revolver and dug in the paddle, the dugout moving faster now, Culhane aiming for the starboard side amidships.

In the prow of the riverboat was another bandit. "Fanny—the front of the boat!" Mulrooney's rifle cracked, then cracked again, the bandit's rifle discharging into the water on full-auto, the body crumbling, tumbling overboard. After what seemed like only a second, the bones floated to the surface.

"Jesus! What's that?"

"Piranha."

"Aren't they the fish that eat people?"

"They're not that picky. They eat anything."

Mulrooney's rifle cracked again, but the direction sounded different to Culhane. She would be firing toward the pirate boat, or perhaps at one of the small skiffs.

Ten yards now. Culhane dug in, propelling the dugout toward the portside gunwales. A face peered up, blood-smeared, a pistol in the right hand. One of the bandits. Culhane drew his revolver and emptied the last two rounds toward the face above the gunwales, at the same time hearing the rifle crack once, then once again in Mulrooney's hands.

The face wasn't there anymore, but there was a smear of blood on the gunwales.

Culhane pulled the paddle once more and they were beside the riverboat. Culhane drew his second revolver and shouted to Fanny Mulrooney, "You're gonna have to go first—I have to hold the canoe here. Hurry—and be careful!"

Mulrooney, her purse slung across her body like Culhane wore his Norwegian bag, started clambering over the edge of the canoe, the rifle in her hands.

Sebastiao and the Greek girl were coming. "Hurry!" Culhane shouted it in Greek; after all, the girl was doing the paddling.

Culhane grabbed up his backpack and canteen, heaved them onto the riverboat, then got up, letting the canoe drift from under his feet as he rolled over onto the deck planks. He heard Mulrooney's rifle discharging, and he wheeled to his knees, the four-inch stabbing outward. Mulrooney had killed one of the bandits, the body flopping back and over the gunwale into the river.

Culhane was up and moving, firing the revolver as armed men rushed for him.

And the revolver was suddenly empty.

Culhane stabbed the useless revolver into his belt and found the Bali-Song. He grabbed Mulrooney, and dragged her toward the cabin bulkhead. "Stay here—here!" Culhane gave her the engineer's bag and both revolvers. "Load 'em up—use this until you do." He handed her the big Gerber.

"But Josh—"

"Stay here, dammit!"

A man came at him with a revolver turned backward to be used as a bludgeon. Culhane blocked the blow, ramming the Bali-Song in under the armpit and into the chest, wrenching it out, kicking the man in the crotch and throwing him over the gunwale.

More of the bandits were coming now in the skiffs. Culhane shook his head, turning to the cabin roof. Santini was locked in combat with a man with a machete; two others were hammering at him with their fists.

Culhane flipped up to the cabin roof.

"Damascus!" Culhane hurled himself at the nearest

of the bandits, prying the man away from Santini, ramming the knife into the man's kidney, kicking the body over the side of the cabin roof. Culhane wheeled to one of the others, but a pistol raked down across Culhane's right wrist, the Bali-Song clattering to the roof, skidding down across it.

Culhane's left foot snapped up and out, catching his attacker in the groin, his aching right hand slamming across the man's face, his left fist hammering up into the bandit's Adam's apple.

Santini's man flew past him, screaming as he skidded off the cabin roof, across the companionway and over the gunwales into the water.

Culhane's left hauled back and plowed into his own assailant's face. Santini's right shot forward, Culhane seeing it in a blur, both of them connecting on Culhane's man, forcing him down.

Santini crossed himself. "God forgive me—I caused that man's death."

Culhane just looked at him and blinked. He felt his balance going and steadied himself. The riverboat was underway, the captain at the tiller, a pistol in one hand, blood streaking down from his right temple.

And Culhane saw why. The bandits in their camouflaged boat were almost alongside now, the two boats less than ten yards apart.

The bandit boat to starboard, Culhane jumped from the roof to port.

"Lose this?" It was Mulrooney and she had his Bali-Song.

Culhane took it and smiled. "We've got trouble."

"Why didn't you write romance novels? We could just stay at home and make love to research them and—" Then she noticed Santini and actually blushed. "Oh—hi, Father!"

"You must be Fanny. I'm pleased to meet you." He offered his hand as he crouched beside them behind the cabin exterior bulkhead.

"You're the military expert," Culhane said to Santini. "What now?"

"Wait. If they cross to this boat, we fight them—but I don't think they will."

"The suitcases?" Culhane asked.

"The suitcases? You're worried about your luggage?" Mulrooney squeaked.

"The suitcases," Santini said, smiling, gesturing belowdecks.

"Right," Mulrooney said. "Don't anybody tell me anything."

"You should talk about the books I write. If it weren't for your crazy books, we wouldn't be in this mess. We wouldn't even be in Brazil. I would have gone back to Miami after the Russians sank *Seacutter*."

"Sank *Seacutter*?"

"Tell you later."

Culhane took his revolvers from Mulrooney, and his other knife. He took the bag, leaving her the rifle.

The riverboat shuddered, but there was no gunfire.

Culhane peered over the cabin roof. The bandits' boat was locked beside their starboard side, pushing them, its engines evidently more powerful. Culhane looked forward. The river split again, forming another downstream fork. And there were rapids.

"We're going to work again," Culhane snapped, pushing past Mulrooney.

The rain poured down now, washing off the wide brim of Culhane's Stetson in rivulets. Mulrooney was soaked, her blouse clinging to her breasts and almost transparent.

Culhane heard a scream. He ran from behind the

cabin bulkhead, and behind the packing crates aft, Magdelena was bandaging the Japanese, his left arm and bare chest smeared with blood. "Look—"

Bandits were poised by the gunwale of their own riverboat. The gap had closed to less than six feet. Culhane started to go for his gun, but he didn't make it. A hail of gunfire peppered the bulkhead near him, Culhane throwing himself down beside Magdelena and the Japanese. There was more blood now: the Japanese man was dead, shot through the head. The Brazilian girl was screaming. "This is crazy—this is—"

Culhane pulled her close to him, shielding her body with his. "Santini—get some fire laid down to cover us!"

He couldn't hear a response; he could barely hear himself. The deck shuddered violently under him, and he looked up. The gunfire slackened, then stopped.

Both riverboats were locked together, jammed somehow or perhaps lashed together by the bandits. Culhane looked ahead. They had gotten into the other stream, both boats now sucked along in the powerful downstream current, spray lashing over the bows, the rapids ahead.

There was a shouted curse and Culhane looked to the bandits' boat. They were boarding. Culhane grabbed Magdelena and dragged her back around the corner of the cabin. Fanny Mulrooney was still there, clutching the rifle.

"Who's she?"

"Magdelena. A passenger. Take care of her, Fanny." Culhane ran past them, searching for Santini. A wall of packing crates had been built to shield the captain and his tiller in the stern, his two remaining crewmen. The third lay dead on the deck, flanking him, guns drawn.

Santini and Sebastiao were completing another wall of packing crates.

Culhane raced back along the deck, grabbing Mulrooney by the forearm, hustling her aft, then Magdelena, as well. Where was Helene Chavez, he wondered.

Gunfire ripped through the air from the prow where a half-dozen bandits had come aboard and from the stern where the captain and his two crewmen were returning fire. He heard the crack of Sebastiao's rifle.

Culhane started aft.

"Fanny!" He couldn't see her anymore, the rain and the spray of the river water combining to make a gray veil covering the boat. The roar of the rapids was deafening. "Fanny!"

Santini was at his arm. "Below! I sent her below with Magdelena—Helene Chavez is down there—she's scared to death!"

"She's more sensible than I thought."

Culhane edged along beside Santini, bullets peppering the packing crates and the cabin bulkhead, skid marks from spent slugs marking the deck planks, the deck itself ice-slick with spray and rain.

Culhane held his six-inch in his right fist, settling between Santini and Sebastiao behind the first pile of crates, the captain and his two crewmen behind the second. The crates were higher behind Culhane, Sebastiao and Santini, and the captain's two crewmen were firing over them from standing positions. Sebastiao put down his rifle and drew his pistol.

"They're rushing us!" Santini shouted over the cacaphony of gunfire and the roar of the water.

The boat rocked and swayed and bounced. Culhane leveled the six-inch, firing as the first wave of bandits came over the cabin roof, hurtling themselves down. Culhane caught one on the fly, and then the fighting was hand to hand, Santini locked in combat with one of them, gunfire coming from behind Culhane as he wrestled one of the bandits on the deck between the packing crates.

Culhane heard the boom of a rifle and felt the body over him go limp.

Mulrooney held his rifle in the cabin doorway. "Look out!" From the cabin roof another of the bandits was aiming a pistol toward her. She started to turn. Culhane snatched up his revolver from the slick deck and fired twice, the bandit's body flipping back, out of sight and gone.

Culhane holstered his revolver and ran to Mulrooney, shoving her back through the cabin door, giving her his four-inch revolver. "Take this—just in case—"

"I know. Save three rounds for the other two women and myself. Where's Fred?"

As if on cue, Culhane saw her. She had carried the fight to the bandits' boat itself and was surrounded by a half-dozen river pirates.

"Stay here!"

"Bullshit!"

Culhane shook his head, took back his four-inch, and holstered it.

He ran, half skidding, toward the locked-together gunwales, jumping like a hurdler, crashing down into a knot of bandits on the far deck, his right fist hammering out into a face, his left losing itself in an enemy abdomen, his right knee smashing upward into a groin.

There was a shot, and a man with a machete collapsed inches from Culhane's right side.

Mulrooney was on the far deck of the riverboat, the rifle to her shoulder.

Culhane jumped from the cabin roof, grabbed on to one of the bandits, and wrestled the man to his knees.

Culhane's right knee smashed into the man's mouth, knocking him to the deck.

Fred wheeled, her spear hacking across the neck of one of them.

At least eight of the bandits still remained. The camouflaged boat was like the very tiny car in the clown act at the circus: more and more men kept coming out.

Culhane grabbed at the girl. "Fred—Me-em-ef!" He pointed to Mulrooney. The Greek girl nodded and jumped from the cabin roof, using the spear like a club over the head of one of the bandits as she leaped over the locked-together gunwales.

Santini, Sebastiao, and the two crewmen, one of them wounded now, were fighting more of the bandits on the riverboat deck between the walls of packing crates.

From his vantage point atop the cabin roof of the bandits' craft, Culhane could see the full extent of the rapids ahead. Walls of rocks, like massive tombstones, rose from the foam and spray, and in the distance he could see horizon only, as if the river dropped away from sight. "Holy Jesus!" A waterfall.

Culhane jumped down to the deck, almost losing his footing. One of the bandits charged him, but Culhane drew his revolver and fired into the man's chest.

Grappling hooks locked the two vessels together at the bows. The hooks were secured to the deck of the camouflaged riverboat with massive lines. Culhane drew the Gerber and hacked at the nearest line, but hacking did no good. He began working the sawtooth edge over the rope, the blade biting through it now, one of the ropes nearly cut, and then it snapped, the rope snapping back and cutting his right side.

Culhane reeled, staggering back against the cabin bulkhead. He shook his head, a cascade of water rolling off the brim of his Stetson.

He dragged himself from the cabin bulkhead, gunfire sporadically hitting the deck.

If he was hurt, he was hurt, he told himself, but he had to finish the job. Locked together, both vessels would be powerless to avoid going over the falls to certain death. Culhane began working at the second rope holding the second grappling hook in place. One strand snapped, then a second, then a third. Culhane stepped back as he hacked at the last strand, the rope whipping past his face inches from him.

The boats were still wedged together, but if he could cut the last rope and get the captain to give the riverboat all it had, they'd break clear. They had to break clear, Culhane told himself.

He began working the third rope.

Behind him he heard the bolt of a submachine gun, the click barely audible, and he spun around. It was the bearded man, the one named José Maria de Jesus. "You die, *senhor*!"

Culhane reached out his right hand with the knife in it, as if for a thrust, but he wheeled left, dropping to the deck to his left hand and left knee, his right leg snapping up and out, the Uzi submachine gun flying upward, discharging in a long ragged burst. Culhane's foot again snapped out, smashing into the bandit leader's crotch, the bandit leader crashing back along the deck, his head colliding with the cabin bulkhead, the body sagging. Culhane was on his feet, the knife ready. The bandit leader was out cold.

Culhane sawed and hacked frantically at the third and last rope, the rope nearly cut through.

One final swing with all his strength and the rope snapped, Culhane reeling back, the rope flying past his face. And the two boats began to separate.

"Culhane!" Fanny Mulrooney lay spread-eagled on the cabin roof opposite him. "Culhane!"

Culhane sheathed the knife and started into a dead run for the prow. He threw himself over the prow of the bandits' vessel, his hands reaching out, grasping for the gunwale of the riverboat, but his finger slipped and his left hand lost its grip. He hung there, dragged through the water now, but the water was too rough here for piranha, he kept telling himself. He got his right hand up, spitting water as it washed over him, his hat brim dropping low over his eyes. He pulled his body up and got his right arm over the gunwale. He hauled himself up, rolling onto the deck planking.

One of the bandits stood above him, an assault rifle in his hands, the barrel aimed at Culhane's head. "American!"

But the bandit's body trembled, shuddered, then fell forward, the rifle discharging over Culhane's head.

A single patch of red appeared dead center in the man's back. Culhane looked to the cabin roof. Mulrooney was there, holding his rifle.

"Thanks, kid!"

Culhane started aft to warn the captain that the falls were only a few hundred yards ahead now.

Fighting was still hand to hand on the riverboat. The Greek girl was wedged between two bandits, Santini ripping one of them from her, punching the man in the face, sending him sprawling across the deck. Both crewmen were dead on the deck. Sebastiao was hitting another of the bandits with the butt of his rifle.

Culhane could not see past the packing crates to the captain. He had to get to the captain and get him to alter course if he could, or he'd have to take the tiller himself.

"Culhane!"

Culhane wheeled. One of the two bandits Santini and the Greek girl had fought was rushing Culhane with a machete. Mulrooney fired, but the machete-wielding bandit didn't stop.

Culhane reached to the deck, picked up a packing crate—it was heavier than he thought—and launched it against his attacker. As it struck the man down to the deck, Culhane read the nearly washed-out stenciled labeling on the crate: KITCHEN SINK.

He'd always wanted to throw in the kitchen sink.

The captain was shouting in Portuguese, and Culhane raced to the tiller to help. The rapids were straight ahead.

The captain, blood pumping in tiny spurts from a head wound, wrestled the tiller as though it were an enemy. He was shouting over the roar of the water, "I cannot control the helm!" Culhane reached for the wheel, fighting it now as the captain did. The captain was sagging.

From behind him, Culhane heard Sebastiao shout, "The boat is almost at the waterfall!"

Culhane ran forward. "Damascus—get Fanny below! Hurry!"

"Right!"

The tiller wasn't responding.

The falls were less than a hundred yards ahead.

The pirate vessel, being somewhat lighter, had shot ahead. It was going over, the underside visible for one sickening instant and then the vessel was gone.

As the captain sank to his knees, he shouted, *"Bandidos. . .Malditos!"*

And his tongue lolled out, his eyes rolling open and back. He died cursing the bandits who had brought him to this.

Culhane threw his weight against the tiller. There was no speed control, but he might be able to guide the vessel into the rocks. If he could, there might be a chance to abandon her and get to safety.

Fifty yards to the falls.

Culhane felt new weight on the tiller—Sebastiao. The tiller was starting to move.

Santini was soon beside him. Then, inserting herself between Sebastiao and Culhane was Mulrooney. "Get below!"

"I can die here just the same. Anyway, I'm with you. So shut up and push!"

Culhane threw his weight against the tiller. It could snap and then all would be lost. But it moved, the four of them pressing their body weights against it, the prow turning.

"We will not make it, *senhor*!" cried Sebastiao.

"Like Fanny said—shut up and push!" Culhane gritted his teeth, feeling the tendons in his neck distending. The prow was turning. "Damascus—when we hit those rocks—if we do—you and Sebastiao get the other women and any gear you can salvage."

They weren't going tó make it, Culhane realized. The tiller had not moved enough.

And suddenly it did move. Culhane looked to his right. Beside Sebastiao stood the Greek girl Fanny Mulrooney called Fred, her well-developed muscles straining, her face set. And beside Fred was Magdelena, her teeth gritted, her lips drawn back over them.

Culhane threw himself against the tiller, shouting, "All together—now!"

The tiller moved hard to port, and the prow turned to starboard with a jerk.

And the riverboat crashed toward the rocks. Culhane loosed the tiller and took Mulrooney in his arms, throwing their bodies to the deck. "Sebastiao—get Fred!"

There was a shudder and the sound of cracking timbers.

And the boat stopped.

Culhane looked up, then got to his knees. Ahead lay the falls, some ten yards away.

Culhane hauled Fanny Mulrooney to her feet. "Damascus, you and Sebastiao get Helene and the gear! Fanny, tell Fred with your sign language to take Magdelena and my pack and my rifle. And hurry!"

Culhane was up, rushing toward the cabin. The cabin was awash with water a foot high. Culhane found Mulrooney's gear he and Sebastiao had stashed aboard before setting out after her. He threw her pack over one shoulder and her stuff sack over the other. Sebastiao was loading sacks on his body. Helene Chavez was screaming, and Culhane slapped her. She looked around her quietly, then fainted.

Culhane held a suitcase in each hand. Sebastiao, laden almost beyond belief, followed him. Santini was still packing gear.

The boat was breaking up. Culhane helped Mulrooney over the smashed gunwale and onto the rocks, throwing gear and the suitcases after her.

He picked Helene Chavez up in his arms like a rag doll and put her over onto the rocks.

Sebastiao was throwing gear over the side, then he clambered over.

Culhane looked to shore and saw Fred and Magdelena picking their way on hands and knees along the rocks toward the riverbank. Fred was loaded with gear.

Culhane helped Santini with his gear, then Santini flipped the rail one-handed and landed beside Sebastiao. The two men divided their burdens and started out along the rocks.

Culhane flipped the rail. If Santini could do it, so

could he, he told himself. He almost lost his footing, but Mulrooney was there beside him.

Culhane grabbed up the two suitcases. Mulrooney had her things and some other gear. They started along the riverbank. The rocks were slippery, and to navigate them it was necessary in some spots to crawl. Behind them there was a mighty groan and then a roar. The riverboat broke in half and disappeared from the rocks where it had been wedged. Over the falls. Gone.

Chapter Twenty-Seven

Culhane had cleaned his three guns and Mulrooney's revolver as well. The captain's gun had been a .38 Special, and among the gear Santini had grabbed when evacuating the vessel had been a box of 158-grain Round Nose Lead Remingtons.

Mulrooney sat beside him, wrapped in a blanket from head to foot.

"A million bucks?"

"Yeah—in gold."

"Can I see it?"

Culhane looked at her and smiled. "That's what Santini and I buried while Sebastiao and you and Fred and Magdelena set up camp."

"Later?"

"Yeah—later."

"Why does Helene Chavez just sit there—staring? She didn't do a damned thing to help on the riverboat. And she didn't do anything once we reached the riverbank."

Culhane looked at Helene Chavez across the fire. Mulrooney was right. The woman just sat and stared. "Some people, well, you know—some people just can't handle a crisis of any kind. They fall to pieces. I guess she's one of them. Poor character trait for a doctor out here, though."

He looked up from the holster he was polishing, and started to work on the belt with the leather cream.

Mulrooney smiled, saying, "Give her her due. Maybe she's hell on wheels in a medical emergency."

Culhane only shrugged. He looked at Mulrooney's face. What he could see of her hair was nearly dry and she was clean again—and so was he. The soaking they'd gotten had taken care of that. She was a pretty girl—the prettiest, he thought.

Sebastiao interrupted his thoughts. "I have been trying to remember, *senhor*."

"What, Sebastiao?"

"The girl—the one the *menina* calls Fred?"

"What about Fred?" Mulrooney asked.

"Twelve—maybe thirteen years ago. . . How old you say Fred is?"

"Twenty-five—maybe twenty-six," Culhane volunteered.

"Try twenty-one or twenty-two," Mulrooney said. "I've been around her a lot more than you. And I had a twenty-one-year-old woman's body once. Neither of you guys did."

Culhane started to laugh. "Depends on how you use the word 'had,' kid—" And he felt her elbow ram him in the rib cage.

"I'm serious—she's just little more than a teenager."

"If the *menina* is right, *senhor*," Sebastiao said, cleaning his revolver's bore with a brass rod and a patch, "then Fred is the one."

"The one what?" Mulrooney asked, leaning closer to Culhane, Culhane feeling her breath against his cheek.

"The one from the crash. Twelve or thirteen years ago—I do not remember exactly—this very rich Greek businessman—he owned mining properties and was a very famous flier—"

"Ah. . .wait a minute," Culhane cut in, trying to recall the name. "Name's on the tip of my tongue."

"Zorba?" Culhane just glared at Mulrooney and didn't answer her.

Sebastiao suddenly said it, "Archimedes?"

Mulroony shouted, "Lindy Archimedes! That's what they called him 'cause he did all those long-distance solo flights."

"Yes—and his plane crashed in the jungle on the way to one of his mining properties that was not yet developed. He had his wife and daughter with him. The little girl was eight or nine."

"And she's his daughter," Culhane murmured, looking across the fire at Fred. She had put on a shirt Sebastiao had given her and had helped Santini as he sorted through the medical supplies. Santini spoke some Greek; a Greek family had lived next door to his family when he was growing up and he'd picked up a few phrases.

"Then she's one of the richest women in the world, isn't she?" Culhane looked back to Mulrooney.

"She's a good girl—I'm almost happy she isn't a real Amazon," Mulrooney said after a moment. "It's gonna be tough for her to get used to civilization."

"She's going to need a friend most of all," Culhane said, putting his left arm around Fanny Mulrooney's shoulders. "And she's already got that." Mulrooney rested her head against his chest, content.

Magdelena had been preparing dinner, boiling the

water to be added to the freeze-dried meals Sebastiao
had stockpiled for Culhane and Mulrooney's originally
planned upriver trek. Magdelena had gathered together
firewood with Mulrooney's help and then volunteered
to handle everything. "It's time to eat," she announced.

"Sounds good to me," Culhane said.

"Hey, Fred, let's eat!" And Mulrooney stood, pulling her blanket around her more tightly and doing her
sign language again.

Culhane could have told the girl in Greek. So could
Santini. But Culhane looked at the smile on Fanny Mulrooney's face as she gestured, and said nothing.

CULHANE HAD EATEN THE BEEF STROGANOFF and the
chicken tetrazini. He leaned back on his elbow now,
popping a handful of M&Ms, washing the chocolate
down with a canteen cup a quarter filled with rum that
he and Mulrooney shared. M&Ms had been invented
during World War II to provide G.I.'s with a candy that
would not melt under tropical conditions. The guy who
had invented it, Culhane decided, knew his stuff. Culhane had stashed the Myers's rum among his socks and
underwear inside his pack, and was pleased to discover
that the bottle hadn't shattered.

Mulrooney took a handful of M&Ms and through a
mouthful of candy said, "The one advantage of being
an adult is you get the chance to act like a kid and you
don't have any parents around to tell you not to."

"Very profound," Culhane said. He picked up the
canteen cup and took another swallow of the dark rum.

"I'm serious," she said, Culhane lighting a cigarette
for her. "Here we are—stuffed—and now we're eating
candy."

"Later we're going to make love."

"Right. Later we're gonna—" And suddenly he

could see her teeth sparkle in the firelight as she shifted closer to him. "Later we're gonna make love."

He folded his arm around her.

In the years of pursuing his research, in the years of missing deadlines because of it—whether fighting a human adversary or a page count for a manuscript—Culhane had learned that if you worked hard at whatever it was you were doing, you had to relax hard, too.

Over dinner, Santini, Culhane and Sebastiao had worked out a watch schedule. Mulrooney had complained, but not too vigorously, that excluding the women from taking a tour on guard was chauvinistic. Culhane had agreed with her and told her to be quiet. Sebastiao had the watch now, Santini would be next, and Culhane would take the last shift from four until eight.

They would set out then, eat along the trail as needed, and head upriver to the mission station near the small town of Ontem. Culhane was not yet late with the gold, and despite the setbacks, a hard day's travel would bring the two suitcases to their rendezvous almost on time.

To have set out on the trip at night—there were painted jaguars, margays and snakes roaming the jungle—could have been insanity. And all of them were exhausted.

Culhane stubbed out his cigarette and started to reach for the cup of rum.

"Do not move!"

The English was good. The accent was Russian.

Culhane started for his four-inch 629 beside him. Helene Chavez screamed, and there was a burst of assault rifle fire into the air. "Do not move or the women die first!"

Culhane didn't move. He looked at Mulrooney. "Your Russians?"

"I guess so."

"Aww, nuts—"

The riverbank campsite was ringed now with men stepping from the shadows. But Culhane didn't feel so bad being taken totally off guard, because he recognized the fatigues—and even some of the faces: Soviet Special Forces. These were the same people from the freighter, some of them the same people who had attacked *Seacutter* and killed Jake and Melissa Burroughs.

"What do you want here?" Santini asked.

The man who had spoken—Culhane had seen the face before. He stepped forward more into the light, no weapon visible except a pistol in a flap holster at his right hip. "I am Major Fyodor Kruglovitch. The identity of the unit that I command is not for your consideration at this time."

He looked down toward Culhane and Mulrooney. "And you, young lady, you must be the bothersome American journalist Miss Mulrooney."

Mulrooney said nothing.

The major stared at Culhane. "And who are you?"

"Josh Culhane. How are ya?"

"Well, sir—quite. You are apparently the gentleman who was to be aboard *Seacutter*. I wonder how we missed you."

"Don't blame yourself—you tried real hard."

"Thank you very much." The major bowed slightly. He strode across the campsite to where Fred stood. "And you must be the Amazon girl Miss Mulrooney was looking for."

Fred spit at his boots.

"She's no Amazon. I thought she was, but—" Mulrooney began.

"Quiet!"

"No, dammit—*you* be quiet and hear me out. She's

the daughter of a Greek hotshot whose plane crashed in the jungle a dozen years ago—''

A voice Culhane had not heard before—the English excellent, the accent Greek or Armenian—interrupted Mulrooney.

''The missing daughter of Lindy Archimedes. The plane wreckage was found, as were the bodies of Archimedes and his wife, but never their daughter.''

Culhane's eyes flashed toward Fred. At the mention of the name Archimedes, tears began to roll down her cheeks.

''It appears you are both right,'' the major said.

''We still have the map,'' the gray-bearded, gray-haired man who had mentioned Archimedes's name said. ''She knows of this.''

''What map?'' Mulrooney snapped.

One of the Soviet troops took the revolver from beside Culhane, snatching up his gun belt and his rifle, as well. ''Where's the man who was on guard?'' Culhane demanded.

''He had a slight accident and hit his head. Probably fatal.''

Culhane started to get to his feet. ''You son of a bitch—'' But the muzzle of an AKS-74 was jabbed toward his face, and he sat back down beside Mulrooney.

''Professor Xanthos—'' the major began.

Beside him Culhane heard Mulrooney hiss, ''Xanthos! He's—''

The major was still talking. ''Your estimate is that this Amazon capital is a day or a day and a half's march. We will take these people with us. They can be disposed of later.''

''What are you after?'' asked Santini.

The major turned to him. ''That question is more properly addressed to Professor Xanthos.''

Culhane looked at Xanthos. "Gold? Archeological treasure? What?"

Mulrooney laughed. "I know what he's after. He's searched for it all over the world. Before he became a Communist he was all over the Florida Everglades. When he gave up on that, he was in Africa. He doesn't want gold or anything like that. He's after one thing. The Fountain of Youth kinda fizzled on him, and he thinks the Amazons live forever and he wants to know how come—so he can, too."

Chapter Twenty-Eight _____

He had spent the early evening hours in Miami, Florida. He had been there before, but he had never been to Chicago and he sniffed the air—crisp and cool, much like the air in Argentina in the wintertime. Mounds of snow were piled in the distance beyond the runways, and as he walked toward the gray car waiting some distance away, the American FBI agent said to him, "Watch your step, Inspector. It can get a little slippery out here on the runways."

"I shall endeavor to do so."

"I don't imagine it gets like this very often in Brazil, right?"

"Wrong, *senhor*. It *never* gets like this in Brazil." Hoevermann chuckled and clapped the man on the shoulder. He shivered in his khaki trench coat. He hoped it would be warm in the car.

"I bet you've got the giant jet lag that attacked the earth," the FBI man said, and smiled good-naturedly.

He was under thirty, red-haired, and scrubbed looking, like so many Americans always seemed to be to Hoevermann.

"No—but I will tomorrow or the next day. As soon as I conclude my affairs here, I must return to my country with all possible speed."

"We have been briefed, sir. The Florida Department of Law Enforcement transmitted copies of the statement from the Palmer Industries pilot regarding his cargo."

"There was a second plane—a small one. It landed in the Keys—your customs authorities assumed them to be smugglers of drugs. Your federal drug people discovered that the cargo was machine tools from a Palmer factory. This is where the Palmer pilot picked up his shipment—*not* at its supposed point of origin. This is what worries me."

"Then you think Palmer was too cheap to come up with the million dollars in gold for the ransom of his wife?"

Hoevermann stopped walking, looking at the FBI agent. "Agent—"

"Summerfield, sir. Robert Summerfield."

"Senhor Summerfield. I do not doubt Senhor Palmer's sincerity in the slightest. I am sure he fulfilled the demands of the terrorist kidnappers to the letter."

"But you just said—"

"What they demanded, I fear, was—if you will forgive a mixed metaphor—a pearl of far greater price. And if he gave it to them—" He sighed. "The story of Pandora from Greek mythology—do you know it?"

"Yes—yes, I do."

An aircraft was taking off at the far end of the field and neither of them spoke for a moment. Hoevermann stared at the sleek business jet he had been provided with to fly north. As the aircraft noise died, he said, "Pandora opened a box and loosed evil upon the world. I fear it will be the same with Senhor Palmer's suitcase—his Pandora's boxes, as it were." He was very cold now, and he walked more quickly toward the waiting car.

Chapter Twenty-Nine

Culhane had told Mulrooney where he and Santini had buried the gold. As they moved through the jungle now, darkness still upon them but their way clear, bats, giant moths and birds fluttering at the massive hand-held spotlights of the Russians, Helene Chavez came up beside him. "Where did you put the gold—in case we don't all make it."

"Father Santini knows. I know. That's enough."

It was actually easy enough walking. The floor of the rain forest was brighter than it was in daytime with the artificial lighting. And all of his gear and his weapons had been taken by the Russians. Even his watch and his belt had been taken. They had left him his cigarettes and his lighter. But they had also left him something else; Soviet Special Forces needed to upgrade their prisoner-search techniques, Culhane thought happily. Before leaving the United States he had made a small purchase. It was a stainless-steel, razor-sharp knife the size and shape of a ballpoint pen, and looked totally innocent. And it was still in the left breast pocket of his army-surplus olive drab shirt. The blade was long enough to be damaging in a fight.

But the question was how to use it—if he could use it at all.

He kept walking, holding Fanny Mulrooney's right hand in his left. Helene Chavez fell back behind them.

"Why didn't you tell her I know?" Mulrooney whispered.

"I don't trust her to hold up if the Russians get rough. Somehow I don't think she likes you too much." Mulrooney wore faded blue jeans much like Culhane's and a new khaki shirt, her hat as wet as his and looking it, but pulled down over her eyes. "Just hang loose," Culhane told her.

"I'm loose already. What are you going to do?"

"Why do you awlays expect me to know what to do?"

"You write adventure novels. I write about the occult and the supernatural and unexplained phenomena—right?"

"Right," he told her, lighting a cigarette, then taking her hand again.

"Fine. If we bump into one of these bats and it turns into a human vampire, I know just what to do. That's my department. We run into Russian army bad guys, that's your department."

"Oh," Culhane said, and nodded.

"I've still got my copy of the map. I put it in a Ziploc bag and sewed it inside the lining of my hat."

"So let's escape from the Russians and find the lost Amazon city, right?"

"Well—"

Culhane started to say something, but he stopped himself. They walked on.

MARY FRANCES MULROONEY JUDGED they had been walking for nearly two hours, and her feet hurt in her wet boots. But Culhane still held her hand.

Things could have been worse, she reminded herself.

All the Russians would do when they killed her was kill her, not boil her first to torture her. She shivered at the thought, remembering the Uruente village.

At least she and Culhane would die together. She felt sorry for Fred who would never really know her own background, her own identity. And as for Sebastiao... such a gentle, good little man. And now dead.

She heard some animal noises in the jungle beyond the glow of the lights, and she held Culhane's hand a little tighter. She'd ask the major before he had them shot, and maybe he'd be decent about it. Could she hold Culhane's hand. A last request.

Under her breath she told herself, "All right, M.F., don't give up."

Beside her, Culhane said, "You say something?"

"No, just thinking out loud." She smiled at him.

He would think of something. He always had in the past. Or she would think of something. And there was Father Santini. An ex-Green Beret, a jungle fighter. He'd think of something. And Fred, she was a warrior, a fighter. Maybe Fred would think of something. Even Magdelena, who now walked alongside Helene and Fred, might think of something.

Her spirits rose. Somebody would think of something.

Then her spirits fell. A spear suddenly impaled the Russian guard just a few yards in front of them. It went through the chest, nailing him to the ground, his body wriggling, gurgling sounds coming from his lips.

It had to be the Uruentes. Maybe...

Culhane pushed Mulrooney into the underbrush and out of the light. "Stay low—get outta here if you can, Fanny. I love you!" And she fell and rolled into the darkness and he was gone. When she looked up, Culhane had the guard's assault rifle and was firing into the trees as tall, leggy, beautiful brunets wearing glittering gold breastplates and golden bracelets swung down from the trees, screaming war cries she could not understand.

These had to be Amazons, she told herself. *Real* Amazons. The Russians opened fire and some of the women went down, but spears and arrows filled the air, Culhane's assault rifle firing until it was empty.

She started for him, but Culhane threw himself between Helene Chavez and one of the Amazons wielding a massive war club. Culhane's rifle butt cracked and broke away, and the war club struck him down. Mulrooney pushed herself to her feet but felt something tackle her.

She rolled back into the undergrowth. It was Fred, and Fred's voice hissed in her right ear: "Amazonas!"

Mulrooney tried to move, but Fred pinned her arms and legs. She could only watch. The word Amazon meant "breastless," because according to legend they would cleave off their right breasts in order to better fire their bows. But from their low-cut armor one thing was clear: they all had unbelievable figures, everything intact. She tugged against Fred, trying to free herself to go to Culhane.

Santini was fighting with his hands and feet. A club smashed down across his back and he fell. Some of the Russian soldiers ran off into the jungle. The older man Josh Culhane had said was most likely some kind of sergeant was stabbed through the heart with a spear. Dead.

Mulrooney stared at one of the women whose armor was set with jewels. She wore a golden collar that covered the front of her neck and looked centuries old. She was as tall as a fashion model, but strong muscles rippled as she moved, her hair wild as if it had a life of its own. Mulrooney wished her hair would do that.

The statuesque woman—their leader, Mulrooney decided—swung her war club and downed the Russian major.

Three of his men were still standing, the rest dead, wounded or gone. Ringed now by Amazon women armed with bows and spears and clubs, the three men lay down their weapons. Outside the circle, crumpled in a ball, blood running down her left arm, was Magdelena.

Mulrooney sagged against Fred. She wanted to weep. And she wanted to kill.

Santini was rolled face up. The Amazon leader bent over him, touched at his hair, then ripped the clerical collar from his neck. One of her women drew back on her bow, but the leader pushed the arrow from the bow and threw down the collar. They walked from Santini to the Russian officer. Again, she felt the man's hair and turned his face from side to side as if studying it. She bent over him and forced open his mouth. The Russian stirred, but a spear was put against his throat and he didn't move anymore. The Amazon leader nodded, and the Russian was hauled up to his knees, his arms drawn behind him, his wrists lashed together.

Mulrooney noticed the three remaining Russian soldiers who had surrendered. Their teeth and hair were inspected. One of them—very slim, almost effeminate looking—was held by two of the Amazons and his trousers and underwear were cut away. One of the Amazons pointed at his genitals and laughed. Then she drew her knife and slashed it across the Russian's throat. Mulrooney sucked in her breath to scream, but Fred's hand covered her mouth and she could not. Mulrooney nodded, and the pressure eased.

The Russian boy's body sagged to the ground and his wrists were unbound. Mulrooney guessed that the rope was not to be wasted.

She had seen Professor Xanthos fall when a club was smashed against his legs. His head bled, and his left leg seemed twisted and bent. The women dragged him to a standing position, and the man screamed with pain. The Amazon leader laughed.

His throat was slit, blood spurting like—Mulrooney didn't know like what. It was the sort of thing Culhane described so graphically in his books. Fred's hand was over her mouth again, but Mulrooney made no attempt to scream.

Culhane.

Culhane was dragged to his feet, his hands bound behind him by two of the Amazons, Culhane shaking his head as though trying to clear it.

As the Amazon leader approached, he was pushed down to his knees. She stood before him.

"Bite it, lady!" Culhane snarled.

The Amazon cuffed him across the face and a knife was pressed to his throat. Mulrooney fought against Fred to break free, to do something, anything. But Fred's hand was still over her mouth.

She could not break free, could not scream.

Culhane was not killed.

The Amazon leader forced open his mouth, two more of the women holding his head. She checked his teeth. She knotted her hand in his hair and jerked his head back. There was laughter from the leader.

For a moment Mulrooney felt shame for him—to have women do this to him. Would they cut away his pants as well?

They did not. He was dragged to his feet and shoved beside the Russian major, then forced down to his knees again. The two Russian soldiers were placed beside them.

The Amazon leader kicked at the body of Helene Chavez and rolled it over. She placed her hands on her impossibly slim waist and laughed out loud. She bent over Helene Chavez and tore at her blouse, ripping the fabric away. The knife came out, but she only cut away Helene Chavez's bra. The leader called to some of the others. Several of the other women came and stood around Helene Chavez, laughing at her body. One of them spat on her, and they all walked back to the four male prisoners.

A longer rope was taken from one of the other women, the leader handing it to still another of the Amazons. The rope was tied into nooses that were placed around the necks of the four men: first the Russian major, then Culhane, then the two others.

Spears prodded them to their feet, and the Amazons, slinging their own dead and wounded over their shoulders, dragging their male prisoners, disappeared from the light of the fallen floodlights and into the jungle night.

It was several minutes before Fred eased the pressure over Mulrooney's mouth.

"You can let go now, Fred. Let go, dammit!"

But Fred did not let go for what seemed to Mulrooney like at least fifteen minutes, perhaps longer, holding her immobile. Fred was saving her life, Mulrooney knew, and she could not hold anger for it.

But there was another life to save. She would get him back, she vowed as she stared into the night.

And then Fanny Mulrooney saw something that almost made her heart come to her mouth. Creeping into the light, his hat gone, no rifle, no pistol, only a large rock in his right hand was Sebastiao, the right side of his head at the temple clotted with blood.

"Sebastiao!" Fred let go of her now and Mulrooney—stiff, muscles cramped—half crawled from the shadowy underbrush into the light.

"What did this?"

"Amazons," Mulrooney said. "Not like Fred here, but the real McCoy."

Santini was awakening. Fred was bending over Helene Chavez, who was still unconscious. Mulrooney told Sebastiao, "Let me take a look at your head."

"I am fine, *menina*—Senhor Culhane?"

"A prisoner of the Amazon women. But I'm gonna fix that." She walked over to Santini. He was sitting up now, holding his clerical collar in one hand and rubbing his head with the other.

"Were, ah, they what I think? Ohh, my head."

Mulrooney knelt beside him and examined the back of his head. He winced as she touched it but did not move away. "Amazons—the real thing. They took Josh, the Russian major and two of his men. Their leader—"

"The one with the jeweled breastplate?" Santini began.

"Yeah—the looker. She slit the throat of one of the Russians, then did the same thing to Professor Xanthos. The rest of the Russians escaped into the jungle, running like hell. Some of the ones here might still be alive. Helene Chavez is unconscious. But Sebastiao's alive, see?"

"Are you okay, Fanny?"

"You know, only Josh calls me that. But I'll give you a special dispensation." She smiled as Santini laughed a little.

"Thanks, Fanny." He tried standing up and sagged back. "I don't work too well yet. We have to get these people looked after and go after Josh."

"No," Mulrooney told him. "You speak enough Greek—ask Fred if she'll guide me through the jungle to the city. I've still got the map. If these are real Amazons, then the map should be real, too. Fred can stay outside, but I'm going in after Josh. You're the only one of us with enough medical training to maybe save a few lives here, considering Chavez is out of commission."

"You're crazy, Fanny."

"No, I'm not crazy. Who better to penetrate a city full of women than another woman? The Russians left all their gear when they ran. Culhane's stuff should be here—his weapons, my gun. I'm doing it. The guy always rescues the girl from a fate worse than death in Josh's books. Well, this time it's the other way around. We'll start a new trend maybe, right?"

Mulrooney stood up. To no one in particular she said, "I'm getting him back. So help me I am."

She started looking at the bodies on the ground to separate the dead from the wounded. She found Culhane's Rolex on the wrist of the man Culhane had labeled the sergeant.

She removed it, opening the flip-lock clasp.

She held it tight in her fist. It would be back on her man's wrist if she died getting it there.

Book Two _____

Prisoner of the
Amazon Women

Chapter Thirty _____

The net was pulled over the top of the massive two-wheeled cart. The horses in harness ahead of the wagon were pawing the earth and the wagon shuddered with their false starts.

Culhane, his hands bound behind him, had been shoved into the wagon between the Russian major and the two Russian enlisted men. Two planks were lashed across the top of the cart and secured at the rear. One of the Amazons stood on the two planks, a spear at her side.

Kruglovitch whispered beside Culhane, "I cannot believe this happens."

"Yeah, well, it wouldn't have happened as easily if you and your guys hadn't killed Sebastiao our guide and hadn't kept the Greek girl from scouting ahead and hadn't taken all our weapons. And if we hadn't walked through the jungle at night with those damned flood-lights."

"This is no time for recriminations."

"'This is no time for recriminations,'" Culhane mimicked. "Okay, fine. When it's time for recriminations, tell me so I can tell you what an asshole you are."

"We must be allies at least for the moment if we wish to get ourselves from the clutches of these bitches."

"Good thing for you they don't speak English. Speak any Greek?"

"No."

"How about your two buddies?" Culhane asked, nodding at the enlisted men.

"Anton speaks only Russian. Ivan speaks Russian and Lithuanian."

"That's going to help us a lot. I agree—we have to work together to get out of here if we can. But since I speak some Greek and understand more, it looks like you and your guys do what I say or don't do anything at all."

"But there are three of us," the major murmured.

"And who knows how many of them." Culhane nodded toward the warrior standing over them.

"What do they plan for us?"

Culhane sighed loudly. The wagon was moving now. He could see through the crack in the boards that comprised the wagon's sides. "I think you can kiss off the immortality routine with our charming hostesses. They need men. Why do you think they were checking our teeth? It was like buying healthy breeding stock."

"You are insane." Kruglovitch began to laugh.

The warrior above them struck the shaft of her spear against the boards on which she stood. "We're disturbing her," Culhane rasped.

"These women intend to—"

"Rape us," Culhane told him.

"A woman cannot—"

"Wanna bet? You think about it. Mulrooney told me what that stuff Xanthos found was concerned with. The Amazons traveled from Africa due west and found this place. They traveled inland and found a city. Pretty smart people...they had to be to cross the ocean like that. It was logical for them to assume that they'd need men here. What if this land were devoid of human life, or the racial composition was wrong for them? Do any of them look Indian to you?''

''Well, no, but—''

''So they brought men with them,'' Culhane said. ''Probably over the centuries explorers, soldiers—missionaries who've disappeared—have added to the gene pool. Fresh stock for breeding.''

''Why didn't they take the Catholic priest?''

Culhane smiled. ''Catholic priests are pretty tough guys sometimes. They take their vows seriously. Why take a man prisoner for one reason only when you know he won't cooperate?''

''The one who is the leader—she pulled off his collar, then threw it down and left him. That must be why.''

''Too bad Damascus didn't have enough clerical collars to go around for all of us.''

Kruglovitch laughed again. ''I am good with women. We shall be all right. I will teach whatever Amazon I make love to how it feels to be with a real man. I will get her to our side to help us escape, and we can take her with us.''

Culhane just looked at the man, then shook his head. As obvious to him as the fact that the four of them had been taken only for sexual purposes, was the fact that the Amazons viewed men as necessary *only* for this. Death after procreation? Or would they be penned up like animals and executed when their healthy days were gone? Culhane closed his eyes. Perhaps Kruglovitch saw some kinky fantasy in this, but Culhane did not.

And he thought of Fanny Mulrooney. He had not seen Fred after the fighting had started. Perhaps Fred had gotten Fanny away to safety. He prayed she had.

But he thought of the title of Fanny's book, *Warrior Women*.

Culhane settled back as comfortably as he could. It would have been possible to work with Kruglovitch to get their hands free. But to what purpose? Amazons rode on horseback on all sides; others walked, their burnished golden armor gleaming in the moonlight. They were incredibly beautiful, incredibly tall for women, muscular, fit, raven haired, deeply tanned. There was a look in their eyes that too few women in the outside world held. Confidence, strength. Culhane had never found it an unpleasant look. Fanny Mulrooney had it.

And these women were tough. He had seen them in battle. They were from another age, an age where survival depended on fighting skill alone. An age where slitting a man's throat was not considered barbaric. It was simply the way.

He thought of his brother's stories of Vietnam, and he knew why Santini had become a priest and still had to wrestle with his conscience.

He had listened to these women speak. To the best of his knowledge, it was ancient Greek.

Culhane heard water splashing, and he peered through a crack beneath the cart. They traveled along a rocky stream bed, the Amazons who had been walking now clinging to the sides of the wagon in which he rode and the wagon ahead of them. The dead and injured Amazon women were in the first wagon.

They had not counted on assault rifles in the hands of their prey.

Culhane considered the possibilities, letting his mind wander. The Amazons were so close beside him through the walls of the wagon against which he leaned, he could smell their bodies, the distinctively unwashed feminine smell of them.

If these women had modern weapons, he wondered

how they could be thwarted. They fought without mercy, with total efficiency. They were raised for battle if the legends held any truth.

Civilized barbarians, they had their own totally distinct, totally untouched culture.

He thought of Fanny Mulrooney again. What a book this would make for her! At the moment he doubted the chances of getting back with notes. But it was part of his nature to try.

One of the Russian enlisted men beside him shouted something Culhane could not understand. He assumed it was Lithuanian.

And from above, the Amazon shouted, cracking a whip over the net.

"What did she say?" Kruglovitch asked Culhane.

"She said for the slave to be quiet or be whipped for his insolence."

It sounds like a line out of a bad movie, he thought. But accuracy was the burden of a good translator. . . .

CULHANE STARED AHEAD through a crack in the boards and over the rumps of the horses. A waterfall divided into a main cataract and several small ones, the water seeming phosphorescent in its whiteness against the pinnacle of black rock over which it cascaded. It was nearing dawn, and the water beneath the cart was streaked with gold. Rapids churned beyond the falls to the left of the wagon. On either shore there was deep rich green—the jungle.

Culhane's attention was suddenly drawn back to the waterfall. A raven-haired woman, the dim light reflecting on her gold bracelets, dived nude from one of the lower cataracts into the foam-flecked pool at the base of the falls.

The beauty of what he saw amazed him.

Culhane peered beyond the falls. What appeared to be a cavern was carved out of the foliage and the rock. Beyond the cavern opening, he could see trees washed in a golden light, the light reflected in the water that flowed from the cavern.

There were cascades of water beyond the cavern mouth, the water dripping almost lazily into the foliage that surrounded it.

They were past the falls now, crossing beneath the cavern roof. The water was higher here, splashing up between the cracks in the base of the wheeled cart.

And everywhere there was gold.

Massive veins of it streaked the black rock itself, and as some of the water splashed between the boards, Culhane saw flecks of the shining yellow metal.

The cart moved up out of the stream, along black rocks worn smooth, Culhane surmised, by the centuries and by the women who had trod them. The ride was even bumpier now.

One of the young Russian soldiers was making sounds as though he were about to throw up.

Culhane didn't fault him; he himself was terrified, as well. An alien landscape populated by an alien people. But perhaps it was a writer's detachment, the ability to step away from oneself and be the observer. Culhane told himself that if he survived, he would write about this place. At least he promised himself that.

His mind was like a camera. It always had been. Photographing the detail beneath the microscope of observation and intelligence.

The wagon moved at a steep angle now, Culhane saying what he could in Russian to calm the boy but not hearing his own words, watching instead. The wagon leveled off, the black rock smoother still, and then he heard the clatter of hooves and wheels on wood. Ahead of them was a drawbridge, and Culhane strained to get his face closer to the crack in the boards to see more. Fortifications cut from the living rock—jagged, grotesque, beautiful, streaked with gold—rose on both sides, towering beyond the point where he could see.

The wagon in which he rode crossed onto the draw-bridge now, the clatter of hoof and wheel and wood almost deafening where he lay.

Gold was everywhere.

On the bodies of the warriors guarding the entrance from the pinnacles of the fortifications, adorning their sun-bronzed flesh, sparkling in their hair.

And the bracelets. He remembered the legend of Hercules. Hercules had defeated the Amazons and forced them to wear the bracelets to calm their savagery.

Culhane smiled. "Where's Hercules when you really need him?" he murmured.

The first cart stopped, and Culhane shifted his position as the cart in which he rode stopped, as well.

The warrior above cracked her whip again and spoke.

"What did she say?"

Culhane looked at Kruglovitch in the glinting yellow light that filtered through the slats of the wagon. The major's face was crosshatched with the shadow of the net over the wagon top. "We are to get out of the wagon and stand on the right with our heads bowed, facing the draft animals. Or we will be punished."

"She can go to hell."

"*You* tell her that."

The boards were worked away, the net withdrawn. Culhane stood, his muscles aching from the cramped position the ride had forced him to assume. He tried swinging his leg over the side but could not, and the Amazon hauled Culhane up by his hair and the collar of his shirt, dragging him bodily over the side of the cart, letting him tumble to the ground.

Culhane shook his head to clear it and stood up. A whip cracked in the air once and then across his back, Culhane gritting his teeth against the pain.

One of the warriors shouted for him to turn his eyes down. He did.

Something else filled him now besides curiosity and the desire to escape: the desire for revenge.

Kruglovitch tumbled from the wagon.

Then after him came the young Russian who had been so afraid. Culhane watched from the corner of his eye, his back stinging where the lash had struck.

The third Russian was down, struggling to his feet.

And then the boy who had been terrified screamed something incomprehensible and started to run. Culhane shouted after him, *"Nyet! Nyet!"*

But it was too late. A half-dozen arrows penetrated the boy's back, and his body sagged to the rock.

Culhane looked into the gray eyes of the Amazon leader, her bejeweled armor shining as she walked toward him.

She grabbed Culhane by the hair and jerked his head back. He didn't know any insults in ancient Greek— only in modern—but being a smartass, he thought, could get him killed. He'd wait. He said nothing.

The woman laughed to her guards and shoved Culhane ahead, Culhane barely keeping his footing. He was stopped and lined up with the two remaining Russians. The noose of rope was placed around his neck again, and as he glanced back, saw one on the neck of Kruglovitch and on the other Russian.

Culhane looked into the Amazon leader's eyes again as she raised his head. She was smiling. It was his fatal charm with women, he guessed, laughing inwardly. He smiled back. She slapped his face hard. The Amazon leader took hold of the rope and started leading him ahead, the other two men behind him.

It was the same scene he'd seen in countless movies, read in countless books: victorious military leader enters city with prisoners in total subjugation. He considered kicking her in the rear end. He decided not to.

They were definitely entering a city. And what a city.

Gold was everywhere, trimming every wall and every roof. Jewels studded every ornament and statues of what appeared to be solid gold, the sculpture fine in its detail. Women—fighting men and conquering. Women—fighting animals and conquering. Women—fighting huge anacondas and conquering. Women—sitting at the feet of another woman, learning.

The Amazons were born propagandists, Culhane decided, walking behind his captor.

Women lined the main street on both sides, the street paved—and not just proverbially—with gold.

The structures towered as far as he could see with his head bowed.

He sneaked a peek upward once and saw spires rising toward the height of a vast cavern, the cavern with hundreds of openings in the roof, the early-morning sunlight filtering through.

A whip cracked. In full daylight, the sun would dapple the streets and the buildings and the occupants. The whip cracked again, and he felt it across his back. He lowered his head.

A city that had never been seen from the air. A city where plants grew along the sides of the streets in ornamental boxes and gardens. Sunlight without sky. A city truly of gold, the rock itself seamed with it.

Culhane kept walking, glancing up more surreptitiously this time. He saw more of the women, these not dressed as warriors, but dressed like women in ancient-Greek sculpture, draped, hair carefully arranged. They watched dispassionately, it seemed to Culhane.

Culhane kept walking. The woman with the whip—he'd wring her neck with it, he promised himself.

The rope around his neck was jerked down, and Culhane stopped.

He looked ahead. The Amazon leader dropped the rope carelessly into the street and walked ahead, ascending a flight of seemingly endless low steps.

He followed her with his eyes. She was breathtakingly beautiful, he had to admit.

A spear was shoved at him, against his neck, forcing him to his knees. But he still followed the Amazon leader's steps with his eyes.

At the top of the stairs, before a classic Greek temple, stood a tall, exquisitely beautiful woman. Culhane somehow realized the woman was in her late forties or early fifties, but the years had not tarnished her looks. Her black hair was streaked with silver and the robes she wore were of gray cloth trimmed with gold and interwoven with gold thread.

Surrounding her were other women, dressed less lavishly, younger by at least twenty years but somehow not as beautiful.

It was clear, Culhane thought. She was their queen. The younger women were her attendants.

That regency and religion would be intertwined did not amaze him. The Amazons according to legend had worshiped Artemis.

They were her cult—forever, it appeared.

The Amazon military leader stopped three steps below the queen, dropping to one knee, raising her right hand in something almost identical to a Nazi salute.

The queen touched the leader's shoulder, and the

leader arose, falling in beside the queen and slightly behind as the queen descended the steps, her attendants walking slowly behind her, one of them carrying the train of her robe.

Culhane watched as they descended the steps.

They approached. Culhane looked down. The woman's sandals were trimmed with gold.

Culhane felt a hand knotted into his hair. His head was snapped back and he was pulled to his feet. He saw the queen full face, but it was the leader of the miltary party who held him. He saw the resemblance in their faces: mother and daughter—it was obvious. The older woman tugged at his chin, and Culhane let his mouth fall open. She was inspecting his teeth. He knew now what a horse felt like at a claiming race. His jaw was let go, but the leader still held his head back by his hair.

The older woman ripped open his shirt, Culhane hearing the buttons as they clattered to the stone street beneath him.

He felt her hands on his chest, felt as she twisted his shirt down from his shoulders to his elbows. Her hands kneaded at his muscles.

And then he felt her hands at his crotch, kneading. And there was laughter and then she let go, and the hand that held his hair twisted harder in it and he was pushed to his knees.

He looked up quickly once. The queen was smiling to her daughter. Culhane didn't smile.

THE ROPES ON HIS WRISTS had been replaced with chains, his hands now in front of him, and a metal collar had been placed around his neck. A chain with something like a lock was attached to the collar, and he had been led away by the chain, the two Russians taken, as well, up beyond the temple, the city following the natural formation of the immeasurably huge cavern.

There were private dwellings, girl children in evidence playing near them but no boys. Perhaps those legends were true: male infants were killed, only the females raised to adulthood.

How they had perpetuated their race in the centuries that lay between their arrival in Brazil and the eventual arrival of Europeans whom they could kidnap and use he did not know and could not guess. Perhaps as an emergency measure they had let the fittest of the male children live.

They traveled upward, the leader gone now, one of the warriors leading him, other warriors ringing them with bows poised and spears ready. They went up past the houses and into the rough and rocky area near the height of the cavern.

Then down into a rock pit. In it were metal cages, and in the cages were men. Culhane counted perhaps fifty of them.

He was led past several of the cages, the Russian major taken away, then the young Russian soldier, Culhane still being led on.

He was stopped, and the chain dropped. He stood before a cage larger than the others, a very old man sitting smiling in the farthest corner.

"Do you speak English?" the old man asked.

Culhane nodded.

"They will not strike me, but they will strike you. So be quiet until they leave. You are at once lucky and unfortunate."

The cage was opened, and Culhane was shoved toward it, the chain removed from the collar around his neck. He was pushed inside, and he stood there on the closely barred cage floor hearing the cage door closed behind him. He closed his eyes.

"So the queen's daughter has finally chosen. It was time for Litra."

Culhane opened his eyes. "What do you mean?"

"You see, I've made quite a study of them. They mate twice only, at the age of twenty-one and at the age of twenty-eight. Litra is twenty-eight. She is very beautiful. You have some interesting nights in store for you. Seven nights precisely. And then, like all the other used men of the royal house—except for me and I never could discern for what reason they keep me alive—you shall die. But do not despair, sir. If you service the princess well, it will be a quick death. But if you fail to perform...well, it's most unpleasant." The old man laughed. "Perhaps they keep me alive because I sired the princess. Who knows? But that was a long time ago. It was 1957 when I came here. And the queen, I found out later, was having trouble bearing. At her twenty-first year—nothing. Poof! So be of good spirit, and get some sleep. You won't get any once the ritual begins. She's a demanding girl. Seven years ago...the poor fellow."

Culhane sat down and closed his eyes.

Chapter Thirty-One

Santini had translated, and Fred had agreed to guide Mulrooney to the city of the Amazon women. But Fred had warned her that no one ever returned from that part of the jungle—*ever*. Fred had also insisted she would guide Mulrooney only on one condition: that she be allowed to penetrate the city with her if they found it. Mulrooney was her friend. She had saved her from Sergio Celini who had kept her caged like a wild animal for weeks, his men repeatedly trying to rape her, the animal sounds, the clawing, the scratching all that had saved her.

She remembered the horrible crash. She remembered her mother and her father's mangled bodies. She had stayed with the plane until there was no food and no water, and she had set off into the jungle to survive. Fred had learned the ways of the hunters, watching them from the treetops but avoiding the natives, avoiding all human companionship after a group of natives had found her once and tried to assault her. She had killed two of them, injured several others and escaped.

Until being discovered by Celini—she had fought with a giant anaconda and nearly died—she had had no real human contact. And though Celini had saved her life by killing the anaconda and feeding her while she had recovered from the giant snake's embrace, he had treated her like no human being should treat another, or even treat an animal.

It was for this reason she insisted that if she accompanied M. F. Mulrooney, she would aid her in recovering Josh Culhane. Mulrooney had taught her that friendship could exist, had shown her that love—the love Mulrooney displayed for Culhane—was not just some distant memory from the days of her parents.

She did not understand the concept of being rich, of being the heiress to the Archimedes fortune. Fred did not even remember her own first name.

Mulrooney had gathered up Culhane's belongings—his guns, his binoculars, his engineer's bag, his pack. She had sat holding his hat while Santini had simultaneously translated and worked to help the wounded. Santini had commented that it was easy for him to speak with Fred in Greek, although he had not used Greek to any real extent since his childhood and had spoken only with children. And Fred's understanding of Greek was at that level, her vocabulary the same.

Few of the wounded had survived; only three of the Russian soldiers were alive. As Mulrooney and Fred had started their trek, Helene Chavez had started coming around. Mulrooney had not waited to talk with the woman. Magdelena aided Santini now, her left arm bandaged from the spear wound, her spirits better. Magdelena was all right, Mulrooney had decided. But Helene was something else again.

Fred jogged through the misty grayness of the jungle, Mulrooney keeping pace with Fred as best she could.

From a great distance Fred had seen the outer reaches of the Amazon capital—a huge cave open to the east and to the west, a fast-moving stream running through it, a waterfall cascading over it and joining the stream. The cave was apparently a hollow mountain, pock-marked on the top, the holes admitting sunshine and rain.

Mulrooney conjectured that such a formation would render the city invisible from the air. As Mulrooney ran, she tried to focus her attention away from the weariness of her body, the heaviness of her burdens. For a hollow mountain to have such holes at its top and not to be volcanic... Nothing Fred had said indicated that, nor had anything in the retelling of the Amazons' migration by Balthazar Muhammed. For the cave to be that way, perhaps ages before the Amazons had come, there had been a meteor shower that had hit with such force... Mulrooney smiled. Maybe Culhane was right and she should try a novel.

She kept running. Forming a plan. There would be guards around the city. Fred had recounted that this was the way she had seen Amazons the one time before, guarding the exterior of the city. They roamed the rocks and the jungle, patrolling.

Fred was the right height and the right build. She even spoke Greek. If they could overpower two of the guards—which would not be easy—they could take their clothing and weapons and walk into the Amazon city.

Mulrooney considered her own build and wondered if the Amazons kept around the runts of their litters.

But they could enter the city that way. Leaving it would be another question.

Once, when they stopped for a rest after following the wagon tracks for a half hour, Mulrooney had noticed something clearly indentifiable to her. A hoofprint. She liked riding and seeing the hoofprint further fed her plan. The Amazons had horses. The animals would be descendants perhaps of horses brought to Brazil by early explorers. Culhane was a really good rider. She didn't worry about Fred—Fred would learn quickly enough. Horses could be stolen for their getaway.

They stopped again, Mulrooney searching for a way with hand signals to convey to Fred that there was no time to rest.

Fred walked ahead slowly, her bow poised to fire.

Mulrooney held Culhane's rifle, following after her through the dense vegetation. Fred disappeared for an instant, and Mulrooney felt panic. Mulrooney broke through the undergrowth, instantly dropping to a crouch, then flattening herself out along a rocky promontory. Below them was a valley, and Fred was stretched out along the rock nearly to its edge.

Mulrooney set down the rifle and took up Culhane's binoculars, focusing them.

What she saw looked like paradise, but it was the Amazon capital and could well be hell instead....

As THE SUN ROSE, Culhane watched the Amazon city take on a still greater glow. From the cage where he was imprisoned, he could see to the lower ground, to the city itself, shafts of brilliant light filtering through the holes in the cavern ceiling. He realized that the mountain was hollow—perhaps once volcanic but aeons ago. The holes could have been caused by some bizarre geological happening, but he doubted it; they were too evenly spaced. Too even in size. He credited Amazon engineering instead—and labor. Perhaps the labor of men like himself. Culhane wondered.

The old man—his name volunteered during another spasm of conversation as Dr. Jules Sutton—began to speak again. "You see, the rest of the Amazons will share their mates. Someone is always coming into season—twenty-one or twenty-eight—and then a mate is needed at the precise time. That's why these other men are here. Some of them have been here for maybe a dozen years. Pretty soon some of them will begin to fail. I'll regret that."

Culhane looked at the man. His white hair was shoulder length and surprisingly clean looking; his beard flowed to his waist, also white. He wore a knee-length shift of some coarse cloth, and he was barefoot. The old man kept talking. "The ones selected to mate with the princess are killed. Lucky you." Sutton cackled. Culhane imagined the old man had gone bonkers after all the years of imprisonment. "You see, I think they don't want to risk another woman being born who has half the blood of the princess—a pretender to the throne. That may be the rationale. The others are kept, fed, bred with, and eventually executed when they are no longer sexually useful."

"What's the greatest number of men you've ever had here?"

"Fifty—like now. They don't let the numbers get too high."

"That means they're afraid of rebellion."

"Rebellion? Be serious, lad..."

Culhane looked away from the old man, studying the city, the entrances on the east and west. "What's so crazy about rebellion?"

"You could never get out of your shackles, for one thing. The woman who claims you has the key on a chain around her waist. Princess Litra has yours right now. When they take you away, they strip you naked. Even if you were able to make some kind of a weapon, they'd find it. When they have you, you're chained to the bed. There's never a chance."

"Then the best chance is when they come for you—right?"

"Best chance—but you're crazy, lad."

Culhane nodded. He wanted a cigarette. The Amazons had not searched him. His cigarettes and his lighter were still in his shirt pocket. He reached up with both manacled hands and got them—and he felt his little knife. "You ever smoke?"

"Used to. You offering?"

"If you want."

"No, you keep them. It's the last pack you'll ever see. Smoke 'em really slowly, lad."

"What kind of doctor are you? Medicine?"

"A dentist, would you believe that? Maybe that's why they keep me around, come to think of it. They take me out of the cage sometimes for that. The captain of the queen's guard lost most of her teeth in battle once and they cause her some pain. I do what I can with homeopathic remedies and some crude tools. If I had a real lab..."

"If we get out of here, you'll find dentistry has

changed a lot in twenty-eight years.'' Culhane looked away, shaking his head. ''If we get out of here...''

''You'll bring the whole world in on them, won't you? Destroy all this?''

''Maybe—but maybe not. They have anything like trial by combat?''

''Once I saw it. Took a woman prisoner. The woman was some kind of police officer, I think. She killed a couple of them with her gun—that's the rumor that went around in the wash pits.''

''Wash pits?''

''Once a day you get out of the cage and get taken down to the wash pits and strip and clean yourself, and once a week you get a new tunic to wear.''

''Sounds lovely,'' Culhane said. ''What about the woman cop?''

''Cop—haven't heard that word in years, lad. Anyway, since she fought them, they had to give her the right to trial by combat. It was the only time I ever saw the queen without her bracelets—that was maybe fifteen years ago. The queen and this lady policeman were fighting, and the lady cop knew some tricks, you know?''

Culhane nodded.

''That's when the queen removed her bracelets. She was like an animal. I saw it all, 'cause when there's a fight they haul out the slaves to watch—to scare us I guess. But the queen—she ripped the lady policeman apart.''

''How about if I kill one of them—trial by combat?''

''Execution—they won't fight a man. Had a man here once who tried it.''

''They can't be afraid they'll lose, not the way they're built,'' Culhane conjectured.

''That isn't it, lad. A man doesn't deserve to be fought. It is a thing of honor.''

"The world turned upside down," Culhane remarked.

"But for them it's the way it has been for thousands of years."

Culhane reached into his pocket, finding his little pen-shaped knife. He didn't let Dr. Sutton see it. He didn't trust the man after all these years of confinement.

Culhane waited, watching the movement of the city, observing the daily life from his vantage point in the cage. He photographed it in his mind.

The old man had not spoken for some time. Culhane did not care, smoking through his package of Pall Malls; it was a psychological thing with him, smoking the cigarettes rather than hoarding them. In his mind he figured that he would get out into the real world again and live, and if he wanted more cigarettes he could just hop in the car and drive to the store and buy some.

There was a rattling sound on the bars behind him and he turned around.

Litra, the princess, the military conquerer. With two other warriors she was opening the cage door.

Culhane stood up, letting his cigarette fall through the bars beneath his feet.

Litra stepped into the cage, holding a coiled bullwhip of braided leather in her right hand, slapping it against her thigh like a military man might carry a swagger stick.

She touched the coiled whip against Culhane's cheek.

Culhane looked up and smiled, then swept her leg with his right leg, causing Litra to lose her balance. He started opening the knife, to put it to her throat as she fell.

But the old man shouted in Greek to the guards, "He has a knife!"

Culhane tried to move as the two Amazon guards

rushed him, but Litra was up now, the guards pinning Culhane to the cage side, his head and shoulders aching where he had been struck with the club during the battle, Litra wrestling the knife from his right hand. It was open and she flicked it past his face, then snapped off something in Greek too fast for Culhane to follow. And suddenly before he realized it, one of the Amazon guards had her knife to his throat. His pants were pulled down, and he felt the cold of his own steel against his testicles.

"Sutton, you bastard!"

"She's my daughter, lad!"

Litra shrieked for silence. Culhane didn't breathe, feeling the knife there at his crotch.

Litra's gray eyes stared up at him. She was nearly as tall as he was.

She said nothing, but she started to laugh, Culhane feeling the pressure of his knife gone. Litra looked at the blade, laughing. Then suddenly she stopped laughing and slapped him across the face. She fired off a command, again too rapid for Culhane to make out clearly. The two warriors released him and he sagged back. Litra walked from the cell, her warriors behind her, and the cage closed. Culhane stood there, watching as she walked away.

Sutton laughed. "Have to get up pretty early in the morning to get the better of her. My daughter's tough!"

Culhane started breathing again. Somehow, he told himself, he'd get his hands on her neck and wring it. . . .

MULROONEY WAS TERRIFIED. She had seen how the Amazon women fought. This was great material for *Warrior Women*, but she could have lived without it. Armed with her revolver and Culhane's Bali-Song knife, she moved ahead, immediately behind Fred as the Greek girl stalked the Amazon guard.

Culhane's gear and weapons were cached near the promontory from which she had first seen the Amazon city's shell. With Fred, Mulrooney had worked her way down into the valley out of which the hollow mountain rose.

Fred reached behind her, signaling Mulrooney to stay. Mulrooney obeyed. Fred moved ahead, a lasso she had made of creeping vines coiled in her hands, the loop ready to swing. Mulrooney watched, huddled in the foliage, holding her breath.

The Amazon guard was tall and exquisitely beautiful. And suddenly Fred was standing to her full height, the lasso making a whistling sound as the Amazon wheeled toward her. The loop snaked out, Mulrooney's heart in her mouth for an instant, thinking Fred missed, but the loop dropped to encircle the Amazon woman's neck. Fred jerked the lasso tight as the Amazon made to raise her spear. And suddenly Fred was shinning up into a tree, holding the vine lasso as she jumped toward the ground.

The Amazon's body was hauled skyward, the neck cracking with an audible, sickening sound. The body hung there, lifeless. Fred smiled.

Mulrooney swallowed hard.

Fred let go of the vine, and the Amazon warrior fell to the jungle floor, Fred immediately beginning to strip the woman of her armor and weapons and clothing.

They needed to kill one more, the shortest one they could find, Mulrooney reflected. And the most flat-chested one.

Chapter Thirty-Two _____

Something called a court order—Hoevermann had broader powers in Brazil in emergencies—had been needed to have a search warrant issued against Palmer Industries.

It had taken into midmorning to get the judge to hear the request, Hoevermann catching some sleep on a couch in a small waiting room in the Dirksen Federal Building in downtown Chicago, changing into fresh underwear and a clean shirt in the men's room.

Robert Summerfield, the red-headed FBI agent who had met him at the airport, had offered to buy him breakfast, and Hoevermann had opted for McDonald's. He had never been to one.

They were sitting in a booth eating when Hoevermann began hearing a beeping sound. Summerfield, looking quickly from right to left, opened his coat and took a pager from his belt. A voice crackled over the device, "We've got it." Summerfield smiled, his blue eyes flashing. "Another American custom, Inspector Hoevermann—eating on the run. They've got the court order. Let's go!"

The men got up, and Hoevermann followed Summerfield past the preschool-age children, the shoppers, the workers on a break, past the trash receptacle—Summerfield pausing there to discard the things from the table—and into the street.

The FBI man looked up along the street. "There—that's the car. Come on—and drink some of that coffee down, Inspector. Special Agent Cashman is doing the driving, and he watches too many cop shows on television.''

"What do you mean?" Hoevermann was barely keeping up with the considerably younger man, and now he was trying to swallow some coffee through a last mouthful of food.

"Fast accelerations—fast turns—you know." Summerfield stepped out into the street, a car narrowly missing him, and a gray Ford stopped for them, blocking traffic behind it. Summerfield held open the right-hand rear passenger door for Hoevermann, then climbed in the front.

"Inspector Hoevermann, this is Roger Cashman, Special Agent. Watch the coffee, Inspector—hit it, Roger!"

OTHER FBI SPECIAL AGENTS, representatives of the Illinois State Police, and officers from the Chicago suburb in which Palmer Radionics was located were waiting for them. It was Saturday, and Palmer Radionics was closed. The company's director, Arthur Dzikowski, had already gone inside, arriving there an hour earlier, before the court order had been issued and search warrant given. Hoevermann shook hands with the state policeman and walked past several uniformed officers and into the building. There was a receptionist's desk beyond the glass doors, but today there was no receptionist. The state policeman had indicated that the executive offices were on the sixth floor. Summerfield led the way to the elevators, and a state policeman stood beside the open elevator doors.

"What sort of man is Arthur Dzikowski?" Hoevermann asked the policeman as the elevator doors closed.

"No criminal record—not even a traffic violation. That's all I can say."

Hoevermann nodded. As soon as the elevator doors opened, he lit a cigarette.

On the sixth floor the reception desk was at the far end of the hallway to his right, and Hoevermann and the FBI agent started toward it, the state policeman staying by the elevator doors.

"I imagine he's inside. I'll knock," Summerfield volunteered.

Hoevermann studied the reception area. It was very plush, very modern, very efficient looking.

"No answer," Summerfield said, turning the knob.

Hoevermann followed him inside, making note of everything. The inner office was paneled, and a wilted carnation sat in a glass vase on the secretary's desk. The typewriter, computer terminals and telephone switching equipment—it all looked bafflingly efficient to him. Hoevermann tapped Summerfield on the shoulder. "You are armed, just in case?"

"Yes, sir, I am. But I doubt it will be necessary."

"Those have been the last words of some fine late friends," Hoevermann remarked.

Summerfield knocked on the inner office door. Hoevermann heard the faint sound of a toilet flushing. "Open the door!" he said to the young man beside him.

"But, Inspector—"

"Open the door—now!" Hoevermann pushed between the red-haired FBI agent and the door, and tried to knob. The door was locked. "Force the door, Senhor Summerfield—I'll assume full responsibility."

"But, Inspector—"

"Obviously you have not been fully briefed. We are talking not about gold ingots, but something vastly more important. Palmer Radionics—think, *senhor!* Nuclear material!"

Summerfield's blue eyes went wide, and he stared at Hoevermann for an instant. Then he threw his shoulder to the door, twisting at the knob. "Mr. Dzikowski—this is the FBI! I have a search warrant for these premises. Destruction of any material vital to our investigation could result in criminal prosecution, sir!"

The door did not budge.

"While traveling from my country to yours, I read through various publications and reports. I believe Scott Palmer is paying off the terrorist kidnappers with a substantial amount of nuclear material—enough for a bomb. We cannot wait!"

Summerfield stepped back from the door and kicked at it once. "Always works in the movies. . ."

The state policeman had come from the elevator to the inner office. "What's the racket?"

"Gimme a hand here. The Inspector thinks we're talking about nuclear materials being transferred to terrorists, and Dzikowski may be destroying evidence in there. Come on! I'm responsible!"

The policeman and Summerfield threw their shoulders to the door together, but it didn't budge.

Hoevermann cleared his throat. "Have you ever shot the lock off a door?"

"No, sir."

"And you, Officer?"

"No, sir."

"I have. Would one of you kindly give me your weapon, please? Millions of lives depend on what we are doing. There is no time to waste now!"

The FBI agent drew his weapon. Hoevermann enjoyed firearms and shooting, and recognized the firearm. A Smith & Wesson Model 13, standard FBI issue. "I'll do it. Should I aim for the lock plate or the door-jamb?" Summerfield asked.

"The doorjamb should do with this type of lock. Hurry!"

"Stand back!" Then Summerfield raised his voice, "Mr. Dzikowski, I warn you again. This is the FBI. If you do not open the door I'll be forced to shoot off the lock!"

There was no response from inside, but Hoevermann thought he smelled smoke. "Flushing apparently didn't work. I smell something burning, I believe," Hoevermann said calmly.

Summerfield nodded, clutching the revolver in both fists, arms outstretched, his body in a combat crouch. "I'll be firing at the count of five, Mr. Dzikowski. Stand well clear of the door for your own safety, sir!"

Summerfield looked at Hoevermann, then leveled his revolver. "One. Two. Three." He steadied the revolver. "Four—Mr. Dzikowski, I'll be forced to fire—five!" The weapon discharged, Hoevermann's ears ringing with it in the confined space, the state policeman drawing his gun.

"Kick the door and it should open," Hoevermann snapped.

The FBI men stepped to the door and kicked at the lock plate, slamming himself against the doorframe as the door opened inward. "Please have your hands where I can see them, Mr. Dzikowski," Summerfield shouted as he went through the door. "Holy shit!"

Hoevermann went through the door ahead of the state policeman.

Dzikowski lay back in his leather executive chair, palms upturned on the chair's arms, blood spurting from the left wrist like a garden hose under full pressure that had suddenly sprung a leak.

"Get an ambulance!" The state policeman grabbed at the telephone on Dzikowski's desk. Summerfield bent over the man, trying to staunch the blood flow, but Hoevermann knew it was useless. He kicked over the still-flaming metal wastebasket instead, stomping on the flames with the soles of his shoes.

Something caught his eye—a piece of paper not quite consumed. He bent over and picked it up, blowing on it because it was still smoldering. It was apparently a memo, and across the top he read the words "Dynamic Plat." The rest was burned. He turned to the FBI agent. "Summerfield, the man is dead or about to be. Nothing you can do will change that. Instead of standing there, check through his Rolodex and see if there is mention there of a Dynamic something."

The FBI agent looked at Hoevermann. "He just—"

"Killed himself. Yes, I know. And that means my suspicions are confirmed."

The police officer who had called for the ambulance set the telephone receiver down and began flipping through the Rolodex. "Dynamic Plating?" And he read the address.

"Will the search warrant cover Dynamic Plating?"

"No."

"We have to go there anyway—now!"

Summerfield nodded. Hoevermann could see the words "I am losing my job" written in the young man's eyes. He hoped it wouldn't be true. Hoevermann started for the door. "You told me this Cashman fellow drives fast?"

"Yes. A maniac."

"You memorized the address?"

"Yes."

"Let's go!"

Chapter Thirty-Three _____

Fred used a similar technique to kill the second Amazon guard, but lassoing her from a position in one of the trees made the taking of the second guard easier. Mulrooney looked down the front of her burnished golden breastplate. They had picked the smallest of the Amazon guards they had seen that could be gotten easily. Mulrooney still felt as flat chested as a boy. She inhaled, trying to fill the armor more. It was hopeless.

She looked at Fred and grinned.

Fred looked the part: tall, big breasted, muscular, raven haired, the bracelets on her wrists gleaming dully in the light.

Mulrooney looked at herself. She could not see her hair but knew it was the wrong color, several shades too light. She had a decent tan but looked white as a ghost compared to Fred and the real Amazons. She was also several inches too short, and though she considered herself as strong as most women, she had no rippling muscles. She was soft, which was the way she had been raised to think she should be.

And her breasts...

She shrugged, and the breastplate almost became dislodged. Making a mental note not to do that, she bent over to pick up her spear and almost fell out of the breastplate doing it. "This isn't going to work, Fred," she told her strapping companion. Fred's eyes looked puzzled. Mulrooney smiled at her, then gestured across her upper body and inhaled. Fred laughed. "Thanks, you're a real pal," Mulrooney muttered. The breastplate was so big for her that she had secured the little revolver and Culhane's Bali-Song knife between the armor and her upper abdomen; the really rotten part about it, she thought, was she could have hidden a larger gun just as easily.

Fred gestured toward the cavern entrance, and Mulrooney nodded. Even the bracelets on her wrists were too large. The sandals fit, but the golden armor for her shins was too large. It clanked when she walked, and she forced herself to a wider stride, carrying her spear in her left hand as she had seen the Amazons do, her quiver of arrows across her back, the bow sheathed beside it, her curved-blade knife at her waist on a thin belt of gold-colored metal. Amazons wore pierced earrings, and she had removed her own small gold balls and inserted the ones taken from the dead guard. The necklace around her throat seemed positively heavy with gold. And talk about skimpy clothes, Mulrooney thought. No top was worn under the breastplate, and the panties were like the bottom half of a string bikini.

She felt horribly self-conscious. But her hair, even though it wasn't the right shade, was about the right length. She wondered what the Amazons used on their hair. When she had removed the dead warrior's earrings, the hair had seemed so alive, so full.

Mulrooney followed Fred into the cavern mouth. There was gold everywhere, veins of it in the black rocks. The sunlight that glittered on the stream beside which they walked made the water itself appear gold.

An Amazon warrior on the other side of the stream waved a hello to Fred, Fred answering it, Mulrooney nodding, but sure the guard had looked at her strangely. She kept walking along the stream, the fortifications looming ahead now, toward the drawbridge—and more warriors....

CULHANE HAD DOZED OFF, and he heard the old man hissing at him as he opened his eyes.

"What?"

"It's your time, lad. Those are Litra's personal guards. They'll take you to the temple after they take you to the wash pits."

Culhane looked behind him, through the bars, and watched as the two women—both enormously tall—strode past the cages, once stopping to shake the bars of one of the cages and frighten the men inside. He watched as the women laughed.

Culhane tested the length of chain between his manacles. A weapon?

He stood up.

"Don't try it, lad."

"Look, Doctor—I'm not like you. I don't like it here, and if what you say is true, I've got seven glorious nights ahead of me and then the ax falls, right?"

"Yes, that's true, lad."

"Don't get in my way," Culhane advised.

The two warriors stopped at the entrance to the cage, watching him. Neither carried a spear. He smiled. They smiled and the cage door opened.

He started for the cage door, hoping to catch them off guard, but each drew her long, curved blade. In English he said, "You wouldn't cut me—Litra wouldn't like that." Culhane swatted the chain downward against the nearest knife blade, thrusting his body weight against the woman, but he could almost feel it coming, and he doubled forward and rolled to the ground.

The two warriors were laughing, Culhane's hands grasping his crotch. They got him hard enough to momentarily cripple him and stop the fight, but not hard enough to do any permanent damage. They knew their stuff, Culhane thought bitterly. Apparently he wasn't the first male prisoner to try rebellion. They hauled him up to his knees, a knife going to his throat, then threw him forward, laughing again.

Culhane rolled onto his back. "Up your ass, lady," he growled at the one who had kneed him. One of them kicked him and he got to his feet. They gestured beyond the cages and he started walking.

As he walked past the cage where Kruglovitch was, the Russian major waved and laughed. Culhane was not amused. He kept walking, turning higher up into the rocks as directed, then clambering down toward a stream with a waterfall. He assumed these were the wash pits. One of the Amazons grabbed at him and he stopped. She gestured to the waterfall—a natural shower. Culhane shrugged. He could stand a cleaning up. He raised his manacled hands and made a gesture of futility. One of the knife blades flashed, and his left shirt sleeve was slashed, then his right, the shirt tugged up over his head and ripped away. Culhane started for them, but the blade flicked past his face and he snapped his head clear of it, a hand knotting into his hair, another hand at his neck, his body numbed under the finger pressure and he could barely breathe. He could hear ripping sounds; his pants and shorts were being cut away.

The pressure was eased. He stood there, naked except for his combat boots. One of them gestured down to his feet. Culhane shook his head. Again the hand in the hair and the pressure at his neck and he was forced to his knees, then into a sitting position. One of the knives slashed and then slashed again. The pressure was released, but the hand was still knotted into his hair. His combat boot laces had been cut. He kicked off the boots, then he was dragged to his feet and shoved forward, down and toward the waterfall.

The water was icy cold as he stood in it. He would wait until he was alone with Litra. It would be his only chance... Or was he deluding himself...?

THEY HAD FOLLOWED THE OTHER WARRIORS, Mulrooney wondering if the old aphorism about safety in numbers held any truth to it. And they approached now what was clearly a Greek temple, a temple to the goddess Artemis. After entering through the cavern mouth and traveling up toward the fortifications and over the wooden drawbridge, Mulrooney had planned that they hide and wait until nightfall, but a gong had begun to sound and smoke had begun to rise from the temple's entrance, and Mulrooney had fallen in with the Amazon women, Fred beside her. There seemed to be several thousand of them, and Mulrooney imagined that except for the most important guard posts, everyone would go to the temple. She planned to break away from the group then: it would be the optimum time to find Culhane and set him free.

But that hope died as she neared the temple. Incense burned in a brazier, the smoke having a very sweet smell to it. And standing beside the brazier, naked, manacled at the wrists, around his neck a golden collar with a chain leading from it that ended in the hands of the woman who had led the Amazon attack in the jungle, was Josh Culhane. Mulrooney muttered, "Oh, boy." Some of the women standing near her and Fred looked at her oddly. She focused her attention on Culhane. He looked kind of sexy naked and all chained up like that. The warrior leader who held Culhane's chain in her hands began a chant and Mulrooney, although she did not understand a word, knew its meaning. Culhane's chain was tugged at and the two warriors flanking him pushed at him. Culhane didn't move. *Good for you,*

Mulrooney thought. Then one of the warriors knotted her free hand into his hair, the other putting her hand to his neck. It was some kind of nerve pinch, Mulrooney realized, but it didn't make Culhane pass out. He fell to his knees and the hand was removed from his neck, but the one who had knotted her fingers in his hair still held him that way, forcing his head down.

The press of women around her grew. Mulrooney estimated that as many as two thousand warriors crowded the steps before the temple.

Behind the brazier, her palms raised toward the cavern ceiling and the sky above it, stood a woman, strikingly beautiful but older than the warriors. Mulrooney guessed that the woman—gray streaking her black hair, her pale-violet robe not hiding a spectacular figure—was their ruler.

The queen took up the chant now, the Amazons surrounding Mulrooney raising their palms skyward in prayer. Mulrooney had read of rituals such as this. She raised her hands, as well, and Fred did the same.

Mulrooney cast her eyes down, bending her head forward, looking down her chest to her feet. In her research for *Warrior Women* she had uncovered an obscure reference to Artemesian ritual. And she froze for an instant. At the conclusion, Culhane would be ritually joined to the woman who held his chain. Because as Mulrooney sneaked a peek toward the altar, she could see the woman kneeling beside Culhane, palms upraised like those of the queen.

Mulrooney felt tears in her eyes, but she could not move her hands to brush them away without drawing attention to herself. She sniffed. She was watching, powerless, while the man she loved was being joined in marriage to an Amazon warrior. *Shit,* she said to herself.

The chanting continued, the smell of the smoke sweeter, and Mulrooney heard the clapping of hands by the queen who was also the high priestess. Instinctively she lowered her hands and raised her head and stared ahead.

Culhane was to his feet, and the warrior woman who was his bride held the chain close to her, Culhane close to her. And around the woman's neck was the strange necklace she had worn in battle. As the queen stepped from behind the brazier, the smoke of the incense dissipating, Mulrooney could see that only she—the queen—wore the same necklace. Culhane was the husband of the princess. And Mulrooney was terrified. Another obscure reference she had found to a matriarchal society that had flourished for a time in Asia centuries ago came to mind. The mate of the princess was brought to her chambers, and after the marriage was consummated the mate was killed. Like the praying mantis, Mulrooney thought. Since entering the Amazon city, she had not seen one man.

Culhane, flanked by the two warriors now, their spears poised on either side of him, was led away by the princess. Mulrooney knew for what. . . .

CULHANE WALKED BEHIND HER. He understood enough Greek, despite some of the archaic pronunciations and vocabulary, to realize he had just been married to Litra at a temple of Artemis. He had never been married. He had of late planned on someday marrying Fanny Mulrooney. He had never planned on being led in chains to the nuptial chamber with armed guards flanking him, his wife wearing jeweled golden armor and holding his leash. Culhane shrugged. Life was full of surprises.

And he had a surprise for Litra.

Litra stopped and so did Culhane to avoid bumping into her. One of the guards stepped forward and opened the double doors. They were in the palace now, on the upper floor, and Culhane looked to his right. He could see the thousands of Amazon women returning to their duties from the temple steps. He wondered fleetingly if Mulrooney had made it to safety.

He felt the pressure at his neck as he turned away from the view over the railing. He was led ahead and stopped for a moment at the double doors to Litra's suite. A low platform about twice the size of a king-size bed dominated the far wall between the window openings. Cushions were scattered about the huge bed, and at the headboard was a large golden-colored ring. He felt a jerk at his neck and moved forward, the guards flanking him again.

Litra had moved off now, and Culhane checked out the guards. As if they had read his mind, the hair again, fingers knotting in it, the pressure at his neck, the pressure heavier now as he collapsed forward. The pressure was not released, and he felt himself being dragged. He was on the bed. He heard the sounds of metal scratching metal, and suddenly the pain on his neck eased and his body felt alive again. The warriors stood on each side of the bed, laughing. Culhane tried sitting up, but his body would not raise up, and he realized that the collar around his neck had been chained to the ring on the headboard. His wrists were still manacled together. The warriors started spreading his legs, holding his ankles, and Culhane looked down along the length of his body. There were manacles near the foot of the bed on long chains, and the manacles were closed around his ankles but not locked. He tugged at them. He could not pull free, could not close his legs.

Culhane swallowed. He was about to be raped.

He heard a door close and looked to his right. Litra. Her armor was gone. She was nude except for her bracelets and a golden chain at the waist, a large golden key there. She clapped her hands—one of them clutched a coiled bullwhip—and the two warriors bowed to her and left, Culhane watching her eyes now, hearing the giggling of the two guards, then doors closing.

"My name is Josh Culhane. D'you come here often?"

Litra cracked the whip, the fall of it stinging at his left thigh.

She wasn't interested in small talk, he decided. It would have been a perfect situation for someone into kinky sex, Culhane reflected—whips, chains, all that was missing was that Litra should have been wearing high boots. But it wasn't something he was into. A plan suddenly formed. If he could keep himself from getting an erection, she would either kill him or call the guards to have him removed. A fifty-fifty chance.

Litra sat on the bed beside him, and he looked down the length of his torso at her hands as they began to explore him. And he felt something happening. There went his plan. . . .

But what she was doing to him hurt now, and she was laughing. He promised himself that when he had the chance he would wring her neck. He closed his eyes, imagining his hands around Litra's neck, closing, tighter and tighter, the fingers gouging into the arteries, the thumbs closing the windpipe.

He opened his eyes. She had stopped kneading his crotch and was slipping her body over his, her mouth coming down over his, her tongue penetrating his mouth.

He did it. He bit her, hard.

Litra screamed and jumped back to her feet, taking up the whip into her hands, snapping it back, hauling her arm forward, Culhane shouting at her in English, "Go fuck yourself, lady—not me!"

The whip stopped. There was noise outside the doors leading to the long balcony and the doors suddenly burst open.

Standing there, dwarfed by the doors, the golden armor impossibly big for her, a spear poised in her hands, was Mary Frances Mulrooney.

Litra spun toward the doorway. Behind Mulrooney, Culhane could see two Amazons locked in combat, but he recognized one woman's face. It was Fred.

Mulrooney shouted from the doorway, "I'm here to rescue you from a fate worse than death!"

Culhane looked down at himself. "Couldn't have waited another five minutes, huh?"

The whip cracked, the spear in Mulrooney's hands sailing through the air and across the room. Mulrooney ducked back into the doorway and reached under her breastplate, the little stainless-steel .38 appearing in her right hand.

The whip cracked again, and the revolver flew from Mulrooney's right hand and landed on the bed, between Culhane's legs. He was powerless to reach it. And the hammer was cocked and the muzzle was pointed at his crotch.

Mulrooney murmured, "I think we're in trouble, Ace."

"The key, Fanny! Around her waist on the chain! The key!"

Mulrooney drew the curved dagger from her waist, then clumsily opened the Bali-Song knife from beneath her golden breastplate. A blade in each hand, she advanced on Litra.

Litra laughed, throwing down the bullwhip, letting Mulrooney come. "Look out, Fanny! She's fast and she's as strong as I am—maybe stronger!"

Mulrooney kept coming, slowly, crouching. Litra sprang forward and Mulrooney was thrown to the floor, one knife sailing across the room, the Bali-Song still in Fanny's left hand. Litra's right hand locked on Mulrooney's left wrist as they rolled across the floor, Mulrooney's head snapping back as Litra punched her across the jaw, Mulrooney's body going limp for an instant, the Bali-Song falling from her fingers. Litra hauled Mulrooney up into her arms, then over her head, balancing Mulrooney over her head in a straight-armed lift like a wrestler. She spun, hurling Mulrooney across the room. She landed across Culhane's legs.

"The gun, Fanny! Get the gun!"

But Litra lunged as Mulrooney, still dazed, rolled onto her back. Then Litra was on her, Culhane's legs feeling as though they would break. Mulrooney's right knee smashed up into Litra's stomach, and Litra rolled back, Mulrooney on top of her for an instant. Culhane's left foot was beside Litra's head, and he twisted his toes into her hair, kicking at her abdomen with his right foot.

Mulrooney gave Litra a right cross, the Amazon princess's head snapping back, Culhane knotting his toes tighter into her hair, hammering his right heel down into her midsection.

Mulrooney tore at the thin gold chain around Litra's waist, breaking it. "I got the key!"

Litra's left hand flashed up, punching Mulrooney in the throat, then she snapped a backhand slap across Mulrooney's face, sending Fanny reeling back to the floor, the key falling from Fanny's left hand.

Clumps of Litra's hair pulled out as she snapped her

legs out and down, standing. She grabbed the key from the floor, but Mulrooney was up, throwing herself against the Amazon like a high-school freshman charging a tackling dummy. Litra was thrown off-balance for an instant, the key falling from her grasp to the bed.

Litra wheeled, backhanding Mulrooney across the face. Mulrooney slid along the floor and came to a stop against the far wall, a table overturning, a bowl of fruit spilling to the floor.

Litra started toward her, fingers flexing, muscles rippling along her naked body.

Culhane could see the key on the far right of the bed. He tried reaching for it, but it was inches beyond the farthest extension of his right hand. His hands were still shackled and separated by only eighteen inches of chain.

Mulrooney was on her knees, hurling pieces of fruit from the floor at Litra, a pear smashing as it struck Litra's face.

Litra stopped in midstride. Her right hand reached to her left wrist. Litra flicked away the bracelet that was there, then her left hand moved to the right bracelet. "Fanny! Get outta here! Now!"

The right bracelet was thrown to the floor.

Culhane blinked. There was no physical change except perhaps for a tightening of the musculature, a shift in balance. But Culhane could feel it, sense it. Litra crouched now, almost on all fours, a loud hissing issuing from her throat, her lips drawn back, her teeth bared, snapping as she advanced on Fanny Mulrooney. A furious she-cat.

"Culhane! Do something!"

Culhane swung the eighteen inches of chain toward the key and missed.

Litra, her nails like claws at the tips of her fingers, poised to rip and tear, lunged. Mulrooney sprang to her feet and threw herself to the left. Litra landed like a cat on all fours, wheeling toward her, hissing, spitting, slashing the air with her claws, her teeth snapping.

"Fanny! Get the hell outta here! Do it, dammit!"

"No—not without you!"

Litra was getting ready to spring. Culhane swung the chain and it looped the key. Slowly so he would not lose it, he started dragging the key toward him. Another few inches. . . .

He looked up for an instant. Mulrooney had the spear again, thrusting toward Litra, Litra recoiling, swiping at it with her claws, swatting at it. Mulrooney grasped it now like a bar between both hands, her arms upraised.

Culhane had the key. He dropped it onto his chest. He snatched at it, tearing some of the hair from his chest that had caught in the slender gold chain.

Litra sprang into the air and crashed down, both feet against the spear shaft, snapping it, Mulrooney falling to the floor.

Culhane had one manacle opened.

Mulrooney inched back. The second manacle.

"Culhane!"

Culhane's hands were free. He reached to the collar around his neck and twisted the key into the lock hole. Then he undid the shackles around his ankles.

Free, at last, Culhane sat up, the little revolver in his right fist.

Litra sprang and Culhane was about to shoot, but Mulrooney dodged between him and his target.

He lowered the hammer and dropped the revolver to the bed, crossing the room in three strides, grabbing Fanny by the arms and throwing her aside. Litra leaped toward him now, Culhane bunching both fists together as though he held an invisible baseball bat in a death grip. As Litra's body hurtled toward him, his bunched-together fists slammed into the left side of her face at the jawline, the head snapping around. Culhane hauled both fists back across his left shoulder and hammered them out again against the tip of Litra's chin and up, her head snapping back, her body back-flipping through the doors into her changing room, crashing down upon a couchlike piece of furniture, the long, low settee smashing under her force and her weight, blood trickling from the left side of her mouth as her head lolled back against the wall.

She didn't move.

Culhane wheeled toward the doors leading to the long balcony, stepping through the doorway. Fred was still battling the Amazon guard. Culhane reached out, grabbing the guard by her hair, dragging her head back with his left hand, his right fist punching forward, straight-arming her in the jaw, his own body shuddering with the impact, the Amazon's legs buckling under her. She started to reach for him as she fell, but Culhane's left hand was still knotted into her hair. He jerked her head back, backhanding his right across the Amazon's face, hammering her down.

She lay unconscious at his feet.

He turned around and ran back into Litra's apartment, Fred right behind him.

M. F. Mulrooney was picking herself up off the floor. She smiled. "Hey—talk about finding your boyfriend in a compromising position, huh?"

Culhane, naked and streaming sweat, folded her into his arms. Even if she didn't fill the Amazon armor very much at all, she was woman enough for him. "I love you," he whispered.

Chapter Thirty-Four _____

If he lived a thousand years, Culhane thought, he would never understand Fanny Mulrooney. Despite what Litra had tried doing to him, despite what Litra had tried doing to *her*, Mulrooney had carefully replaced the Amazon princess's bracelets on her wrists, explaining to Culhane as he shackled Litra onto her own bed, "Without these, she would be in a wild rage until she exhausted herself and died."

"It's psychological—that's all it is. The bracelets symbolize self-control, and when she removes them, she lets herself go into the rage."

"Whatever," Mulrooney answered.

Culhane posted Fred outside the doorway, having dragged in the two unconscious Amazon guards. He tied one of them with Litra's whip. "You didn't bring me any pants, did you?"

"I didn't think you'd be naked in bed with some princess when I got here. I mean, I saw the wedding ceremony. You made a beautiful groom."

"Thanks, you're sweet, too. Tie up the other one, okay? Use my knife and cut up some of the bedding or something."

"She's got clothing in this changing room. I can twist some of that into ropes."

"Right," Culhane told her, hog-tying the Amazon warrior, drawing the ankles up almost to the wrists. He was tempted to put a Capone noose around her neck but didn't. He had always prided himself on not being vindictive.

Mulrooney was binding the other one with the

twisted-up sarilike robes the women wore over the ankle-length sleeveless tunics. "Are you sure that's sturdy enough?"

"I'm sure."

Culhane only nodded, going back to the bed. Something like a thin sheet was across the bed under Litra's unconscious body. Culhane started pulling at it, tugging it from under the princess and free of the bed. It was a white, linenlike material. Culhane dragged it across the room to where his Bali-Song knife had fallen. He cut a section slightly larger than a bath towel, then dropped the rest, holding the knife in his teeth as he wound it around his waist like a kilt.

"Ohh, you look cute," Mulrooney said, standing up from the Amazon warrior she had just tied. "Nice knees," she added with a smile.

"Knock it off," Culhane said through the knife in his teeth. Finished, he took the knife and closed it one-handed. "Now, rescuer person, have you and Fred there figured out how we're getting out of here?"

"Yup," Mulrooney said, grinned. "You still have that key?"

"It's over there at the foot of the bed." Mulrooney nodded and walked toward the bed.

A jewelry box had fallen to the floor during the fight, its contents spilled. Culhane saw his pen-shaped knife among the items and bent to pick it up, closing it. He clipped it at his waist, then watched as Mulrooney undid the collar and its chain lead from the head of the bed. "What are you doing?"

"You are going to be our prisoner. We'll walk you right out of here."

"I don't think it'll work."

"Got a better idea?"

"No," he admitted. He raised his chin as she came toward him, feeling the coldness of the metal around his neck again. "Don't lock it."

"I won't, don't worry. Fred and I saw where they keep their horses. We can make a break for it as soon as we get to the corrals."

"Little detour, Fanny. We have to get up to where they keep the rest of the prisoners."

Mulrooney's jaw dropped. "Those Russian guys? They would have killed us!"

"Are you ready to leave them here?"

She shrugged. "It's rough being one of the good guys. Heavens, no—we couldn't mistreat those guys just because they planned to kill us and got us into this mess to begin with."

Culhane smiled at her. "There are about fifty other guys up there. If we spring them all, it'll just make things that much more confused, and give us a better chance to get away."

"Who're you kidding?" Mulrooney smiled. "You'd never leave those other fifty guys up there. Our getting out of here is just a bonus after our good deed of the year."

"All right, so I'm transparent..."

Mulrooney laughed. "Don't stand with your legs spread apart. That thing around your waist is pretty transparent too." She tugged at the chain. "C'mon, let's get this show on the road."

THEY HAD IMPROVED ON MULROONEY'S PLANS, taking the shackles from the still-unconscious princess's wrists and tying her instead. The shackles were now back—unlocked—on Culhane's wrists, Mulrooney holding the end of the neck chain, walking slightly ahead of him, carrying her spear, her bow and quiver across her back.

Fred walked beside him, similarly armed. He had given Mulrooney her gun, and it was hidden again under her breastplate. Clutched in his right fist, Culhane held the Bali-Song, the lock disengaged for a fast, one-handed opening.

They left the palace and began to make their way through the city, Culhane keeping his eyes down, trying to look the model prisoner, Mulrooney walking quickly, but to Culhane, not quickly enough.

They passed the temple, the sweet smoke of the brazier still in the air. When he had first smelled it he had thought they were planning to drug him. But he had dismissed the idea just as quickly. Drugging someone into submission wasn't the best way to heighten sexual prowess.

They kept walking, past the temple now, turning up into the rocky area above the city and toward the prisoner compound and the cages. No one looked at them. He guessed maybe there really were a few shorter, blonder Amazons. It was funny watching Mulrooney. Looking down to the ground as he was, he could do little else but watch her feet. She was walking on her toes, as if wearing invisible high heels, to make herself appear taller.

As they turned off toward the prisoner compound, Mulrooney whispered hoarsely, "What's the plan?"

"They don't keep too many guards there. I noticed two, sometimes three. But a lot of the warriors seem to like to stroll around the place, checking out the stock. If we're lucky, just the guards'll be there. Then we get up as close as we can and start bashing heads. Don't use the gun unless you have to."

"Noise—gotcha."

"Can you tell Fred?"

"She'll follow my lead."

"*I* can tell Fred. I just remembered that." Under his breath he started assembling the right words in Greek to tell her the plan, Fred grunting her understanding when he was through.

They were at the edge of the compound now. Culhane stole a look up: two guards. Their luck was holding.

"Steer me close to the two warriors. You and Fred take the one on the left, and I'll take the one on the right," Culhane said in a stage whisper. They kept moving, Mulrooney walking him right up to the Amazon guards. One of the women turned. She seemed to be staring at Mulrooney. Fred stepped beside Mulrooney and stopped. Mulrooney dropped the end of the chain and rammed her spear down on the instep of the guard nearest her, Culhane reaching up and out, swinging both manacled wrists in a tight arc, the manacles smashing the Amazon nearest him on the side of the head. He stepped back, and Fred's fist shot into the first Amazon's jaw, the woman keeling over. Mulrooney was shaking her right fist. "I slugged her in the stomach— forgot about the damned armor!"

Culhane undid the manacles and threw them down at his feet. He worked open the collar around his neck, snatching back the rest of the chain as he removed it. "This could be a handy little weapon."

"They don't have any keys."

"Litra's guards had the keys to the cages. I never saw what they did with them. Each of you grab a big rock and hand it to the biggest guy in each cage. Have him smash the lock, then use your spears to pry it apart."

"Right."

"Meet you back here." Culhane took off at a trot toward the cage and the old man.

He ran past Kruglovitch who shouted, "Culhane— free us!" He waved but kept running.

When he reached his cage, the old dentist was still sitting in his corner. Culhane stopped at the cage door. "What about it?" he asked, catching his breath. "Coming back to the real world?"

The old man stood up, walked over to Culhane, and handed him his cigarettes and lighter. Culhane lit a cigarette.

"No."

"Why?" Culhane asked, but he thought he knew.

The old man laughed. "Because in my heart, lad, I do love the queen. Here, I can see her now and then from a distance. Once in a while she stops by my cage and smiles at me. Who knows? Maybe someday, well..." And there was a light in the old man's pale eyes for an instant. And then the light faded. "Out there—hell, here I'm a sex symbol, lad. And here I can see her. You didn't kill my daughter, did you?"

"No, Doctor, I didn't kill her. She'll have a sore jaw—and might even get you sprung to check out her teeth."

The old man extended his right hand through the bars. "Good luck, lad. Hell, that girl you came in with—not the tall one—the girl too puny to be an Amazon. She your girl?"

"Yeah—and she's just right for me," Culhane said. "Good luck to you, sir."

"One more thing. Don't send the Brazilian army in here to destroy all this."

Culhane smiled, inhaling on his cigarette. "Yeah, well, I don't think the Brazilian army would stand a chance against these broads anyway." Culhane shot the man a wave and ran for the cell with Kruglovitch and the young Russian soldier.

OF THE FIFTY-THREE MEN IMPRISONED, only eighteen had chosen freedom. There was a best-seller in this somewhere, Culhane mused.

They ran down from the cages where the men had been penned, Mulrooney chattering to him between breaths. "And so Fred kept me pinned down, and I couldn't do anything to help you out and then Sebastiao came along."

"He's all right then?"

"Father Santini's taking care of him. He had a nasty head wound, but he'll be okay."

"How're Santini and the others?"

"Helene was hit on the head, but she was coming around. That girl is really useless, Josh. And Magdelena is fine—wounded in the left arm but okay."

Culhane raised his right hand, signaling a stop to his ragtag army. The men behind Culhane, Mulrooney and Fred were armed with rocks and sticks from the firewood pile.

Viewed from the edge of the compound, the city shimmered below them. Torches had been lit, the sunlight now gone from above, and the city was nearly as bright as day, the gold veins in the rock and the gold trim of the buildings and the gold statuary glittering in the torchlight.

No, Culhane decided, he wouldn't betray the presence of the city. He had learned something. And the men with them—however many survived—would not either, he knew. What man would admit to being held prisoner by Amazon women and used as a sexual slave? And what man—if he said it—would even be believed? Culhane laughed. Another experience totally useless for Sean Dodge. But not for Josh Culhane. He reached out and placed his right arm around Mulrooney, holding the

Bali-Song in his right fist, the chain and the collar that he would be able to use as a flail in his left.

Some of the men spoke English, some Spanish, most Portuguese.

He said the English word that was nearly the same in Spanish and Portuguese—"Liberty"—and he gestured toward the corrals on the far edge of the city.

He started jogging easily, Mulrooney at his side, Fred behind them, then the eighteen freed prisoners, the Russian major and his young soldier bringing up the rear.

They were at the edge of the city proper when Culhane heard the shouted war cry that he had first heard less than twenty-four hours ago in the jungle before the battle.

Culhane wheeled toward the sound. Amazon warriors were on the roofs of the flanking buildings, their bows poised. "Run for it!" Culhane shouted.

Arrows filled the air, spears hurtling downward, Culhane grabbing at Mulrooney, his knife in his teeth now, open, Fred pausing, turning, firing. Culhane glanced back, one of the Amazons felled with an arrow.

Culhane grabbed at the Greek girl. "Move it, Fred!" Culhane dragged her by the arm, running now, Mulrooney stopped ahead, edging back, Culhane running up beside her. Where the street curved, a wall of Amazon warriors stood, their clubs poised for battle.

"Josh?"

"Yeah, yeah, I know." Culhane looked behind them. The Amazons on the rooftops had ceased firing. But their bows were poised.

Culhane held the Bali-Song in his right fist. "All right," he shouted. Some of the men could understand, some couldn't, he knew, but he hoped they'd follow the others. "If we stay, they'll slaughter the two women—

and probably kill us, too. That's if we surrender. I won't.'' He stepped in front of Mulrooney.

The wall of Amazon women broke at the center, and walking through the opening in her jeweled armor, the left side of her face puffed, discolored and swollen, her hands holding her spear in front of her horizontally, was Litra.

Culhane watched her gray eyes. They focused on Fanny Mulrooney and then she laughed.

"Bitch," Mulrooney hissed under her breath.

"Why are you whispering? She doesn't understand English.''

"Why is she whispering to her mother? I don't understand Greek.''

Mulrooney was right. Litra had been joined by the queen. The queen, wearing white robes trimmed with gold, was staring at Culhane.

Kruglovitch called out, "We shall attack—go down fighting like men!''

"Wait," Culhane said. Something strange was happening here.

The queen stepped forward, speaking slowly. "What's she saying?" Mulrooney hissed.

Culhane tried translating. "That, oh, that she is amazed. No man has ever defeated an Amazon for thousands of years.''

"What the hell does she mean?" Mulrooney snarled. "You just helped—''

Culhane held her hand, squeezing it. He shifted the knife to his left hand with the chain. "She's saying that Litra's honor must be served.''

"Oh, no," Mulrooney moaned.

"She's saying that—'' He looked at Mulrooney. "What?"

"She's saying that the skinny girl and the tall woman

who looks like she should be an Amazon are welcome to stay and live as Amazons, even though the skinny woman..." Culhane fought back a laugh.

"What'd she say?" Mulrooney demanded.

"Even though the skinny woman has breasts the size of grapes and legs like twigs."

Mulrooney started to step forward, but Culhane held her back. "She's saying that all three of us have proven ourselves as warriors and must be treated as warriors, or Litra's honor will never be restored." And Culhane watched as the queen reached to Litra and started to take Litra's spear. Litra did not let go. The queen slapped Litra across the face.

Litra released the spear. The queen snapped the spear as effortlessly as if it were a toothpick. She threw both ends to the ground.

The queen began to speak again. "We are all free to go—including the rest of the men who have chosen to go with us. But we must raise our hands to the sky and pledge to Artemis never to reveal the city."

Slowly, Culhane bent to set down the chain, closing the Bali-Song and securing it at his waistband. He raised his hands palms upward to the sky. Beside him, Mulrooney put down her spear and raised her hands. He looked behind him. Fred had done the same, and slowly, one by one, the eighteen men began to throw down their rocks and sticks.

Kruglovitch and the other Russian soldier had taken up the weapons of the two fallen prison compound guards. Kruglovitch did not throw down his weapon.

Culhane called to him. "Kruglovitch—put down the spear!"

"They will kill us!"

"We can trust them and maybe get out of here, or be killed. If they cross us, then we fight."

"No! A man does not trust his enemies!"

"Kruglovitch!"

"Nyet!"

Culhane smiled at the queen, lowered his hands and walked toward Kruglovitch, the young Russian soldier holding fiercely to his spear, as well. "Please—do this. We don't have anything to lose. Honor is important to these people. The queen pledged before her warriors that we'll be freed. She'll stick with it."

"This is what I think of your trust in this female barbarian!" And Kruglovitch hauled the spear up to throw it, Culhane shouting at him not to. Culhane hurled himself toward Kruglovitch, but the Russian's eyes suddenly glazed, and blood bubbled up from his mouth. Kruglovitch tumbled forward, the young Russian beside him casting down his spear. Kruglovitch's back had at least a dozen spears protruding skyward, the Russian major facedown in the dirt.

Culhane raised his palms upward, standing beside the young Russian now and reciting with the queen the pledge to the goddess Artemis.

Chapter Thirty-Five _____

Mulrooney had been allowed to keep the bracelets. She had changed into her own clothing and sat on a flat rock studying them in her hands, Culhane near her, changing into the things from his backpack. His combat boots had been returned, and he sat down beside Mulrooney, threading his spare boot laces into them. "What are you going to do?" Culhane asked her.

"You mean about the Amazons?"

"Yeah."

"Well," she answered, looking at him and smiling, "I took that pledge, didn't I? Just like you did."

"That you did."

"So I can't very well—"

"No, you can't. Not very well."

"No."

Culhane put his right arm around her and drew her close. "Do you think the Russian will tell?" she asked him.

"No. I talked to him about it while we were walking. He very much respected Major Kruglovitch. Kruglovitch died in battle and was never taken prisoner. Kruglovitch died so that he—the kid—could get away. Whoever it was that attacked the column last night— well, they were just ordinary natives with long hair and flashy weapons. There are no such people as Amazons. The guys who ran off into the jungle won't be specific— they'd face court-martial. They had a rendezvous point set and he'll make his way toward it. He's sticking with the rest of the guys we sprung from the cages until he gets downriver near Manaus. All the Russians had Brazilian money, ID—counterfeit ID of course—and civilian clothes. He'll make it."

"What about you?" Mulrooney asked, her voice very low, soft.

"We have to get that ransom delivered. That's what I came here for in the first place. Then let's go home, okay?"

Mulrooney buried her head against his chest. "Let's go home," she whispered so softly that he could barely hear her.

After a while he returned to lacing up his combat boots. Mulrooney used her cigarette lighter to burn her copy of the map to the Amazon city and the original she had taken from the body of Professor Xanthos.

As Culhane, Mulrooney and Fred finished digging the hole to bury the Amazon armor, Mulrooney whispered, "I wonder if this is the way all legends die," and very gently she placed her Amazon bracelets into the hole and mounded dirt over them with her hands.

Book Three

The Golden Death

Chapter Thirty-Six _____

It was called forcible entry, with or without the accompaniment of an FBI agent, Hoevermann reflected. The president of Dynamic Plating, a Palmer Industries subsidiary, insisted that it was illegal. Hoevermann and Agent Summerfield stood in the underground executive garage with the corporate officer Ryan Burns and the two state policemen who had invited him to the facility for questioning. And with Ryan Burns stood his lawyer, a Mr. Ashton. "My client needs to tell you nothing, sir. You represent no official interests in this country. And as for the FBI, entering Dynamic Plating without a warrant is simple burglary, and I shall ask for both of your arrests, and prepare criminal and civil charges."

Hoevermann looked at the lawyer. He was cold standing on the concrete floor of the underground parking lot. "Arthur Dzikowski took his own life after flushing and burning evidence. Part of the evidence was a memo from Dynamic Plating. We are talking about thousands of lives that may be lost involving nuclear material originating at Palmer Radionics."

"We have nothing to say," Ashton said grimly.

"What about you, Senhor Burns?" Hoevermann looked directly at Dynamic Plating's president. The chin was weak, the hair thinning, but the body looked lean and fit. It went with the expensive jogging clothes the man wore, Hoevermann supposed.

"My client will tell you nothing," Ashton answered for Burns.

"What I have to say should not be said in front of these two gentlemen from the state police." Hoevermann lit a cigarette.

"Wait outside," Summerfield said.

The men nodded and walked off.

After a long moment, Hoevermann, Summerfield, Burns and his lawyer Ashton stood alone in the parking garage. Hoevermann spoke to Summerfield. "Do you trust me? I mean, based upon our limited knowledge of each other since we met at the airport?"

"Yes, sir."

"Give me your gun."

"Wait just a damned minute," Ashton snapped.

"I can't give you my gun, sir!"

"I will fix everything, *senhor*—trust me." Hoevermann looked long and hard at his young American ally. "I will say it again: the lives of thousands of my people hang in the balance. If the situation were reversed, and you were in my country pursuing nuclear terror, I would trust you. I feel that."

Summerfield swallowed hard. "What the hell—I can kiss off my job anyway. And I guess I'm looking at jail already. Why not?" The FBI agent shrugged, his eyes suddenly smiling. He reached under his coat.

"Just a goddamned minute," Burns started. "Ashton—do something!"

"My client—"

Ashton fell silent as Hoevermann took the gun and pointed it at Burns, the muzzle less than two feet from the man's head. "Senhor Burns, you received nuclear material from Palmer Radionics, then shipped it from here. How much and how was it disguised?"

"You're bluffing," Ashton snarled.

"The gun is not pointed at your head, *senhor*, but at the head of Senhor Burns." Hoevermann inhaled on the cigarette in the left corner of his mouth, waiting. He was not bluffing. There would be no hope of prosecuting Burns after doing this, and if Burns failed to reveal the information, Burns had to be punished. "The worst that will be done to me is that I will be deported and forced into early retirement. I am quite well off, and being deported to Brazil—my family home is in a lovely spot—is hardly being exiled, is it? I have nothing to lose." He started to squeeze the trigger, very slowly, so Burns would see the cylinder start to rotate.

"You wouldn't kill an innocent man—" Burns stammered.

"I hardly consider someone who knowingly cooperates with nuclear terrorism innocent," Hoevermann said, smiling good-naturedly.

At the very measured rate of the trigger pull, he calculated Burns would be dead in less than a second.

"Wait!"

"Yes?"

"Fifty pounds of plutonium. It was encased in lead ingots the size of building bricks when—for God's sake, put down that gun!"

Hoevermann stopped the trigger pressure, but he didn't move the muzzle from Burns's head.

"We made up lead ingots that were hollow inside. The stuff was inside. And then we plated them with a five-hundredths-of-an-inch-thick layer of gold. When the process was completed, they weighed one hundred forty-six pounds. That's all I know. They were picked up and taken away."

Hoevermann lowered the revolver. "Enough, from what I have read, to construct a thermonuclear device. The lead will shield those near it. But if the ingots come in contact with water, the shielding will be insufficient if the exposure is for a sufficient length of time. There could be a radiation burst. Or an uncalculated blast. These lead ingots are currently being brought upriver along the Negro, a branch of the Amazon. An American who thinks he is merely delivering an ordinary ransom carries them. One of my agents—a very lovely young woman—accompanies him. As do, I am told, several other innocent people. Now I must order them to be stopped at all costs from delivering this ransom, even if it means killing them. My country will press no charges. Your involvement in the incident, Senhor Burns, will be swept under the rug—in exchange that no charges be brought against this young man." Hoevermann returned the revolver to Summerfield.

"I don't know about that—" Ashton began.

"Shut up," Burns whispered, his voice hoarse, tight. "You want to do something, Ashton? Draw up a letter of resignation for me." And Burns turned and walked away.

Hoevermann only watched for a moment. "It is time," he told Summerfield, "for your friend Cashman to once again exhibit his driving skills—to the airport. I will need to be put in contact with my country's ambassador and I need transportation arranged. Can we do that on your police radio?"

"Yes, sir, I think we can."

Hoevermann nodded and clapped the young man on the shoulder. He was very tired and felt very old.

Chapter Thirty-Seven _____

The Russians who had not died in the jungle attack had only had superficial wounds. Santini had treated worse, seen worse, his medical training in Special Forces comprehensive. They had drifted away from the battle site, and he had made no attempt to stop them. He had prayed over the graves of their dead comrades, prayed for their souls. And at dawn, with no sign of Culhane, Mulrooney or the Greek girl, he had announced his decision to take Helene Chavez and Magdelena and return to the original campsite by the river and dig up the gold in the two suitcases. The ransom needed to be paid, or Amelina, Scott Palmer's bride, would be killed.

Santini had seen enough death. He would keep his promise to Culhane. He would deliver the ransom himself.

It had taken several hours to reach the campsite, Santini taking a different route to avoid any further complications. There were still the river bandits to consider: some could have survived. And the Uruentes. With Sebastiao on the drag spot, guarding their rear, Santini had forged his way ahead, a machete from one of the dead Russians in his hand, one of the AKS-74 assault rifles slung across his back. He had no idea if he could use it and kill intentionally again. But he had removed his clerical collar.

Sebastiao and Magdelena watched while he dug, Helene Chavez showing no interest. She sat at the far edge of the campsite, looking out into the water.

He raised the suitcases from the hole in which he and

Culhane had buried them. Already the damp soil had begun to attack the metal on the cases. Each case carried a combination lock, and Culhane had shared the combinations with him. Damascus Santini opened one of the cases.

He lifted back the material beneath the case lid and stared. Gold ingots the size of bricks. He took one in his hand. He had no idea what gold should weigh.

"My God," Magdelena murmured.

"Some people's God, yes." And then Santini began to laugh and couldn't stop.

"Father—there is something wrong?" Sebastiao asked.

Magdelena crouched beside him. "What is it, Father?" she almost whispered.

Santini finally controlled his laughter. "That cheap bastard—Scott—too cheap to pay his wife's ransom."

"What do you mean, Father?"

Santini looked up from his knees. Sebastiao stood beside him, holding the bolt-action rifle, staring out into the jungle. "Are you Catholic, Sebastiao?"

"Yes, Father, I have always—"

"A Catholic priest handles gold, right? Altar vessels, candlesticks, cups?"

"But, of course, Father."

"And gold doesn't tarnish, does it?"

"No—"

Santini took the bayonet for the AKS-74 from the utility belt he had taken off one of the dead Russians. He picked one of the more corroded spots and scratched at the ingot with the blade of the bayonet. A dark substance—it was soft to the knife edge—was beneath the gold. "Lead. We've been risking our lives—causing other people to die—all for a bunch of lousy lead bricks because Scott wouldn't cough up the real gold to ransom his wife!'' Santini threw the ingot into the suitcase, then bent his head to his chest and closed his eyes.

Beside him, he heard Magdelena murmur, ''Perhaps we should take the suitcases to the meeting with the kidnappers. Perhaps we can fool them and save Amelina.''

''To Ontem?''

''Yes, Father.''

Santini looked at her. ''Yes—we can do that. It's her only hope now.''

''We will pray, Father. Will you lead us?'' Sebatiao asked.

''I, ah, I can't do that, Sebastiao. I'm sorry—more than you know,'' Damascus Santini got to his feet and stared for a while longer at the suitcases. He decided that the ingots with the most obvious tarnish should be packed into the bottoms of the suitcases. He could add deception to his other sins.

And lying. He told Sebastiao and Magdelena, ''Say nothing about this to Helene Chavez. If she asks, let me take care of it.''

''But, Father—'' Sebastiao began.

''Just do as I say.''

Chapter Thirty-Eight

When he had been a boy, he had wanted to be a pilot. He became a policeman instead. But he could close his eyes and then open them and suddenly he was a boy again. The controls were in front of him. Real. Glowing. He flew the SR-71 instead of the American whose flight uniform showed no rank or unit and was the same black color as his plane.

The clouds were endless. He was free of the earth. But then he returned, the pilot's voice coming into his headset: "Inspector Hoevermann, your government has been patched into our radio network. I have a message. I'll not monitor it if you like."

"No—your government has been more helpful than I could have imagined," Hoevermann said into the microphone near his lips. It had been impossible to find a flying suit that properly fit him, and instead of a standard high-altitude suit, he wore a two-piece astronaut suit that had been waiting for him in Miami after the conventional military-jet flight out of Chicago.

And the voice came in, but he could barely recognize it. "Inspector—can you hear me? This is Manoel do Reis."

"Yes, Manoel—I hear you."

"We have arrested Palmer. Repeat—arrested Palmer. He has admitted that the ingots contain plutonium. His engineers indicate enough for a bomb. Our scientists agree. He has told us that one of the members of the party who travels with the American writer Culhane is an agent of the kidnappers. He will not say who. Over."

Hoevermann made a mental note to correct his counterterrorist people on their rather sloppy radio procedures.

"Manoel. About Culhane—where are they?"

"Our observation helicopters haven't picked them up yet, *senhor*."

"If they can land, they are to alert Senhor Culhane to the situation and solicit his help. If they cannot land, they are to use their loudspeakers. If this fails, they are to stop Culhane at all costs. Kill him if necessary. Are the substitute ingots being prepared?"

"*Sim, senhor.*"

"If Senhor Culhane can be intercepted and the ingots substituted for the ones he carries, perhaps at least Senhora Palmer can be saved."

"Senhor Hoevermann?"

"Yes, Manoel?"

"Several bodies have been washed ashore since the storm. One of the bodies was partially devoured by a shark, but enough remained of the left hand to get a print check. Interpol was contacted in your absence, *senhor*. The fingerprints match those found on a fragment of a bomb planted by terrorists in West Germany. The man has been identified as Angelo Guttierez, a Cuban who is suspected to have been trained by the Soviet KGB in terrorism. Guttierez always works with a woman. Her name is not known, but it is assumed she also is Cuban or from one of the other Central or South American nations."

"That could be the person traveling with Culhane. If that is the case, we must be doubly cautious. She could activate the nuclear material—she would know more about it than we. I should be landing in Manaus in an hour. Have my helicopter ready. Dispatch our strike force by floatplane to Ontem. It is the only logical place for the ransom to be delivered."

"*Sim, senhor.*"

"Hoevermann out."

Try as he could, Gunther Hoevermann could not return to his fantasy of flight.

Chapter Thirty-Nine

Culhane looked up, hearing the rotor blades overhead. It was the sort of thing he would do in his books: Sean Dodge in terrible trouble, racing through the Amazon jungles with two women, a fortune in gold buried somewhere up ahead, a rendezvous with terrorists to attempt to free a terrified kidnapped woman. Because the good guys always win.

But the helicopter was real.

Fred crouched low to the ground, raising her bow as if to fire.

"What do we do?" Mulrooney shouted over the heightening noise of the rotors.

"It'll be Hoevermann, but we don't have any choice. The ransom was to be paid in Ontem this morning. Let me do the talking!"

"Who the hell is Hoevermann?"

Culhane tried to answer, but the PA was braying, the English heavily accented, "Stay right where you are, Senhor Culhane, or we will be forced to open fire. The ransom you carry is in reality fifty pounds of plutonium. Stay right where you are!"

The helicopter hovered. Ropes were let down and armed men in jungle fatigues started rappelling down on either side of the chopper.

"Put my rifle down on the ground, Fanny," he shouted as he walked over to her and put his lips beside her right ear.

She set the rifle down and then dropped to her knees beside Fred, using her hand signals again to get Fred to lower her bow. Culhane just stared up at the men descending from the chopper. "Nuclear material—plutonium—oh, shit," he murmured....

DAMASCUS SANTINI CARRIED ONE OF THE SUITCASES, Sebastiao the other, the two women between them. Santini led the way as they walked within a hundred yards of the river toward the rendezvous with the terrorists. Santini wondered what he would do. He would stay at the mission—if he ever reached it—until another priest could be sent out to replace him. And then . . . his bishop had told him once that he was too worldly for the church. Santini had insisted that he fought to curb his impulses.

But the bishop was right.

Santini considered why he had joined the priesthood. To retreat, he wondered. He pondered this as he heard Helene Chavez's voice from behind him. "Father?"

"Yes?"

"I think we had better stop for a moment."

Santini stopped, turning around to face her and setting down his suitcase. It was incredibly heavy. "Yes?"

"You wish to deliver the ransom?"

"We don't have any choice if we're going to save Scott Palmer's wife."

Helene Chavez smiled. "Sebastiao," she called without looking at the guide. "Check your map and take a compass reading if you need to. We should be very close."

"*Sim, menina.* Close to what?"

Santini sat down on his suitcase. He started to laugh. "All along—you aren't a doctor, are you?"

"No," Helene Chavez said, and smiled.

Magdelena grabbed her by the shoulder and swung her around. "You—"

Helene Chavez pushed Magdelena's hand away.

"Close to what, *menina*?" Sebastiao insisted.

Damascus Santini answered for her. "We aren't going to Ontem. We never were. That's why Helene was sent to accompany Culhane. Get him close to Ontem, then tell him the real rendezvous site, right?"

"Yes." She smiled again.

"And you're one of them."

"Yes."

"Why don't I kill you?"

"Because you are a priest."

"I took my collar off back there, remember?"

"If you kill me, the ransom will never be paid, and Scott Palmer's lovely wife Amelina will be raped and then beaten to death."

Helene Chavez still smiled. Damascus Santini stood up from his perch on the suitcase, then backhanded her across the smile. She staggered back, a trickle of blood from the right side of her mouth. "You make up your mind, priest," she sneered. "Right now. You play the hero all that you wish—and Amelina dies the way I said she would die."

"Give Sebastiao the map references. Let's get this thing over with."

Despite the blood still dribbling from her mouth, Helene Chavez smiled again.

JOSH CULHANE STARED AT THE HOLE.

"What now, Ace?" Fanny Mulrooney whispered.

Culhane turned around to face the cunterterrorist force group leader. "Well, it *was* here—honest."

Culhane, Mulrooney and Fred had been led a half mile to a clearing for pickup by the chopper, which had landed them on the river near their original campsite. Informed aboard the aircraft that substitute ingots were being prepared, Culhane had decided to cooperate rather than attempt to commandeer the helicopter.

He now reconsidered. "What's the plan, guys?"

"If Father Santini has the plutonium, that is regrettable. He must be near to the point where the ransom is to be paid," the counterterrorist leader told him. The leader held no submachine gun; he carried only a pistol holstered at his belt. The other two had submachine guns slung under their right arms, the bolts closed. The fourth man was the pilot, and he lounged beside the chopper, standing on the starboard side float, smoking a cigarette. Culhane began to calculate. "But the ransom cannot be paid, I am afraid. We shall attempt to stop him as we did you. If we cannot—"

"But Father Santini has one of the terrorists with him—you said that," Fanny Mulrooney interrupted. "Santini will be killed either way."

"It cannot be helped, *menina*. The plutonium cannot be surrendered to the terrorists."

Culhane lit a cigarette. He walked over to stand beside Mulrooney. Fred sat on a log some distance away. "He's right. We can't let those terrorists get their hands on enough plutonium for a bomb. Hell, they wouldn't even need a detonator if it's encased in lead ingots like they say." Sean Dodge had fought nuclear terrorists more than once, and Culhane had done a lot of reading on the subject. "I don't even want to think about it." Mulrooney was looking at him strangely now. "You see, water retards the natural and very necessary neutron radiation, and with all the plutonium in two suitcases—hell." He sucked in his breath. "Just tie the two suitcases together—and drop them from an aircraft into a reservoir or a river, and instead of a radiation burst, you'd have enough for the plutonium to go critical—and explode." Culhane flipped his cigarette into the chest of the counterterrorist strike force leader, then wheeled, his right foot snapping up and out into the man's abdomen. "Fred!" he yelled.

Culhane wheeled right as one of the officers went for his submachine gun. Culhane took one long-strided step and crossed the man's jaw with his left, hard. Fred had pinned the third officer to the ground and was strangling him with the sling from his submachine gun.

Culhane snatched up the fallen man's Uzi and threw it to Mulrooney. "Pull the bolt back and point it at 'em—don't let Fred kill that guy." Then Culhane was running toward the riverbank, the pilot clambering back into his machine, Culhane jumping from the muddy bank and almost missing the pontoon, his legs into the water. He grabbed at one of the support struts, wrenching himself up, the helicopter's rotor speed increasing, Culhane throwing himself into the machine through the open doorway, wrestling the pilot from his seat, Culhane's right arm snapping out, crossing the pilot's jaw, hammering him back. Culhane cut the power, the pilot coming for him, Culhane's left moving pendulum fashion into the pilot's groin. Culhane rasped, "Sorry, pal," and as the man doubled up, the knife edge of Culhane's right hand chopped him lightly behind the left ear.

Culhane moved from the cockpit into the fuselage. The pilot had been weaponless.

Culhane opened the chest by the portside of the fuselage. Emergency flares and rappelling ropes and other items were stored there. So were his guns and Mulrooney's little revolver. There was a third Uzi, and he grabbed it and one of the loaded magazines, ramming the magazine up the well.

He looked to the riverbank. Mulrooney had her subgun aimed at the three men, one of them holding his throat, doubled over. Fred stood over him holding the submachine gun like a club.

"All right, ladies, let's get rid of our friendly pilot here, leave these nice gentlemen a gun and a hand-held radio, and get on our way." Culhane didn't quite know what he was going to do, but it was the sort of thing Sean Dodge would have said.

Chapter Forty

"We cannot go there, Father."

Santini turned to look at Sebastiao. The man's eyes were pinpoints of fear, and then he looked down into the dish-shaped valley. It looked like an ordinary cave except for the markings on the stone near the entrance. The cave was set at the top of a rise at the center of the small valley. "Why not? What do those markings mean?"

Sebastiao made the sign of the cross. "It is an Uruente burial cave, Father."

"And it's where the ransom will be paid," Helene Chavez said. "We had trouble with the Uruentes. They don't like submachine guns. You'll be safe—from them."

Santini looked at her and nodded, saying nothing. Then he turned to Sebastiao. "You take Magdelena and get her upriver to Ontem."

"But, Father, I cannot—"

"He's right," Magdelena volunteered, Santini looked at her. "I'm going with you, Father."

"Me, too!"

Santini looked at both of them and smiled. "Al
right! Let's do it, then!" He picked up the suitcase and
started down the incline and into the valley.

SANTINI STOPPED AT THE BOTTOM of the rise.

"You must bring the gold inside," Helene Chavez
said beside him.

"No," Santini told her softly. "They bring Amelina
to the entrance of the cave. I assume they're waiting for
us."

"That is not the way it is to be done."

"I'm getting a little tired of following their instructions. Josh Culhane probably lost his life over this.
Fanny Mulrooney and that Greek girl, Fred—they're
probably all dead. The riverboat crew, the captain. The
American engineer, the Englishman. The Japanese. All
the others. Those bandits. No. You tell your buddies that
if they want the gold, I see the girl first—and *then* we
make a transfer. And don't be too heavy on me being a
priest." Santini set down the case and moved the AKS-74
forward on its sling. "Tell them I took off my collar
when I picked up this. Tell them I got ninety-two regis-
tered kills in Vietnam shooting scum like them. Tell them
they can have their gold, but only when I get the girl."

He caught Sebastiao's eyes, then looked away. There
was no gold—but Helene Chavez didn't know that.

Helene started up toward the cave mouth, up the incline from the valley floor, Santini calling after her,
"Far enough, lady—you call from there."

Beside him, Magdelena whispered, "I will pray for
you, Father."

"Don't," he told her. He held the assault rifle tight in
both fists.

Helene Chavez called from the midway point between
Santini and the cave mouth. "The ransom is here!"

He was surprised that she was using English, but he read it as denoting an international force. He wondered if he would again see the Frenchman who had set the charges aboard the cruise ship, causing the death of all those people.

Santini remembered seeing Captain Porter in the water. Why had he seen him? He asked himself what was God's purpose. The captain of the ship had already been dead, yet Santini had seen him in a lifeboat that was not there, beckoning to him so he'd keep swimming a little longer. He had racked his brain to think how the ransom demands had been placed in his pocket. When had the captain done it? He could not understand how they had gotten there.

What was his own purpose? Why was he here?

And then he saw the Frenchman standing in the cave mouth. He recognized the voice as the Frenchman spoke. "Priest—I remember you."

"And I remember you."

"Did you pray for my immortal soul, priest, since I am such a sinner?"

"No. But if the girl's harmed, I'll kill you—you can bank on that."

The Frenchman laughed, reaching out of sight, then dragging a woman in a tattered and stained wedding dress into the entrance. A cloth sack was over her head, a chain around her neck, her wrists handcuffed in front of her. "Here she is, priest. Where's my gold?"

"Amelina!" Santini called. "Are you all right?"

"We gagged her, priest. She kept moaning all night and robbing us of our much-needed rest." The Frenchman laughed. "She can talk to you all she wants, but only after the gold is up here—with me."

Santini looked at Sebastiao. "Sebastiao, take one

suitcase up to Helene. Leave it beside her and return. Do it!''

"Yes, Father."

Sebastiao started forward, Santini shouting up to the cave mouth, "Sebastiao is bringing up half of the gold. You bring Amelina down to where Helene is."

"Are you threatening me, priest?"

"I promise you," Santini said.

The Frenchman laughed, then started down from the cave mouth with the hooded and chained girl in the tattered wedding dress. Santini watched the man. He had always prided himself on never breaking a promise.

Chapter Forty-One _____

The headphones not only served as speakers for the radio, but they muffled the sound of the helicopter. He was glad of that. Hoevermann adored fixed-wing aircraft, reading about them, flying in them whenever possible. The experience of flying in one of the American SR-71s, perhaps the fastest jet in the world, certainly in the Free World, was something he would forever dream of.

But Hoevermann hated helicopters with a passion. They went up and down and sideways too much. They made incredible noise.

Manoel's voice came through his headphones, "Calling Inspector Hoevermann. Calling Inspector Hoevermann. Come in, Inspector."

Hoevermann spoke into his teardrop-shaped microphone: "What is it? Word of Culhane?"

"Yes, Inspector. After Culhane and the two women were picked up by group leader de Rocha and his men, things did not go well."

Hoevermann shook his head. "What did not go well, Manoel?"

"The gold was not where it was supposed to be buried. Culhane and the two women took group leader de Rocha by surprise, disarmed him and his men, then stole the helicopter. Group leader de Rocha thinks they plan to warn the terrorists."

Manoel's voice ended. Without proper radio protocol, Hoevermann noted again. "De Rocha is insane. Tell him I said so. Where is he now?"

"Culhane left him a radio and a submachine gun. De Rocha used the radio to call us. They raised another of the helicopters. Uruente raiding parties have been sighted on their side of the river, and they never cross the river unless for burial ceremonies—"

Again, Manoel's voice just cut off. Hoevermann said into the microphone, "Try to locate Culhane and the stolen helicopter. He is a lucky man if he is alive so far. He may be lucky enough to find the plutonium. I doubt he would have stolen the helicopter otherwise. He knows the contents?"

"De Rocha told him, Inspector. But de Rocha became suspicious. The North American Culhane seemed to know a great deal about nuclear materials."

The voice died again. Hoevermann spoke into his microphone. "He is not with the terrorists. He writes adventure stories. That is how he knows about such things. Find him! We are proceeding toward Ontem."

He stared at the jungle canopy beneath him. Where was Culhane? And where was the plutonium?

Chapter Forty-Two _____

Amelina stood trembling, Helene Chavez holding her by
the shoulders but not comforting her. Santini stared at
Amelina. There was something wrong. The Frenchman
flanked Amelina on the other side, Sebastiao moving
down now, stopping at the base of the incline from the
cave mouth. "And now what, Father?"

Santini considered the question. He didn't want to
lose the initiative. "Now—you send her down, and I'll
bring up the second suitcase myself."

"How can I trust you, priest?"

"You can't," said Santini. He didn't wait for further
conversation. The AKS-74 in his right hand, he picked
up the second suitcase with his left. As he walked between Sebastiao and Magdelena, he rasped under his
breath, "Once the girl is down, get her away—quickly!
Very quickly! Remember—this isn't gold."

Sebastiao murmured, "God be with you, Father."

Santini said nothing, walking. The incline was a
ramp, built to reach the cave mouth, built of hard-
packed dirt and stone. On either side it dropped off to
the level of the natural terrain, in places quite steeply.
He realized that dense ground cover and heavy tangles
of vines obscured the real level of the ground. He kept
walking, the AKS-74 aimed ahead of him.

The Frenchman was taunting him. "With all this
priest business, I'll bet you do not even remember how
to fire a gun."

"If you think I've lost my flair for this sorta thing,
gimme a try." Santini kept walking. He could see the
woman in the wedding dress more clearly now. He

blinked; he remembered the almost lily-whiteness of Amelina's hands when Scott Palmer had placed the wedding ring on her finger. The ring was there, but the hands were dark brown. The dress was so long he could not see her feet.

But the hands. . . it was not Amelina. Santini stopped. "What is it, priest?"

"The girl's an Indian. Where's Amelina?"

"Right here, Damascus." Santini looked to the cave mouth and saw Amelina in jungle fatigue pants and a tight-fitting T-shirt. She held an AK-47 aimed right at him. She laughed. "You're very sharp, Father, very sharp. The color of her hands, right?"

Santini stared at her. The bound-and-hooded girl, whoever she was, would be in a crossfire now if there were gunplay. "That's why the Uruentes are on the war-path, right?"

"You *are* good," Amelina said, smiling. There was a pistol at her right hip, a thin, short cigar in the left corner of her mouth. "We needed someone to give back when we got our little shipment from my husband Scott. How is Scott?"

"Ohh—he's terrific," Santini told her. But it sickened him. Amelina had betrayed Scott. And Scott had betrayed her by substituting lead ingots for the gold. Life sickened him. "You sure fooled Scott, didn't you?"

"Yeah, didn't I though."

"Is Amelina your real name?"

"Good as any."

"You've certainly improved your English since the wedding."

"I used to hop up to the States all the time when I studied in Havana."

"Are you really Brazilian?"

"Yeah—that's how I got the idea for all this. I grew up out here. My father—" she moved the cigar from her teeth and spat on the ground "—was a mining engineer—a real capitalist pig. But that's how I learned about explosives."

Santini looked at the suitcase beside the Indian girl, then to the one in his left hand. "Scott didn't—didn't—"

"Did some of the gold rub off?" She laughed.

"Amelina! *Fermez la bouche*!"

Santini shouted to the Frenchman, "Why should she keep quiet? What is she going to tell me?"

"You aren't leaving here alive, Damascus, so we may as well tell you. You are the proud bearer of fifty pounds of American plutonium that is going to wind up right under the main hall of the Latin American Economic Conference. American plutonium, Damascus, supplied by an American capitalist pig who doesn't want the people of Latin America to determine their own economic destiny. He smuggled the plutonium in from America to a group of right-wing mercenaries. Trouble is, Damascus, all the mercenaries get away after the explosion, and poor Scott—I don't know what they'll do to him."

If the devil were a real force in the physical world, like an old priest had told him once and he had thought was superstitious nonsense, the devil stood in the entrance of the cave, and she laughed at him, the priest, who had just delivered to her an instrument of unspeakable evil.

He started walking, still carrying the suitcase, saying nothing but getting closer to the trembling Uruente woman. "What have you got up your sleeve, Damascus?" Amelina called down to him. "Gonna rescue the Indian slut there and take the plutonium off into the jungle and bury it? What are we gonna do while you're doing all that? Hmm? We won't let you. And plutonium like that is pretty bulletproof. What are you gonna do, Damascus? Pray for God to open the clouds and destroy us with thunderbolts or some other crap like that? Or maybe God'll throw some impenetrable shield around you and the man and woman down there? And the Indian girl? Bullshit—on you and your God!''

Santini stopped. He was nearly beside the Indian girl now. He set down the suitcase. He knew now why he had not drowned, why the ransom note had been placed in his pocket.

He knew more than he had ever known in his life.

And he felt greater peace than he had felt since the killing had started bothering him and entering his dreams back in Vietnam.

He set down his rifle, letting it fall to the ground.

He slowly reached into the right-hand outside pocket of his ripped and mud-stained black suit jacket. His clerical collar. With his left hand, he released the buckle of his utility belt, letting it and the bayonet there drop to the ground at his feet.

He started to put the collar on.

He would die. But for the first time in his life, death meant nothing to him.

He walked the few steps to the girl and undid the wire binding the chain around her neck. He undid the chain.

He tugged at the hood on the girl's head, pulling it off. He looked into her face and smiled. He made the sign of the cross over her and whispered even though she understood no English, "Go down there, my child— you'll be safe." And he started her toward the foot of the incline where Sebastiao stood beside Magdelena.

Magdelena spoke. "Inspector Hoevermann of the counterterrorist strike force has been monitoring our movements through the jungle. He'll be closing in."

Helene wheeled toward Magdelena. "You! I knew Hoevermann would put a spy on the boat—you!"

"He'll never let you get away with it!" Magdelena shouted now. "Never!"

Santini just stood, summoning energy from all parts of his body into his center, where he could control it. "Magdelena, take the Indian girl, and you and Sebastiao go from here. Go from this place—now!"

Santini had set his suitcase right beside the first suitcase. He stared at the Frenchman. "I hated you. Forgive me."

The Frenchman laughed. Santini shrugged. "Can't win 'em all," he said, and in his mind he released the energy that he had called into his center, shouting, "Run, Sebastiao!" He sprang up, his left foot smashing into the two suitcases, driving them over the edge of the incline and down. His right arm shot out, the heel of his hand hitting the base of the Frenchman's jaw, snapping the head back. As his left foot settled, his right leg came up in a side kick that knifed into the Frenchman's groin, his left hand hammering forward, straight-arming Helene Chavez in the chest, his right elbow snapping up into the Frenchman's face as the Frenchman doubled over forward.

And Santini jumped over the side of the incline, into the underbrush, the AK-47 rattling death from the mouth of the cave.

Santini landed and rolled, his left shoulder striking something hard, one of the suitcases. He snatched it up. The other suitcase was beside it. He started to run, tripping, catching himself, the underbrush around him shredding under the impact of assault rifle fire and submachine guns now, too.

He kept running, on the level of the valley floor now, into the savannah, running.

He could hear Amelina shriek after him, "Goddamn you!"

Santini kept running. All those times in the school gym, all those times he had run in the streets. Running.

He stared ahead of him. The trick was to focus the mind away from the running, away from the two suitcases that pulled his arms from their sockets, away from the gunfire. Run—but don't think of it. Just run.

Ahead of him. A shrieked war cry. Uruentes.

He wanted to call out to them that their woman was safe. But he ran, veering left now, running, the Uruentes closing in, gunfire and arrows flying through the air around him.

Running.

Running.

He was lost now in fantasy, unaware of his legs moving, unaware of his burdens, unaware of it all. He was back in Vietnam for some reason. He could hear the rotor blades churning in the air almost overhead.

Running. Santini focused on the rotor noises. Running.

Running. . . .

"THAT'S HIM! And I see Sebastiao—and that must be Amelina! You said she was wearing her wedding dress when they took her."

"Anybody else?" Culhane called.

"Magdelena. But I don't see Helene."

"That's good enough. Do it right, Fanny—cut a line behind Damascus to let the terrorists or whoever they are know we mean business. The chopper should frighten away most of the Uruentes, especially once you open fire on the terrorists. 'Great bird from sky spits death'—that routine. Let's do it!" Culhane started taking the chopper down for a pass, glancing behind him

once. Mulrooney was strapped in, half suspended out the
open fuselage door, one of the Uzi submachine guns in
her hands, ready. Beside her, strapped in, as well, he
could see Fred, almost blocking Mulrooney from view,
the bow poised in Fred's hands, an arrow ready. Culhane
wondered if the downdraft would deflect the arrows.

He leveled off, crossing perhaps fifty feet over the
ground, the savannah grass blowing as if a hurricane
were upon it, Santini running, terrorists and Uruente
tribesmen exchanging fire at one another but running
behind him.

"Now, Fanny! Now!"

He heard the rattle of the subgun. She had never fired
a submachine gun before. A wild zigzag ripped across
the savannah grass, dirt flying, the Uruentes slowing
their charge, Mulrooney firing again, two of the terrorists going down, falling to their knees, then lost in
the high grass.

Santini was still running.

Mulrooney fired again as Culhane finished the pass,
another terrorist going down, assault rifles raised
toward them now, Culhane shouting, "Fanny—you and
Fred—duck back inside! Fast!"

Bullets pinged off the fuselage, a spiderweb appearing
suddenly where the cockpit bubble was hit. The machine
wasn't crashing, so Culhane assumed nothing vital had
been hit. As he came up, turning the chopper a full 180
degrees, he saw them coming over the horizon. Helicopters.

Culhane looked to his right. The river was visible
below, and floatplanes were landing there now. "Hoevermann! Way to go, Hoevermann! Right on!"

Culhane started into his second pass, finding the
radio switch. "This is Culhane. Can anybody hear me?
Over."

"This is Hoevermann. Go ahead. Over."

"Father Santini has the plutonium in the two suitcases. He's down there running himself into a heart attack. Uruentes are chasing him, but most of them are breaking off. Terrorists are still after him. Our guide, Sebastiao, and Magdelena, one of the passengers, have Amelina over by the rim of the valley. Over."

"Magdelena is one of my agents. We're closing in on the terrorists now. My ground forces will be moving up from the river to cut them off if they reach the rain forest. Stay clear. Hoevermann out."

"Bullshit, Inspector! You stay clear yourself! Santini was my brother's best friend. Culhane out!"

Culhane shut off the radio, coming in for the pass, shouting to Mulrooney, "Fanny—go for the ones closest to him this time. Hear me?"

He had displaced one earphone so he could hear her.

"Yeah—what the hell do you think I was doing last time, Josh?"

Culhane leveled off, hearing the chatter of Mulrooney's submachine gun. One of the terrorists fell with an arrow in his chest, those around him going down.

Santini was still running.

Three terrorists were close at his heels now. Hoevermann's half-dozen helicopters were closing, as well. Culhane shouted, "We're going down—hang on and stay back!" Santini was into the jungle now, the three terrorists entering behind him, Culhane setting the chopper down between Santini and the other terrorists. From the seat beside him, he grabbed his special rifle, rotating the set screw as he cleared the pilot's seat and framed himself in the open doorway of the cockpit. He started working the lever, hosing the .44 Magnum toward the remaining terrorists, hearing Mulrooney opening up with her submachine gun, Fred's arrows finding targets faster than he would have thought she could have shot.

The terrorists were falling back. Culhane grabbed up his four-inch revolver from the seat behind him, ripping it from the holster he hadn't had time to put on, firing it out at the fleeing terrorists. Hoevermann's strike-force teams were rappelling from their choppers now, a PA system blaring in Portuguese, *"Mãos ao alto! Mãos ao alto!"* The terrorists obeyed, laying down their weapons, surrendering, hands over their heads.

Culhane threw down his empty revolver to the cockpit seat. He started to run with only the six-inch revolver and his knives. Santini was out there in the jungle—and three terrorists were, too. One of them looked like a woman.

Culhane jumped a deadfall and thrashed into the brush, running, hearing a shouted plea from behind him, "Wait for me, Josh!"

He looked back. It was Fanny Mulrooney. Culhane stopped and drew his revolver, the barrel catching a ray of the sun, glinting brightly.

In an instant Mulrooney was beside him. "What the hell's wrong with Damascus? Why didn't he stop?"

"He knows what he's got! Come on!" Culhane broke into a run, looking for signs of Santini's trail, his eyes moving about the rain forest, the sun bright in patches where it penetrated the shadowy darkness. Mulrooney was beside him.

Culhane kept running. Santini was somewhere out there. He heard gunfire and veered right, swatting aside a low-hanging branch. "Watch your face, Fanny!"

He kept running, Mulrooney panting from slightly behind him now. "Did they get him, d'you think?"

"If they did, I'll kill them with my bare hands—so help me!" Culhane kept running, more gunfire ahead now. He almost tripped over the body. He fell to his knees, Mulrooney crashing into him.

Culhane rolled the body over. It was one of the terrorists. He pushed himself to his feet, running. He heard more gunfire and ran in that direction now, Fanny crashing through the underbrush beside him, his revolver in his fist.

There was a shout, and Culhane's Portuguese was just good enough to understand what was said. He froze, Mulrooney crashing into him again.

"What did they say?" Mulrooney gasped, breathless.

"From over there—the priest is dying." Culhane started toward the sound of the voice.

It came again, *"O padre esta morrendo!"*

Culhane broke through a wall of broad-leafed foliage into a small clearing. Damascus Santini lay in the arms of one of the jungle-fatigue-clad counterterrorist strike force team, his face white, blood pumping from his neck. The Brazilian soldier started for his pistol.

Culhane rasped, "I'm not a terrorist—relax! I'm the American who stole the helicopter. Hear of me? Josh Culhane?"

"Yes—the man Inspector Hoevermann trusted."

Culhane crossed the clearing and dropped to his knees beside Santini. Santini opened his eyes. "Hey—Josh—"

"Don't talk, buddy."

"They got the suitcases...heading for the river... Amelina is the terrorist leader... Maybe..." And his head fell back.

He was still breathing. Culhane asked the soldier, "Are you Catholic?"

"Yes."

"Pray for him." And Culhane was up, running toward gunfire from the river beyond the jungle, Mulrooney beside him again.

The gunfire grew more intense, closer, and then came the sound of rotor blades almost overhead and Hoevermann's voice over a PA system, saying in English, "Lay down your weapons! You haven't got a chance! Lay down your weapons!" Culhane broke from the jungle, Mulrooney beside him, Hoevermann's helicopter landing, and on the river armed helicopters were hovering over the surface. Two of the terrorists—a man and a woman—were poised on the float and in the open fuselage door of one of the floatplanes Culhane had seen landing.

The woman—it had to be Amelina, Culhane figured—held a pistol to the head of a man dressed in the uniform of the counterterrorist strike force.

Rifles were swung toward Culhane, submachine guns leveled at him and Mulrooney. But he heard Hoevermann's voice over a bullhorn, telling his men that Culhane and the woman were not terrorists. Culhane broke into a run toward Hoevermann, Mulrooney still beside him.

Hoevermann stood at the edge of the riverbank. He'd taken cover behind a tree trunk, and men of his strike force team were positioned around him.

Hoevermann was on the bullhorn again, "I guarantee that if you release the pilot and throw down your weapons you will not be harmed!"

Culhane edged over to Hoevermann. "You know what you've got out there—they've got the suitcase from Father Santini!"

"I know that."

"Do you know what happens if those things go into the water anywhere near each other?"

Hoevermann looked at him. "They can explode, can't they?"

"Vaporize this whole section of the river and us with it."

"I told you I read one of your books. That sounds like the sort of thing your Senhor Dodge would say. And then the police inspector looks at him meaningfully and asks, 'Do you have a plan?'"

Mulrooney laughed.

Culhane nodded, still catching his breath. "Yeah, I got a plan. They're going to take off with that plane—" And as if punctuating his words, the propeller started to turn.

"That was obvious, *senhor*."

"I'm taking one of the other aircraft. I can fly it, but I'll need a pilot for what I've got in mind. Once they start their takeoff, order your choppers to fly over them. Keep that plane from getting airborne! I'll jump from my plane to theirs. I can get aboard—maybe. And I can kill them and stop the plane. If they keep the pilot, so much the better—he can stop it faster."

"That is insane, but it might work. Take that plane there—Fuentes is my best fixed-wing pilot. Take my submachine gun."

"No, thanks—I couldn't hold onto it and get across. I got this." Culhane tapped at the holster at his hip with the six-inch .44 Magnum.

"We have a saying in my country—but you wouldn't understand it." Hoevermann extended his right hand. Culhane took it, starting for the aircraft, hearing Hoevermann shouting from behind him, "Fuentes—do exactly as this man tells you!"

Culhane realized Fanny Mulrooney was beside him. "Get behind some cover, will you—please?"

"Bullshit! You go up in the airplane, so do I. I can

cover you. And if the bomb goes off, we both go to
gether.''

He stopped and looked at her, Fuentes's aircraft pro
starting to turn. ''All right,'' he told her. ''All right.'
And he took her hand in his and started for the aircraft

The helicopters were going airborne now as Culhan
made the jump out to the float, small rubber boats dot
ting the river surface, armed men in them, the capture
plane starting to taxi along the river downstream. H
caught Mulrooney as she jumped.

''What are your orders?'' the pilot asked Culhane.

''Get as close to that plane as a flea on a dog. I'n
jumping from this one to theirs, and Hoevermann is us
ing the helicopters to keep them on the river, from get
ting airborne.''

''You are crazy, *senhor*.''

''He knows that,'' Mulrooney said.

Culhane slid into the copilot's seat; Mulrooney go
into the seat behind. The pilot was already strapped in.

Culhane stripped off his bush jacket and hat, passin
them back to Mulrooney, the aircraft Fuentes pilote
starting into the stream.

The helicopters were making low passes at th
terrorist-occupied craft, the floatplane making slov
progress over the water. Through a bullhorn, Culhan
could hear a woman's voice shouting from the ope
fuselage door, ''If these helicopters are not recalled,
will detonate the plutonium immediately!''

It was Amelina. Scott Palmer's bride. Santini wa
right.

Culhane rasped to Fuentes beside him. ''Hurry
We're running out of time!''

But Culhane's aircraft was already almost parallel t
the hostage aircraft now, running slightly behind it
''Give her more speed!''

He felt Mulrooney's arms around his neck for an instant. "You die, you're in big trouble, Culhane!!"

He looked at her. "Love you, too." Already, Culhane began wrenching open the starboard-side fuselage door. "Keep down—they'll start shooting as soon as they figure out what I'm doing, so be careful."

Culhane twisted the handle and started out, the wind lashing at him now, river spray blown back by the propeller thrashing his face and hands as he balanced his feet in the doorway frame, his hands knotted to the wing strut midway out from the wing stem.

Amelina was in the fuselage door of the larger floatplane. There was a pistol in her hand. Culhane edged out as far as he could, his feet swaying free now, his hands grasping the frame of the wing, a shot pinging off the wing over him as he edged outward. Another shot sounded, then there was gunfire from the starboard door he had just left. Culhane looked down and back. Mulrooney was firing her little .38.

"Get back inside before you get shot, Fanny!"

She didn't do what he said. She rarely did, he reflected, edging farther along the wing. Gunfire again, Culhane feeling heat and pain and then numbing cold along his left rib cage. He kept moving, hand over hand, nearly to the wing tip now, the float for the larger plane perhaps ten feet away. Another shot, then answering fire from Mulrooney.

Culhane swung himself outward, the fire again by his rib cage, letting go, in midair now, then his legs and torso crashing against something, his hands groping out—

His legs were dragging through the water, but his hands grasped the float. Gunfire perforated the float beside his hands now, more answering fire from Fanny Mulrooney.

Then a clicking sound, barely audible. She was out of ammo.

Culhane looked at his legs, dragged through the water now, skimming the surface, the water around his legs foaming white, Culhane feeling something tearing at his blue jeans. The wake of the aircraft as it changed direction slightly made the water clear for an instant. Piranha.

Culhane reached out with his left hand to get a better grip on the float.

There was blood on the water—his own from the wound in his side. Culhane dragged himself up onto the float, throwing his weight forward, half collapsing there.

In the fuselage doorway now, Culhane could see Amelina. There was a submachine gun in her hands. Culhane sagged back, his legs barely out of the water, his right hand finding the flap of his holster, unsnapping it as she leveled the subgun to fire.

The butt of the revolver in his fist, chunks of the float were spraying upward as the submachine gun in Amelina's hands fired. Culhane's revolver fired again and again and again. The gunfire stopped. Amelina's body twitched, then fell forward through the doorway into the river, the river white with foam as the piranha surrounded her.

Culhane turned to his left, still perched upon the float, the plane veering wildly. He could see through the windshield. The male terrorist had pushed the pilot aside, and the pilot was struggling with him, the aircraft out of control. Culhane looked ahead. The aircraft was heading for the opposite riverbank, on a collision course.

Culhane raised his revolver, the plane vibrating maddeningly.

The pilot and the terrorist were locked together in combat in the pilot's chair.

Culhane fired. The terrorist's head was suddenly no longer visible, the interior of the cockpit was washed with red—

Culhane rammed his revolver into the holster and shouted toward the cockpit, "Turn her!"

Culhane looked to the water at the piranha. Culhane jumped from the float, reaching, his left hand finding the fuselage doorframe, his body dragging through the water. His right hand groped up, getting a grip, Culhane wrenching his body upward, falling through into the fuselage, stumbling forward. The pilot's body had fallen forward over the controls. Culhane threw himself toward the man, stumbling over the nearly headless body of the terrorist.

Culhane jerked the pilot from his seat and threw himself down, the controls sticky with blood under his hands, the interior of the windshield smeared with it. Culhane throttled back, turning the craft to port, feeling it, hearing it—a tearing sound as the craft dragged bottom. The starboard wing snapped and was gone, the aircraft spinning out, Culhane throttling down.

And suddenly it stopped.

Culhane sagged forward onto the floor. The pilot was still breathing, and Culhane smiled. He was, too.

He tried lighting a cigarette, but his hands shook too much and he gave up. "Bad for your health," Culhane murmured.

Chapter Forty-Three _____

Culhane stood holding Fanny Mulrooney's hand. He turned and looked at her. She had a better tan than he'd ever seen her have. And the white sundress and the white shawl around her shoulders really set it off.

He looked back to the hotel driveway.

A cool breeze blew over the white sands from the river Negro. In the driveway, a Mercedes was parked, the trunk open.

He heard the voice from behind him and turned around to match the voice to the face. It was Hoevermann, and walking beside him, tall, lovely, her hair up, gold hoops in her ears, a gold bracelet on her right wrist, her left arm through Hoevermann's right arm, was Fred.

She wore a pink suit. It looked like linen and looked very expensive.

Because of the high heels she wore, she was taller still, and when they stopped a few feet before them, Culhane realized he was looking up into her eyes.

"Fred," Culhane said, smiling, extending his right hand to her. She left Hoevermann's arm and stepped closer to him, not taking his hand but folding her arms around his neck. She kissed him full on the lips.

And she stepped back. She looked at Fanny Mulrooney, and then the two were in each other's arms.

Culhane watched, smiling, as their embrace broke and they began to talk using their improvised sign language, not a word spoken.

He looked away from them to Hoevermann. Hoevermann said, "I will personally put her on the plane at

Belém. But a representative of the Archimedes family will be there to meet her. Then she will be on her way to her new life.'' Hoevermann smiled, lighting a cigarette, cupping his hands over his lighter against the breeze.

Culhane looked again at Frederica Archimedes. She had remembered enough of her name to draw the name "Fred" from Mulrooney's saying the word "friend." Mulrooney had explained to Culhane the origin of "Fred," and after returning to Manaus, Mulrooney took her on a shopping spree all afternoon. The morning of the next day, a communication from the sister of Lindy Archimedes had arrived. The missing girl, Frederica, was a millionairess many times over.

Culhane wondered absently how come his charge cards had paid for Fred's clothing when she was the multimillionaire and he was not. He was certain Fanny Mulrooney would explain the logic of it all to him.

"We must be going, I'm afraid," Hoevermann began, extending his hand. Culhane took it. "And don't worry about your friend Scott Palmer. Life has punished him more than the Brazilian government ever could. We are simply deporting him. The American authorities won't prosecute—the publicity in the world press would be murderous."

Culhane nodded, searching the pockets of his khaki suit and lighting a cigarette of his own.

"The Frenchman you shot—the man aboard the aircraft? He was wanted for bombing a synagogue in Paris—not a nice man. You did the world a favor by killing him."

"It's still killing somebody. It's a lot easier for Sean Dodge than for me," Culhane said laughing, suddenly remembering his rib cage hurt whenever he laughed where he had been grazed by Amelina's bullet.

"An admirable way of thinking, Senhor Culhane."

And Hoevermann turned to Fred. "Menina Archimedes?"

She smiled, nodding. And then she looked at Mulrooney once more and laughed. "Fred—Me-em-ef—" And Mulrooney burst into tears and hugged the girl.

They had stood by the driveway until the Mercedes was gone from sight, and then started back into the Tropical Hotel Manaus, past the jungle plants where the tropical birds made their strange chattering sounds and into the lobby. It was a twenty-minute ride from the hotel to the airport. Soon Fred would be on her way to Rio, and from there to Athens. Mulrooney hugged his arm.

"What's the matter, Fanny?"

"Oh, nothing."

"How about we take a vacation in a few months—I'll promise you not to chase down anything for a *Takers* book and you promise me not to chase down weird legends and unexplained phenomena."

"Where to?" She looked up.

"How about Greece? Maybe take in the Greek islands, and while we're there, we can visit Fred."

Mulrooney leaned up to him and kissed his cheek as they walked. "I'd like to see Fred again. She's a nice girl—she really is."

"I know that."

Mulrooney smiled. They turned into a corridor and walked toward their room. "And I'll make you a deal." Mulrooney laughed a little, still hugging his arm. "We can come down to Brazil and go upriver past that town with the funny little name that means yesterday—"

"Ontem?" Culhane interrupted.

"Uh-huh—and we can spend some time with Damascus."

"I've been thinking about that. I make pretty good

money. How about I get a chunk of royalties set aside— from the next *Takers*, maybe—and funnel it into that mission Damascus is running?''

"Well, now that you mention it," she said, walking slowly beside him, "*Warrior Women* should do pretty well—and I'm getting into a kind of strange tax bracket."

"I know what you mean," Culhane told her.

They stopped at the door to their room. Culhane took the key from his jacket pocket and turned it in the lock, Mulrooney entering and Culhane following her. The afternoon sun flooded through the windows overlooking the central garden. Culhane set the key down on the dresser top, then took his wallet, his money clip and his knife from his pockets.

Mulrooney stood beside him and Culhane turned toward her. He took her in his arms, drawing the shawl tight around her, holding her close against him. "One day," she whispered, "we'll have to try what that Amazon princess was going to try with you."

"Hmm," Culhane murmured, kissing her neck.

She looked up at him, the shawl falling to the floor. Culhane bent over to pick it up, and he threw it across the bed on top of Mulrooney's blue purse. "Make love to me," she asked.

"Like the Amazons...?"

"No—not like that at all." And Culhane enfolded her in his arms.

Sundresses were wonderful garments, Culhane mused. They came off women very easily.

The bathrooms at the Tropical Hotel Manaus in the heart of Brazil were very unique. Specially made glazed tiles bore the motifs of Amazon plants and flowers. They were very pretty.

But as Josh Culhane leaned Fanny Mulrooney's back

against them, the warm water splashing across their bodies, her hands doing things to him that the Amazon princess had never imagined, he thought fleetingly that nothing was as pretty to him as Fanny Mulrooney. And she stood on her toes in the water, Culhane supporting her with his hands as their bodies became one body.

As she held him tightly, their bodies moving, she whispered in his ear, and he could barely hear her over the running of the water. "You know, ohh, if we get to Greece, on one of the islands there, there's—ohh—a cave—and when the wind blows just right, they say you can hear human voices speaking in ancient Aramaic—I love you."

He knew she did.

About the Authors _____

JERRY AHERN, linguist, survival expert, magazine editor and the successful author of such landmark action-adventure series as Track, The Survivalist and They Call Me the Mercenary, lives in a small Georgia town near Atlanta where he writes, tests firearms and restores an ancient but honorable house. **S.A. AHERN**, who has collaborated with her husband since their high-school days in Chicago, is a photographer in her own right, has held a lifelong interest in the occult and the unexplained, and shares Jerry's passion for archaeology. Resisting the lure of the word processor— "You process food, not language"—the Aherns work side by side on equally ancient typewriters that are threatening to become archaeological artifacts themselves.

Readers and reviewers talk abou
THE
TAKERS

The best I've read in a long time!
—*M.A., Junction City, Orego*

I can hardly wait for the next installment of *The Takers*.
—*J.M., San Diego, Californi*

The Takers was everything it was advertised to be. Truly
a stunning book. It kept me up at night because I could
not put it down. Now that's the way I like them!
—*M.M. (NR*

I enjoyed it immensely. —*E.B., Nogales, Arizona*

Indiana Jones has nothing on Josh Culhane
whatsoever.... Ingenious.... I look forward to seeing
more exploits of *The Takers*.
—*T.D., Pepperell, Massachuset*

Jerry and Sharon Ahern are one of the best writing teams I've come across. . . . I could not put the book down. —*P.O., Cameron, Louisiana*

✳

A spectacular and sensational novel . . . the best book I've ever read. —*R.D., USAF*

✳

The Takers would make a fantastic movie. . . . Indiana Jones, eat your heart out!
—*T.M., Douglasville, Georgia*

✳

A break with tradition. . . . Compelling action!
—*El Paso Times*

✳

The action moves rapidly and tightly!
—*Publishers Weekly*

✳

Takers takes off! It's a whopper of a story.
—Victoria, Texas, *Advocate*

✳

Hours of exciting suspense! —*The Daily Independent*